Regency

RUMOURS

Regency
RUMOURS

ANNE
ASHLEY

MILLS & BOON

REGENCY RUMOURS © 2019 by Harlequin Books S.A.

The publisher acknowledges the copyright holders of the individual works as follows:
THE VISCOUNT'S SCANDALOUS RETURN
© 2010 by Anne Ashley
Philippine Copyright 2010
Australian Copyright 2010
New Zealand Copyright 2010

First Published 2010
Second Australian Paperback Edition 2019
ISBN 978 1 489 27741 1

BETRAYED AND BETROTHED
© 2005 by Anne Ashley
Philippine Copyright 2005
Australian Copyright 2005
New Zealand Copyright 2005

First Published 2005
Second Australian Paperback Edition 2019
ISBN 978 1 489 27741 1

MIX
Paper from
responsible sources
FSC
www.fsc.org FSC® C001695

Published by
Harlequin Mills & Boon
An imprint of Harlequin Enterprises (Australia) Pty
Limited (ABN 47 001 180 918), a subsidiary of
HarperCollins Publishers Australia Pty Limited
(ABN 36 009 913 517)
Level 13, 201 Elizabeth Street
SYDNEY NSW 2000 AUSTRALIA

Printed and bound in Australia by McPherson's Printing Group

CONTENTS

ANNE ASHLEY

was born and educated in Leicester. She lived for a long time in Scotland, but now lives in the West Country with two cats, her two sons and her husband, who has a wonderful and very necessary sense of humour. When not pounding away at the keys of her computer, she likes to relax in her garden, which she has opened to the public on more than one occasion in aid of the village church funds.

The Viscount's
Scandalous Return

Chapter One

September 1814

Miss Isabel Mortimer's return to her farmhouse-style home coincided with the long-case clock's chiming the hour of eleven. She had been out and about since first light, and so might reasonably have expected a more enthusiastic welcome than the decidedly reproachful glance her ever-loyal housekeeper-cum-confidante cast her.

'Oh, Lord, miss!' Bessie exclaimed, as she watched her young mistress deposit the gun and the fruits of her labours down upon the kitchen table. 'You've never been a'wandering over Blackwood land again? I've warned you time and again that there steward up at the Manor will have you placed afore the magistrate, given half a chance. Heard tell he weren't best pleased back along, when them there high-and-mighty legal folk came up from Lunnon, asking questions about the night of the murders, and he discovered it were you had stirred things up again after all these years.'

'No, I don't suppose he was pleased.' Not appearing in the least concerned, Isabel collected a sharp knife from a drawer and then promptly set herself the task of preparing the rabbits for the stew-pot. 'What's more, young Toby told me, this very morn as it happens, there's been no sign of Master Guy Fensham these past two weeks. Which I find most revealing in the circumstances. After all, what had he to fear if he told the truth about the happenings on that terrible night?'

'Well, that's just it, miss. He couldn't have done, now could he, if what the old master set down on paper be true? And I would far rather believe the old master, 'cause there were nought wrong with him at the time of writing.'

'Well, I, for one, never doubted the truth of Papa's version of events. As you quite rightly pointed out, he wrote his account before he suffered that first seizure.'

Whenever Isabel thought of her late father she experienced, still, an acute sense of loss, even now, after almost two years. They had always been wondrous close; more so after he had become infirm and had come to rely upon her for so much. Yet nothing in her expression betrayed the fact that she had nowhere near fully recovered from his death. If anything, she seemed quite matter-of-fact as she said,

'So you've no need to fear I shall fall foul of Fensham, especially as I didn't take one step on Blackwood land. I've been in the top meadow, as it happens. Besides...' she shrugged, emphasising her complete unconcern '...what would it matter if I had been trespassing? If and when his lordship does return, I shall make it perfectly plain that he owes me a deal more than the few fish I've removed from his trout stream for all the damage his overgrown ditch has done to my vegetable garden during his long absence. Why his father ever employed such a lazy ne'er-do-well as Guy Fensham as steward up at the Manor, I shall never know!'

Thoughtfully drying her hands on her apron, Bessie joined her young mistress at the table. 'Well, miss, no matter what folks may say about the old Viscount—and you'll find plenty hereabouts who never liked him—you'll never hear anyone say he neglected either the land or the Manor. When the old Lord Blackwood were alive the steward did his work, and toed the line.' She shook her head sadly. 'Now look at the place! It's a year and more since you went to Lunnon to seek out Mr Bathurst,' she reminded her mistress. 'And never a word since!'

'Now, that isn't strictly true,' Isabel corrected, striving to be fair. 'We've never been precisely kept abreast of developments, I'll agree. Even so, Mr Bathurst did take the trouble to send that one letter, confirming he'd set the wheels in motion, as it were, and thanking me once again for the trouble I'd taken in seeking him out personally in order to pass on Papa's written account. And he fully re-imbursed me for all the expense of travelling to London and remaining there for those few days. He was most generous, in fact!'

Isabel cast a long, considering look at the large dresser that almost covered the entire wall opposite. 'How very fortunate it was that so many hereabouts recalled that it had been none other than Mr Bathurst himself who had sold this very property to my father, and had gone to London to study law. Fortunate, too, that so many remembered he and the Honourable Sebastian Blackwood had been upon the very best of terms in their youth. He was the ideal person for me to seek out and pass on what Papa had revealed about the Viscount's younger son.

'And you must remember,' Isabel continued, after a further few moments' consideration, 'Mr Bathurst was in something of a precarious position. Just how much of a hand he had in effecting his friend's escape from the authorities, after Sebastian Blackwood had been accused of murdering both his father and brother all those years ago, I can only speculate. All the same, for some considerable time Mr Bathurst has been a well-respected barrister, a veritable pillar of the community and a staunch upholder of the law. He would need to be circumspect and surely wouldn't wish his name to be too closely connected with a man who, as far as we know, is still accused of committing the atrocities.'

After listening intently to everything her young mistress had said, Bessie nodded her head in agreement. 'But do you know, Miss Isabel, long afore you found your father's papers about the happenings on that terrible night, I never for a moment thought young Master Sebastian had gone and done that wicked deed. And I weren't the only one who disbelieved it, neither. Now, I ain't saying he were a saint, 'cause he weren't. For a start, he were a devil for the ladies, young as he was. Not that I ever heard tell he got any round these parts into trouble—think he preferred painted doxies, or maybe those nearer his own class.

'Oh, but he were right handsome, so he were.' Bessie continued reminiscing, her plump cheeks suddenly aglow at some private thought. 'I can see him now—so tall, so proud, riding by on that fine horse of his. Why, he used to send my heart all of a-flutter, to be sure!'

'Get a hold of yourself, woman!' Isabel admonished lovingly. 'I remember him too. And I'll tell you plainly we're far beneath his touch. Why, he'd never give the likes of you and me a second glance!'

'Not me he wouldn't, that's for sure,' Bessie acknowledged a moment before a surge of loyalty, borne of an ever-increasing loving respect, prompted her to add, 'But you're quite another matter. Well, you would be, if you'd trouble yourself about your appearance once in a while,' she amended, frowning at her mistress's shabby, worn attire, and windswept chestnut locks, numerous strands of which had escaped the confining pins.

Isabel responded with a dismissive wave of one hand. 'I've better things to do than sit before a mirror for hours on end preening myself. I might have been born the daughter of a gentleman, and raised to be a lady, at least when dear Mama was alive, and had a hand in my upbringing, but even so I never was the sort to attract the attentions of any aristocratic gentleman, least of all one so high on the social ladder as the son of a viscount. And I've always had sense enough to realise it! I'm far too managing for a start. Besides…' she shrugged '…I'm not altogether sure I really wish to marry. I'm happy enough as I am, and I enjoy my independence. No, if and when Lord Blackwood does return to take his father's place up at the Manor, my only interest in him will be to see how long it takes him to improve the drainage on his land, and to improve, too, the lot of those unfortunate wretches who rely upon the estate for a living, not least of which, as you very well know, is poor old Bunting.'

At this Isabel became the recipient of a hard, determined look. 'Now, miss, the old butler up at the Manor be none of your concern. I know 'tis a sinful shame he weren't pensioned off years ago, and given one of the estate cottages promised to him by the old Lord Blackwood. I think it's wicked, too, that a man of his years should be alone up there in that great house, hardly seeing a soul. Why, if it hadn't been for you and the young curate visiting him so regular last winter, I swear the influenza would have taken him off.'

'You did your share of nursing too,' Isabel reminded her.

Bessie, however, steadfastly refused this time to be won over by the warmth of her mistress's lovely smile. 'I know I did. But that don't change matters. You simply can't afford to take on any more waifs and strays. You've too many folk depending on you as it is.

'And it's no earthly good you looking at me like that!' Bessie exclaimed, totally impervious to the reproachful glance cast in her direction. 'I know you feel grateful to Troake for all the care he took over your father during those last years. And there's no denying he worked well enough when the old master were alive. But even you can't deny he's become dreadful slow of late, not to mention a bad-tempered old demon. And then there's young Toby. Now I ain't saying the lad ain't worth his weight in gold,' Bessie went on, thereby successfully cutting off the protest her mistress had been about to utter. 'The boy's nothing less than a godsend, so he is, the way he repaired the barn roof last winter. But the wages you pay him could be put to better use.'

Bessie's brown eyes slid past her mistress to the large shaggy dog lying sprawled on the floor, close to the range. Before she could voice any condemnation of the hound, which had been saved from a watery grave in the millpond, and which had become totally devoted to the mistress of the house, his rescuer forestalled any criticism by announcing,

'Don't you dare say a word against him! I won't deny there is some justification in what you've said about both Troake and Toby Marsh. But I would never be without my darling Beau! Why, if it hadn't been for him the house would have been broken into on at least three occasions that we know of these past months. Furthermore, but for him, we wouldn't be having rabbit stew for supper. He managed to root out half a dozen in the top meadow.'

Bessie, ever sharp, wasn't slow to pounce upon this interesting snippet. 'In that case, where be the other two?'

Isabel had the grace to look a little shamefaced in view of what had been mentioned already. 'I let Toby take them home to his mother.'

Bessie cast a despairing glance up at the ceiling. 'Now, why doesn't that surprise me none, I wonder! I don't suppose you took a moment to consider we've an extra mouth to feed, now that young cousin of yours has taken refuge in the house. Now, I ain't saying you shouldn't have taken her in the way you did, she being the only child of your papa's dear sister, and the only close kin you've left in the world that's ever had any dealings with you. And there's no denying she, too, be worth her weight in gold,' she hurriedly conceded. 'I do declare the house has never looked so clean and tidy for many a long year. I defy anyone to find a speck of dust about the place! And sew…? I've never known anyone set a neater stitch than Miss Clara, not even your sainted mother. It's a pleasure to show folk into the front parlour nowadays, what with the new curtains, and all.'

It was clear that Bessie was at least a staunch supporter of the young woman who had surprisingly turned up on the doorstep late one evening a month before, almost begging sanctuary. Isabel hadn't recognised the beautiful stranger as the young cousin she had seen only a few times in her life, and then many years ago, when her aunt and cousin had paid the occasional visit to London. None the less, she hadn't doubted her authenticity. Nor did she regret for a moment the decision she had made to help her hapless relation, who had been fleeing from a forced union with a man old enough to be her father. All the same, she couldn't help feeling that her act of kindness might bring trouble in the future.

She tried not to dwell on this uncomfortable possibility as she enquired into the whereabouts of her relative, and by so doing gave rise to a look of comical dismay in her ever-faithful companion.

'The young curate were round here again, bright and

early this morning, with a few more newspapers from up at the vicarage. It's good of him, I suppose. But it do put queer notions into your cousin's head. Now, I ain't saying Miss Clara ain't in the right of it not wishing to be a burden on you,' Bessie went on, somehow managing to preserve a serious countenance. 'But what wife and mother in her right mind would ever employ such a beautiful girl as a governess? She seems to suppose someone will, though, and begged a lift with the local carrier into Merryfield so that she might visit the sorting office with her reply to an advertisement she spotted in one of them there journals.'

Smiling wryly, Isabel shook her head. 'Yes, you're right. Clara has the sweetest of dispositions. She's hardworking, can set a stitch better than most, and she is far from dull-witted. Sadly, though, she isn't very worldly.'

She was suddenly thoughtful. 'I just hope she doesn't come to regret this determination of hers to find employment. I cannot help but feel that the fewer people who know her present whereabouts the safer it will be for her. Should her stepmother discover where she is, I'm not altogether sure I could prevent her from removing Clara from under this roof.'

The application of the front-door knocker successfully brought an end to the conversation. The housekeeper made to rise from the table, but Isabel forestalled her by saying she herself would go. Although mistress of the house, she had never been too proud to answer her own front door, should the need arise.

Consequently, as soon as she had washed her hands, removed her soiled apron and made herself reasonably presentable by repositioning a few wayward strands of hair, she went along the passageway to discover a man of below-average height awaiting her on the other side of the solid oak barrier.

Everything about him suggested a professional man, so Isabel wasn't in the least surprised to have a business card thrust into her hand bearing the names of Crabtree, Crabtree and Goodbody, a firm of lawyers based in the metropolis.

'And you are?' Isabel enquired, her great fear that he might have come in connection with her cousin Clara's present whereabouts diminishing somewhat by the fact that the notary was flanked by two young children. By their clear resemblance to each other, Isabel felt they must surely be brother and sister.

'Mr Goodbody, ma'am,' he answered promptly, doffing his hat, whilst all the time favouring her with a scrutiny that was no less assessing than her own had been. Evidently he had decided that, although not in the least stylishly attired, she bore all the other characteristics of a young woman of refinement, for he added, 'Would I be correct in assuming I have the pleasure in addressing Miss Mortimer, daughter of the late Dr John Mortimer?'

Isabel would have been the first to admit that she had been reared to conduct herself in a genteel manner, at least for as long as others had had an influence on her behaviour. Years of increasing responsibilities had tended, however, to persuade her to disregard social niceties, and adopt a more forthright approach when dealing with her fellow man. Some, it had to be said, found her abrupt almost to the point of rudeness, whilst others considered her no-nonsense approach commendable.

Seemingly Mr Goodbody fell into this latter category, for he betrayed not a modicum of disquiet when she demanded to know precisely why he had called, and answered promptly with, 'I am here at the behest of the present Lord Blackwood, ma'am.'

Although intrigued, and quite naturally interested to

discover the seventh Viscount Blackwood's present whereabouts, Isabel couldn't help experiencing a feeling of disquiet where the two children were concerned. She could
detect no resemblance whatsoever to the dapper little lawyer, which instantly begged the question of whose children they were. An alarming possibility instantly sprang
to mind. None the less, although renowned for her no-
nonsense manner, she was also known for her innate acts
of kindness. The little girl, clearly weary and afraid, clung
to the older child like a limpet, instantly rousing Isabel's
sympathy.

'In that case, sir, you'd best bring the children into the
house, and we'll discuss the matter which has brought you
here in the comfort of the front parlour.'

Bessie had not exaggerated about the transformation
that had taken place since Clara's arrival in the house.
Tirelessly she had worked on making new curtains. She'd
repaired all the upholstery where she could, and had even
taken the trouble to embroider new covers and cushions
to place over those worn areas that had been beyond her
skill to repair. Clearly Mr Goodbody was favourably impressed, for he cast an admiring glance about him the instant he entered the largest room in the house.

After settling the two children on the sofa, and furnishing the lawyer with a glass of Madeira, Isabel once again
asked for an explanation for the visit, adding, 'And would
I be correct in assuming that his lordship's whereabouts is
no longer a mystery, and he is presently in the country?'

All at once the little man's expression became guarded.
'I'm afraid I am not in a position to divulge his lordship's
current whereabouts, Miss Mortimer. All I am able to reveal is that a successful outcome to the enquiries regarding past—er—unfortunate happenings will not be long
delayed now. In the meantime, his lordship feels himself

unable to take up his responsibilities with regard to these two young persons.'

There wasn't so much as a flicker of compassion in the glance Isabel cast the children this time, before fixing the notary with a haughty stare. 'And what, pray, has that to do with me, sir?' she enquired in a voice that would have frozen the village pond on the warmest summer's day. 'His lordship's private domestic arrangements are entirely his own affair.'

'Indeed, yes, Miss Mortimer,' he readily concurred, having seemingly realised in which directions her thoughts were leading. 'Perhaps if you were to read his lordship's letter first,' he added, delving into the leather bag he had carried into the house. 'It might set your mind at rest on certain matters.'

Still very much on her guard, Isabel, with some reluctance, took the missive from the notary's outstretched hand, and broke the seal to read:

My dear Miss Mortimer,

I am fully cognisant of the debt of gratitude I already owe you, and the charge I would settle upon you now. Believe me when I tell you the decision to place my wards into your care was not taken without a deal of consideration, and I can only trust to your forbearance in this matter.

The estimable Mr Goodbody is in a position to answer any questions you might have with regard to my wards, and has been instructed to reimburse you in advance for the expenses you will undoubtedly incur whilst the children are in your care. If, however, you feel unable to burden yourself with the responsibilities of a surrogate guardian, I shall perfectly understand.

And will have the honour to remain,
Your obedient servant,
Blackwood

Although there was a certain familiarity in the tone of
the missive, Isabel couldn't find it within herself to be offended. At least it had vanquished the idea that she was
being asked to care for the Viscount's by-blows!

After reading the letter through again, she raised her
eyes. 'So these children are Lord Blackwood's wards.'

'Indeed, they are, ma'am,' the lawyer duly confirmed,
before instructing the boy to stand and make his bow. 'This
is Master Joshua Collier, who has recently celebrated his
ninth birthday, and his young sister, Alice, who is six.'

Isabel, having had little experience of children, was at
a loss to know what to say to the siblings to put them at
their ease, while she considered more fully the errant Viscount's request. The boy stared back at her now with an
almost defiant gleam in his dark eyes, as though he was
more than ready to challenge any authority she might in
the future attempt to exert over him, while his little sister
merely stared, awestruck, as though she were looking at a
being from another world. Fortunately the slightly embarrassing silence was brought to an end by Isabel's cousin
unexpectedly entering the room.

'Oh, I'm so sorry. Bessie quite failed to mention you
had visitors.'

'No need to apologise,' Isabel assured her. 'Your arrival is most timely.'

She was now quite accustomed to the effect her strikingly lovely cousin always had on members of the opposite sex, most especially those who came face to face with
her for the very first time. And Mr Goodbody was no exception! Although he refrained from gaping, there was no

mistaking the look of appreciation he cast the stunningly lovely girl who glided towards him in order to clasp his outstretched hand.

Few gentlemen, Isabel suspected, would be proof against such wide, brilliant blue eyes, and the sweetest of smiles, set in a heart-shaped face. It was a countenance truly without flaw, and crowned with the brightest of guinea-gold curls.

'Would you be good enough to take Master Joshua and his sister into the kitchen and provide them with something suitable to eat and drink, Clara? I'm sure they must be hungry after their journey.'

'Of course,' she obligingly replied, holding out her hand to the little girl who, after a moment's hesitation, seemingly decided she would be happy to go with the pretty lady with the kindly smile. Her brother, evidently less impressed by Clara's physical attributes, frowned dourly up at her before following them from the room, the prospect of plum cake and apple tart seemingly having won the day.

'Now that we are able to discuss the matter more freely, Mr Goodbody,' Isabel began, the instant they were alone, 'perhaps you would be good enough to enlighten me as to why his lordship felt himself unable to place the children with a relative or friend? After all, I am neither. His lordship and I have never exchanged so much as a pleasantry.'

'And that, I strongly suspect, is one of the main reasons why he chose you above anyone else.' Frowning, the lawyer considered more fully for a moment. 'Given what you have unselfishly done on his behalf, his lordship must be satisfied as to your integrity. Naturally, he has the children's best interests at heart. Until such time as he is able to undertake the duties of his guardianship, he wishes his wards kept well away from their uncle's sphere—their late mother's brother, that is.'

'Does his lordship believe the children's uncle means them harm?'

'I shall be diplomatic here, Miss Mortimer,' he responded after a further moment's consideration, 'and say that neither his lordship nor myself believe the gentleman to be in the least trustworthy. He resided with his sister throughout the last year of her life, during which time certain irregularities came to light with regard to her finances. One can only speculate as to why so many large sums were withdrawn from her bank during this period. Furthermore a letter, supposedly written by the children's mother, unexpectedly came to light shortly after her death. In it she requested an adjustment to her will, naming her brother sole guardian to her children, and sole beneficiary in the event of their deaths, giving the reason for the changes as a staunch belief that the present Lord Blackwood would be an unfit guardian. I am now in possession of certain letters written over the years by Sarah Collier to his lordship, the last one penned no more than three months ago, that clearly refute this. Therefore, it is my belief that either pressure was brought to bear upon the lady, when she was not in full possession of her faculties, to make adjustments to her will, or the letter is a complete forgery. I strongly suspect the latter.'

'There was nothing suspicious about her death, though, surely?' Isabel asked gently.

'Nothing whatsoever, Miss Mortimer,' he assured her. 'She died of typhus.'

Isabel was far from sure that she wished to burden herself with the responsibilities of caring for two recently orphaned children. After all, what would happen if the uncle should happen to come to Northamptonshire in search of his niece and nephew?

'I think that most unlikely, Miss Mortimer,' the lawyer

assured her, after she'd voiced this fear aloud. 'The uncle, Mr Danforth, is completely unaware of his lordship's present whereabouts. If he chose to make enquiries, all he would discover is that the Manor and his lordship's town house are still unoccupied, as they have been for more than eight years, save for one reliable servant in each. Furthermore, Danforth knows I removed the children from their home. I know for a fact that my own house has been watched during this past week. I strongly suspect that he believes, you see, I have the children safely hidden in London. By the time he has exhausted every possibility, and I have several sisters residing in the metropolis, it is fervently hoped that his lordship will have been cleared of all charges against him, and I myself shall have proved beyond doubt that Sarah Collier's supposed adjustment to her will is entirely fraudulent.

'But until such time, and if you are agreeable,' he went on, when all Isabel did was to stare at him in thoughtful silence, still unsure what she should do, 'his lordship has instructed me to give you this, in advance, in the hope that you will accept the responsibility he would place upon you.'

Delving into his bag once again, he drew out a bulging leather purse, which he promptly deposited on the low table between them. Isabel could only speculate on how much it contained. None the less, she suspected it held a considerable sum, perhaps more than she'd seen at any one time in her entire life.

'His lordship will ensure that a draft on his bank is sent to you at the beginning of each month, until such time as he is able to make alternative arrangements. He wishes the children to be as little trouble to you as possible, and therefore requests that a governess be engaged, and any other help you deem necessary. I had no time to engage a suitable person, but if you are happy to accept the responsibility, I shall gladly do so on my return to London.'

'No, there's no need for you to trouble yourself, sir,' she countered. 'I happen to know of the very person.'

'Do I infer correctly from that, Miss Mortimer, that you are agreeable to his lordship's request?'

'Yes, sir, you may be sure I am.' The bulging purse on the table having comprehensively silenced the voice of doubt.

Although Clara had little difficulty in winning the trust and affection of little Alice Collier, her stronger-willed brother proved a different matter entirely. As Isabel had suspected, young Joshua had little appreciation of Clara's beauty and, as things turned out, he wasn't above taking wicked advantage of her innate good nature either.

On several occasions during those first weeks, Isabel was called upon to restore order to the upstairs chamber that functioned as a schoolroom-cum-nursery. Which she did in a swift and very effective fashion. Whether it was because she would tolerate no nonsense, or the fact that she was happy to take him along with her whenever she went out hunting or fishing that quickly won the boy's respect was difficult to judge. Notwithstanding, by the time autumn gave way to winter, it was clear to all at the farmhouse that Master Joshua Collier had grown inordinately fond of the mistress of the house.

Naturally, having a young boy and girl residing under the roof resulted in a much more relaxed and cheerful atmosphere about the place. Bessie, however, considered there was more to it than just having two very contented children round the house.

The prompt payments sent by Mr Goodbody early each month had brought about numerous beneficial changes.

Clara's employment as governess had resulted in her feeling a deal happier knowing she was able to contribute something towards household expenses. The extra money had meant that items, once considered unnecessary luxuries, had been purchased, making life at the farmhouse so very much easier and agreeable. Most gratifying of all, as far as Bessie was concerned, was the non-appearance of those troubled frowns over financial matters that had from time to time creased her young mistress's intelligent brow during recent years, whenever money for large bills had needed to be found.

Although he made no attempt to return to the farmhouse to see how the children fared, Mr Goodbody never failed to enquire after their welfare in the accompanying letter he always forwarded with the promissory note; Isabel duly replied, attesting to their continued well-being, and assumed he must surely pass these assurances on to the children's guardian.

Of his lordship himself, however, Isabel saw and heard nothing; until, that is, the arrival of Mr Goodbody's December letter, wherein he apprised her of the fact that the seventh Viscount Blackwood had finally been cleared of all charges against him, and was now at liberty to take up his rightful place at the ancestral home.

Isabel received this news with decidedly mixed feelings. On the one hand she knew it would greatly benefit many in the local community to have the Manor inhabited again; on the other, she would miss the children, most especially Josh. She was honest enough to admit, too, that she would miss the generous payments she had received over the past months for taking care of the orphans.

The New Year arrived with still no sign of the Viscount. Nevertheless, it was common knowledge that an army of local tradesmen had been hired to work in the Manor. So it stood to reason that Lord Blackwood was planning to take up residence at some point in the near future.

An unusually dry January gave way to a damp and dismal February, and brought with it no further news of his lordship. Then, in the middle of the month, an unexpected cold spell struck the county, making travel virtually impossible, even the shortest journeys, for several days. The vast majority of people, of course, were glad when at last the thaw set in, and they could go about their daily business unhindered; but not so Josh and Alice, who returned to the farmhouse with their governess, looking most disgruntled.

'My snowman's dying,' Alice lamented, close to tears.

Both Isabel and Bessie, who were busily preparing the luncheon, tried to appear suitably sympathetic, unlike Alice's brother, who was far more matter-of-fact about it all.

'He's not dying, you goose!' Josh admonished. 'He's just melting. Snowmen aren't alive, are they, Miss Isabel?'

She was spared the need to respond by Beau's timely intervention. He had risen immediately the children had entered the kitchen, and was now receiving his customary pats and strokes.

It never ceased to amaze Isabel how differently the hound behaved towards the children nowadays. When they had first arrived at the farmhouse, it had to be said that he hadn't been at all enthusiastic and had growled at them both whenever they had attempted to venture too close.

Quite understandable in the circumstances when one considered his life had very nearly been terminated by a group of village urchins, she mused. It hadn't taken Beau very long, though, she reminded herself, while continuing to watch the by-play, to realise that children divided into two distinct factions—those who would cruelly tie a brick round his neck and hurl him in a pond; and those who offered tasty treats, and threw sticks in lively games.

Beau, now, was quite happy to accompany Josh and Alice whenever they went out to get some exercise under the watchful eye of their governess. More often than not, though, he would return in search of the mistress of the house, if she failed to put in an appearance after a short time.

'Come, children, let's go back upstairs to the school-room,' Clara announced in her usual gentle way, making it sound more like a request than a command. 'We've time enough, before luncheon is ready, to finish reading the story we began earlier.'

Both children obediently rose to their feet, and were about to accompany their governess, when there was an imperious rat-tat-tat on the kitchen door.

It wasn't unusual for callers to use the rear entrance. More often than not it was the young lad whom Isabel employed to help her about the place seeking instructions on what work needed to be done. Toby Marsh had quickly become a firm favourite with Josh, who rushed across the kitchen to answer the summons, only to discover a forbidding-looking female standing there, dressed from head to toe in sombre black, accompanied by an equally unprepossessing gentleman, standing directly behind her.

Confronted by two such daunting strangers, Josh quite naturally fell back a pace or two, as did his governess, who also let out a tiny whimper, which not only captured Isabel's attention, but also that of the unexpected female caller.

'So there you are, you wicked, ungrateful gel!' the visitor exclaimed, striding, quite uninvited, into the kitchen, with much rustling of wide bombazine skirts.

Although Isabel had never seen the middle-aged matron

in her life before, her cousin's suddenly ashen complexion and wide terrified eyes, as she fell back against the wall, gave her a fairly shrewd notion of who the harridan must surely be. Unless she was much mistaken, this was Clara's stepmama, the woman her cousin's loving father had married in the hope of replacing his beloved first wife. Well, it might have been beneficial for the late James Pentecost to remarry, but from things Clara had revealed during recent months her lot had not been improved by her late father's second marriage, and the arrival in the family home of a selfish stepsister.

After calmly wiping her floured hands on her apron, Isabel placed herself squarely between her cowering cousin and the woman who was causing her young relative such distress. Evidently her resentment at having her home invaded by two complete strangers had conveyed itself to her faithful hound. Beau's hackles rose as he let out a low, threatening growl, which had the effect of bringing the fleshy-faced man to a stop, as he made to follow into the kitchen, and even induced his equally unwelcome companion to retreat a pace or two.

'My name is Isabel Mortimer, Clara's cousin and mistress of this house,' she said, managing to convey a calmness she was far from feeling.

Although she detected the sound of the front doorknocker being applied, Isabel considered she had more than enough to cope with at the present time without becoming sidetracked by a further caller, and so ignored the summons, as she turned to her cousin.

'Would I be correct in assuming this female, who has dared to invade my home without the common courtesy of at least introducing herself first, is none other than your stepmama?'

'Yes, I am Euphemia Pentecost,' the woman responded,

when all her stepdaughter did was to nod dumbly, and stare at her strong-willed cousin in awestruck silence for daring to remind such a formidable matron of basic good manners.

If Mrs Pentecost had been slightly taken aback, her discomfiture was not long lasting. 'If I seem rude, miss, then I apologise!' she snapped, sounding anything but chastened. 'But let me tell you I have been sorely tried these past months in attempting to trace this wicked, ungrateful gel, who left her loving home without so much as a word to anyone!'

She gestured towards her companion who, keeping a wary eye on Beau, had been attempting to edge ever closer to her. 'And poor Mr Sloane, here, has been almost out of his mind with worry over his fiancée's well-being.'

'Really?' Isabel raised her finely arching brows in mock surprise as she studied the fleshy-faced gentleman closely for the first time, noticing in particular the lack of neck and wide, thick-lipped mouth. 'Now, that is most interesting, because I have been led to believe that my cousin flatly refused to marry Mr Sloane, and that she was obliged to flee the family home because of the pressure being brought to bear upon her by you to form the union, ma'am,' Isabel countered, the accusing note in her voice all too evident. 'Which begs the question, does it not, of who is speaking the truth?'

Having seemingly appreciated already that she was having to deal with a young woman of character and determination, the antithesis of her stepdaughter, in fact, the widow adopted a different tack, becoming nauseatingly apologetic and ingratiating as she bemoaned her widowed state, and the extra burdens placed upon her since her husband's demise.

'Believe me when I tell you, Miss Mortimer, it is my one

cherished wish to do everything humanly possible to ensure my stepdaughter's future happiness,' she continued in
the same fawning tone, 'and I would be failing in my duty
if I didn't attempt to arrange the best possible match for
dear Clara. I'm sure a sensible young woman like yourself
must appreciate that it is much better to marry an upright
gentleman of property, like Mr Sloane here, who can offer
a future wife most every creature comfort in life, than to
retain foolish, girlish dreams of meeting a dashing knight
in shining armour whose interest would very soon wane.'

'I couldn't agree more, ma'am,' Isabel quickly intervened before the widow could develop the theme. 'But that
doesn't alter the fact that Clara doesn't wish to marry Mr
Sloane. Nor, indeed, any profligate in armour, as far as
I'm aware. Let me assure you that she is more than happy
to make her own way in the world, and not be a burden
on you any longer, by engaging in a genteel occupation.'

Hard-eyed and tight-lipped, the widow transferred her
gaze to her stepdaughter. 'I am fully aware of it,' she un-
locked her nutcracker mouth to acknowledge, thereby
clearly heralding the return to her former inflexible stance.
'How do you suppose we managed to locate your whereabouts, you foolish girl! The gentleman with whom you
attempted to attain employment several months ago just
happened to read the notice we were eventually obliged
to place in the newspapers regarding your disappearance
and, recalling the name, wrote to Mr Sloane, providing us
with this address.'

She looked her stepdaughter up and down, the contempt
in her eyes all too discernible. 'Governess, indeed! Who
would ever employ you as a governess?'

'It might surprise you to learn, ma'am, that somebody
already has,' Isabel informed her, experiencing untold delight, before she turned to her cousin, who was holding a

now, tearful Alice to her skirts. 'If you have no desire to accompany these persons back to Hampshire, Clara, perhaps you would be good enough to return to the schoolroom with your charges.'

'You stay precisely where you are!' the widow instantly countered as Clara made to leave the kitchen. 'Until you attain your majority, my girl, you remain under my control, and you will do precisely as I tell you.'

Whether this was true or not did not alter Isabel's resolve to protect her cousin at all costs from such a harridan. Very slowly she moved across the kitchen and, by dint of using a low stool, was able to reach up far enough to remove the pistol that she always kept ready for immediate use on top of the dresser, much to Josh's evident astonishment.

'No, you didn't know I had this, did you, Josh? I keep it primed and ready for just such an unfortunate occurrence as this.' Smile fading, Isabel turned to face her unwelcome visitors again. 'You shall both leave my house at once, otherwise I shan't hesitate to use this.'

Even the case-hardened widow fell back a further pace or two when the pistol was levelled in a surprisingly steady hand. 'You've not heard the last of this, young woman,' she threatened in return, though keeping a wary eye on the firearm. 'You may force us to leave now, but we shall be back with the constable, you mark my words!'

'Spill her claret, Miss Isabel,' Josh urged with bloodthirsty delight.

A moment's silence followed, then, 'I sincerely trust you will refrain from doing any such thing, my dear young woman,' a softly spoken voice from the doorway strongly advised.

Chapter Two

Apart from his superior height and faintly haughty bearing, Isabel could detect no resemblance whatsoever to the handsome young aristocrat whom she had glimpsed all those years ago riding by on a fine bay horse. Yet instinctively she knew that the elegantly attired gentleman framed in the doorway was none other than the late Viscount Blackwood's younger son, home at last to claim his inheritance and take his rightful place up at the Manor.

His unexpected arrival had an immediate effect upon all those present. Silence reigned as all eyes turned on the distinguished gentleman who came sauntering languidly into the kitchen, removing his gloves as he did so. Out of the corner of her eye Isabel saw Bessie check in the act of reaching for the rolling pin, which undoubtedly her trusty housekeeper had intended brandishing as a weapon. Surprisingly, even Beau ceased his growling to turn his head on one side to study the new arrival, and Isabel found herself automatically lowering the pistol on to the table, somehow sensing that its use now would not be necessary.

She continued unashamedly to study him intently as his ice-blue eyes, betraying no emotion whatsoever, flickered briefly over the two unwelcome visitors. Even when he turned his head to study her cousin, still clutching the little girl to her skirts, incredibly there was nothing to suggest that he was possibly viewing one of the most beautiful females he had ever seen in his life. Only when his eyes finally came to rest upon her was there a suggestion of a slight thaw in those cool, strikingly blue depths a moment before he whipped off his hat to reveal a thick, healthy crop of perfectly arranged black locks.

'My name is Blackwood,' he announced in deeply rich cultured tones.

'Yes, I rather thought you must be,' Isabel returned candidly, as she felt Josh press against her. Instinctively she raised her left arm to place it reassuringly about the boy's shoulders, and surprisingly glimpsed what she felt sure was the faintest of twitches at the corner of the Viscount's thin-lipped mouth.

'Would I be correct in assuming that at last I have the felicity of making the acquaintance of Miss Isabel Mortimer, daughter of the late Dr John Mortimer?'

'Indeed you would, sir,' she answered, reaching for the hand that was extended to her. She felt it close briefly round her own, warm and comforting. Since his arrival she felt as if she had experienced the whole gamut of emotions. Foremost now was a sense of relief, and an overwhelming belief that this impressive aristocrat would offer assistance if she had the gall to request it of him on so slight an acquaintance. But dared she…?

'And your arrival, my lord, is most opportune,' she told him, before she experienced any second thoughts. 'Just prior to your own welcome appearance, my home was invaded by these two persons who are intent upon removing my cousin from under this roof… My cousin who just happens to be in your employ as governess to your wards, sir,' she finished artfully.

But would the gambit work? Study him though she did, she could detect no change in his expression, not so much as a suggestion of sympathy in his eyes before they turned from her to the boy still clasped against her, and then flickered briefly in the direction of his younger ward.

'Indeed?' he said at last in a tone that hovered so perilously close to boredom that Isabel was almost obliged to accept that her audacious attempt to attain his support must surely have failed, when assistance came from a most unexpected quarter.

'And I shall take leave to inform you, sir, that I have every right to do so!' Mrs Pentecost announced boldly.

Instantly his lordship's expression changed. He stared down his long aristocratic nose at the widow, a contemptuous curl to his lip. 'If I evince any desire to converse with you, madam, you will be under no illusions about it.'

Even the case-hardened widow was not proof against such a superb put-down, and automatically closed her unpleasant mouth as she retreated a pace or two.

His lordship's gaze again returned to Isabel. The contempt had vanished completely from his expression, though just what had replaced it was impossible to judge.

'You have no reason to doubt the authenticity of this person?'

'No, my lord,' she responded promptly, while dropping her arm from about Josh's shoulders, as though to convey to the boy that he need have no fear of the tall man standing before them. 'I have no doubt that she is indeed my cousin's stepmama. What I do challenge is her right to remove my relative from under this roof. Miss Pentecost was obliged to flee the family home because she was being coerced into marriage with this person.'

If Isabel's look of disdain was nowhere near as accomplished as his lordship's had been a short time earlier, Mr

Sloane was left in no doubt about what she thought of him personally. 'Any man who resorts to coercion in order to attain a wife is beyond contempt. My cousin came here desperately seeking my help, not looking for charity, my lord,' she assured him, gazing earnestly up at him once more. 'She is more than prepared to earn her own living and make her own way in the world. Surely she should be allowed to do that?'

'Perhaps,' was all he said before turning to the widow and her companion, who had gone very red about the jowls since Isabel's condemnation of his conduct.

'I shall obtain your direction, madam, from Miss Pentecost, and you shall be hearing from my lawyers in due course. No, be silent!' he commanded, holding up one shapely hand against the protest the widow had been about to utter. 'If it should come to light that you are indeed legally responsible for Miss Pentecost, be assured she will be safely returned to your home at my expense. If, however, I discover that, for whatever reason, you have been attempting to exceed your authority, then you may be sure I shall take matters a good deal further should Miss Pentecost request me to do so. In the meantime, you have my assurance that your stepdaughter will receive my protection for as long as she remains in my employ.

'Now, if Miss Mortimer has nothing further she wishes to say to you, you may leave,' he continued curtly. 'I have matters I wish to discuss with her in private.'

After being so summarily dismissed, not even the hardened widow dared to utter anything further. Isabel watched them closely before they finally departed and thought she could detect a troubled look in Mr Sloane's eyes, even if the widow's remained hard and defiant.

Lord Blackwood waited only for the housekeeper to close the door behind them before turning once again to

Isabel. 'Clearly I have not chosen the most auspicious of occasions to become acquainted with you, Miss Mortimer,' he announced, a ghost of a smile hanging about his mouth as he uttered this gross understatement. 'So I shall call again tomorrow, if I may—say, at eleven, when I shall hope to spend a little time with my wards and discuss certain matters with Miss Pentecost.'

'I assure you, my lord, that will be most convenient,' Isabel answered for her cousin, who seemed to have lost the power of speech since her stepmother's unexpected appearance. 'Please allow me to show you out.'

Isabel's final farewell was not protracted, as she too needed time to reflect on the unfortunate happenings of the morning. After closing the front door behind the distinguished visitor, she headed for the kitchen once more, pausing briefly as she did so before the large mirror in the passageway.

'Why on earth didn't you tell me I look such a fright, Bessie! she exclaimed the instant she had returned to the others. 'Not only is half my hair dangling about my ears, I'd flour on the end of my nose!'

Bessie almost found herself gaping. In all the dozen or so long years she had known her young mistress, not once had she ever heard her voice the slightest concern over her appearance. Furthermore, she very much doubted the first two callers were behind this surprising show of disquiet over grooming.

'Chances are he never noticed,' she returned above Josh and his sister's impish chuckles. For all the effect the assurance had, however, she might well have saved her breath.

'Not noticed...?' Isabel was momentarily lost for words. 'Lord, Bessie! Where have your wits gone begging? I've no notion where or what Lord Blackwood has been doing in recent years. But by the look of him I'll lay odds he hasn't been enjoying life's luxuries. What's more, I'd wager those blue eyes of his miss nothing!'

Isabel's assessment was remarkably accurate. As it happened his lordship hadn't enjoyed a comfortable existence during the past half-decade or so out in the Peninsula, spying for Wellington. Working mostly alone, he had needed his wits about him at all times, and had become intensely observant as a consequence.

Determined to discover the answers to several puzzling questions, Lord Blackwood returned directly to the Manor, and sent for his aged butler, the person he considered most able to satisfy his curiosity over certain matters.

He awaited his arrival in the library, which had been the first room in the house to be redecorated in readiness for his eventual return. Although age-old tomes still completely lined the shelves on two of the walls, everything else was new. His lordship had even ordered the painting of a hunting scene, which had graced the area above the hearth for many a long year, removed and replaced with one of his adored mother resting her arm about the shoulders of a handsome boy with jet-black locks and strikingly blue eyes. The pose instantly conjured up a much more recent memory, and his lordship smiled to himself as he poured a glass of wine.

The door behind him opened, and he turned to see his aged butler, who had now officially retired and was remaining at the Manor only until such time as his promised cottage on the estate was ready for habitation.

Knowing Bunting was a rigid upholder of the old order, whereby a servant knew his place and never attempted to get on a more familiar footing with his master, his lordship neither offered him a glass of wine, nor the chance to rest his aching joints in the comfort of one of the easy chairs. Any such consideration, he felt sure, would have made the retired major-domo feel distinctly ill at ease, and therefore very likely less forthcoming with information.

Consequently, maintaining the status quo, Lord Blackwood took up a stance before the fire, and rested one arm along the mantelshelf. Outwardly he appeared completely at ease in his surroundings, every inch the relaxed, aristocratic master of the fine Restoration mansion, even though he had utterly loathed his ancestral home as a youth.

'I recall, Bunting, shortly after my long-awaited return here yesterday, you mentioning that you are acquainted with Miss Mortimer,' he said, getting straight to the point of the interview. 'Naturally, I'm curious about her. Not only was she instrumental in clearing my name, but also, as you may possibly be aware, she has been responsible for my wards these past months.'

'Although Miss Mortimer didn't make the children's true identities commonly known, sir, she did confide in me,' the aged butler confirmed, before frowning slightly. 'I believe the children have been happy enough living with her, sir,' he then added, having quickly decided that this must surely be what his master wished to know. 'At least I've not heard anything to the contrary. She brought them up to the house a few weeks back, and asked me to show them round, as it would be their home sooner or later. She wouldn't look round herself, sir. Not one to take liberties, Miss Mortimer isn't. Never known her attempt to venture any further than the kitchen and my rooms on the ground floor, sir, in all the times she came up to the Manor last winter, when I was poorly. If it hadn't been for Miss Isabel and that housekeeper of hers, I think the good Lord would have taken me. She's an angel, sir, that's what she is…an angel!'

His lordship could not forbear a smile as his mind's eye conjured up a clear image of the so-called angel brandishing a serviceable pistol in her right hand. And appearing as if she was more than capable of using it too!

'Evidently a lady of many contrasting talents,' he murmured, though loud enough for the butler to hear.

'Well, sir, the poor young lady was obliged to manage for herself from quite a young age. Seem to remember she lost her mother a year or so after the family moved into the house, sir,' he revealed, falling into a reminiscing mood. He cast his master an uncertain glance. 'Then, not long after the terrible happenings here, the good doctor took bad, and poor Miss Mortimer, little more than a slip of a girl herself at the time, was obliged to care for him.' He shook his head. 'She's not had an easy life, sir. Maybe if her mother had lived, she might have met and married some nice young gentleman by now. But as things turned out…'

His lordship had little difficulty in conjuring up an image of a face boasting more character than beauty; of a pair of large grey-green eyes whose direct gaze some might consider faintly immodest, of a determined little chin above which a perfectly shaped, if slightly overgenerous, mouth betrayed a lively sense of humour, even when confronted by adversity. When compared to her beautiful young cousin, she did perhaps pale into insignificance. Yet it was strange that it was the face framed in the disordered chestnut locks that should be more firmly imprinted in his memory.

And yet not so strange, he countered silently. After all, he owed that young woman a great deal, perhaps more than he might ever be able to repay. He felt a sudden stab of irritation. That didn't alter the fact, though, it had been grossly impertinent of her, not to say outrageous, to have embroiled him in an affair that had absolutely nothing whatsoever to do with him. Had it been anyone else he might well have just walked away and left her to her own devices. Yet he had found he could not withstand the look of entreaty in those large eyes of hers.

He shook his head, wondering at himself. 'I must be getting old,' he murmured.

'Beg pardon, sir?'

'Nothing, Bunting, merely thinking aloud.' He fortified himself from the contents of his glass whilst he gathered his thoughts and focused on what he wished to know. 'Now, the cousin who's living with Miss Mortimer has been acting as governess to my wards, so I understand. The girl, Alice, seems to have become quite attached to her.'

'That wouldn't surprise me, my lord, though I couldn't say for sure,' the aged servant responded, scrupulously truthful as always. 'I've only ever met the young lady once, and then only briefly. But she seemed a very gentle-mannered young woman. What I can tell you, sir, is the boy is very fond of Miss Isabel. Why, I've seen her time and again striding across the park towards the home wood, Master Joshua skipping happily alongside, and that great dog of hers not too far behind.

'Not that I think they were up to no good, my lord,' he hurriedly added, suddenly realising he may have revealed more than he should have done.

The Viscount, however, merely smiled to himself before dismissing the servant with a nod.

The following morning Isabel spent far more time over her appearance than she had ever been known to do before, a circumstance that certainly didn't escape the keen eye of the housekeeper, when her young mistress finally came down to the kitchen shortly before eleven.

The new gown her cousin had made for her suited her wonderfully well, emphasising the perfection of a slender, shapely figure, the colour enhancing the green flecks in her large eyes. Around her shoulders she had draped one of her late mother's fringed shawls, a stylish accessory she rarely donned, and her radiant, dark locks, although not artistically arranged, were for once neatly confined in a simple chignon.

Bessie almost found herself gaping at the transformation. Although it couldn't be denied that in looks she was a mere shadow of her beautiful cousin, few would deny that she was a fine-looking young woman in her own right, and one who never failed to make a lasting impression on more discerning souls.

Bessie might have been slightly concerned, though, about the obvious attempts to impress had she not been very sure her young mistress had a sensible head on her shoulders, and had made every effort for the most self-less reasons. Unless Bessie very much mistook the matter, there was no thought to attract the aristocratic gentleman's interest, merely a desire for all members of the household to appear in a more favourable light.

As the application of the door-knocker filtered through to the kitchen, Bessie made to break off from her task in order to answer the summons, but was forestalled by her young mistress who insisted on going herself.

'I'll give him one thing at least—he's punctual,' Isabel remarked as she headed for the door leading to the passageway. 'Let's hope he's also fair-minded.'

The housekeeper's silent judgement had been uncannily accurate. Isabel didn't wish Clara to be dismissed from her post, simply because of yesterday's unfortunate occurrence, if she could possibly do anything about it. Although she would have been the first to admit that her cousin was not very worldly, and could never be described as a blue-stocking, she was far from stupid, and was at the very least quite capable of teaching little Alice all the necessary female accomplishments.

After pausing only briefly before the passageway mirror, Isabel opened the front door, very well pleased with her appearance. Yet there was nothing, not even so much as a faint widening of blue eyes, to suggest that the Viscount noticed anything different about her from the day before. Had she been in the least conceited she might easily have taken umbrage at such a blatant display of indifference towards her as a woman. The truth of the matter was, though, she was more interested in whether she could persuade him to overlook yesterday's débâcle and retain her cousin's services as governess.

She invited him to step into the parlour, and could see at a glance that this at least met with his approval, even before he said, 'I've always considered this a most charming room, Miss Mortimer. I was a frequent visitor when my good friend Charles Bathurst resided here with his parents. You are to be congratulated. There is a wonderful homely quality about it still. One senses it at once. Would that the Manor could feel so welcoming!'

'It is mostly thanks to my cousin's efforts that the room is now so pleasing, my lord,' she returned promptly, thereby not wasting any opportunity to point out Clara's accomplishments, while at the same time wondering what had been at the root of his remark about the Manor. Surely he was happy to be back in the ancestral home? Or was the realisation of what had taken place there just too harrowing to forget?

'Do sit down, my lord,' she invited, realising suddenly

she was staring at him rather intently. What was worse, she was receiving close scrutiny in return! 'May I offer you some refreshment? I have a rather good Madeira here I'm sure you'd enjoy.'

'Only if you join me, Miss Mortimer,' he returned in that deeply rich velvety voice that was both oddly reassuring and faintly disturbing at one and the same time.

She had already decided that his years away hadn't been altogether kind to him. He was still the same fine figure of a man she well remembered, perhaps a little more so now that sinewy muscle had replaced any slight excess of flesh he might have been guilty of carrying in his youth. Nevertheless, of those handsome, youthful looks there was precious little sign now. His features had grown markedly more severe. The hawk-like nose, the thin-lipped mouth and the square line of his jaw might not have seemed quite so harshly defined had they been tempered by doe-like orbs of a softer hue. Furthermore, the thin line that now ran from the corner of his left eye down to his top lip gave his mouth a slightly contemptuous curl. Yet, for all that, Isabel didn't consider him unattractive. In fact, the opposite was true. There was about him a sardonic quality that she found strangely alluring.

Although she refrained from imbibing in strong liquor as a rule, at least so early in the day, she decided in this instance that it might be wise to humour him, and so settled herself in the chair directly opposite before sampling the contents of her own glass.

'My lord, I am glad to have this opportunity to speak with you in private,' she announced, at last giving voice to the well-rehearsed speech she had been mentally practising since early morning. 'It offers me the opportunity to ask your forgiveness for my behaviour yesterday. I cannot apologise enough for the way I quite outrageously embroiled you in that fiasco. The truth of the matter is, though, sir, I was at a loss to know just how to proceed.'

Once again she thought she could detect the faint twitching of a muscle at the corner of his mouth, before he sampled the contents of his glass and then gave his assessment by a nod of approval. 'On the contrary, Miss Mortimer, you appeared to be in full control of the situation. I'm reliably informed you are no novice where the use of firearms is concerned.'

'Oh, pray don't remind me, sir!' she begged, her suddenly heightened colour proof of the mortification she still felt over her behaviour. 'I should never have threatened them in such an outrageous fashion had I known how to proceed. But the fact is, sir, I didn't know whether Mrs Pentecost could legally remove my cousin from this house, as Clara does not attain her majority until the middle of May. And I simply couldn't allow that to happen! Poor Clara has looked to me, quite five years her senior, to protect her since her arrival here.'

His lordship stared across at her in silence for several moments, his cool gaze revealing nothing except, perhaps, a flicker of sympathy. 'The widow may well be within her rights, ma'am,' he told her bluntly. 'But do not be too disheartened,' he didn't hesitate to assure, when she appeared slightly downcast. 'If she had proof of guardianship with her, I believe she would have been back with the authorities. As this quite obviously didn't occur, I rather fancy there's nothing official in writing. It may well be that the late Mr Pentecost merely expected his wife to take care of the child from his first union. However, it might be that he did make provision for his daughter in his will. I'll wager that female was concealing something. And her companion didn't appear altogether comfortable either!'

'Ah, so you noticed that too!' Isabel returned, feeling

inordinately pleased that she hadn't imagined those wary expressions just prior to her unwelcome visitors' departure. 'Mrs Pentecost certainly seems determined Clara should marry Mr Sloane.'

'Well, she could do worse,' his lordship pointed out, ever the pragmatist. 'His dress alone would suggest he's a man of reasonable means. Your cousin would no longer be obliged to earn a living.'

Isabel was appalled at the suggestion, and it clearly showed. 'My beautiful young cousin married to that portly tailor's dummy...?' she returned in disbelief. 'Why, it's obscene! Not only is he more than twice her age, and therefore old enough to be her father, he also has a most unpleasant, wet mouth. Besides,' she continued, ignoring the odd choking sound emanating from the chair opposite her own, 'Clara and I might not have a great deal in common, but neither of us is avaricious, and would never consider marrying for financial gain.

'And speaking of my cousin,' she went on, when all he did was to stare thoughtfully down into his glass. 'I'm sure you wish to see her and your wards.' So saying, Isabel rose and went over to the bell-pull.

Soon afterwards Bessie was showing the children, followed by their governess, into the room. Isabel herself made to leave, but his lordship forestalled her by requesting her to remain. She was then able to observe his treatment of his wards.

Clearly he was more at ease with Josh who, after an initial hesitancy, began to ask numerous questions about his late father, a gentleman who had been one of his lordship's closest friends, and who had died almost three years before during the capture of Badajoz. Alice, of course, couldn't remember her father in the least, and it rather amused Isabel when his lordship, betraying a faint disquiet when innocent brown eyes stared fixedly up at him, attempted to converse with the little girl.

Yet, as had happened the day before, Isabel could detect nothing in his lordship's demeanour to suggest he was in the least impressed by Clara's loveliness. His tone was quite impassive when he questioned her about the various subjects she had been attempting to teach his wards during the time they had been in her care, and although he showed no reluctance in retaining her services, at least where Alice was concerned, he evinced no delight whatsoever when his offer was readily accepted.

'I do not think there is anything further we need discuss at this time, Miss Pentecost,' his lordship said, at last rising to his feet. 'If you would have the children's belongings packed, my carriage will be here to collect you in the morning, and will return you to the Manor later in the day.'

He then took his leave of his wards and their governess, before surprising Isabel somewhat by requesting she accompany him round to the stable to collect his horse.

'For the time being it would be best if your cousin remains under your roof.' The Viscount registered the look of mingled surprise and doubt in her eyes. 'I know what a censorious world we live in, Miss Mortimer. It wouldn't be too long before your cousin's hitherto spotless reputation suffered as a result of residing permanently under my roof. But that hopefully will be avoided by her returning to your protection each evening.'

Easily guessing the reason for the lingering concern she cast up at him, he added, 'And pray do not trouble yourself over any possible actions of the stepmother's. I think we can safely rely on the excellent Mr Goodbody's abilities to delay proceedings until such time as your cousin attains her majority, should it prove that Mrs Pentecost is within her rights to remove her stepdaughter from under your roof. I shall write to him on my return to the Manor, requesting his help in the matter. He hasn't failed me yet.'

This admission brought something else to the forefront of Isabel's mind. 'And the children, sir—are they now safe from any claims to guardianship their uncle might make?'

His lordship's smile was not pleasant. 'The last I heard of Danforth, he was making for the Channel in an attempt to flee the authorities. He was proved to be the very worst kind of scoundrel. What might have happened to the children had they been left in his care, I shudder to think. Suffice it to say, he'd be unwise to show his face again in this country for a considerable time.'

Having reached the yard, Isabel noticed his lordship surprisingly frowning at the lad whom she employed to do odd jobs about the place, as Toby emerged from the stable, leading his lordship's fine bay.

'Is there something amiss, my lord?'

'I seem to recognise this lad.'

A thought occurred to Isabel. 'Possibly a family resemblance. His brother worked up at the Manor for several years, so I understand. He disappeared around the time of the murders. Is that not so, Toby?'

The boy confirmed it with a nod of his head. 'Disappeared on that selfsame night, so Ma said. Went out for a tankard of ale, and never came 'ome again. Not a word been 'eard of 'im since, neither.'

After learning this his lordship raised his head and stared across the meadow into the far distance. 'Yes, I remember, now, my friend Charles Bathurst mentioning something about young Jem disappearing on the night of the murders. I suppose I thought he'd just upped and left and got himself another situation somewhere else. Couldn't have blamed him in the circumstances.' His frown deepened. 'But he would never have gone without a word to a soul.'

'That 'ee wouldn't,' Toby confirmed. 'Ma were expecting 'im back that night. She reckons 'ee must 'ave been set on by footpads, or such like. But I don't reckon that be right. 'Cepting for that watch you give 'im all them years back, m'lord, 'ee couldn't 'ave 'ad more than an odd penny in his pocket.'

'I'm sure you're right, Toby,' Isabel agreed. 'But it is strange, is it not, that no one has seen or heard anything of him since. Don't you agree, sir?'

His lordship, however, continued to stare silently at some distant spot, his mind locked in the past.

Chapter Three

It was only to be expected that the children's removal to the Manor would result in a return to normality at the farmhouse. Isabel was obliged to admit that it was much quieter for a start. A little too quiet sometimes, she increasingly began to feel as the days passed.

She couldn't deny that their departure had resulted in a much lighter workload for both Bessie and herself. They were no longer obliged to slave over a hot range for hours a day in order to satisfy the appetite of a rapidly growing boy, not to mention his healthy younger sister. There was far less laundry to deal with each week as well. Yet, for all that the children had been hard work, Isabel missed not having them about the place.

Of course she looked forward to her cousin's return to the house each evening. Over supper, Clara would regale them with all the latest gossip from up at the Manor, and keep them abreast of the improvements to the house that were, apparently, daily taking place. None the less, even her cousin's continued presence at the farmhouse couldn't suppress the ever-increasing discontent Isabel was for some obscure reason experiencing.

As February gave way to March, even seeing evidence

that spring was not too far away quite failed to lift her spirits. She was reminded of how she had felt during those first weeks after her dear father had passed away. Then, of course, there had been a good reason for the malcontent that had gripped her. What excuse was there now for her feeling totally dissatisfied with her lot? There was none, of course. Yet, try as she might, Isabel simply couldn't shake off the mood of despondency.

A week of heavy rain did little to improve her spirits. Nor, it had to be said, did waking up one morning to discover her vegetable patch under a considerable amount of water.

Her prized garden had produced sufficient quantities of root and green vegetables to feed the household throughout the previous year, not to mention sufficient soft fruits during the summer months to preserve for leaner times. She doubted very much that this would be the case for the present year, for she very much feared that her attempt to produce early crops had been completely washed away by the deluge.

'That is it!' she declared, reaching for her cloak and stout, serviceable boots. 'I'm not prepared to put up with this any longer! I'm mindful of the fact that his lordship has been most generous to this household already, especially where Clara is concerned. But that doesn't give him the right to neglect his duties as a landowner. So don't you dare try to stop me, Bessie!'

The thought never crossed the housekeeper's mind for an instant. She knew well enough that, when her mistress had reached the limits of her patience, only a forceful airing of views would restore calm, and return her to her normally sensible and controlled state. None the less, Bessie sensed that more lay behind this present show of fiery tension in her young mistress than the washing away of a few vegetable seedlings. All the same, she was at a loss to know quite what it might be.

From the kitchen window she followed her irate young employer's progress up the drove to the meadow. Then she watched her clamber, in a most unladylike fashion, over the boundary fence that divided his lordship's deer park from her own property, her faithful Beau padding along at her heels. Bessie smiled to herself as she recalled a story she'd heard many years before about an ancient warrior queen, fearless and determined, setting forth to do battle with her enemies. Which was exactly how Miss Isabel looked right now! And there wouldn't be too many souls brave enough to stand in her way, she mused.

Although Mr Tredwell, the new butler up at the Manor, did not view the rather ill-groomed young woman, demanding to see the aristocratic master of the house at once, in quite the same reverential way as did her own devoted servant, her overall demeanour, quite frankly, did puzzle him. Had he been in town he maybe wouldn't have thought twice about denying admittance. But this was not London. And unless his adroitness at assessing a person's station in life had deserted him entirely, this was no country bumpkin either. Nor, he felt sure, was she a female of a certain disreputable calling.

None the less, having been in his lordship's employ a few short weeks only, Tredwell had no intention of jeopardising his superior position in the household by not fulfilling his role as major-domo. He had a duty to deny admittance to all those who might importune his lordship. And this young woman, he strongly suspected, was more than capable of doing precisely that!

Consequently, he was on the point of demanding to know the caller's name and business, when a high-pitched squeal from behind captured his attention, and he turned to see his master's elder ward bounding down the main staircase.

The boy knew well enough that he was only ever supposed to use the back stairs, unless instructed to do otherwise, and Tredwell was on the point of reminding him of this fact, when he was almost thrust rudely aside by Josh in his enthusiasm to reach the caller.

'Miss Isabel! Miss Isabel!' he cried joyfully, almost launching himself into her outstretched arms. 'You've come to see us at last! Why has it taken you so long? Have you come to take me fishing?'

Josh's enthusiastic greeting and subsequent barrage of questions had contrasting effects on the two adults: a look of enlightenment immediately flickered over the high-ranking servant's long, thin face, for he was very well aware that the children's surrogate guardian during past months had been none other than a Miss Isabel Mortimer; whereas the lady herself, after a brief glowing smile down at Josh, cast a look of comical dismay above the boy's head in the general direction of the butler.

'The truth of the matter is, Josh, I'm here to see his lordship. There's something I need to discuss with him urgently. But I haven't forgotten my promise,' she assured him. 'I will take you fishing. But we'll need to seek his lordship's permission first, and wait for warmer weather, of course.'

Out of consideration for the servants, Isabel first removed her boots, which not surprisingly had become caked with mud after her brisk hike across the sodden park land, before accepting the butler's invitation to step inside the hall, and leaving her trusty hound to await her return in the shelter of the roomy, stone-built entrance-porch.

'Why are you not at your lessons, Josh?' she asked him,

thinking it most strange that he should be wandering about the house by himself at this time of day.

'Oh, I just happened to leave my book in the kitchen,' he answered, raising wide, innocent eyes, which didn't fool Isabel for a second. 'I often do, you know.'

'Yes, I can imagine,' she responded, favouring him with a quizzical look. 'And what prompts these lapses in memory—plum cake or apple tart?'

He chuckled impishly. 'Plum cake. But it isn't as good as yours.'

'Artful little demon!' she admonished lovingly. 'You'd best run along then, and have your mid-morning treat, before Miss Pentecost wonders what's become of you… although I expect she's a pretty shrewd notion already of why you're so forgetful.'

This touching exchange was witnessed by more than one person, as Isabel quickly discovered, when the butler requested her to take a seat whilst he discovered whether his lordship was available to see her.

'Don't trouble yourself, Tredwell. I'm quite at leisure,' a smooth voice assured him, and Isabel swung round to see the master of the fine Restoration building leaning against a door jamb, his arms folded across his manly chest.

'This is an unexpected pleasure, Miss Mortimer,' he declared, after moving to one side in order that she might precede him into the room. He then looked at her intently, studying her from head to toe, and paying particular attention to the wild and shining windswept locks, the glowing colour in her cheeks and her unshod feet, whilst all the time she took stock of her surroundings, in blissful ignorance of his scrutiny.

'Had I not happened to witness that touching little reunion between you and Josh, I might have been forgiven for imagining some personal calamity had befallen you. I shall take leave to inform you, young woman, you look a positive fright! In fact, little better than any ill-groomed labouring wench!'

'And so would you, if you'd traipsed across the park in this wind,' she defended abruptly, clearly nettled by the criticism, though she did whip off the red ribbon that had earlier confined her locks at the nape of her neck and re-tied it as best she could without the aid of a mirror.

Secretly he had thought she looked stunningly attractive with her rich chestnut locks framing the healthy glow in her face. She was so different from so many of those high-born society ladies who made full use of any artificial aid to beauty. Miss Isabel Mortimer might never be considered by some to be a gem of loveliness, a pearl beyond price. But she was certainly out of the common way, he decided, and quite refreshingly natural.

'Do sit yourself down, Miss Mortimer, and tell me how I may serve you,' he invited, while pouring out two glasses of wine. 'Here, drink it,' he added, when she attempted to refuse the Madeira. 'It will calm your nerves.'

'There's absolutely nothing wrong with my nerves,' she assured him, reluctantly accepting the glass. 'I'm merely damnably annoyed.'

'About what, may I ask?' he enquired, not wholly approving the unladylike language, which was strange, considering that he never objected to plain speaking as a rule.

'For the past six years, my lord, the ditch on the western boundary of your property has repeatedly overflowed on to my land, after any prolonged spells of rain, to the detriment of my vegetable crops. Time and again I approached the last steward, Guy Fensham, to do something about it, but to no avail. Why your family ever employed such a lazy—' Isabel pulled herself up abruptly, realising suddenly that she was going beyond what was pleasing by voicing opinions on matters that were absolutely none of her concern.

Taking a moment to fortify herself from the contents of her glass, she peered up at him through her lashes. He didn't seem in the least annoyed by her outburst. But then it was sometimes very difficult to judge what was passing through the mind of this enigmatic aristocrat, she reminded herself. 'But you do not need me to tell you how he neglected his duties during your time away, sir.'

Without uttering a word, his lordship went over to his desk and proceeded to write a brief note. The silence in the room was punctuated by the scratching of the quill across the sheet of paper, the steady ticking of the mantelclock and a distant low and eerie howling. Which Isabel did her best to ignore whilst taking further stock of her surroundings.

It really was a very masculine room, with its dark wooden furnishings, and heavy leather-bound tomes lining two of its walls. The claret-coloured curtains at the window matched almost perfectly the shade of the leather upholstery on the heavy chairs. Only the fine painting of the woman and the boy above the fireplace might have been considered by some to be out of keeping with the rest of the room. Yet the more Isabel peered up at the portrait of the striking dark-haired woman, with her arm lovingly placed round the shoulders of a handsome boy, the more she considered it provided a necessary relief to the library's ambience of rigid masculinity.

As his lordship rejoined her by the hearth, and Isabel watched him reach for the bell-pull, her eyes automatically returned to the portrait above his head. Then stark reality hit her like a physical blow, almost making her gasp.

'Good Lord! That's you, sir!'

He raised his eyes briefly to the likeness of himself as a boy. 'Yes, handsome young rogue, wasn't I?'

'Indeed you were,' she acknowledged. 'And that woman is your mother, I assume? You certainly favour her in looks… Well,' she amended, 'at least you did. I believe, like myself, you lost your mother when you were quite young?'

Just for an instant his eyes betrayed a flicker of sorrow before he tossed the contents of his glass down his throat, and placed the empty vessel on the mantelshelf behind him.

'Yes, I was fourteen, and away at school when I learned of her death from typhus. She had been visiting one of the families on the estate, and contracted the infection there.' He released his breath in an audible sigh. 'The house was never the same after she'd gone. I grew to hate the place.'

Isabel felt saddened to hear him say this. 'That's a great pity, sir,' she responded softly, echoing her thoughts. 'It's a fine old house, and this room is both elegant and comfortable.'

'I had it completely refurbished before my arrival,' he enlightened her. 'I knew I should be obliged to spend at least part of each year here, and I had no intention of suffering constant reminders of my late father.'

She had heard rumours, of course, of how much he had loathed his father and half-brother, and now she'd had confirmation of the fact from the man himself.

She couldn't help wondering from where the hatred had sprung. It would have been true to say that his father hadn't been universally liked, and there were plenty round these parts who certainly hadn't mourned his passing, she reminded herself. But to be disliked so intensely by one's own child…? It was all so very sad.

She raised her eyes to discover him staring intently down at her. There was a decidedly saturnine smile playing about his mouth, an indication, perhaps, that he had guessed precisely what had been passing through her mind. She felt acutely uncomfortable, and for the first time in his company felt unable to meet that knowing gaze. Fortunately the butler came to her rescue by entering the room a moment later, thereby instantly capturing the Viscount's attention.

'Get one of the footmen to take this note over to my new steward without delay, Tredwell,' his lordship instructed, handing over the folded sheet of paper. 'I want as many of the estate workers as can reasonably be spared taken off other duties and sent down to the western boundary to clear the ditches down there.'

The butler was on the point of departure, when his lordship forestalled him by demanding to know, 'What on earth is that confounded noise?'

Isabel acknowledged the butler's apologetic glance with a smile, before she said, 'I'm afraid I'm to blame. It's my dog, Beau. I'd better leave.'

'Nonsense, child! Sit down, and finish your wine,' his lordship countered, as she made to rise. 'Leave the library door ajar, Tredwell, and let the misbegotten creature in. I don't doubt he'll locate his mistress's whereabouts without causing too much mayhem.'

It was a matter of moments only after Isabel had detected the sound of the front door closing that Beau came bounding into the room. After satisfying himself that she had come to no harm, he did something that she had never known him do before. He stood on his long hind legs and placed his front paws high on his lordship's chest. A lesser man might well have staggered, or at the very least betrayed signs of alarm. His lordship did neither. He merely looked appalled when the hound appeared as though he was about to lick his face by way of an introduction.

'Oh, no, you don't, you abominable creature! Get down at once!'

Although the dog surprisingly enough obeyed the command, his immediate compliance didn't appear to impress the Viscount, who followed the hound's subsequent exploration of the fine library with a jaundiced eye.

'What did I hear you call him…? Beau, was it?' At her nod of assent, he rolled his eyes ceiling-wards. 'A singularly inappropriate name. A more ill-favoured brute I've yet to clap eyes on!'

More amused than anything else by this most unjustified criticism of her beloved hound, Isabel smiled up at him. 'Ah, but you see, my lord, you do not view him through my eyes.'

He regarded her in silence, his expression, as it so often was, totally unreadable. Then he said, 'What on earth possessed you to acquire such a breed? You know what it is, I suppose?'

'Yes, a wolfhound—er—mostly,' she responded. 'When a pup he was discovered scavenging for food round the cottages in the village by some urchins, who then considered it would be wonderful sport to tie a large stone about his neck and throw him in the millpond,' she explained. 'I happened along at the time, rescued him and took him back with me to the farmhouse. Naturally I made enquiries about the village, and in Merryfield, too, to see if anyone had lost a wolfhound pup, but no one came forward to claim him. So he's been with me ever since.'

While she had been speaking Lord Blackwood had seated himself in the chair opposite. Not many moments afterwards Beau had returned to the hearth and had settled himself on the rug before the fire, making use of one of his lordship's muscular thighs to rest his head.

Isabel watched as his lordship raised one long-fingered

hand and began to stroke the hound gently. He appeared perfectly relaxed, and she would have been too, strangely enough, had she not been convinced that striking blue orbs were avidly scrutinising her from behind those half-shuttered lids.

'Well, I'd better not waste any more of your time, my lord,' she said hurriedly, suddenly feeling embarrassingly aware that the hem of her skirts and cloak were caked in mud.

Although she had always remained particular in her personal habits, she would have been the first to admit she had never spent an inordinate amount of time before her mirror, simply because being perfectly groomed at all times had never ranked high on her list of priorities. Yet she couldn't deny that being likened to an ill-groomed country wench had touched a very sore spot indeed. Why suddenly should her appearance matter so much? More-over, why should this aristocrat's approbation all at once be so important to her?

'It was good of you to see me,' she added, 'but now I'll be on my way.'

'Nonsense, child!' he countered, when she made to rise. 'Sit and finish your wine. As I mentioned before, I'm quite at leisure.'

She was forced silently to admit that he looked it too. Sitting there, with his long, muscular legs stretched out before him, and his eyes fully closed now, he appeared totally relaxed, completely at ease with himself. Had she needed more proof that he could never have committed that terrible crime all those years ago, she was being given it now. Surely no man who had carried out such a dreadful deed could look so at peace with himself?

Yet the murders did take place, she reminded herself, once more taking stock of her surroundings. There was no refuting that fact. Could the grisly events have taken place here, in this very room? She couldn't help wondering.

'Something appears to be troubling you, Miss Mortimer,' he remarked, his eyes once again fully open and as acutely assessing as her own had been only a short time before. 'I trust you are not concerned about being in here alone with me. You are in no danger, I assure you. And if, for any reason, I should experience an overwhelming desire to lay violent hands upon you, I'm sure your trusty hound, here, would come to your rescue.'

'Ha! I'm not so very sure he would!' Isabel returned, quite without rancour. She was more amazed than anything else that Beau had taken such an instant liking to someone. It had never happened before. Which just went to substantiate her belief that his lordship was not the black-hearted demon he had sometimes been painted.

'So, what were you thinking about a few minutes ago that brought such a troubled expression to your face?'

Lord! Isabel mused. Was he always so observant? 'Well, since you ask, I was experiencing a surge of morbid curiosity,' she finally admitted. 'I was wondering whether your father and brother were killed in this room.'

'No, in the drawing room, as it happens. Should you like to visit the scene of the crime?'

Had she not witnessed it with her own eyes she would never have supposed for a moment that those icy-blue orbs could dance with wicked amusement. He really was a most attractive and engaging gentleman when he chose to be. And, she didn't doubt for a second, a damnably dangerous one, to boot, to any female weak enough not to resist his charm! Was she mad even to consider remaining with him a moment longer?

'Well, yes, I would, as it happens,' she answered, curiosity having rapidly overridden sound common sense.

Rising smoothly to his feet, Lord Blackwood escorted her and his new-found friend across the wood-panelled hall and into the large room situated at the back of the house. Of all the ground-floor rooms, the drawing room boasted the most commanding view of the formal gardens at the rear of the house, which could be reached by means of tall French windows leading out on to a wide, stone terrace.

His lordship recalled vividly the many large parties held in the drawing room when his mother had been alive. It had once been, without doubt, the most elegant salon in the entire house. Sadly this was no longer the case. It smelt musty through lack of use, the wallpaper and curtains were tired and faded, and what few bits of furniture remained scattered about the floor were sadly worn and heralding from an age long gone by.

As she moved about, noting the dark, intricately patterned carpet and the elegance of the marble fireplace, Isabel didn't experience, strangely enough, any sense of disquiet because of what had taken place in the room. If anything, she felt saddened by its neglect. Undoubtedly the carpet, the wallpaper and the curtains had been expensive. All the same, they were far too dark and oppressive, an ill choice for such a room as this in her opinion.

His lordship, easily detecting the tiny sigh of discontent, smiled ruefully. 'No, not the most pleasant of atmospheres, is it, Miss Mortimer? Such a dark, depressing place!'

'I couldn't agree more,' she returned at her most candid. 'But it has little to do with what took place here. I do not know who might have chosen the décor, my lord, but whoever it was betrayed a sad want of taste, if you'll forgive me saying so. The wall-coverings are far too dark, and totally at odds with the patterned carpet. And as for the crimson curtains…'

Isabel went over to the French windows, where the offending articles hung. Once it must have been a wonderful view. Now even the gardens were showing clear signs of neglect. As the windows were securely bolted, both top and bottom, denying access to the terrace, she wandered over to the windows in the east-facing wall, and was instantly reminded of how windy it was outside.

'Great heavens! Little wonder it strikes so cold in here. This window, here, is very ill fitting, my lord.'

He came to stand beside her, and tested the catch himself. 'That is something that must be put right without delay,' he remarked. 'The Lord only knows how long it has been like that. I've seldom set foot in here since my father had it redecorated some eighteen years ago.' He looked about him with distaste. 'You're quite right, the room is damnably depressing. I dislike it intensely!'

No one could have mistaken the disdain in his voice, which she felt was a great pity, because it could have been made into such a lovely bright and airy room without too much effort.

Conscious of his nearness, and the fact that he was staring at her in that intensely disturbing way once more, she put some distance between them by wandering about again, noting what items of furniture were left in the room and, perhaps, more importantly, those that were quite obviously missing. Maybe the furniture had not been to his taste either. Or perhaps certain items still bore the evidence of what had taken place. After all, the old butler had told her once that it had been nothing short of a bloodbath.

Something in her expression must have betrayed her train of thought, for when she happened to glance in his lordship's direction once more, she caught him staring back at her, that cynical curl to his lips very much in evidence.

'My father, by all accounts, was found over there in his favourite chair.' He pointed in the general direction of the impressive fireplace. 'My brother somewhere over here, so I understand, on one of the sofas.'

She frowned. 'So you never...?'

'Saw for myself?' he finished for her. 'No. As soon as the bodies were discovered, Bunting, I believe, sent immediately for the local Justice of the Peace, Sir Montague Cameron, and the constable. I was still sound asleep when they arrived, covered in blood, with a bloodstained sabre on the floor by my bed.' The cynical smile was suddenly more pronounced. 'Pretty damning evidence, wouldn't you say? Had it not been for your intervention, and the help of some good friends, I might still be living in obscurity across the Channel. But when one has none other than Wellington as a staunch ally, other influential people begin to take notice.'

Isabel's ears pricked up at this. 'You know the Duke personally?'

'I was with him throughout most of the Peninsular Campaign,' he revealed so casually that one might have supposed he had found the whole experience quite uneventful and dull. 'I was on his staff, as it happens, one of his Exploring Officers. As you might already be aware, my mother was a Frenchwoman. She taught me to speak her native tongue so well that I could pass for one of her fellow countrymen. Which, as I'm sure you can appreciate, proved most useful when I was obliged to ride deep into enemy territory.'

It took Isabel a moment only to assimilate what she was being told. Then a feeling of bewilderment, not to mention irritation, gripped her. 'You were a spy, you mean. You spied for Wellington. You put your life at risk attempting to discover things he needed to know?'

His faintly ironic bow confirming this only served to irritate her further. 'Then why—for heaven's sake!—with all your experience, have you never attempted to discover who tried to frame you for the murder of your father and brother? Your name has been cleared, yes. But mud sticks,' she reminded him bluntly. 'There will always be those who will wonder.

'No, you might not care, my lord,' she continued when all he did was to raise his broad shoulders in a shrug of complete indifference. 'But your wife might, should you ever choose to marry. More importantly, so would any children you might one day be blessed to have. Do you suppose they would ever wish to hear their father called a murderer?'

He stared at her for so long in silence, his expression, yet again, totally unreadable, that she was convinced her words had fallen on deaf ears. Then he astonished her by asking, 'So, where do you suggest *we* begin? The events, may I remind you, took place almost nine years ago. All the old servants were discharged soon afterwards, and found new positions, I know not where.'

'With one exception,' she reminded him.

'Bunting was questioned at the time by Sir Montague. He neither saw nor heard anything,' he responded.

Isabel, knowing this to be true, acknowledged it before adding, 'I'm certain what he did reveal was the absolute truth. But I should still like to know how the murderer managed to get into the house without using force, and left it again, without anyone being any the wiser.'

'In that case, Miss Mortimer, we'd best go and ask him.' Leading the way back into the hall, his lordship gave orders for the carriage to be brought round to the door as soon as possible, before he turned to discover an expression of doubt flicker over a finely boned face. He guessed at once the reason behind the troubled look. 'Had you come here alone, ma'am, I wouldn't have hesitated to consider the proprieties. However, as you have your own four-legged duenna to hand, I think we might dispense with the services of a maidservant for the short journey to Bunting's cottage, don't you?'

Chapter Four

The journey to the old butler's cottage on the edge of the estate was conducted almost in silence. His lordship couldn't quite make up his mind whether this was because his fellow passenger felt uneasy at being in the close confines of a carriage alone with him, or she was merely not garrulous by nature. Whatever the reason, he considered her a restful young woman for the most part. For instance, he could never envisage her getting into a state over trifles. Or ever succumbing to a fit of the vapours, come to that. None the less, he could well imagine she could be a managing little madam on occasions, if not sufficiently bridled.

He couldn't resist smiling to himself. Few in his life had ever exerted sufficient influence over him to bestir him into doing something he had no real desire to do, or to persuade him to look at something from a totally different viewpoint. Miss Isabel Mortimer had succeeded in doing just that, however. No mean feat! he was silently obliged to concede. Whether he would thank her for it in the long run was another matter entirely. But he had embarked, now, on this quest to solve the mystery of who had killed his father and brother, and he had no intention of changing his mind.

'You may relax now, Miss Mortimer, we've arrived at our destination,' he teased gently, as the carriage drew up before a double-fronted cottage at the end of a row of newly limewashed dwellings. 'You'll not be obliged to suffer my baneful presence alone any longer.'

The implication was clear. 'I do not feel in the least ill at ease in your company, sir,' Isabel assured him. 'Why should I? You've never given me any reason to mistrust you. I apologise, though, if I seemed a little distant. It's merely that I've never travelled in such a comfortable carriage before, and I've been enjoying the experience hugely, not to mention travelling across part of the estate where I've never ventured before.'

As he threw wide the door to allow Beau to jump out, his lordship felt something within him stir. It wasn't pity, he felt sure. What she had revealed was the simple truth, not an attempt to arouse compassion. Yet it had moved him none the less.

He let down the steps himself, and as he helped her to alight, and she placed her hand briefly in his own, he could feel the calluses in the palm. His old butler had revealed that, for a gentleman's daughter, she hadn't enjoyed the most favourable existence. The elderly retainer clearly had not lied.

Yet again something within him stirred.

Making use of his silver-handled walking stick, the Viscount made their presence known, and it wasn't long before Bunting answered the summons.

'Why, your lordship!' he declared, clearly astonished. 'This is a most unexpected pleasure! And Miss Isabel, too! Oh, do come in, please!'

'Don't wait for Beau,' Isabel advised the old man as she stepped over the threshold. 'He's obviously picked up the

scent of a rat, or something or other. He'll come and find
me when he's ready.'

'So long as he doesn't present any vermin he does happen to locate to me on his return,' his lordship remarked
drily, which resulted in Isabel gurgling with mirth.

The Viscount's immediate smile in response held the
old butler transfixed for a second or two before he turned
to close the door. Not since his lordship had been a boy
had he seen him smile so naturally or so warmly.

His astonishment was no less marked than Isabel's when
she stepped into the low-ceilinged front parlour and first
glimpsed the elegant furnishings. She had a fairly shrewd
idea from where they had come. At least his lordship had
put some of the old drawing-room furniture up at the
Manor to good use, and no doubt Bunting had been most
appreciative. Undeniably it was a deal more respectable
than hers at the farmhouse, and she couldn't help feeling
a twinge of envy.

After taking a seat, but refusing the offer of refreshment, his lordship didn't waste time in coming to the reason for the visit, which resulted in the old man's smile
instantly disappearing.

If the truth were known, it was something the ex-butler
would far rather forget. A lifetime in service, however,
could not be so easily forgotten. He would never consider
disobeying one of the Viscount's requests, even though,
strictly speaking, he was no longer in his lordship's employ. None the less, the young master had been generous
since his return by providing a comfortable little home,
fully furnished. It was little enough to ask in return, Bunting decided.

'What precisely do you wish to know, my lord?'

'I'd like you to go through the events of the evening before, when my cousin Francis came to dine. That much I

can remember, and storming out of the house in a rage just prior to his arrival, after a—er—slight altercation with my sire.' His lordship's teeth flashed in one of his saturnine smiles. 'Which I'm positive you must surely have overheard, or, at the very least, learned about later.'

'Quite so,' the old butler acknowledged apologetically.

Something occurred to Isabel as rather odd at this point in the discussion, but she decided to keep her own counsel for the present, and listened intently to what the old man had to say.

'Mr Francis Blackwood arrived around six. Dinner that evening was not what you might term an enjoyable affair, as I recall. His lordship was still angry with you, sir. And I have to say your brother didn't help the situation by reminding his father of certain of your past—er—misdemeanours, though Mr Francis came to your defence on more than one occasion, as I recall, suggesting a career in the army might be the best thing for you.'

'How very magnanimous of him!' his lordship put in, still smiling faintly. 'I must remember to thank him when next we meet. And thank him, too, for taking some responsibility for the Manor during my absence.' His lordship ceased to contemplate the logs in the hearth, and looked across at his old servant once more. 'But I interrupted you, Bunting. Pray continue.'

'Your father, of course, wouldn't even consider it. Said something about, if you wished to join the army, you could work your way up the ranks, because he'd never purchase a commission for such an ingrate. In the next breath he threatened to disinherit you.' Bunting shrugged his thin shoulders. 'You must remember, though, sir, he'd worked himself up into a passion, and was drinking more than usual.

'Well, they eventually repaired to the drawing room,

where Mr Francis and his lordship played cards,' he went on, after a moment's silence. 'Your father was wont to say, if you remember, sir, that Mr Francis was the only decent player in the family. He blamed you for not being there to make up a fourth at whist, but Mr Francis managed to console him with a few hands of French ruff.

'It was very late, well after eleven, nearer midnight, when Mr Francis finally rang for his carriage,' he continued, once again having taken a moment or two to gather his thoughts. 'Master Giles was already dozing on the sofa, and your cousin was pouring his lordship a final brandy, as I recall, but didn't have one himself. His lordship ordered me to show Mr Francis out, then bolt all the doors and retire. His lordship sounded weary, I seem to remember. At the time I assumed he must have dropped off to sleep, like Master Giles.'

'And you did check all the doors and windows before you retired?' Isabel asked him.

He confirmed it with a solemn nod. 'I always checked the windows before I drew the curtains earlier in the evenings, miss, never failed, and I always checked that all doors were locked at the same time. I only ever threw the bolts across them just before retiring. If I knew Master Sebastian was out of an evening, I wouldn't bolt the side entrance. He always entered that way on account of it being nearest to the stables. But on that particular night I went round and bolted them all.'

Isabel's ears pricked up at this. 'What, even the side door?'

'Yes, miss,' he confirmed, before casting Lord Blackwood an apologetic glance. 'It was his late lordship's own orders, sir. He muttered something about you could sleep in a hedgerow for all he cared.'

The Viscount's response to this was to smile that

crooked smile of his. Isabel, on the other hand, thought it extremely callous, even though, with hindsight, she realised that it was a great pity her father and the others had somehow managed to sneak the present Lord Blackwood back into the house by way of the side entrance and up to his room, before the side door had been securely bolted for the night, and echoed her thoughts aloud.

'About what time was this feat accomplished?' his lordship asked her, having no memory of anything that had taken place after he had visited the local inn.

'I seem to recall Bessie telling me Papa was home just as the long-case clock in the kitchen chimed midnight. So I suppose it must have been some time around eleven. Papa mentioned, in his written account, about using the back stairs, and seeing no servants about.'

'He wouldn't have done, miss, not at that time,' Bunting confirmed. 'I'd sent them all to bed long before then. Neither his lordship nor Master Giles required their valets at that time of day. They always got themselves ready for bed, as indeed did you, my lord,' he continued. 'I could manage well enough on my own at that time.'

It was little wonder not one of the old servants at the Manor would ever say a word against Bunting. He had always been so considerate to them all, she mused, before asking him if he'd heard anything himself. After all, attempting to get an inebriated man, who was incapable of walking, up to his room must have caused some commotion, she reasoned, but he shook his head.

'I was keeping myself occupied at the other end of the house, miss, tidying the dining room, and setting the table in the breakfast parlour in readiness for the morning. I never went anywhere near the back stairs until I first checked the side entrance door was locked earlier in the evening. Then, of course, later, when I threw the bolts and retired to bed.'

'And you discovered the bodies at what time, Bunting?' his lordship asked.

'Oh, it wasn't I who first saw the terrible sight,' he enlightened his visitors. 'No, it was the poor young scullery maid, when she went into the drawing room to lay the fire. It might have been early May, sir, but it could still get quite chilly of an evening.'

'About what time would she have begun her work?' his lordship asked, thereby betraying his complete ignorance of such household practices.

'About half past six, sir. That's what time she always began laying fires, and always started with the one in the breakfast parlour. Then she did the library, and then the drawing room. So I suppose it would have been about seven, or soon afterwards. I was then informed of the tragedy, and sent for Sir Montague Cameron at once. He wasn't best pleased, I seem to recall. Apparently he'd had little sleep the night before.'

'I'm not surprised. My father was there until quite late delivering his sixth child,' Isabel revealed. 'It had been a difficult confinement and he had been there since the afternoon. It was while he was making his way home, sir, that he came upon Jem Marsh and your old steward outside the village inn attempting to get you on to your horse. Without much success, I might add. In the end my father took you back to the Manor in his gig. You couldn't even stand on your own two feet, let alone wield a sabre, for heaven's sake!'

His lordship couldn't forbear a smile at the clear note of derision in her voice, and silently acknowledged that his behaviour that evening, what he could remember of it, didn't redound to his credit. None the less, he was obliged to point out that several hours might have elapsed before his father and brother were murdered. Time enough, surely, for him to have sobered up sufficiently to commit the deed?

Isabel, however, wasn't so sure. Her father had witnessed more than one man in a drunken stupor, and his lordship, according to her father's statement, had been as good as unconscious, and would have remained so for a good many hours. 'The murders could only have taken place after Bunting had retired, and before the servants rose the following morning,' she reminded them. 'My father was convinced that you would have been still sleeping off your excesses when the servants rose. But just let's suppose you did recover from your drunken stupor and went downstairs and murdered your relatives, would you then have gone back up to your room and calmly gone to sleep again? I hardly think so,' she told him, when he didn't attempt to respond. 'You'd have to be totally insane to do such a thing, and I do not imagine anyone would consider you a candidate for Bedlam.'

'Well, my lord, I remember quite well that it took me quite some time to rouse you that morning, as it so often did when you had been—er—imbibing quite freely,' Bunting disclosed, clearly thinking on the same lines as Isabel. 'And you didn't seem best pleased when I did. You swore at length, advising me to go stick my head in a bucket.'

'Ha! That's rich!' Isabel muttered. 'You'd have been well advised to have done that to yourself.'

Ignoring the aside, his lordship frowned, trying desperately to recall just what had occurred that morning. He remembered waking with the worst head he'd experienced in his life. The next thing he knew, Sir Montague and the constable were in the room, staring aghast at his clothing. 'When did you first realise I was in the house, Bunting?'

'Not until I entered your bedchamber, sir. It was Sir

Montague who suggested I should check you weren't in your room. Of course, I thought you hadn't returned.'

'And there was no sign of a break-in, Bunting, you're sure of that?' Isabel asked him to confirm, knowing as she did that it had been this one fact, and the evidence of Guy Fensham, the former steward at the Manor, that had so incriminated the gentleman seated opposite her.

'Miss Isabel, I'd stake my life on it. I wasn't myself that morning, I'll admit, but I swear all the doors were still securely bolted when the servants rose. Cook assured me the kitchen door was as it should have been, a footman said the same about the side entrance. He unbolted it himself when he went for Sir Montague, and I unbolted the front entrance later that morning, when Sir Montague arrived. No, all the doors were secure and none of the windows had been broken or forced, except…'

'Except what?' Isabel prompted when all the old servant did was to frown heavily.

'It was something that struck me as odd at the time, although it might have been nothing. I noticed the key was still in the lock of the French windows, and yet I felt sure I returned it to the usual place in the top drawer of the bureau the evening before, when I closed the curtains.' He shrugged. 'Perhaps his lordship or Mr Francis wandered out on to the terrace for a breath of air. The door was certainly locked and securely bolted, so no one could have gained entry by that means.'

'Thank you for your time, Bunting,' his lordship said, when his delightful companion appeared to have fallen into a meditative mood. He rose to his feet, exchanging one or two more commonplaces with his old servant before he returned Isabel and her faithful hound to the carriage.

The return journey seemed as if it too would be undertaken in stony silence. Only this time his lordship sensed it was for an entirely different reason. The increasingly endearing Miss Mortimer wasn't so much interested in the passing countryside as attempting to solve a conundrum, if the deep furrow drawing her charmingly arching brows together was anything to go by.

'Something certainly appears to be troubling you this time, Miss Mortimer, even if it was not the case on the outward journey.'

'What…? Oh, I do beg your pardon, my lord.' She cast him an apologetic smile, which he secretly thought was lovely. 'I do have a habit of drifting into a world of my own when something is troubling me, and not sharing my thoughts. It comes from having been so self-reliant for so many years, I suppose.'

Again he found himself in the grip of that strange sensation, but ignored it as he said, 'Would I be correct in assuming your puzzlement stems from something discovered from the estimable Bunting?'

'Several things, as it happens,' she disclosed, staring at him fixedly, and without seeming in the least self-conscious about it either. 'You must have taken a key with you that night. Bunting said he made a point of locking the doors when he went about drawing the curtains and checking the windows in the evenings. He only ever threw the bolts across just prior to retiring, and then not those on the side entrance as a rule, if he knew you were out, except on that particular night.'

'Well, what of it? He was merely following my father's orders.'

'The door would already have been locked by the time Papa and the others returned you to the Manor. You must have had a key about your person, otherwise they couldn't have got you back into the house. The side door must have been re-locked by someone. Bunting said he checked it and it was locked,' she reminded him. 'So who relocked it? It wasn't Papa, that I do know.' She frowned. 'Could the person who retained the key have returned to the house shortly afterwards, before Bunting had thrown the bolts, and hidden somewhere?'

Lord Blackwood agreed it was certainly a possibility before adding, 'So we're looking at Jem Marsh, and the former steward, Guy Fensham, neither of whom is here to question.'

'True,' she acknowledged. 'I wasn't acquainted with Jem Marsh, but if he was anything like his young brother, I cannot imagine he'd hack someone to death with a sabre. What was the motive? Nothing was taken from the house, was it?'

'Not as far as I'm aware. And, as you surmise, Jem was a good lad, one of the best. My father liked him too, and was all for him becoming head groom one day. He had no reason to kill any member of my family. And neither did Guy Fensham.

'Yes, I'm well aware he's been lining his pockets from the estate these past years,' he added, when it looked as though she would disagree. 'And I'm also aware that his account of what took place that night differed considerably from your father's. But let's try to be fair and suggest he might not have been perfectly sober himself that night, and maybe became confused. Furthermore, he did his job well when my father was alive. I cannot see how it would have benefited him to murder his employer, and incriminate me. The next holder of the title just might have brought in his own people.'

Having no in-depth knowledge of his family, Isabel asked, 'And who is next in line, after you, my lord?'

'My dissolute and debauched Uncle Horace. I came across him in London a few weeks ago. He hasn't changed.'

Suppressing the strong urge to suggest deplorable behaviour must surely run in his family, Isabel concentrated her mind on something else that had puzzled her whilst in Bunting's cottage, and asked his lordship outright if it had been the norm for him to storm out of the house in a rage after a disagreement with his father.

Easily detecting the note of censure in her voice, Lord Blackwood smiled crookedly. 'I was a hot-headed youth who grew into an angry young man. I'm not proud of my past behaviour, but there's nought I can do about it now.' He turned to stare out of the window, but was oblivious to the pleasing landscape flashing past. 'Whenever I paid a visit home to the Manor during my years at Oxford and, indeed, after I'd left university, there was hardly an occasion when my father and I didn't argue about something. I was nothing like my older brother, who would agree with our father over everything in order to remain in his good books. Sometimes I would return to London after one of our rows; on other occasions I would find solace in Merryfield.'

Realising he had disclosed more than he had intended, he turned to look at his companion again, and easily detected the rising colour before she hurriedly turned her head away. How very revealing! he mused. An innocent she might be, but she was not naïvely stupid. She knew well enough what went on in the world, and the desires of the opposite sex, even if she didn't approve.

'But I digress,' he added, when she resolutely continued to stare out of the window on her side of the carriage. 'On that particular night, I chose not to stay away, but drown my sorrows at the local inn.'

This surprisingly caught her attention, and forced her to look across at him again. 'That is what I find so confoundedly puzzling,' she revealed. 'Why didn't the murderer kill you too that night?' She frowned deeply, at a loss to understand. 'Instead, he did his utmost to have you hanged for the murders. So was it his intention all along to make you suffer most of all? Or was he merely taking advantage of the fact that you had returned to the house to make doubly sure that the finger of guilt wasn't pointed in his direction? But if the latter is true…' she shook her head, totally perplexed '…how on earth did he know you'd returned to the house, and in such a condition that it was highly unlikely you would rouse even when your clothing was being smeared with your relatives' blood? Furthermore, unless the murderer knew the precise whereabouts of your room, my lord, he took an awful risk wandering about the house at the dead of night. He might so easily have woken one of the servants. Which suggests to me that the murderer knew the layout of the Manor, and also possessed a good knowledge of your character. Which also suggests to me that he is someone you know.'

'Well, haven't you given me a great deal to mull over, Miss Mortimer?' he said lightly. 'How fortunate it is that I had already decided not to offer my support to Wellington again.'

Although disappointed because his tone had suggested he wasn't particularly concerned about the events of years ago, his latter remark did puzzle her. 'What do you mean, sir? The war with France is at an end.'

His brows rose. 'Evidently, my dear Miss Mortimer, you haven't heard. It was all over the newspapers a few days ago… Napoleon is once again in Paris, undoubtedly gathering more of the faithful about him as we speak.'

So stunned was she by the shocking revelation that she almost didn't notice when the carriage went past the turning to the Manor. 'Oh, but, sir, surely your coachman has missed the turning?'

'Clegg might be new to the area, but he's finding his way about remarkably well. No, Miss Mortimer, he is merely following instructions.' His crooked smile appeared. 'My, my, what a very poor opinion you must have of me, if you thought I'd expect you to walk home.'

Nothing could have been further from the truth. In fact, Isabel's regard for the Viscount was increasing every time she was in his company. He was undoubtedly intelligent, and a most charming companion when he chose to be. She just wished he would apply himself and use the fine brain with which the good Lord had seen fit to bless him, and uncover his father's murderer. She was not a pessimist by any means. All the same, she couldn't help feeling, as they arrived at the farmhouse, that unless the mystery was solved, there would always be a dark cloud hanging over Blackwood Manor and its occupants.

Little did Isabel realise that, far from taking a light-minded view of the whole business, the Viscount was determined to unravel the puzzling events of that eventful night all those years ago. Throughout the short journey back to the Manor he mulled over everything he had discovered that morning.

As soon as the carriage drew up before the front entrance, he made his way directly to the scene of the crime, pausing only to hand his outdoor garments to a waiting footman and to give orders for the butler to join him in the drawing room as soon as possible.

His expression of distaste as he entered the large room had little to do with the events that had taken place all those years before. It was simply that he clearly recalled how it had looked when his dear mother had been alive: an elegant salon, tastefully decorated in pale greens and cream. It was almost as if his father had wished to obliterate all memory of Louise Carré, his very pretty second wife. Not many weeks after her untimely death, he had either given away or sold most of her clothes and other personal belongings. He had replaced all the elegant couches and chairs in the drawing room with solid, heavy pieces. Dark blue and gold had replaced the pale green on the walls, tasselled crimson curtains had been chosen for the windows and a garish multicoloured carpet for the floor.

His lordship closed his eyes, thereby momentarily blocking out the offending décor. Dear God! He'd been in more tastefully decorated houses of pleasure! he decided, striding down the length of the room to the spot where the only piece of furniture his mother had brought with her from France all those years ago stood against the wall.

Pulling open the right-hand drawer he saw the key to the French windows; just where, according to the old butler, it had always been kept almost from the day his mother had become mistress of the house. The rose garden had been her pride and joy, and she would often throw wide the French windows enabling the fragrance to waft into the room on warm summer evenings. At least, during his lifetime, his father had never neglected the garden his second wife had so loved, his lordship was obliged to acknowledge. He shook his head. His mother would have hated to see it, now, looking so overgrown and neglected.

After making a mental note to interview the head gardener in the very near future, his lordship slipped the key in the lock of the French windows. That was where Bunting had found it on that fateful morning. Yet he swore it had been in the drawer, just where it should have been, when he had come into the room to draw the curtains the evening before. So what did that suggest?

He ceased his deliberations the instant his new butler entered the room, and wasted no time in discovering what he wished to know. 'And you're absolutely certain about that, Tredwell—there are only three keys to all the outside doors, including the French windows here?'

'Most definitely, my lord,' he confirmed. 'The keys are kept in the doors themselves, or close by. Then, I have a set, as does the housekeeper. The spare keys in my charge are kept on hooks just inside my rooms, should one of the other staff have need of them.' He glanced briefly at the French windows. 'That key is always kept in the bureau, according to what Mr Bunting told me. And I assumed you would not wish that changed,' he added, after noting the key was in the lock.

The Viscount assured him this was so, before adding, 'And you are sure you haven't come across a fourth key to the side entrance? I had an extra key made some years ago, but it seems to have disappeared.'

The butler appeared concerned. 'I shall instigate a search, my lord.'

'No…no, don't do that,' his lordship countered. 'But if you, or any other member of the staff, should come across it somewhere, perhaps you'll be good enough to let me know.'

'Of course, my lord. Will there be anything else?'

'Yes. When I was in here with Miss Mortimer, earlier, we noticed one of the windows here is very ill fitting and letting in the most confounded draught.'

'I shall have it attended to at once, my lord.'

'Very good, Tredwell, you may go. No, wait a moment,' his lordship corrected, when a thought suddenly occurred to him as he studied the offending window.

Reaching for the catch, he raised it, and then let it go. 'I wonder,' he murmured. Then, much to his butler's surprise, he threw the window wide and, raising one long leg, stepped over the sill on to the gravel path outside. For a tall man it was no difficult task. More importantly, neither was closing the window securely from the outside, as he discovered a moment later when he raised the catch until it was upright. Then he very carefully pushed the window closed, before giving the wood a hearty thump with his fist.

The bemused butler came to his rescue in a trice. 'Oh, my lord, you've shut yourself out,' he declared, throwing the window wide once more, thereby enabling his lordship to step back inside.

'Yes, didn't I just!' He studied the window from behind half-shuttered lids. 'A very tidy means of escape, and undetectable, wouldn't you say, Tredwell? But that still doesn't solve the conundrum of how he gained entry.'

'Does it not, my lord?' Tredwell ventured, appearing more bemused than ever.

'No, it does not,' his lordship confirmed, smiling to himself. 'I think it behoves me to consult with the estimable Miss Mortimer again before too long. Delay having the window repaired, Tredwell, for the time being at least.'

Chapter Five

The following morning, directly after breaking his fast, Lord Blackwood repaired to his library as usual to deal with those estate matters requiring his attention. It was a routine to which he had swiftly grown accustomed; moreover, one he thoroughly enjoyed.

The love of the land was in his blood, and it was to his credit that never once during his youth or early manhood had he felt any jealousy towards his older half-brother, who, in the normal course of events, would have inherited both title and land.

It would also have been true to say that, although he hadn't felt the least envious of his brother's more favourable position, he and his sibling had never been close. The twelve years' difference in their ages had been too great, he supposed. With one exception, they had had absolutely nothing in common, which had resulted in each pursuing his own interests without involving the other. Only the love of the land had been common to them both. Sadly, instead of binding them together on occasions, it had had the opposite effect. Giles had resented the interest his younger brother had taken in what he had considered was destined to be entirely his own domain, and numerous heated arguments had resulted.

His lordship sighed as these memories, quite unbidden, came back to haunt him, and he turned to stare out of the window at the many acres of deer park that Fate—capricious jade!—had decreed would be his.

There was no refuting the fact that he had disliked his father and elder brother. But had this antipathy induced him to murder…? No, he didn't believe so. In fact, he had never thought it was so, not even on that fateful morning when he had woken to find himself smeared in his relatives' blood. As he had revealed to the enterprising Miss Mortimer, his response to any heated family argument had always been to storm out of the house, either to return to London and his friends, or to find solace in the arms of a very understanding young widow residing in Merryfield. On the odd occasion he had been known to drown his sorrows at the village inn before returning to the Manor. He wished now he and his father had enjoyed a better understanding. He doubted they would ever have become close. All the same, he bitterly regretted much of what he had said and done in his hot-headed youth.

He shook his head as he was assailed by further bitter regrets. Sadly, it was impossible to undo what had happened. All he could do was ensure that he enjoyed a better understanding with his own son…with all his children, should he ever be blessed to have any.

He smiled wryly as a thought then occurred to him. But he had two already, of course. At least, he amended silently, two children to whom he stood in place of a father.

Their natural father had been one of his closest friends. Daniel Collier had been one of the first to come to his aid when he had been most in need of help. In fact, it had been none other than Daniel and his darling wife, Sarah, who had safely hidden him away in their home, until such time as others had managed to get him safely across to Ireland. The least he could do in return was honour his obligation and take the very best care of the Colliers' children, he decided, leaving his library to make his way up the stairs to the old nursery.

He had had little contact with his wards since their removal from the farmhouse to the Manor. Not only had he been extremely busy dealing with long-neglected estate matters, he had also wished to give the children time to settle to life at his ancestral home. He had felt, too, that Miss Pentecost's reputation would be less likely to suffer if he refrained from visiting the nursery too often. Added to which, he had never been given any reason to suppose his presence there was at all necessary, until the day before, when he had witnessed the touching little interlude between Miss Mortimer and Josh. It became quite obvious then, of course, that a lack of discipline was prevailing above stairs.

He couldn't deny that, ordinarily, he would never have dreamed of offering the position of governess to Miss Pentecost. He would have much preferred someone older, with a deal more experience. And someone far less pleasing on the eye, come to that! He didn't doubt that she was competent enough to teach little Alice most all she needed to know. Josh, on the other hand, was a different matter entirely. He clearly needed more control, a firmer grasp on the reins than the gentle Miss Pentecost was able to exert.

The lovely girl he employed to care for the children betrayed a moment's surprise when he entered her domain. She rose at once to her feet, thereby offering him an unfettered view of her charming figure. She was undeniably a rare specimen, certainly one of the most ravishing girls he'd ever clapped eyes on in his life. Yet it was strange, that, apart from a healthy masculine appreciation of her evident charms, he experienced no very real attraction. Unlike that managing little baggage of a cousin of hers, Miss Pentecost singularly lacked the power to retain his interest!

Briefly his eyes slid to his younger ward who, at her governess's prompting, had risen to her feet to execute an awkward little curtsy. 'Forgive the interruption,' he said, returning his attention to the ethereal being with the guinea-gold locks and limpid blue eyes. 'I'm here merely to satisfy myself that you have everything you need.'

'Everything is just perfect, my lord, I thank you.'

The Viscount moved forward to study the picture his younger ward had been creating. If little Alice did indeed possess any artistic ability, patently it hadn't manifested itself quite yet, and it was left to her kindly teacher to reveal the subject of the picture.

'And a most remarkable flower it is too!' his lordship declared, with only the merest trace of a tremor in his voice. 'I declare I have never seen one quite like it before! Perhaps, when the weather becomes a little warmer, you and your governess would care to explore the home wood and pick some wild flowers for the nursery. I know in the spring there are carpets of bluebells.'

Trusting brown eyes were raised to his. 'Would you like me to pick some for you too, sir?'

It pleased him to think that the little girl was gradually becoming less shy of him. 'I shall be honoured to accept them, Miss Collier,' he assured her, executing a graceful bow.

His response had clearly earned the governess's approval. Unfortunately her charming smile was, a moment later, replaced by a slightly concerned look when the door opened, and her other charge came striding boldly into the room, still bearing the evidence of the real reason for his absence around his mouth.

'Ah, so the truant finally returns!' his lordship quipped, instantly capturing the boy's attention and causing him to stop dead in his tracks.

'He's been away only a very short time, sir,' Clara Pentecost assured her employer, thereby instantly coming to her charge's aid. 'He just popped out to collect his book.'

'Via the kitchen, I do not doubt,' his lordship responded, favouring his elder ward with a stare of evident disapproval. 'These frequent absences from the schoolroom during lessons must cease, Master Collier, is that understood?'

His lordship then returned his attention to the teacher. 'If the children should require extra sustenance mid-morning, then send down to the kitchen for milk and shortbread, Miss Pentecost, or anything else Cook can supply. That is why I employ a nursery-maid—to cater for your needs. While Josh remains in your care, I expect you to maintain discipline.'

Although he had not spoken harshly, his wishes could not have been made more clear. 'However, I shall deal with the matter this time,' he added. 'Josh, come along with me.'

His lordship did not miss the look of alarm Josh exchanged with his governess before accompanying him out of the room. The fact that the boy dragged his feet as they walked down the long length of the picture gallery didn't escape his notice either, and eventually the Viscount relented.

'For heaven's sake, lad, stop looking so anxious!' he ordered. 'I've no intention of wielding a birch rod,' he assured him. 'I merely have things I wish to discuss and make clear to you.'

Reaching the door of the room that had once been his bedchamber, his lordship threw it wide to allow his ward to precede him. 'Would I be correct in assuming that it was none other than the estimable Miss Mortimer who maintained discipline whilst you resided at the farmhouse?'

The boy's impish grin was answer enough. 'I rather thought as much. Boxed your ears, did she?' He slanted his ward a warning look. 'Well, you just be aware of one thing—I can cuff a good deal harder. So, until such time as I can find a tutor to educate you, we'll have no more taking advantage of your governess's good nature. Is that understood?'

Josh appeared nonplussed for a moment. 'Am I to have my own tutor then, sir?'

'You are,' the Viscount confirmed, as he went across the room to a large chest, which stood at the foot of the bed. 'I rather think you would go along much better under a male's guiding hand. I would insist he involves you in more outdoor pursuits for a start. I hardly think you'll be vastly entertained going into the home wood to pick flowers.

'No, I thought not,' his lordship went on when his ward grimaced. 'But until I can find someone suitable, I shall take you out myself as often as I am able. I shall purchase a suitable mount for you within the next few weeks so that we might go out riding together. And we'll go fishing, too, if you would like?'

Josh instantly brightened. 'Can Miss Isabel come too?'

Smiling softly, his lordship favoured the boy with a searching stare. 'Do you really think she'd like to come?'

'Oh, yes, sir,' was the instant response. 'She's a great gun! She taught me how to shoot. Like Mama, she never gets into a grand fuss about things.'

This was the first time the Viscount had heard the boy mention either of his parents. 'I should tell you, Josh, that you and I have something in common,' he revealed. 'We both lost our mothers unexpectedly. Like yours, my mother too died of typhus. I was very fond of your mama. She was like a sister to me…just as your father was like a brother. I have some things of his here that I brought back with me from Spain.'

It was clear that he had captured the boy's full attention, and when he opened the trunk and handed Josh his father's sword, his lordship felt moved by the reverential expression on the child's face as he held it in his small hands.

For a few moments Josh appeared lost for words. 'Can I keep it, sir?' he managed finally to ask, whilst transferring his awestruck gaze to the Viscount.

'It is yours, Josh,' his lordship didn't hesitate to assure him. 'Just as all those other things in that chest are yours—the pistol, dress uniform, and your father's watch, among other items. But I should like to keep them here safely for you until you come of age. But you may come and look at them as often as you please, providing you do not attempt to do so during your lessons, and you do not attempt to take them from this room.'

Nodding dumbly, Josh placed the sword carefully back inside the trunk before reaching for the pistol. 'Miss Isabel has one of these, too. She keeps it on top of the dresser in the kitchen.'

'I'm very well aware of it,' his lordship responded, his disapproval all too evident. Unlike his ward, he had not been at all impressed to see a young lady wielding a serviceable firearm. Then, surprisingly, he found himself relenting when questioning brown eyes were raised to his. 'You're very fond of her, aren't you, boy?'

As Josh nodded, the Viscount had no difficulty recognising the shadow of sadness flitting over the boy's features. 'But she doesn't come to see me at all. Maybe she's too busy.'

His lordship placed a reassuring hand on one small

shoulder. 'I well imagine she's most always busy. But that isn't why she doesn't come to see you. I suspect there are many reasons, and mostly to do with me. I'll see her again quite soon, perhaps even tomorrow, and try to persuade her to come and see you. Then you can arrange to go over to the farmhouse to visit her. Why not Saturday afternoon, weather permitting, of course?'

The following morning Isabel received a surprise visit from the young curate, Benjamin Johns. She had liked him from the first. He had been a regular visitor to the house when her father had been alive. The visits, understandably, had lessened after Dr Mortimer's demise, though there had been a noticeable increase in recent months. It was quite evident to Isabel just what the attraction had been.

'I'm sorry I've been unable to call round with these before,' he said, depositing the pile of newspapers he'd brought with him from the vicarage down on the kitchen table. 'I've been so busy since poor Mr Walters has taken to his bed with that terrible chill. He doesn't seem to be improving at all. In fact, I think he's a good deal worse. It's gone to his chest.'

Isabel couldn't resist casting a sceptical glance in her housekeeper's direction. Unlike his curate, the Reverend Mr Cedric Walters had never earned her approval. Whether his present malady was serious or not, she couldn't have said with any conviction. What she did know, however, was that the local vicar was a self-seeking, indolent man who cared only for his own creature comforts and little for the trials of his parishioners. It had been none other than Mr Johns who had done nearly all the good works in the parish since his arrival in the village some three years before.

'I suppose you've heard the dreadful news by now,' he remarked, after accepting the offer of a seat, but declining the offer of refreshment, declaring he couldn't stay very long.

'If you're referring to the events across the Channel, then, yes,' Isabel responded. 'It so happens Viscount Blackwood told me the other day.'

The handsome boyish face across the table looked thoughtfully back at her after learning this. 'Oh, did you visit the Manor? Did you, perchance, call to see Miss Pentecost? Is she well…happy in her post?'

Having always been quick-witted, Isabel required few things explained to her, and she guessed what truly lay at the root of the curate's questions in a trice.

'Mr Johns, let me assure you my cousin returns here to the farmhouse each evening, and seems remarkably content in her post. Not to put too fine a point on it, I do not believe Lord Blackwood has ever attempted to seduce her, or cause her the least discomfiture in any way, come to that.'

As so often happened, Isabel's plain-speaking had once again caused embarrassment, if the curate's expression was anything to go by. 'I'm sorry, Mr Johns, if I shock you, but I see little point in prevaricating. Personally, I truly believe that much of what is said about his lordship is totally untrue.' Ignoring her housekeeper's surprised glance, Isabel added, 'I have been alone with him, and he behaved like a perfect gentleman, not attempting to take advantage of the situation.' She didn't add that she suspected this was because she was not in the least to his taste.

'I'm sure that is true,' he hurriedly concurred. 'Indeed, I have heard nothing but praise for him whilst I have been about my duties. I know already that he has improved the lot of his estate workers, ensuring that necessary repairs have been made to their cottages, and offered several local people employment, not to mention engaging the services of local tradespeople. I believe I'm right in thinking also that Toby Marsh's young sister is now employed up at the Manor as nursery-maid.'

Isabel was aware of this herself, just as she was very well aware that Mr Johns's regard for her cousin had grown over the months. He had always behaved with the utmost decorum towards her, and it was clear that Clara favoured his society. Isabel felt that her beautiful cousin could do a great deal better for herself than become attached to a penniless curate. But, then, what right had she to interfere? In less than two months Clara would attain her majority—old enough, surely, to make her own decisions?

'Why don't you visit Clara on Saturday afternoon? His lordship has been most generous where she is concerned. Not only does he allow her a half-day every Sunday, he allows her to leave early on Saturdays too, and she's usually home by mid-afternoon. I'm sure she'd be pleased to see you.'

'Well, you've certainly changed your tune, I must say!' Bessie declared, the instant she had closed the door behind the contented young man. 'I thought you said you'd try your best to discourage that attachment.'

'Did I?' Isabel was nonplussed for a moment. 'Well, if I did say that it was very presumptuous of me. Who am I to interfere in Clara's personal concerns? If she seeks my advice that's a different matter, because I cannot deny she could do rather better than to tie herself to an impoverished clergyman,' she readily revealed, echoing her thoughts. 'That said, I would far rather see her wed to a man like Mr Benjamin Johns than that ill-favoured roué her stepmama had selected for her!'

'Now, who's that, do you suppose?' Bessie said irritably, when a further knock on the kitchen door obliged her to interrupt her task yet again.

'Why, if it isn't Mr Clegg!' Isabel declared, recognising at once Lord Blackwood's bow-legged coachman.

'Aye, that's right. Tom Clegg be the name.' At Isabel's invitation, he took a step into the kitchen, casting an admiring glance over the housekeeper's well-rounded figure as he did so. 'His lordship's compliments, miss. And could you spare time to visit up at the Manor?'

Isabel was on her feet in a trice, instantly fearing the worst. 'Why, what's wrong?' she demanded. 'Has something happened to his lordship…the children…my cousin?'

The head groom shrugged. 'Not that I know to, miss. His lordship just strolled round to the stables earlier and said as 'ow I were to bring you back with me, if convenient. But I can come back later if you'd prefer, like?'

'No, no, that's all right,' Isabel assured him, more intrigued than anything else as to why her presence should be required up at the Manor. She was on the point of collecting her serviceable cloak, when a somewhat embarrassing recollection gave her pause for thought. She then changed direction and headed across the kitchen to the door leading to the passageway.

'As the matter doesn't appear to be at all urgent, perhaps you'd be good enough to wait a few minutes so that I might change into something more suitable?'

It wasn't so much Tom Clegg's immediate acquiescence to the request that captured her attention as the quizzical look the housekeeper instantly shot in her direction. Isabel, however, was determined not to be swayed by anything Bessie might foolishly suppose.

The truth of the matter was a certain someone's criticism of her appearance had continued to rankle. Yet, at the same time, innate honesty obliged her to admit that she had allowed her standards to fall over the years. Of course, it mattered not how she looked when she was hard at work, dealing with her poultry and other creatures she kept about the smallholding. There was no excuse, though, not to make an effort when she ventured beyond her own property.

Determined never to be found wanting again, she hurried upstairs to her bedchamber and changed into the pretty turquoise day dress her nimble-fingered cousin had created for her, whilst all the time studying the poor selection hanging in her bedchamber's most impressive piece of furniture.

There was no denying her wardrobe was sadly lacking even the basic commodities a gentleman's daughter ought to possess. Yet she was sensible enough to appreciate that it would be foolish to suppose that she could ever attempt to ape the elegance of the fashionable ladies of the *ton*. A light purse would always prove a bar to success. Furthermore, she had absolutely no desire to become a fashion plate either. Nor try to win his lordship's approbation, come to that, she told herself firmly. No, it was simply that it had been made clear by certain persons, Bessie included, that she had been woefully neglectful over her appearance in recent years, and she was determined to rectify the fault.

By the time she returned to the kitchen, her hair had been neatly confined beneath a charming straw bonnet trimmed with ribbon of the exact same shade as her dress. With the black-velvet pelisse that she kept for Sunday best neatly buttoned over her gown, and her work-roughened hands perfectly concealed in a pair of kidskin gloves, she knew her appearance this time could not be found wanting. Not only did Bessie's look of approval confirm this, but also Tredwell's glint of appreciation as he bowed her into the Manor a short time later.

'His lordship awaits you in the garden, Miss Mortimer,' he informed her, slightly to her chagrin.

Had his lordship been so sure she would instantly obey the summons? The mere idea that it might be so irked her, and a determination to make it clear at the earliest opportunity that she would not be at his beck and call in future quickly followed.

This firm resolve was instantly forgotten, however, when she first caught sight of the master of the house, standing in the centre of the sadly neglected rose garden, in earnest conversation with an older man.

His lordship's immaculate attire was in stark contrast to the estate worker's raiment. Highly polished top-boots emphasised the perfection of his straight, muscular legs, just as the immaculately tailored blue jacket highlighted the strength in his shoulders. His boyish good looks might have long since disappeared, but there was no refuting he was a fine figure of a man.

The smile of welcome he cast the instant he detected her footfall on the gravel path obliged her to revise her assessment of his looks—perhaps no longer handsome, but damnably attractive, none the less!

'Your arrival is most timely, my dear Miss Mortimer,' he assured her, after dismissing the butler with a nod. 'Monk, here, is my new head gardener, and I have instructed him to supply you with all the seedlings you need to replace your losses.'

Isabel made no attempt to hide her mortification at such a suggestion. 'Oh, my lord, no! No, I simply cannot accept… You…you have done more than enough already. Your people have worked solidly these past couple of days clearing the ditch.'

'In that case, this fresh supply should be in no danger of being washed away,' his lordship responded, before turning to the gardener and instructing him to have the selection placed in the carriage in readiness for Miss Mortimer's departure. Then, without further ado, he entwined Isabel's arm through his and walked away in the direction of the terrace.

Although secretly pleased that she made no attempt to release herself, Lord Blackwood couldn't help thinking that this was mostly due to the fact that her mind was definitely elsewhere.

'What's troubling you, child?' he finally asked, for some obscure reason not liking to see her looking so subdued.

'You make me feel so ashamed,' she revealed promptly. 'You have been generous to us already. That money you sent for Josh and Alice's keep was more than enough. I was able to save a goodly portion of it.'

She might have expected her honesty to please him. Instead, when she chanced to glance up, she discovered him frowning in evident disapproval.

'I am very well aware of it, young woman. And I shall take leave to inform you that I was not best pleased about it! Part of that extra money was to enable you to employ a maidservant, not to be at the beck and call of the children yourself.'

'You don't know the half of it, sir,' she freely admitted, hardly chastened by the reproof. 'We didn't buy them any clothes either. I went into Merryfield and bought all the necessary materials, and dear Clara made all the garments they required.'

He considered her apparel. 'Did she happen to make that dress for you?'

'Yes,'

'I thought it charming the first time I saw you wearing it,' he surprisingly revealed, before adding after a moment's consideration, 'But you'd look better in richer hues—dark green or blue, or perhaps a deep red would suit you best, with your colouring. Which reminds me…'

They had by this time arrived at the terrace. Mounting the stone steps, they entered the Manor by way of the French windows leading to the drawing room.

'I have decided to have this room redecorated next,' he told her, 'and would value your opinion on a possible colour scheme. I totally agree that it is dull and cheerless in here. It needs brightening. So, what would you suggest?'

Although somewhat surprised to have her opinion sought Isabel, none the less, gave the matter some thought. Disengaging herself at last from his gentle hold, she moved into the centre of the long room and looked about her, paying particular attention to the greenish tones in the marble fireplace. 'Well, I'm no expert, sir. But if this happened to be my drawing room I would choose pale green and cream.'

When he made no comment, she turned to find him staring strangely at her, the look in his ice-blue eyes intense. 'My God,' he muttered at last. 'My God…'

Taking this to mean he totally disapproved her choice, she said, 'Well, I did say I'm no expert. It was merely personal preference. You could do it in a shade of yellow, I suppose. That is supposed to be all the rage at the present time, is it not? I believe I read somewhere that the Regent himself is fond of it.'

'Nauseating colour!' his lordship declared, waving his hand in a dismissive gesture. 'I had one of the spare bedchambers done out in primrose.' His eyes glinted with a suspicion of malicious delight. 'I think I shall place my esteemed godmother in there when she pays a visit. It should prove amusing. I know precisely what she thinks of Prinny!'

All at once his expression changed and the look in his

eyes became almost gentle as they rested upon Isabel. 'No,' he said softly. 'I think your suggestion perfect—green and cream it shall be.

'Now, before you disappear upstairs to see the children, there's something I want you to see.'

'Was I summoned here to see the children then, sir?'

'Why, yes, didn't I say?' He appeared nonplussed a moment before he turned and headed down the room to that certain window sited in the end wall. 'They both miss you, Josh especially. He wants to visit you at the farmhouse. I said he might. I hope you don't mind.'

'Not in the least,' she assured him. 'I look forward to it.'

'Why not stay and take luncheon with them? I'm sure they'll all enjoy that, your cousin included. In fact, I might well eat in the nursery for a change myself. Now, come over here and take a look at this,' he went on, with a complete change of tone, and then without further ado revealed what he had discovered about the window catch two days before.

'How interesting,' Isabel murmured, as she reopened the window and leaned out to stare down at the gravel path. 'Someone could certainly have got out that way without anyone knowing about it. But that still leaves us with having to solve just how the murderer gained entry.'

After clambering back inside, his lordship went over to the bell-pull before rejoining Isabel again at the end of the room. 'Tredwell informed me earlier today that he has been able to locate only three keys to the door leading to the stable-yard. I know for a fact there used to be a fourth.'

'So one is missing,' Isabel murmured. 'The one you had with you that night, I suppose?'

'Most likely. But until we are able to question either Jem Marsh or Fensham, we'll not discover what happened to it.'

'Neither of whom you believe committed the crime,'

she reiterated. 'So that still leaves us with the mystery of how the murderer gained entry.'

His lordship's eyes strayed to the French windows. 'According to old Bunting there had been a fire in here that evening, and yet someone must have braved the chill evening air and gone out on to the terrace, otherwise why should the key have been in the lock, when it's normally kept in the drawer over there? Undoubtedly I shall run into my cousin Francis before too long. I shall mention it to him—see if he can recall wandering out on to the terrace that night. If my memory serves me correctly, he has always taken an interest in gardens, especially his own. His passion is for roses, I believe.'

The door leading to the hall opened and the butler entered, instantly capturing his employer's attention. 'Ah, Tredwell, be so good as to inform Cook that there will be a guest for luncheon. Also, Miss Mortimer and I shall be eating in the nursery.'

'Very good, my lord. Will there be anything else?'

'Yes, be good enough to show Miss Mortimer the way up to the nursery now.' His lordship accompanied her to the foot of the stairs. 'I shall look forward to rejoining you presently,' he assured Isabel, and then turned on his heels and went directly into his library, where he helped himself from the contents of one of the decanters.

Taking the filled glass with him, he went to stand before the hearth and stared up at the portrait taking pride of place above the mantelshelf. Smiling enigmatically, he raised the glass in a silent toast. 'Well, well… Who would have thought it, Mama? Who would have believed that I should return and discover the very one for me, here, in this unlikely place…'

Chapter Six

As Isabel walked up the deer park's slight rise towards the Manor, her faithful Beau padding alongside, she spotted Josh awaiting her, at the prearranged spot, by the great oak that had been struck by lightning two years before, and had lost one of its huge branches as a result. The instant he saw her he ran down the slope to greet her, taking time to pet the huge dog, before capturing one of Isabel's hands and retaining it possessively in his own.

As they set off towards the home wood together, they little realised that the entire greeting had once again been witnessed by none other than the owner of the magnificent deer park himself, standing before his library window.

'Why didn't you bring your gun with you?' Josh asked, all at once noticing that it wasn't resting upon her shoulder. More often than not when they had ventured forth together in the past they had hunted for rabbits, and on one memorable occasion had even bagged a brace of pheasants.

'What, with the master of the house in residence!' Isabel stared down at the boy in mock horror. 'Are you trying to get me hauled before the local magistrate for poaching?'

'His lordship wouldn't do that...at least not to you,' Josh responded in all seriousness. 'He likes you, I can tell. I watched him when we all ate luncheon together in the nursery yesterday. He looks at you funny...different, somehow.'

'You're imagining things,' Isabel countered, wondering what on earth the boy could possibly mean. 'We rub along together surprisingly well, it's true. And I suppose his lordship feels grateful to me for helping him to overcome a—er—certain problem he was experiencing at one time. But that is all.'

There was a decidedly unhealthy gleam in the brown eyes that were raised now to hers. 'You mean about the murders, don't you? I hear the servants talking about it a lot. There was blood everywhere—all over the floor, and dripping down the—'

'For heaven's sake!' Isabel exclaimed, successfully bringing the lurid recital to an end. 'You shouldn't listen to servants' gossip, Josh! It's all a lot of nonsense, anyway! None of the servants employed up at the Manor now was there at the time, so how on earth would any one of them know?'

He seemed to consider this for a moment, before asking, 'Did you ever see what happened?'

'Naturally not. I was little more than a girl myself at the time. I doubt his lordship or the other members of his family even knew of my existence. They knew my father, of course. I believe I've mentioned before that, at the time, he was the only doctor for miles around. So the Blackwood family did call upon his services when required.

'Now, where shall we go?' she continued, as they reached the outskirts of the wood. 'Shall we walk towards the southern part? I've never been in that area before.'

Isabel suddenly received a very suspicious look. 'We're not going to pick flowers, are we?'

She couldn't stop herself chuckling at this. 'Not unless

you want to, though I doubt we'll find too many about at this time of year. Remember it's still only March.'

'Thank goodness for that!' he declared with feeling. 'Lord Blackwood knew I wouldn't want to do such silly things with my sister. That's why he's getting a tutor for me.'

'Is that so?' This was news to Isabel, though not entirely unexpected. Had she been in his lordship's position, she would undoubtedly have done the same. 'When is he likely to arrive at the Manor?'

When Josh revealed that he didn't think the post had been filled, Isabel immediately recalled a conversation she'd had with the curate, not so very long ago, regarding Mr Johns's younger brother, and made a mental note to repeat the gist of the conversation to his lordship at the earliest opportunity.

'Well, as you've no desire to go hunting for wild flowers, Josh, shall we just go exploring, instead, and see what we can find?'

This seemed to please him, and he walked happily alongside, lashing out at the odd hapless piece of foliage with the sturdy stick that he had just happened to find lying conveniently on the main path.

As they continued in a southerly direction the wood grew markedly denser, and noticeably darker too. Isabel wasn't unduly troubled, though. They were both sensibly dressed in warm outdoor garments and the day was dry, with little prospect of rain. Her only slight concern occurred when Beau failed to return to her side after one of his explorations.

Pausing along the wide track, she whistled and then called his name, but surprisingly gained no response. Her concerns mounted when she repeated the exercise again to no effect. Beau rarely failed to respond to her bidding.

Either something had succeeded in capturing his interest in a big way, or he was unable to return to her side. A rather disturbing possibility then occurred to her.

Only the day before she'd discovered from her house-keeper, always a mine of local gossip, that his lordship had recently employed a gamekeeper. Throughout Lord Blackwood's long absence from the estate a great deal of poaching had taken place. Why, she'd even indulged in the illegal practice herself on the odd occasion, espe-cially when she'd become enraged over damage to her veg-etables from floodwater. The difference between her and the average poacher, however, was that she'd taken quite openly, and usually from the trout stream. She had never attempted to lay traps in the woods. She didn't doubt for a moment that the practice had been drastically curtailed since his lordship's return; she didn't doubt either, though, that there were traps aplenty still littering the woodland floor. And if Beau had just happened to become entangled in one of those...?

'Josh, we'd best search for Beau. Something must have happened to him.' She looked down at the boy earnestly. 'Now, I want you to walk directly behind me, understand? And for heaven's sake look where you're putting your feet! We'll need to go off the main path and search. And we don't know what we might find lurking there.'

Josh had learned quickly not to disobey one of Isabel's orders, most especially when he knew she was in ear-nest, and dutifully remained a pace or two behind as they ventured along narrow pathways, covered inches deep in leaves. Every so often both she and Josh would call, but to no avail, and Isabel was just beginning to fear the worst had indeed happened, when her call was at last answered by a low howl.

Heading in the direction of the bloodcurdling noise,

they soon discovered the dog, thankfully unharmed, just sitting in the middle of a glade. For once he never made any attempt to greet her, and she soon discovered the reason for the hound's disquiet. Scattered over a considerable area were human remains, possibly the result of animals scavenging in the undergrowth. Beau had stumbled upon a grave... But whose?

Unlike Isabel, who shivered involuntarily, Josh regarded the find with ghoulish enthusiasm, and began to poke around the general area of what remained of the torso with his stick. 'Oh, Josh, come away, do!' she implored him. 'You don't know what the poor fellow might have died from.'

'How do you know it's a man?'

'I'm no expert, Josh, but there is a way of finding out. A doctor would know, of course. I'm merely guessing, I suppose.' Isabel looked at the remains more closely, especially the skull. 'What I can tell you is that I don't imagine the person was very old. He still had many of his teeth when he died.'

'And what's this?' Josh said, having uncovered an object in the peaty soil with his stick.

Even before she knelt down to take the object from the boy's hand, and wipe it with her handkerchief, Isabel could see it was clearly a pocket-watch, and undoubtedly silver, even though sadly tarnished. Quickly locating the clasp, she soon had it opened, and could only stare dumbly as she read the inscription: *With my undying gratitude, S. Blackwood.*

'Oh, my God,' she murmured, suddenly fearing she knew whose remains had lain hidden in the glade for so many years; realised, too, as she once again stared intently at the skull, that it was unlikely his death had been due to natural causes.

'Josh, I want you to return to the Manor, and take this with you.' Carefully wrapping the watch in her handkerchief, Isabel slipped it inside the boy's jacket pocket. 'If his lordship is at home, I want you to seek him out at once, and give him the watch. He'll not be angry. Tell him where I am, and that I need to see him urgently. If his lordship isn't there then…then go round to the stables and see Tom Clegg.'

The Manor's head groom had already favourably impressed her by his sound common sense. He'd impressed her housekeeper a deal more, if Isabel was any judge, though whether for the same reason was debatable. All the same, she knew she could trust Tom Clegg to come to her aid.

'You're to stay on the main track and run all the way, and not stop for anything, or anyone, understand?' she impressed upon the boy. 'And you're to take Beau along with you. He'll stay with you if you keep throwing your stick for him, and he'll be able to lead whoever is able to come back to me.'

Heeding the advice, Josh ran as fast as his young legs would carry him back to the Manor, only pausing from time to time to catch his breath, and to encourage the large hound to stay with him.

Tredwell wasn't slow to respond to the pounding on the front door. Unfortunately he wasn't so eager to permit his lordship to be interrupted, as the master of the house was still ensconced in his library with the steward. Josh, on the other hand, experienced no such qualms and, easily dodging the butler's restraining hand, darted into the room, unannounced, Beau not far behind him.

'I'm sorry, my lord. I wasn't able to stop him,' the butler apologised, while favouring the miscreant with a baleful glance.

His lordship, as Isabel had predicted, was more surprised than annoyed over the interruption. 'Why the need to see me so urgently, young fellow?'

Still breathless after his hurried return, it took Josh a moment or two before he was able to explain, 'It's Miss Isabel, sir. She needs to see you now.'

No one observing the Viscount would have supposed for a moment that something within had suddenly lurched painfully, or that his heart rate had increased dramatically. He even sounded remarkably composed as he asked, 'Has she sustained some kind of injury, Josh?'

'No. But we did stumble upon a body, sir,' he revealed with youthful enthusiasm. 'Well, at least Beau found a skeleton in the wood.' He gave a start as he recalled something else. 'Oh, and Miss Isabel said I was to give you this.'

After removing the square of, now, soil-smeared linen from the boy's outstretched hand, his lordship unfolded it to discover the skilfully formed tarnished piece of silver and knew, even before he took a few moments to examine it more closely, to whom it had belonged.

Although she had little patience for childish superstition or, indeed, for those who allowed foolish imagination to influence their behaviour, Isabel couldn't deny that she didn't feel perfectly comfortable after Josh and Beau's departure. More than once she found herself peering between the trees, expecting to discover someone lurking, avidly watching her. Worse, still, she seemed unable to stop the hairs on the back of her neck standing on end every so often as she continued to study the burial sight, hoping to discover some other clue that might verify the identity of the corpse. And, if that wasn't bad enough, the surrounding area seemed resonant with eerie, unearthly sounds! She knew, of course, it was only the late March wind whistling through the trees. None the less, she couldn't suppress a sigh of relief when she first detected that all-too-familiar deep barking.

She wasn't certain what pleased her more—to have her faithful hound at her side again, or to see that tall figure on horseback fast approaching along the main track.

'Do have a care, my lord,' she urged him, as he securely tethered his fine bay hack and began to approach on foot. 'The Lord alone knows how many traps might be lurking beneath all these leaves!'

'My new gamekeeper has come across quite a number,' he revealed, not altogether pleased. 'I've already made my feelings clear on the matter in certain quarters. What went on during my absence I'm prepared to overlook. But woe betide anyone I find poaching now.'

He reached her without suffering mishap, and looked at her intently for a second or two. She was paler than he might have liked, but apart from this nothing in her demeanour suggested she was in the least perturbed by the gruesome discovery. But then, he reminded himself, she wasn't the type to fall into hysterics. All the same, he made a mental note to take her away as soon as his steward arrived with some of the estate workers.

Squatting down, he studied the remains more closely, noticing as Isabel had done the shattered portion at the back of the skull, a strong indication that the victim had been struck from behind with some violence. 'It looks very suspicious, wouldn't you say, *ma belle*?'

So concerned with the discovery was she that Isabel hardly registered the endearment. 'It's very worrying, certainly, because robbery couldn't possibly have been the motive.' She transferred her gaze to the strong profile that she was increasingly finding more appealing. 'Do you suppose it is Toby Marsh's brother?'

'The discovery of the pocket-watch I gave him many years ago would suggest as much. But I'll need await my new steward's arrival, with some men, before committing myself. They'll undertake a thorough search of the area and see if they can discover anything else.'

He raised his head as he detected sounds in the distance. 'Ah! And unless I much mistake the matter, they're heading this way now. My ward—bless him!—was able to reveal which area of the wood you'd been visiting, as well as providing me with Beau's invaluable assistance. I'm beginning to view this great shaggy brute of a dog of yours in an entirely different light,' he surprised her by admitting.

Together they returned to the main track, thereby enabling the steward, Perkins, who was tooling the cart containing several estate workers, to see them quite clearly. Their progress was of necessity fairly slow and steady. Several days of heavy rain during the month had left the woodland floor soft, not the ideal place to manoeuvre a substantial cart laden with a wooden crate, not to mention several burly men.

Thankfully the small cavalcade arrived without mishap, and his lordship wasted no time in issuing instructions to the small group who knew only too well that they owed their livelihood now to the seventh Viscount Blackwood. All the same, it didn't prevent some slanting curious glances in Isabel's direction as they received their orders. She knew most all of them, of course, at least by sight, and could almost guess what was passing through their minds. She didn't in the least blame them for wondering what she was doing alone in the middle of the home wood with only the Viscount to bear her company. It was hardly conventional behaviour, after all, for a young woman whose reputation had hitherto been spotless to be found fraternising with a member of the aristocracy in such a lonely spot!

His lordship didn't precisely enhance her standing in the locale, either, by grasping her by the waist a moment or so later, and tossing her effortlessly up on to the back of his handsome bay hack. So shocked was she by the totally unexpected manhandling that she inadvertently let out a squeal of alarm. Which naturally only made matters worse, because it instantly captured the attention of all the workmen once again. Her disconcertion increased fourfold when his lordship proceeded to settle himself on the saddle behind her, and it took quite some time before she could regain sufficient control to prise her tongue from the roof of her mouth in order to castigate him comprehensively for his actions.

His lordship regarded her in amused exasperation. 'What the deuce did you expect me to do...? Let you walk back along the track whilst I calmly rode alongside? A very poor opinion you must have of me if you thought that, my girl! Or is it that you suspect I might succumb to my baser instincts the instant we're out of sight, and throw you down on the woodland earth round the very next bend and attempt to seduce you?'

'Well, of course I don't think any such thing!' she countered weakly, all too painfully aware of his nearness, of her left leg resting alongside his and of her back pressed against his chest, not to mention the strong arms brushing against the sides of her waist. 'Nothing like that would ever occur to you,' she added in an attempt to concentrate her thoughts. 'I do realise I'm not to your taste.'

'Now that, I shall take leave to inform you, young woman, is a most provocative remark to make to any red-blooded fellow like me,' he returned in a flash. 'Furthermore, I cannot help wondering whether it was uttered in an attempt to have me prove you wrong. Or were you merely fishing for compliments?'

Suddenly uncaring that her every movement brought her into closer contact, Isabel swivelled round slightly so that she might look into his face, and instantly recognised the wicked amusement dancing in his eyes. He really was enjoying himself hugely at her expense. 'Oh, you're outrageous! You know I never meant any such thing!'

'That's better,' he approved, his smile full of the special warmth it so often contained these days. 'Missish behaviour doesn't suit you, Belle. Instead, turn your mind to something else, and satisfy my curiosity.'

She regarded him with misgiving, suspecting he might be in a deliberately provoking mood. 'About what, precisely?'

'About why it took you so long to reveal your father's written statement about the events of that night? Charles Bathurst mentioned something about it when I stayed with him last year, about your father having suffered a seizure and being unable to speak. But this, so I understand, sadly happened at least a month after the murders had taken place.'

'Oh, I see! Evidently you don't know all the details.' Isabel took a moment to collect her thoughts. 'As I may have already mentioned, my father returned to the house late that night. I had long been in bed. I didn't see him the following morning either, because he'd already left for Hampshire to visit his ailing sister, Clara's mama. Although they had seen each other rarely since we left London, they did correspond often, and Papa knew his sister was dying of the wasting disease. That month-long visit was destined to be the last time they would see each other.'

'Did you not correspond with your father during the time he was away?'

Although his tone had been in no way accusatory, Isabel could understand his puzzlement over her and her father's failure to act on his behalf far sooner, and was more than happy to explain.

'Of course news of the tragedy at the Manor spread quite quickly, as indeed did rumours of your subsequent arrest. After a week or so accounts began to appear in the newspapers. Unbeknown to me Papa must have read one of these during his stay in Hampshire, but he didn't write to me concerning the matter, and I refrained from regaling him with local gossip on the one occasion I did write to him, because I assumed his only concerns at the time were for his sister. I believe I enquired merely about my aunt. You must remember also that, at the time, I was blissfully ignorant of the fact that he had witnessed your condition on that night.'

'Yes, of course,' he acknowledged softly, while surveying the woodland track ahead with narrowed assessing eyes. 'I seem to recall my good friend Charles Bathurst telling me that your father suffered his first seizure on the very night he returned home.'

'Yes. We hardly exchanged more than a dozen words before he retired.' She shook her head sadly at the memory. 'It was a tragedy not only for him, but for you too, my lord. Had he not been so very weary, we would undoubtedly have caught up on each other's news, and he would have almost certainly informed me about what he knew concerning the happenings on the night of the murders.'

Although she shrugged, it wasn't a gesture of indifference, far from it. 'Because his speech was so impaired, he received few visitors during his last years. Which was so sad because there was nothing wrong with his understanding, and when in the mood he was able to play a decent game of chess. I shall always feel grateful to our local curate, Mr Johns. He was one of the few who took the trouble to visit my father regularly during the last year of Papa's life. He took the trouble also to attempt to communicate with Papa by regaling him with various happenings in the district. Indeed, it was none other than Mr Johns who first reminded my father about the events up at the Manor.

'I remember quite clearly,' she continued, after once again pausing to collect her thoughts, 'that I was in the kitchen at the time preparing dinner, when Mr Johns came rushing in, saying that Papa had become very agitated. I understood some of what Papa could manage to say, but not enough to comprehend just what had upset him so much about Mr Johns's disclosures about the murders at the Manor. He suffered a further seizure that very night, and never fully regained consciousness. He died a few days later.

'It was many, many months before I could bring my-self to go through his belongings,' she continued, after a further moment's thought. 'It was then I stumbled upon what Papa had written about that night. The account was written in my father's hand, dated and signed by him. It had clearly been written during the visit to his sister in Hampshire. Perhaps he decided not to send it by post in case it got lost. It's my belief that he intended to present it in person to Sir Montague Cameron on his return here. But Fate, sadly, intervened. The rest you know.'

'I shall for ever be in your debt, *ma belle*,' he mur-mured softly.

'Nonsense!' she returned, dismissing his gratitude with an impatient wave of her hand. Then, 'Oh, what did you call me?'

His only response was to smile provocatively before bringing his mount to a halt at the edge of the home wood, where his carriage stood awaiting them. In his turn dismissing Isabel's assurances that she was more than capable of walking home, he lifted her gently to the ground, and then waited until she was safely inside the chaise before returning to that certain spot in the wood.

By the time the Viscount returned to the Manor, some two hours later, more evidence had been unearthed to confirm the remains were none other than those of Jem Marsh. His mother was able to identify the five pewter buttons found scattered about the body as the very ones she had stitched on to her eldest son's one and only waistcoat.

Having had to break the tragic news to the widowed mother, his lordship, understandably enough, wasn't feeling highly sociable. Consequently he wasn't in the least pleased to find a strange carriage in his stable-yard upon his return, suggesting he had a visitor. Upon learning the caller's identity, however, he didn't hesitate to join his visitor in the parlour.

'Why, Cousin Francis, this is a most unexpected pleasure!' his lordship declared convincingly enough upon entering the room. 'Can I offer you some refreshment…? Ah, no, I see the estimable Tredwell has already seen to your needs.'

The gentleman who immediately rose to his feet at the Viscount's entry was some few inches shorter than his titled cousin. None the less, he was a fine figure of a man, boasting regular features beneath a shock of expertly styled light brown hair, and a physique of such exquisite proportions that his London tailor openly bragged that he had the dressing of Mr Francis Blackwood. Not only that, the gentleman in question was renowned for his innate good taste, his polished manners and his love of the finer things in life.

'My dear Sebastian!' Francis moved languidly across the room to shake his cousin's hand warmly. 'How good it is to see you again. And, if you'll forgive my saying so, much changed,' he added, staring up slightly at the harshly defined features of his tall cousin.

Anyone who was ignorant of their respective ages could have been forgiven for supposing that Francis were the younger, when he was, in fact, the elder by some four years. His boyish countenance had changed little since their last encounter, a circumstance that his lordship was not slow to remark upon, before adding, 'A hard existence, however, leaves its mark, Cousin. Yes, indeed, I have changed. And in more ways than one. Come, let us make ourselves comfortable by the hearth, and you may tell me what brings you here.'

Light brows were instantly raised at this. 'Why, I have come for the pleasure of being reunited with you, Sebastian. Family is everything, dear boy, and I'm determined not to lose touch! There are precious few Blackwoods left nowadays. We have lost several family members since you have been away.'

'All through natural causes, I trust,' his lordship responded, before smiling that cynical smile for which he was now famed, when he received a nod in response. 'I cannot express the relief I feel having the fact confirmed, Cousin. Had it been otherwise, I might have begun to believe there was a vendetta against our family, given the way my father and brother met their end.'

'Yes, a bad business, a very bad business,' Francis solemnly agreed. 'And the devil of it was there was absolutely nothing I could do to help you at the time.' He shook his head. 'It might have been all so very different had I accepted your father's invitation to stay the night, but...' he shrugged '...it was a fine night, clear and bright, as I recall, if surprisingly chilly for the time of year. And I live only a matter of three miles from the Manor. No very great distance, after all. Besides which, I had intended travelling down to stay with some friends in Devonshire the following day. That, of course, was delayed, when I discovered what had occurred.'

'As well you didn't stay overnight. You might well have become the slayer's third victim,' his lordship pointed out.

'But you didn't,' his cousin returned directly.

'How very true… And it is a mystery just why not, wouldn't you say?' This time the Viscount's smile was distinctly warmer. 'As quite a remarkable person said to me only recently—was I the intended victim all along, or merely a very convenient scapegoat?'

His cousin appeared utterly bewildered. 'I'm sorry, Sebastian, that's far too deep for me, old fellow. You'll need to explain what you mean.'

'Oh, it's quite simple, Francis. Someone wanted me hanged for the murders. Was this the intention from the start? Or did the real killer, or killers, merely make full use of my unexpected presence upstairs, and implicate me in order to divert any suspicion away from him, or them? If this was the intention, then it was remarkably successful. Once I was taken into custody, no further enquiries were ever undertaken. Very convenient for the real killer, wouldn't you say?' His lordship peered grimly down into the contents of his glass. 'And a damnable pity in another way. Had a more thorough investigation been undertaken at the time, poor Jem Marsh's remains might not have been left to rot in a shallow, unmarked grave for almost nine long years.'

Francis frowned at this. 'Marsh…? Should I know him? Was he connected with the crime in some way?'

'Oh, not directly, I don't suppose for a moment. But I'd lay odds he knew something the killer didn't wish spread abroad, and that is why he was murdered on that very same night, I suspect.'

His lordship took a moment to sample his wine and collect his thoughts. 'It was one of the few things my father and I had in common—we both thought highly of Jem Marsh. I would frequently invite him to ride out with me. He was good company. Jem was totally uneducated and yet very level-headed—in those days the exact opposite to me, in fact.' His shout of laughter held a distinctly self-mocking ring. 'It was none other than Jem who rescued me when I was foolish enough to attempt to swim across that river near your place, remember? The current was strong, and I had been imbibing too freely. You've always maintained an excellent stock of claret in your cellar. Had it not been for Jem diving in after me, who could say what might have happened?'

'Indeed, I remember the incident well,' Francis acknowledged. 'I tried to dissuade you from doing such a foolhardy thing.' He spread his hands in a helpless gesture. 'But you were foolishly headstrong in those days.'

'My dear Francis, I was not known for my sobriety, either, in my youth,' his lordship reminded him, smiling grimly. 'I was too intoxicated to remember much at all. But I do recall Jem diving in after me. I rewarded him for his courage by presenting him with a fine silver pocket-watch, inscribed. It was found with his remains. So we might safely rule out theft as a motive, wouldn't you agree?'

He did readily, before asking, 'But are you sure he was murdered? Might he have had an accident on his way home? I assume he lived in one of the estate cottages?' he added when his lordship regarded him keenly.

'Yes, he still resided with his mother and siblings. The back of his skull was smashed in. He could, I suppose, have sustained a bad fall. But I strongly suspect he was murdered.'

Francis shook his head, appearing genuinely appalled. 'Well, unless the murderer is overcome by remorse and confesses to the crimes, I don't see there's much the authorities can do after all this time.'

'Perhaps not,' his lordship agreed. 'But there is something you can do for me.' It was clear he had his cousin's full attention. 'Be so good as to cast your mind back and recall, if you can, precisely what it was my father and I argued about before your arrival.' Once again his brief smile was faintly cynical. 'I have it upon the best authority that my beloved sire was consigning me to the devil throughout most of the evening, so you must have some idea.'

'Is it important?' Francis enquired, appearing bemused.

'It might be, yes,' the Viscount assured him.

'Oh, dear…well, let me see.' He frowned, evidently in an attempt to remember. 'It was clear that Uncle Henry was vexed about something, and when your name was mentioned it wasn't too difficult to work out precisely who had annoyed him. But then you were forever at loggerheads, weren't you, Sebastian? And I believe I inadvertently made matters much worse by suggesting it might be best for all concerned if he bought a commission for you, which enraged him even more, if my memory serves me correctly.'

Francis raised his eyes from their contemplation of the hearth to cast his cousin a considering look. 'By the by, Sebastian, is the little rumour I've heard true—that you have been out in the Peninsula during these past years?'

'Yes, perfectly true,' he confirmed. 'But I shan't be offering my services again to King and country should the need arise. Which I very much fear it will. I have far too much to occupy myself here.' He smiled grimly. 'I might have retained certain reservations before, but now, after what I've discovered today, I'm determined to do all I can to uncover the identity of my father's killer.'

Francis Blackwood appeared vaguely surprised. 'Well, I wish you well, Sebastian, old fellow. But I don't see that I can be of much help. What I really remember about that particular evening is that it wasn't one of the most convivial I've spent beneath this roof.'

'In that case, Francis, I shall endeavour to make the next occasion quite the opposite. Although I have every intention of visiting the metropolis in the near future, I have no desire to spend the Season in London this year, and so shall hold a party here in May, and trust you will attend?' His lordship rose to his feet. 'Unfortunately I'm unable to ask you to dine this evening. As I'm sure you can appreciate, I must inform the local magistrate, Sir Montague Cameron, about the unfortunate discovery in the home wood, and know not what time I shall return to dine myself.'

Francis, too, rose at once to his feet, appearing not in the least put out that this their first encounter in many years was to be so short. 'Perfectly understandable, old fellow. And I shall very much look forward to returning to the ancestral pile in a few weeks.'

Chapter Seven

Jem Marsh's funeral took place three days later. Deputising for the vicar, Mr Johns conducted a most moving service. Bessie, who had known the Marsh family all her life, accompanied Isabel, and they, together with a large congregation, including his lordship, saw Jem finally laid to rest in a corner of the churchyard.

Isabel had already guessed that it had been none other than Lord Blackwood himself who had ensured that Jem had not been placed in a pauper's grave which, sadly, had been the fate of so many of the Marsh family's forebears. It wasn't until the following day, however, when she was informed by Mr Johns that his lordship had also provided much of the fare served after the funeral in the Marsh family's cottage, that she realised just how generous his lordship had been.

'The Viscount put in an appearance himself, briefly,' the curate went on to reveal. 'I was invited, and can truthfully say the food, undoubtedly prepared in the kitchens up at the Manor, was excellent. It is little wonder his people think so highly of him. It's a great pity so many of his class are not nearly so benevolent. One ought to consider oneself fortunate to work for such a man.'

This instantly struck a chord of memory with Isabel, and she didn't hesitate to ask the young clergyman if his brother had managed to find himself a position.

'Only temporarily, I'm afraid. For a few weeks only, so I understand. Poor Simon, he's such a capable young fellow too. Sadly our parents cannot possibly provide him with sufficient funds to enable him to study law. He'll come into a little money when he's five-and-twenty left to him by a generous godfather. But until then…' He shook his head. 'I wish I were in a position to help.'

'Well, you might be,' Isabel enlightened him. 'It just so happens that his lordship is looking for someone to tutor Josh until the boy goes away to school. Do you think your brother might be interested?'

'Oh, I'm sure he would!' Mr Johns enthused, but then appeared slightly perturbed. 'I hardly think, though, I'm in a position to put Simon's name forward as a possible candidate for the position.'

'Don't worry,' Isabel responded. 'Write to your brother, and if he is at all interested, I'll speak to Viscount Blackwood on his behalf.'

'Not for a while you won't,' Clara countered, having entered the kitchen in time to overhear the last threads of the conversation. 'His lordship left for London first thing this morning and doesn't expect to be back for at least three weeks. I think he's gone to the capital for some peace and quiet. The house is in a positive uproar. He's having the large drawing room completely refurbished, and four of the larger bedchambers too. There's an army of workmen clumping through the house.'

Perversely, Isabel felt hurt because his lordship hadn't seen fit to apprise her of his plans. Without taking time to consider what the reaction might be, she echoed her thoughts aloud, and was immediately the recipient of several startled looks.

Bessie was the first to recover from the shock. 'Well, why for heaven's sake should he tell you that he's having his drawing room redecorated?'

Isabel dismissed this with an impatient wave of her hand. 'Oh, I knew all about that. But he might at least have mentioned, when we spoke in the churchyard after the funeral, that he was going jaunting off to the metropolis.'

Once again three pairs of eyes regarded her with varying degrees of speculation. 'Well, I shan't be able to approach him now about your brother, shall I?' she added inspirationally, fervently hoping that this would satisfy her listeners' evident curiosity over her show of mild pique.

At least it seemed to satisfy her cousin, who turned to Mr Johns to declare her delighted surprise at finding him at the farmhouse. As the curate had more often than not made a point of calling when he knew full well Clara would be there, Isabel considered the remark the most ingenuous piece of nonsense she'd heard in some considerable time, and was rather relieved when there was a knock on the front door, enabling her to leave the room before she uttered something else she might later regret.

Although she made a point nowadays of always changing her attire after working out of doors, it had also become second nature to check for imperfections in the passageway mirror before answering the door to callers. Consequently, although she was slightly taken aback to discover none other than the ample frame of the august local magistrate filling the small porch, she had no need to feel any qualms about her overall appearance as she cordially invited Sir Montague Cameron to step into the parlour.

Even though her father had been invited to dine numerous times at Sir Montague's fine Georgian mansion, Isabel could recall only one occasion when the Baronet and his wife had taken the trouble to call to see how her father went on during the six long years of his illness.

Yet her father had been more than their physician, he had quickly become a family friend since moving into the area and setting up his practice. Before today the only occasion Sir Montague had graced the farmhouse since her father's demise had been after she'd stirred up something of a hornets' nest by placing into a certain very safe pair of hands her father's written account of what he had known about the happenings on that dreadful night the murders had taken place. The Baronet had been aggrieved, perhaps understandably so, because she hadn't seen fit to pass the information directly on to him; and she very much suspected that resentment because she had apprised the Viscount, and not himself, about her grisly find in the wood was what lay behind his visit now.

'No doubt, Miss Mortimer, you are surprised by my visit,' he began, after accepting a glass of Madeira and seating himself in one of the comfortable chairs.

'Not at all, sir,' she swiftly disabused him in her forthright way. 'I imagine you're here to discuss the skeletal remains of Jem Marsh, which I had the misfortune to come across a week ago.'

Although it would have been true to say that few members of her mother's family had had any contact with her, there was no refuting the fact that her maternal grandmother had been the daughter of an earl. It was perhaps for this reason that Isabel had never felt particularly in awe of such persons as the Baronet. When he had called on that memorable previous occasion to take issue with her for not presenting him with her father's written account, she hadn't been afraid to point out that his initial handling of the enquiry could not withstand close scrutiny. As he had on that occasion turned an alarming shade of puce, she rather thought she would be well advised to exert a little diplomacy this time, if only because she had no desire to cause ill feeling between him and the Viscount.

'When I spoke with Lord Blackwood yesterday, after the funeral, he mentioned he'd apprised you of what had been found. I do not believe there's anything more I can add.'

Within the space of a very short time Isabel once again found herself the recipient of a considering stare. Although she didn't hold the Baronet in particularly high regard, and might deplore the fact that he had possibly allowed past grievances with the present Lord Blackwood's father to cloud his judgement all those years ago when the murders had taken place, she would never have considered him a dullard. Therefore she could only speculate on what was passing through his mind. She wasn't left wondering for long.

'I didn't realise, my dear Miss Mortimer, that you were so well acquainted with Viscount Blackwood.' When she deliberately refrained from comment, he added, 'Because I respected your father very much, I shall take the liberty of proffering a piece of advice—the present Lord Blackwood might indeed have been completely innocent of the sin of murder, and I am inclined now to believe this is so, even though it has yet to be proved beyond question. None the less, Sebastian Blackwood in his youth was guilty of many indiscretions, and earned himself something of an unsavoury reputation. I should guard against too much familiarity in that quarter lest your reputation should suffer as a result.'

Only the belief that the advice had been kindly meant stopped Isabel from telling him outright to mind his own business and not interfere in her concerns. After all, not once since her father's demise had he taken the trouble to call to see how the only daughter of his good friend went on. Notwithstanding, her resolve to maintain her composure remained firm.

'I believe your advice, sir, was kindly meant,' she responded, after fortifying herself from the contents of her glass, 'if totally unnecessary. Lord Blackwood's interest in me is purely in the spirit of good-fellowship, and is based, in my opinion, on misplaced gratitude. I've already told him that he owes me nothing for making my father's account known.'

The Baronet, however, wasn't wholly convinced, as his next words proved. 'What you say might be true. And I must admit when he came to consult with me over the discovery of young Marsh's remains, I was favourably impressed. He is undoubtedly, now, a man of strong character and sound judgement. So I cannot help wondering why he should have entrusted you, someone he'd never met until he returned to the Manor earlier this year, with the temporary guardianship of his wards.'

Isabel at last began to appreciate why the Baronet should believe her association with the Viscount was much closer than, in fact, it was. During the period Josh and Alice had resided at the farmhouse she had made it generally known that they were the children of a close friend. Somehow the Baronet must have got wind of this information. Servants' gossip, she could only suppose.

'You must ask him for an explanation as to why, precisely, he entrusted the children into my care. I can only speculate. But I believe, first and foremost, he desired to keep the children's whereabouts secret. At the time his lordship and I had never met. Therefore no one would have been likely to seek the children here at the farmhouse. I imagine also, because of my past actions, he believed I might be relied upon to care for his wards, if I promised to do so.' She returned the Baronet's steady gaze without so much as a blink, before adding, 'And you must remember, he does now need to be extra careful. Someone intended he should be framed for murder,' she reminded him, 'and that person has yet to be identified.'

Even though he acknowledged this with a nod, he didn't seem altogether satisfied with the explanation, and Isabel was left wondering, as she showed the Baronet out, what had really prompted the unexpected visit.

Her thoughts were momentarily diverted when she returned to the kitchen to discover only Bessie there. 'Has Clara gone upstairs to her room?'

'No, she accepted Mr Johns's invitation to accompany him on a visit to the old lady who lives next to the mill house. Seemingly she's been struck down with the same ailment that has kept the vicar in his bed these past few weeks, though I don't believe her case to be quite so severe.'

Winning no response, Bessie joined her mistress at the table. 'Your visitor didn't bring bad news, I trust?'

'Truth to tell, I'm not quite sure why Sir Montague Cameron called,' Isabel revealed, finally withdrawing her eyes from her frowning contemplation of the plates on the dresser. 'You know I've never held him in the highest regard. Not only did he virtually ignore Papa during his last years, but his handling of the murders up at the Manor left much to be desired.'

She shook her head, unsure what to think. 'Although his long-standing feud with the late Viscount was common knowledge, I don't for a moment suspect he was in any way involved in the crimes himself. Nor do I imagine he achieved any kind of satisfaction from taking the present Lord Blackwood into custody years ago… But I do mistrust Sir Montague, and his motives.'

By the time the Viscount returned to the manor, five weeks later, Isabel had long since thrust the local magistrate's odd visit to the back of her mind. Comfortably settled in one of the chairs in the front parlour, repairing a slight rent in a gown, she was apprised of the news of his return by her cousin, who came into the room, armed with two large packages.

'The children were so pleased to see him, especially Josh,' she went on to reveal, her eyes suddenly lit by a spark of excitement. 'And whilst he was visiting the nursery he revealed his intention of holding a large party in two weeks, a few days after my birthday, in fact. Oh, and he wants me to attend!'

Unlike her cousin, Isabel was faintly troubled by the tidings. After all, it wasn't the norm for employees to be invited to such grand affairs, and she echoed her worrying thoughts aloud.

'Perhaps not,' Clara conceded. 'But he wants me to bring the children down early in the evening, just for a brief period. But he said I might remain, if I so wished.'

Abandoning the sewing, Isabel gave her cousin her full attention. 'And is that what you want? Aside from his lordship, it's unlikely you'll know anyone else present,' she pointed out gently.

'Oh, yes, I shall…you,' Clara countered, and before Isabel could recover from the shock, she had thrust an invitation card into her hand.

For several moments it was as much as Isabel could do to gape down at her name written in the finest copperplate. 'But I cannot possibly attend,' she announced, when she had finally recovered from the shock. A score of reasons for refusing crossed her mind in quick succession, the foremost among them being, 'For a start I've absolutely nothing suitable to wear for such an occasion.'

'Yes, his lordship said you'd say that.' For the first time Clara betrayed an element of doubt. 'He suspected I might too, and as it is his expressed wish I attend he…he took the liberty of buying me a length of material. Oh, and it's so beautiful, Isabel!' she declared, stroking the brown paper package reverently. 'It's white, with a silver thread running through it. His lordship said that he'd discovered what an excellent seamstress I am, and felt sure I was more than capable of creating a suitable gown.' Raising her blue eyes, she cast an imploring glance. 'Oh, do please say I may accept it, Cousin!'

'It has absolutely nothing whatsoever to do with me,' Isabel returned bluntly. 'Your own conscience must decide. Though, I suppose,' she added, when Clara appeared slightly crestfallen, 'as it is at his lordship's expressed wish you be there, then there's some justification for accepting the gift.'

'Indeed, yes,' Clara agreed, brightening briefly before appearing decidedly troubled again. 'And he also said, as you were nowhere near as competent with a needle, you'd better have this.'

Clara almost tossed the larger package on to her cousin's lap. If the truth were known, Isabel wasn't altogether pleased to receive it either. She eyed it for several moments with misgivings before reaching for her scissors and snipping the twine that kept it securely bound.

Several items dropped to the floor in quick succession as Isabel reached for the parcel's major content and, rising to her feet, held it at arm's length. Unlike Clara, who gazed wonderingly at the beautifully made gown, Isabel was anything but impressed.

Only partially successful in stifling a squeal of vexation, she let the garment fall to the floor before fleeing the room, her feelings of wounded pride not precisely lessening when she discovered none other than his lordship's head groom sitting beside her housekeeper at the kitchen table, and working his way through a generous portion of apple tart.

'What the deuce are you doing here?' she demanded to know ungraciously.

Although not one to suffer fools gladly, Isabel could never have been accused of the sin of talking down to those less fortunately circumstanced than herself. Strangely enough, though, neither of the pair seated very companionably at the table appeared in the least surprised by her unusual outburst. In fact, if anything, the opposite was true. After a conspiratorial wink at Bessie, Clegg revealed that his master had instructed him to bring Miss Pentecost back to the farmhouse as she had parcels to carry.

''Ee also said as 'ow I wasn't to 'urry back, on account of 'ee rather thought you'd appreciate a ride in the carriage back to the Manor.'

'Oh, he said that, did he!' Isabel was almost beside herself with rage. She took a few deep steadying breaths before she informed the little coachman that she would require a few minutes only in order to fetch her bonnet.

The sound of that certain pleasantly melodic female voice filtering through from the hall brought a ghost of a smile to his lordship's lips. Setting aside his quill, he rose to his feet and was halfway across to the door when Isabel swept into the room, the clear light of battle flashing in her large grey-green eyes.

'How are you, Belle?' Unperturbed by the lack of response, he added, 'Looking extremely well, I'm pleased to say, if flying a trifle more colour than I like to see.'

He watched the slender hands ball themselves into fists. He felt sure she would derive much satisfaction from administering a sound box to his ears, and could only admire her self-control for resisting temptation.

'Why the heat, child?' he added, deciding not to goad her further. 'Didn't you approve my choice of gown? I chose it with particular care.'

'You shouldn't be buying gowns for me at all!' Isabel admonished, striving to maintain control, and not sound like some belligerent fishwife. 'People will suppose I've become your latest doxy, if ever word gets out!'

'My dear girl, I should never consider buying such a gown for a mistress,' he assured her, with only the faintest betraying sparkle in his eyes. 'It is far too demure.'

'Demure…?' she echoed, nowhere near appeased. 'It's red!'

'On the contrary, the modiste assured me the colour was claret—refined and the Season's must-have shade for any discerning young matron. Of course, I wouldn't have considered choosing such a colour for your cousin, but you will carry it very well.'

Successfully capturing her hand while she was fully occupied in formulating some stinging retort, he led her across to a chair by the hearth, and left her to grapple with her temper and compose herself while he poured out two glasses of wine.

After handing her one of the filled vessels, he took up a stance before the hearth, determined to persuade her to overcome her misgivings. 'The dress apart, tell me what's really troubling you, child?'

'I cannot possibly attend your party, sir,' Isabel finally admitted, suspecting he would eventually get to the truth, anyway. 'I'm not of your world. You're asking me out of kindness…out of gratitude. And I do wish you would not. You've given me so much already.'

When she attained no response whatsoever, curiosity got the better of her, and Isabel raised her eyes to his face. Then promptly wished she had not. His lordship's reputation in his youth, it had to be said, had not been without blemish. He had been hot-headed, unpredictable and an unconscionable womaniser. Yet his behaviour towards her had always been beyond reproach, save for the occasional provocative remark. Now, though, he was revealing that darker side. It was now wholly controlled, and all the more frightening because of it.

Every vestige of warmth had faded from his eyes, leaving them icy-cold and calculating. 'Don't you ever spout such flummery at me again, do you understand!' The threat was all the more disturbing because it had been delivered so softly. 'And before you attempt to say anything further, I should warn you that I had a fairly lengthy conversation with my godmother, Lady Augusta Pimm, during my recent sojourn in the capital, and she knew your grandmother, on the distaff side, extremely well.'

Isabel shrugged, determined to make light of it. 'So, what if I am distantly related to the present Earl of Trowbridge, and members of other notable families? My maternal grandmother had little contact with the other members of her immediate family after her marriage. And now the connections are too distant for me to remark upon.'

'Perhaps,' his lordship agreed, his gaze still assessing. 'But one cannot mistake breeding. I recognised it in you from the first. Furthermore, I'd wager your mother didn't come to the marriage penniless.'

A grey-eyed gaze flew upwards to meet his. Then his lordship watched as she set her glass aside, her hand not perfectly steady, and rose to her feet. He continued to watch her avidly as she went over to the window, moving with a natural grace from the hips. She stood there, merely staring out across the park, much as he had done when he had witnessed her meeting with his ward, on that eventful afternoon when Jem Marsh's remains had been found.

Then at last she broke the silence by admitting, 'You're right. Mama did have a dowry. Perhaps not substantial by your standards, my lord, but certainly not to be sniffed at. Yet it meant nothing to Papa. Unlike so many of your own class, who marry merely for money, my parents' marriage was that idealistic union that sometimes happens—a love match. Papa was the son of a gentleman, and although he was obliged to earn a living, he was what I believe is termed reasonably circumstanced.

'None the less,' she continued, after a further silent contemplation of the view beyond the window, 'he knew well enough that he couldn't afford those luxuries to which Mama had grown accustomed throughout her early life. He could provide her with a roof over her head, and a comfortable home, but not carriages and jewels and the lifestyle enjoyed by members of the *ton*. Those things Mama acquired from her dowry.

'Papa had a thriving practice in London. Unfortunately living there all year round did not suit Mama's delicate constitution, and after several years her health began to suffer. So Papa decided to set up a practice in the country, and eventually got to hear about Mr Bathurst's home. He fell in love with the farmhouse and the area. It seemed ideal. There was room enough to invite family and friends to stay in the house. Indeed there was room enough to keep a carriage and horses. Even I used to ride in those early days, after the move from London.'

A sigh escaped her. 'But everything changed after

Mama died. We lived well enough, but those luxuries I'd enjoyed throughout my early life slowly began to disappear one by one. Mama's carriage and the horses were the first things to go. Papa just kept the one animal to pull his gig. I've since learned that the money Mama brought to the marriage, at least what was left of it, was placed in trust for me. Unfortunately I cannot touch so much as a penny until I attain the age of thirty, or marry. Papa, of course, left me well enough provided for until then. Unfortunately during his long illness his savings became sadly depleted.'

Turning to face him, she shrugged again. 'But I'm no pauper. He did leave money in trust for me. We go along very well at the farmhouse, and shall continue to do so, I'm sure, until I come into my inheritance.'

'You'd go along a deal better if you didn't squander money on wages that are unnecessary,' he returned abruptly, thereby successfully concealing his feelings of admiration and compassion for the stoic outlook she continued to maintain. 'You might easily dispense with young Toby Marsh's services for a start. Do so and I shall offer him employment here. Seemingly Clegg has spoken to him on several occasions during his visits to your home, and has taken a liking to the lad.'

Isabel wasn't prepared to dismiss the offer out of hand, simply because what his lordship had said was true: she could easily dispense with Toby's services. All the same, she was slightly suspicious about his lordship's motives. No matter what the world at large said about him, she knew him to be a most thoughtful and generous man.

'You require extra help in your stables, my lord?'

He nodded as he moved across to his desk. 'Clegg has just one lad under him at present. The boy works well enough, but is far too young to attempt to tool a carriage-and-four. Marsh would be ideal. He's strong and could deputise for Clegg whenever the need arises. Besides which, extra help will almost certainly be needed when guests begin to arrive for the party. And speaking of which...'

He came slowly towards her, stopping so close that she had to resist the urge to take a hasty step away. 'Now that I have successfully dispensed with your nonsensical notions for not attending, I shall assume I may count on your presence.'

'I have given no such assurances,' she returned, the light of battle once again in her eyes.

Which were so unlike his own that only contained the gentle warmth she so often glimpsed there. 'Come, Belle, your cousin will need your support, if only to protect her from the young bucks that will moon over such a beauty. You wouldn't wish to see her fall victim to any such foolish blade?'

'Ha! Not much chance of that,' she assured him. 'Although Clara might never be considered long-headed, she isn't fickle. She's well on the way to falling in love with the local curate, Mr Johns, if I'm any judge.'

'Really?' This was news to his lordship, and he didn't attempt to hide the fact. Secretly he had been very impressed by the moving way the curate had conducted Jem Marsh's funeral service. Whether the young woman before him regarded the clergyman in a favourable light was difficult to judge. She could be quite remarkably circumspect when she chose, and so he decided to ask her outright.

She shrugged. 'It isn't up to me to approve or disapprove. I'm not my cousin's keeper. Sadly, though, unless Mr Johns manages to acquire a living of his own in the near future, I cannot see how they could afford to marry, unless Clara herself does come into some money upon marriage.'

Mention of the curate had jogged Isabel's memory, and she mentioned Mr Johns's brother as a possible tutor for Josh, if one hadn't already been found. His lordship merely said he would bear it in mind, before returning the conversation to his forthcoming party, and giving the impression that he now took it for granted that she would fall in with his wishes.

'I haven't agreed to attend yet,' she reminded him, not hesitating to set him straight on the matter, and just as swiftly discovered that he could be equally determined, if not a deal more so.

'Of course you'll attend. There's absolutely no reason for you not to do so, Belle.'

'My name is Isabel,' she corrected, very much fearing that against her better judgement she would end by acquiescing. Yet, alongside this, she couldn't deny that it would enable her to satisfy a secret and long-standing desire to attend just such a prestigious event as her mother had enjoyed on numerous occasions in her youth. 'And I haven't given you permission to use even that yet,' she added, striving to remain firm.

'Then do so now,' he returned. 'Formality is quite unnecessary between…friends.' He reached for her hand, easily holding it captive in his own as he contemplated the finely tapering fingers. 'Little did I realise when in Spain that my future well-being would one day rest in these hard-working little hands.' He raised his eyes in time to catch the flicker of uncertainty in her own, and released her at once. 'My name is Sebastian, by the way. Sebastian, Arthur, Darcy, George, to be precise.'

'I do know that, sir,' she assured him, hurriedly moving away and inadvertently brushing against the corner of his desk with her cloak, knocking some papers on to the floor. She bent to retrieve them, and in so doing gave herself a moment or two to recover from his lordship's brief and gentle physical contact. Sir Montague Cameron was oh, so right! Lord Blackwood was still a dangerous man, and far too fascinating for someone of her limited experience of the opposite sex. She must be mad even to consider attending his party!

After making a great play of tidying the papers, Isabel finally became aware of what had been written on the topmost sheet, and frowned in puzzlement. It appeared his lordship had been practising his signature just prior to her arrival. It seemed rather an odd thing for him to do, and she echoed her thoughts aloud.

'Look closely, *ma belle*,' he urged her, and watched as she studied the signatures closely. 'Do you see any differences between them?'

'Yes, the formation of several of the *B*s is different. On some you finish the letter with a distinct loop.'

'Clever girl! And that, my dear, was a warning to Wellington and his staff that the contents of any letter received from me must be regarded with great suspicion, because in all probability I had been captured and had been forced to pass on erroneous information regarding French movements.

'Naturally, I was obliged to adopt an assumed name… well, almost assumed…when I was out in the Peninsula. Wellington, of course, and a few others, knew of my true identity. Whenever I sent in written reports, I always initialled them *S.B.* and it was the letter *B* that was of interest to Wellington. Fortunately I was never captured, so I shall never know now if the little ruse would have alerted the Duke to possible dangers.

'And it is so important to have people around you that you can trust, *ma belle*,' he added, after a moment's silence. 'That is why I do so want you, above all others, to attend my party.'

She looked up at him, uncertain. 'I do not perfectly understand, sir. You do not suppose an attempt might be made on your life, do you?'

'I should be most surprised,' he assured her. 'But, also, I must be prepared for every eventuality. There's always the possibility that the murderer of my father and brother might be among the guests or, at the very least, that among them lurks someone with a greater knowledge of what precisely took place that night than has hitherto been revealed. Having given the matter much thought in recent weeks, I'm now convinced the perpetrator of the crimes is someone I know very well. And I need you, *ma belle*, someone I trust implicitly, to be my eyes and ears, and help me bring the culprit to book.'

All Isabel's reservations about attending disappeared in an instant. 'Of course I shall attend your party, sir,' she assured him, and then as a reward had her hand raised and kissed in very much the grand manner.

Chapter Eight

During the following two weeks Isabel saw nothing of her friend the Viscount, though she continued to receive an almost daily recital of the comings and goings at the Manor from her cousin, and from Josh too when he paid his regular Saturday afternoon visit to the farmhouse.

It was in the middle of May when Isabel finally fulfilled her promise to take Josh fishing in his lordship's well-stocked trout stream. The day was so fine that she didn't feel the need to wear even a lightweight shawl, though she wisely took the precaution of donning a broad-rimmed straw bonnet to ward off the danger of freckles.

Considering she had spent so much time out of doors, most especially during the past half-decade or so, her skin had remained remarkably unblemished, save for a liberal covering of freckles on both arms. Her mother had always maintained the prized fairness of her daughter's skin was the result of having been blessed with a substantial amount of natural red highlights in her chestnut hair. Whether this was true or not, Isabel couldn't have said with any real conviction, though she was eternally grateful that the freckles she had carried over her nose as a child had blessedly disappeared with the passage of time.

She glanced down at her young companion. Hatless and coatless, he was happy to leave his skin at the mercy of the elements. Like so many blessed with dark brown hair, the boy's skin acquired a healthy golden tan when exposed to sunlight.

'You look as though you've been spending a deal of time in the fresh air of late, Josh,' she remarked, as they settled themselves on a shaded portion of bank by the stream, and prepared their fishing rods. 'Has Miss Pentecost been taking advantage of the fine weather by spending time out of doors?'

By his grimace she strongly suspected that his periods in the fresh air had not altogether met with his approval. Then he brightened suddenly. 'His lordship has bought me my very own pony. He's my godfather as well, did you know?'

'No, I didn't,' Isabel admitted, though she wasn't in the least surprised. From things Josh had told her over the past months, she knew that his father and his guardian had been very close.

'He said it was to make up for all the birthdays he'd missed not buying me presents while I was growing up.'

Isabel smiled softly at this. How any one could stigmatise his lordship now as being in the least selfish or heartless she quite failed to understand. 'And have you ridden him already?'

Josh nodded. 'His lordship has taken me out twice. He said I may ride every day, if the weather is fine. And he said if he cannot accompany me either Cleggy or Toby will come along.'

'Ah, yes! And how is Master Marsh settling in at the Manor?' In truth, although she had accepted it had been the sensible thing to do, Isabel had been reluctant to dispense with young Toby's services, simply because she had liked him from the first, and he had proved a good and willing worker. When she had approached him he had appeared slightly taken aback, not to say crestfallen; until, that is, she had explained there was a position awaiting him up at the Manor, which she sincerely believed would offer him far more opportunities to better himself.

'All right, I think. He goes about whistling a lot,' Josh revealed innocently. 'Just as he did at the farmhouse. And I think he and Cleggy like each other. They're always laughing and joking, at any rate.'

This was a relief to hear and, contented, Isabel leaned back against a conveniently positioned tree trunk directly behind her, and closed her eyes, whilst attending to her young companion's lively discourse about life at the Manor. Eventually, though, disgruntled by the lack of success, Josh announced that it had been shockingly poor sport that afternoon, and suggested they do something else.

Isabel slanted her young companion a mocking glance. 'And are you really surprised we've not had so much as a bite? You haven't stopped talking since you settled yourself down on the bank,' she reminded him. 'Fish can hear, you know. Especially Big Jake, although I expect he's keeping to the deeper water on the far bank.'

Young eyes, full of wonder, were raised to hers. 'How big is he?'

'Massive!' Isabel spread her arms wide. 'Almost as big as a whale. I very nearly had him once, and almost broke my rod in the attempt.'

Josh regarded the stream with renewed interest. 'See if you can catch him now,' he urged her, but Isabel shook her head.

'As I've said before he keeps to the deeper water on the far bank. But I'll wade in midstream and see if I have better luck there at catching a couple.'

Although Isabel as a rule never bared her lower limbs before members of the opposite sex, she experienced no qualms about doing so in front of Josh who, apart from a cursory glance, paid no heed to a lady peeling off her stockings and tucking her skirts into her waistband so that she might wade into the water, almost up to her knees, without getting her clothes wet. She might not have been quite so unconcerned about her immodest state had she realised that her slender straight legs were being favourably surveyed by someone successfully concealed in the small copse a few yards away.

It took Isabel minutes only before her skill and patience were rewarded, and she tossed a fine specimen on to the bank, much to Josh's delight.

'I want to look for Big Jake.' He began to jump up and down, and was voicing his determination to catch the monster trout, when a much deeper voice echoed a similar sentiment, and Isabel turned to discover none other than the owner of the trout stream sauntering across the grass towards them.

'Wait a moment, Josh,' the Viscount ordered, as his ward, having already divested himself of shoes and stockings, was on the point of joining Isabel in the water. 'Help me off with these confounded boots first.'

Isabel found herself unashamedly admiring his lordship's muscular calves as he peeled off his stockings. Although nowhere near as white as her own, the skin on his legs was several shades lighter than that on his face, and had a liberal covering of fine black hair, as did his arms.

Oddly enough, as he waded into the water towards her, she experienced not a single moment's disquiet at having a gentleman in a state of undress standing so close. In fact, the opposite was true, for she gurgled with mirth when he proceeded to take her to task for spinning Josh such a yarn about the gigantic trout.

'Whale, indeed! If I'd a shiny sovereign for every fishy tale I'd heard…'

'You'd be twice as wealthy as you are now,' she finished for him, grinning wickedly up at him, and receiving the full warmth of his own smile in return. 'I dare say. But it won't do him any harm. Look at him now,' she added, after watching Josh searching the depths on the far side of the stream for the monster trout, 'as contented as can be. He might never find the elusive Big Jake, but there's plenty of prize specimens lurking in these shallows. I can attest to that.'

'Yes, I'm sure you can, you baggage!' he returned and, although not sounding altogether pleased, not fooling her for a moment by the mock show of disapproval. 'I know how you've been making free with my game over these past years.'

'Ah, but only when my garden produce was damaged by your poor drainage,' she reminded him, totally unabashed. 'And never once since your return, until today.' She turned her head on one side, looking, he decided, most adorable. 'I considered it recompense.'

'You did, did you? Well, let us see if we can catch a couple more for your supper.'

Borrowing Isabel's rod, his lordship was more than equal to the challenge, and very soon caught three fine specimens before abandoning the sport in order to join Isabel on the bank. Unlike his companion, who had instantly readjusted her attire on leaving the water, he made no attempt to don any of his, and settled himself on the grass beside her, allowing the sun to dry his legs and bared portion of his arms.

By belatedly thanking him for the fish, Isabel broke the

companionable silence, but his lordship, at first dismissing the gratitude with a wave of his hand, considered her for a moment.

'You can repay me by dancing with me at the party next week. You can dance, I trust?'

Isabel had not missed the wickedly mocking rise of those arching black brows. 'I'm not a complete country bumpkin,' she assured him. 'Of course I can dance! Well, most all the country dances, at any rate.'

'I thought as much.' He tutted. 'So you cannot waltz.'

'Of course not!' she returned primly. 'It has never been danced at the assemblies in Merryfield. Even I know it's frowned upon in polite circles.'

'Not so much now,' he enlightened her. 'It is at last beginning to win approval at private functions. I discovered a good dancing master when in London recently. It just so happens he's agreed to break his journey to Nottinghamshire on Monday, so you can come over to the Manor in the afternoon, and receive expert tuition, if you'd like. In fact, I insist upon it,' he went on, adopting a very dictatorial stance. 'It's the least you can do to reimburse me for all the poaching you've done during my many years away. Besides which, dancing together will afford a golden opportunity to discuss what, if anything, we've been able to uncover at the party, without arousing suspicion.'

As he was lying beside her, with his head resting on his hands, and his eyes closed, Isabel wasn't able to judge whether he was being serious or not. All the same, she had the feeling that more lay behind his wanting her to dance with him than he was willing to reveal.

Decidedly suspicious though she might have been, Isabel, nonetheless, allowed herself to be conveyed to the Manor in his lordship's carriage directly after luncheon on

Monday afternoon. Tredwell escorted her up the imposing wooden staircase to the long gallery, where she discovered not only his lordship talking with a dapper little
man dressed formally in satin knee breeches, white stockings and pumps, but also her cousin, seated at a pianoforte.

'Ha! Miss Mortimer.' His lordship, instantly breaking off his conversation, came forward. 'May I make you
known to Mr Petersham, the owner of the famous Petersham School of Dancing.'

'Enchanted, *mademoiselle*,' the little man greeted her,
bowing low over her hand. 'Already I have observed you
move with ease and grace, and have a lightness of step. It
should be no problem to teach you. Just as I had little difficulty instructing your fair cousin, who has kindly agreed
to remain and provide us with music.'

'Aren't we bold?' Clara whispered, as Isabel placed her
bonnet on the table beside the instrument.

She refrained from comment, though she couldn't help
feeling that her cousin's employment at the Manor had not
been wholly advantageous. One would hesitate to call her
unbecomingly forward, exactly. All the same, her association with the Viscount over the weeks had definitely
boosted Clara's self-confidence.

The little dancing-master's prediction turned out to be
correct. Within the space of half an hour, Isabel had mastered the steps, and was confident enough to hold her head
up, and not stare down at her feet. In fact, she found the
dance exhilarating, and wasn't in the least self-conscious
having a man's hand resting lightly on her waist, until,
that is, his lordship ceased to turn the pages of music for
Clara, and took the dancing-master's place. Then it was
as much as Isabel could do to stop herself from treading
on his feet, while she kept her gaze riveted to the intricate
folds of his snowy-white cravat.

'Come, *ma belle*,' he chided gently. 'People will suspect I've coerced you into dancing with me at the party, if you look so terrified.'

Although she wasn't perfectly certain she knew quite what his touch was doing to her, of one thing she was certain, it had nothing whatsoever to do with fear. It took a monumental effort, but she managed to raise her eyes to his, then promptly lowered them again when she perceived the satisfied glint lurking in those blue depths. The wretch knew—knew full well that his touch was having an adverse effect on her equilibrium, sending her pulse rate soaring, not to mention increasing her bodily temperature to such an extent that the palms of her hands felt sticky, and she was sure she had gone quite red in the face.

Consequently she wasn't altogether sorry when the dance came to an end, and his lordship's attention was immediately afterwards claimed by the unexpected appearance of a very imposing elderly matron, dressed from head to toe in purple, making her way down the length of the gallery towards him.

'Good gad! Lady Pimm!' He placed a dutiful salute on the lined cheek presented to him. 'Didn't expect to see you until Wednesday at the earliest.'

'I cannot recall mentioning precisely when I should be arriving when you visited me in London recently. I trust there are rooms ready for me and my maid,' she added, casting a brief glance in the direction of the dancing-master, before favouring the two females present with her full attention.

Although Lady Pimm had been painfully well aware of her godson's rakish behaviour in his youth, she had never heard it said that he had ever attempted to seduce innocence. Nor could she recall that he had ever been guilty of bringing a light-skirt back to the ancestral pile. She could fully appreciate what might have attracted him to the golden-haired chit. The girl was quite stunningly lovely, and his name, of course, had been linked with several accredited beauties in the past. And not all of them unmarried, she reflected. But just what the attraction might be to the other female escaped her. The young woman was maybe here for propriety, a relative or some such, she finally decided.

'Won't you introduce me to your young companions, Sebastian? Petersham, I know, of course,' she revealed, acknowledging the dancing-master's bow with a slight nod. 'A year or so ago he successfully instructed my flat-footed niece to acquire at least a modicum of grace on the dance floor, for which the family remains eternally grateful.'

His lordship complied with the request with his customary aplomb, introducing Isabel first to his godmother before turning to Isabel's cousin and revealing, much to her ladyship's evident surprise, that Clara was in his employ as governess to his wards.

An awkward silence then followed, during which her ladyship cast such a withering look in the direction of the pianoforte that Clara blushed to the roots of her hair. His lordship didn't appear entirely pleased, either, by his godmother's quite obvious misconceptions, and so Isabel, with great presence of mind, filled the breach before any further needless unpleasantness arose.

'And no doubt, Clara, you are eager to return to your charges. Thank you for playing so beautifully. I could not have managed half so well without you. Nor, indeed, without you, Mr Petersham. I believe now I shall go on very well at the party,' she added, offering her hand in farewell to the dapper little man, before finally taking leave of his lordship's autocratic godmother.

'I shall see you to the carriage,' his lordship said, an offer Isabel hurriedly declined.

'Please do not trouble, sir. I know my way out. And I think, in truth, I should much prefer to walk back home. The fresh air will do me good.'

It wasn't so much Isabel's charming smile of farewell that captured her ladyship's attention as a certain look that just for one moment sprang into her godson's eyes as he followed the cousins' progress along the gallery. But precisely which of the young women had engendered a look of such tenderness her ladyship was far from certain now.

It was not until early that evening, when she joined her godson in the parlour before dinner, that she received her first opportunity to satisfy her curiosity regarding the two young women. Notwithstanding, she thought it might be prudent to begin by apologising for her earlier, possibly, erroneous misconceptions.

'Even so, in my defence, Sebastian, I have to say it was a mistake anyone might have made,' she continued, accepting the glass of wine he held out to her. 'In my day governesses were never so favourably packaged. And you always did have an eye for a pretty face.'

He smiled secretively down into his glass. 'I still do, ma'am. But you'll never hear it said that I attempted to compromise an employee in this, or any other household. Miss Pentecost relies on me for her livelihood. I would never betray her trust.'

She regarded him through narrowed eyes. 'You've changed, Sebastian. You've grown. It would seem your years in the army were the making of you.'

Once again he smiled down into his glass. 'No, ma'am, you err. It wasn't my years in the Peninsula that persuaded me to view certain matters rather differently. Oh, no... It was...something entirely different.'

He raised his eyes to discover himself the recipient of a very penetrating look. 'Tell me, ma'am, are your rooms to your liking? Have you everything you need?'

'Everything is most comfortable, Sebastian,' she assured him. 'I must say the Manor is looking very fine. You've clearly transformed the place since your return. And the drawing room is splendid. Just as wonderful as it looked in your dear mama's day! It is the same colour scheme, is it not?'

'Why, yes, I do believe it is,' he replied, once again smiling that same infuriatingly enigmatic smile.

She would dearly have loved to know what he was thinking about, but as she was fairly certain he would not satisfy her curiosity she decided to steer the conversation back to the other topic that had intrigued her since her arrival.

'And I assume you will be holding the party in there?'

'Yes, indeed, as there is no ballroom here at the Manor, as you well know.'

'And am I right in believing you've invited none other than your governess's cousin?'

He shrugged, maintaining quite beautifully a display of indifference. 'I could hardly do otherwise, ma'am, now could I? Among my guests will be several friends of Daniel and Sarah Collier, who shall be putting up at several different locations in the area. I believe they would wish to see the children. So naturally I shall require the governess to present them. And she could hardly attend the party without the support of the older cousin, Miss Mortimer, now could she?'

Far from satisfied, her ladyship peered owlishly up at her godson, who, save for a glint of amusement still lurking in those strikingly blue eyes, maintained an annoyingly expressionless stance before the hearth.

'Mortimer…? Mortimer?' she repeated. 'Now where have I heard that name before recently?'

'From me, I dare say. You knew her grandmother, Lady Mary Brent,' he reminded her.

'Ah, yes! A spirited minx in her youth, and not altogether wise, but I liked her. She eloped with a handsome young rogue, an inveterate gamester, and bore him a child, a daughter, before he got himself shot in a duel over some gambling dispute. The family never welcomed her back into the fold after her scandalous marriage. Her father, the sixth Earl of Trowbridge, was very high in the instep, and his successors equally so. But I believe Mary went on quite well, mainly due to the generosity of her wealthy godmother, with whom she resided when not visiting the capital. She had a wide circle of friends, and not all the members of the *ton* snubbed her, so she continued to socialise frequently, as did her daughter, I believe. What eventually became of the child, I cannot for the life of me now recall.'

'She married a Dr John Mortimer, and bore him one child. After several years in the capital, he set up a practice here in the local community.'

She regarded her godson in silence for a moment. 'So Miss Mortimer is Mary Brent's granddaughter, is she? I wonder if she possesses her grandmother's spirit?'

'You must judge for yourself, ma'am,' he told her, almost conveying the impression the subject held no special interest for him. But then he said, oh, so very gently, 'She does, however, possess many fine qualities. Had it not been for the selfless actions of that young woman, I might even now still have been wanted for murder. I owe her more than I could ever hope to repay.'

Was it simple gratitude he felt towards Lady Mary's granddaughter? she couldn't help wondering. And what of the other girl, the cousin? Surely he wasn't so indifferent to her? Had she, too, some notable family connections?

'She is the daughter of a gentleman and undeniably a genteel young woman,' he responded in answer to her questions. 'Who her antecedents might have been, I have never troubled to enquire. She is employed as governess in my household, and carries out her duties to my satisfaction. That is all that concerns me.'

Lady Pimm wasn't entirely convinced by the assurance. How could such a red-blooded male like Blackwood be indifferent to such a beauty? Either his character had changed completely during the past nine years, or he was doing his level best to conceal something. She would need to do a little investigating of her own, if only to satisfy her curiosity. Something had happened to her godson. That much was certain! Maybe his experiences in Spain had influenced his behaviour, changing him from a wild and occasionally thoughtless young man into a person of sound judgement and discretion. Or had there been other beneficial influences in his life? Who could say? The only thing she was certain of was that never before had she seen him looking so relaxed, so at ease with himself.

Two days later, however, Lady Pimm was no closer to solving the conundrum of her godson's behaviour, save that she was certain in her own mind that Lord Blackwood's manner was not feigned. He seemed truly contented with his lot.

She paid a daily visit to the nursery, and by the time she had left on the second occasion she was firmly convinced that the beautiful cousin, amazingly enough, held no particular attraction for him. When she had happened to enter a short time earlier, and had discovered him there, she had glimpsed nothing in his expression to suggest he was even remotely captivated by the girl with the gentle blue eyes, golden locks and enviably flawless complexion. In fact, if anything, he had betrayed a deal more enthusiasm at the prospect of taking his elder ward out riding later that morning.

But what of the other cousin? she wondered, making her way back along the gallery to her allotted bedchamber. Did his interest in her stem only from a feeling of gratitude? Or was there, perhaps, something far more meaningful lurking beneath the surface, just waiting to be uncovered? There was only one way she would satisfy her ever-increasing curiosity.

'Dimmock, we are going out,' she revealed, discovering her personal maid of many years standing tidying the yellow bedchamber. 'Arrange for my carriage to be brought round to the door, and get ready yourself. I shall need you to accompany me. Your judgement is second to none!'

Isabel was unable to hide her surprise when Bessie showed her visitors into the parlour shortly before midday. 'Why, Lady Pimm, this is an unexpected pleasure! Won't you sit down?' Her eyes slid briefly to the thin little woman who had seated herself near the door, before turning again to the imposing matron and offering refreshment.

'A glass of port would be most appreciated. My godson is most disapproving of my chosen tipple. But then I do not believe he likes to see females imbibing too freely.'

'I find that hard to believe, ma'am,' Isabel didn't hesitate to confess. 'He's always forcing a filled glass into my hand whenever I go to see him. Which fortunately is not so very often that I stand the risk of becoming a toper.'

For several seconds Lady Pimm studied the young

woman who had seated herself opposite, noting the evenness of her features. There was a confident directness in her gaze, which her cousin's sadly lacked. Not only that, there was no mistaking the intelligence in the greyish-green eyes. She too had been blessed with a flawless complexion, and a healthy sheen to her chestnut locks, which today were merely adequately confined by a ribbon at the nape of her neck. 'Now I come to study you more closely, my dear, I see you have a great look of your grandmother about you.'

'Sadly she died when I was very young, ma'am. I do not remember her at all.'

Once again Isabel found herself the recipient of a long, assessing look. She wished she knew just why she had been honoured with this visit. However, not wishing to appear rude, she refrained from asking outright. Instead, she brought the uncomfortable little silence to an end by enquiring whether other guests had now arrived at the Manor.

'Sebastian said one or two would be arriving this evening, but no family members. I believe they are all arriving tomorrow. Not that I should imagine they'll cause the staff at the Manor too much extra work. There are so few close members of the Blackwood family still living.'

Once again Lady Pimm stared long and hard over the rim of her glass, before sampling its contents and smiling approval. 'And you and your charming young cousin are to grace the event, so I understand?'

Isabel's grimace in response was most intriguing, and Lady Pimm's curiosity was instantly aroused. She immediately sought an explanation for the evident reluctance, and quickly discovered that the young woman who was rising in her estimation with every passing minute was quite capable of keeping her own counsel.

'Oh, there are several reasons, my lady,' was all Isabel

would reveal, only to discover that her visitor was not to be so easily discouraged.

'Oh, come, my dear! Young women of your age love parties and dancing.' She looked thoughtfully at the neat, but clearly provincial day dress Isabel was wearing. 'Forgive my asking, child, but your reluctance doesn't stem from not having a suitable gown to wear for the occasion, I trust?'

If anything Isabel's expression betrayed even more disquiet. 'Oh, no, my lady. I have a gown, right enough!'

Lady Pimm could not mistake the disgruntled tone and, more curious than ever, requested to see the garment. The instant she detected Isabel's light tread mounting a staircase, she addressed the other occupant of the room, who had sat in her chair throughout, quietly observing the young mistress of the house. 'What say you, Dimmock? Not too difficult a task to bring the chit up to scratch?'

The middle-aged abigail didn't pretend to misunderstand. 'She has good features, my lady, and an excellent figure.'

'Yes, and far more character than that cousin of hers. I wonder...? Yes, I'm truly beginning to believe it's possible. I shall rely on you, Dimmock, to bring to bear all your skills.' She raised a warning finger. 'Quiet now, I believe she is returning.'

Lady Pimm, never having been one to conceal her emotions, made not the least attempt to hide her astonishment when Isabel held the gown against her, the better for her visitor to pass judgement.

'I know, ma'am, you do not need to tell me,' Isabel assured her, having interpreted the astonished expression for disapproval. 'But it's too late now for me to have another made. Besides which, I don't wish to offend his lordship.

The gesture was kindly meant, I know. But I have made it quite clear that I shall accept nothing else from him.'

It took Lady Pimm a moment or two to assimilate precisely what she was being told. 'Do I infer correctly from that, that it was none other than my godson who purchased the garment for you?'

Looking plainly guilt-stricken, Isabel nodded. 'And I do wish he had not. The gesture was well meant. But really there was no need. It was my father, not I, who wrote an account of what took place on that eventful night, when his lordship's father and brother lost their lives. All I did was to ensure the information was passed on to the right people.'

Although Lady Pimm had listened to every word, her eyes had remained fixed on the beautiful gown. That her godson had gone to the trouble of choosing the garment himself told her all she needed to know. The dress was beautifully made, and clearly the creation of one of the capital's leading modistes. What a demon he was! she mused. Unless she was much mistaken, he had chosen the colour with particular care. And it suited the chit admirably!

'Well, my dear, it is hardly a suitable garment for a girl embarking on her first Season to wear. But, without wishing to give offence, a young woman in her mid-twenties can scarcely be looked upon in such a light. You will carry the colour extremely well. What say you, Dimmock?'

'Indeed, yes, ma'am,' the maid dutifully agreed, before adding, 'providing it is worn with the correct accessories.'

Feeling decidedly uncomfortable under the two females' continued scrutiny, Isabel informed them that his lordship had seen fit to provide her with silk shawl, evening gloves and slippers, all of which had been dyed the exact shade as the dress. 'And everything fits perfectly. Though the Lord only knows how he managed to judge my size so accurately!'

Her ladyship tactfully refrained from pointing out that her godson was no stranger to the female form. Instead, she asked what, if any, jewellery would be worn to the party.

'Well, I haven't quite made up my mind yet, ma'am,' Isabel admitted. 'I have a fine gold locket, or there's a single string of pearls, which belonged to my mother. Also, I have a garnet necklace.' She smiled reminiscently. 'Papa never objected to Mama buying jewellery. He was no expert, and so when she told him they were rubies, he believed her. She felt so guilty about spending so much money, you see, on a ruby set.'

'I consider any of those would be admirable,' Lady Pimm responded, adding, as she rose to her feet, 'And, my child, if you would not be offended, I should like to offer my maid's services to dress you for the evening. She has quite a remarkable way with hair. Mine, of course, being grey and wispy, can never do justice to her skills. Yours, on the other hand, most definitely shall. So may I send her over to you on Friday afternoon?'

In view of such kind generosity, Isabel considered it would be ungracious to refuse.

Chapter Nine

Throughout her adult life thus far, the nearest Isabel had ever come to having a personal maid had been Bessie, who had helped her to dress for the odd social evening Isabel had enjoyed since attaining the age of sixteen. Before her father had become ill, she had accompanied him from time to time when he had been invited to dine in the more affluent households in the locale. She had also enjoyed the rare evening's entertainment since her father's demise, and felt she had left the house on all these occasions always looking presentable enough, and without suffering the least qualms over her appearance.

None the less, Bessie herself would have been the first to admit that she lacked those special skills inherent in every professional lady's maid. Consequently, she was only too happy to place her young mistress into the hands of the birdlike little woman who arrived at the farmhouse at the prearranged time on Friday afternoon.

Because her cousin had decided not to return to the farmhouse, and to dress for the evening at the Manor, with the young nursery-maid's assistance, Isabel was able to luxuriate for quite some time in the rose-scented water of the hipbath, placed next to the kitchen range, without fear of interruption. Having her hair carefully washed, and then relaxing outside, whilst all the time her locks were drying in the late afternoon sun, was a luxury she had never before experienced. So it was hardly surprising that, long before her long tresses had been piled high on the back of her head, the majority of which fell in a softly waving pony-tail, and her lips and cheeks had been touched with colour, she had already begun to feel extremely special indeed.

As she gazed into her late mother's dressing-table mirror, she barely recognised herself. She had allowed the abigail to do precisely as she wished. With a few judicious snips of the scissors the lady's maid had fashioned several wispy curls to cascade on to Isabel's cheeks, and had strategically positioned a beautiful pearl comb into the glowing chestnut locks.

'I hardly know what to say, Dimmock. I would never have attempted such a style myself. There is almost a Grecian quality about it. Thank you so much.'

'Your hair is beautiful, Miss Mortimer, a real pleasure to dress,' the maid responded, looking rather satisfied with the results of her efforts herself. 'And the comb just adds that extra special touch, do you not think?'

'It certainly does, but… Who does it belong to?'

The maid's expression all at once seemed guarded. 'My mistress brought it with her from London,' she finally revealed.

'Then it is most kind of her to lend it to me for the evening,' Isabel responded, touched by the gesture, for she had nothing in her jewellery box to equal it. 'But I rather fancy it has settled on my choice of necklace—Mama's pearls, I think.'

'If I might suggest putting on your gown first, miss, and then decide,' the abigail suggested, going across to the good quality, if slightly old-fashioned, wardrobe where the dress had been safely stored since its arrival in the house.

With one expert movement the maid had the dress over Isabel's head, without so much as disturbing a single lock of hair. Once she had each fastening secured, she invited Isabel to sit again in front of the mirror, before she reached again for the velvet-covered flat box, which she had brought with her from the Manor.

Inside, resting on a bed of purple silk, were two pearl-drop earrings and the most beautiful matching necklace Isabel had ever seen. Two individual strands of pearls came together in a beautifully fashioned knot and then divided again to cascade over the wearer's chest.

'But surely Lady Pimm wishes to wear them herself?' Isabel suggested, after gazing in awe at the beautiful set.

'On the contrary, miss. Her ladyship would be only too happy if you agreed to wear them. She has always maintained that jewels always look much better when displayed against young skin.'

By the time the necklace had been fastened about her neck, and she had donned the earrings, Isabel was too astounded by the change in her appearance to voice adequately enough her thanks to the little woman who had wrought such a miracle.

Her amazement, however, was as nothing when compared to Bessie's reaction on first catching sight of her mistress descending the stairs. Whipping out her handkerchief, she did no more than burst into tears.

'Oh, Miss Isabel, you look like a princess, so you do!'

With perhaps one exception only, there was no one's approbation that she valued more. Even so, Isabel was nothing if not a realist. She possibly looked the best she'd ever looked in her entire life, but she had not turned into a

ravishing beauty in the space of a few hours, and she had
sense enough to realise it.

'Pull yourself together, woman!' she scolded lovingly.
'And don't you dare to wait up for my return, understand!
Clara and I are more than capable of helping each other
to disrobe. Just leave the lamp burning on the hall table.'

Then, after hurriedly placing a kiss on Bessie's cheek,
she whisked herself outside to where his lordship's carriage
awaited her, before she was infected by her housekeeper's
sentimentality and gave way to a weakness she despised.

The journey to the Manor, of course, took no time at all,
and as there were no carriages waiting to disgorge their
passengers she was able to enter the Manor without further
ado. Tredwell, a prince among butlers, betrayed no sign
whatsoever that he had observed the slightest change in her
appearance, and merely turned to lead the way across the
hall to the drawing room. Isabel automatically followed,
until, that is, she detected an impish chuckle filtering down
from high above her head.

After mounting half-a-dozen stairs, she easily located
the source of amusement. Two small faces were peering
down at her through the banister rails. 'What on earth are
you two doing about at this time?' she demanded to know.

'Our guardian said we might stay to watch the guests
arriving, at least those invited for dinner,' Josh enlightened her. 'But we only really wanted to see you.' His expression revealed that he wasn't entirely impressed with
what he saw, even before he added, 'You do look funny,
Miss Isabel.'

'No, she doesn't,' Alice countered, casting her older sibling a disapproving look. 'She looks as beautiful as Miss
Pentecost. She's been invited to dine as well, Miss Isabel.'

'In that case I'd best present myself to our host, and not keep the other guests waiting for their meal.'

'Indeed you had,' a velvety voice behind her softly agreed, and Isabel turned to discover his lordship at the foot of the stairs.

Never before had she seen him dressed in formal evening attire, and thought he looked magnificent. Secretly she might have preferred to see him in his less formal riding garb, but even so he looked so distinguished in his long-tailed black coat and buff-coloured knee-breeches. What he thought of her appearance was impossible to judge, for apart from a lingering look at the adornment hanging about her neck, his expression revealed little, before he bade the children goodnight, instructing the little nursery-maid, who had remained hovering in the shadows, to take his wards to bed.

'Come, *ma belle*.' He held out his left hand. 'There are several people eager to make your acquaintance, and one other very eager to renew it.'

Once she had reached his side, he did not hesitate to wrap her arm round his so that they might enter the drawing room together. 'Tell me, *ma belle*, from where did you obtain that pearl set?' he asked casually, as they approached the beautifully redecorated room. 'Were they your mother's, perhaps?'

'Oh, no, my lord. They are your godmother's. It was so very kind of her to allow me to wear them for the evening, do you not think?'

'Kindness, I strongly suspect, had precious little to do with it, *ma belle*. And my name is Sebastian.'

'Yes, I know that, my lord.'

'Baggage!' he muttered, but to little effect, for Isabel was too intent on scrutinising the new décor to pay much heed.

'Oh, sir, how different it all looks! It's magnificent! You must be very well pleased.'

'Yes, very much to my taste. I could not have chosen better,' he declared, staring intently down at her. 'And now, *ma belle*, I wish to reacquaint you with an old friend of mine.' And without further ado he led her towards the only man in the room who was fractionally taller than himself.

'You remember Miss Mortimer, do you not, Charles?'

'How could I forget her?' the big man responded gallantly, while taking the proffered slender hand and bowing over it. 'Though, I'm forced to add, I would have been hard put to it, my dear Miss Mortimer, to have picked you out in a crowded ballroom.'

He favoured the Viscount with a surprised look. 'And what are you still lingering for, Blackwood? I do believe Lady Pimm is trying to attract your attention. You may safely leave Miss Mortimer in my care. Go away, do, and see what the formidable matron wants, whilst I look out our friend Staveley and make him known to this charming young lady.'

The Viscount had a fairly shrewd notion why his godmother was so eager for a word, and sauntered over to where she was seated by the wall. 'And how long have you been in possession of Mama's pearls?'

'Since that wretch of a father of yours gave them to me shortly after her death. He said he thought I might like them, as your mother and I were particular friends. Wicked, it was! Just because he never purchased them for her. They should have been added to the family jewels. The Lord alone knows what became of the other fine pieces she brought with her to the marriage! But I always intended to return the set to you. That is why I brought it with me.'

When he continued to stare down at her with lazy affection, uttering not a word, she peered up at him wickedly. 'It has been some years since they have been seen in public, Sebastian… I trust the neck on which they are now being displayed is the right one?'

'Why my mama, who was so sensible as a rule, chose such a devious and wicked woman for my godmother, I fail to understand,' he responded, thereby igniting Lady Pimm's wicked sense of humour.

'I shall tell you why, you young rogue. It is because she knew I was not easily shocked, and therefore would never be scandalised by your future behaviour. Although you have surprised me on this occasion,' she went on to admit. 'Pleasantly surprised me, I might add. That young woman is quite out of the common way. And, unless I much mistake the matter, like myself, not easily shocked. Not that you would ever seek my approval, Sebastian. All the same, I shall take leave to inform you that I think you have chosen wisely.'

For answer all he did was to offer his arm in order to assist her to her feet, a moment after the estimable Tredwell had announced dinner. He had already secured his good friend Charles Bathurst's services to escort Isabel in to dinner, and had been equally successful in persuading the very gentlemanly Sir Philip Staveley to offer his support to Isabel's much shyer younger cousin. Sebastian had also ensured that the position on his governess's left was filled by someone who would undoubtedly put the young woman very much at her ease, a fact that didn't escape Isabel's notice as she took her place between the two very personable gentlemen who had kept her very well entertained soon after her arrival.

She took a moment to stare round the table at her fellow dinner guests, twenty in all. Some she knew well enough, or at least by sight—the curate, Mr Johns, for instance, and Sir Montague Cameron and his wife and eldest son; others were complete strangers. Yet not one among the unknown female guests could she have said with any degree of conviction was likely to be married to either of the very personable gentlemen sitting either side of her.

'Did your wife not choose to accompany you, Mr Bathurst?' she finally asked, curiosity having got the better of her.

'No, unfortunately not. My wife is in, what you might say is, a delicate condition, as is Sir Philip's, I might add.'

'Oh, many congratulations, sir! When do you expect the happy events to take place?'

'Not until the autumn. Both ladies were disappointed not to be here, most especially Lady Staveley, who's a good friend of the Viscount. Sense, however, prevailed, and she, too, considered her unborn child.'

The instant Mr Bathurst's attention was claimed by the lady on his right, Isabel congratulated Sir Philip on his recent marriage, and happy future event. 'I understand your wife knows Lord Blackwood well.'

Not all gentlemen, she felt sure, would have been too pleased to discover that their wives had enjoyed a close association with the Viscount. Surprisingly enough, though, the charming Baronet seemed completely unperturbed.

'Yes, they were both out in Spain together,' he explained, once again displaying the ease of manner that Isabel found most winning. 'My wife was with her father throughout most of the Peninsular Campaign. Beth's father and Lord Blackwood were involved in similar work.'

'I see. And you, sir…? Were you also out in Spain?'

He shook his head. 'But I did know Sebastian slightly many years ago, but I didn't really get to know him well until he stayed in Somerset with my good friend Bathurst last autumn.' He leaned towards her, adding in a conspiratorial whisper, 'It was during that period he had the impudence to propose marriage to the lady who I now have the honour to call my wife.'

Even though Isabel couldn't mistake the wicked twinkle in a pair of attractive grey eyes, something akin to an icy bolt tore through her at the mere thought of the Viscount being in love. It took a monumental effort to rally her disordered thoughts sufficiently to say, 'Well, sir, at least she had the sense to refuse and marry you instead. Clearly a lady of discernment.'

Sir Philip's spontaneous bark of laughter drew the attention of several of those at the table, including the host himself, who favoured Isabel with a half-reproachful, half-quizzical glance.

Thankfully the moment's madness, undoubtedly engendered by an unexpected surge of searing jealousy, was blessedly over. She now had herself well in hand again, and could only wonder at herself for experiencing such an emotion in the first place. After all, wasn't it more than likely the Viscount had been in love with a score of women and more during his incident-filled adult life? Of course it was! And it shouldn't matter a whit to her anyway, she told herself, determined to maintain a practical outlook and concentrate on why she had been invited to the party in the first place.

Consequently, as soon as the delicious dinner was over, and everyone had returned to the drawing room before the majority of guests began to arrive for the party, Isabel requested Charles Bathurst to take a stroll with her about the garden. He was only too willing to comply, and together they slipped out of the French windows on to the terrace, and then down the steps to the rose garden, which had truly been transformed since the last time Isabel had strolled through it with the Viscount himself.

'I do not wish to importune you, sir,' she began, not wasting precious moments alone with him if she could avoid doing so, 'but I could think of no one else here tonight in whom I could happily confide.'

Quickly recognising the concern in her eyes, Charles Bathurst suggested they sit on one of the benches sited at intervals along the gravel path, before asking how he might serve her.

'Sir, you know as much as I do about the events that took place here nine long years ago, now,' she began. 'His lordship has asked me here tonight in order to help him discover something…anything that just might shed some light on the identity of the murderer.'

Masculine brows rose sharply at this disclosure. 'Indeed…? Said that, did he?' There was a suspicion of an amused glint in his dark eyes. 'It would appear my good friend is being remarkably cautious for once. Well, well, well!'

'With good reason, sir,' Isabel pointed out, thinking his reaction strange, 'if among his guests tonight is, indeed, the murderer of his father and brother.'

It was clear she had captured his full attention now. 'And does he suppose this is so?'

She shrugged. 'That I couldn't say. All I do know is that we're both convinced the crime was not perpetrated by a stranger. And I was just hoping for your views on the matter. You know his lordship well, sir, perhaps better than anyone else here tonight knows him. You know far more about his past misdemeanours. You must surely have a better idea of who would wish him harm.'

After an initial show of surprise at her plain speaking, he sighed. 'It would indeed be less than honest for me to pretend Sebastian was any kind of a saint in his youth, Miss Mortimer, for he was not. That said, he wasn't as black as he was sometimes painted, either. The truth lies somewhere between.'

'You misunderstand, sir,' she told him. 'It isn't so much his past that concerns me as his future. You see, I do not perfectly understand why his lordship was spared that night.'

She took a moment to stare down at the painted figures on her fan; yet another present from the gentleman who had come to mean so much to her that if she could in some way help to prove his innocence beyond doubt she would move heaven and earth to do so.

'If the grievance was against the Blackwood family as a whole, why then wasn't Sebastian killed that night too? Instead, the murderer merely tried to frame him. Why? Was Sebastian the main target? Was the intention that he should suffer more by being imprisoned and then hanged for something he didn't do? It's the motive, sir, that continues to elude me. Was it revenge for one of his lordship's past misdeeds, or a grievance against the family as a whole? If the latter, then why didn't the murderer take advantage of the fact that Sebastian was also in the house? After all, there was always the possibility he might be proved innocent. As, indeed, has turned out to be the case.' She shook her head, at a loss, still, to be sure of what the true answer might be. 'If we could only uncover the motive, I'm certain the identity of the murderer must surely follow.'

Charles Bathurst sighed. 'Believe me, my dear young lady, I too have pondered long and hard over those very same questions, and have come up with no conclusive answers.' He raised his eyes as he detected someone's approach. 'Ah, Staveley, the very man! See if that great brain of yours can aid our cause. Our friend Sebastian, it would seem, is at last determined to uncover the identity of the murderer of his father and brother, and has invited Miss Mortimer here tonight—er—ostensibly in order to help him in this task.'

Although she witnessed the two men exchange a look, Isabel was far too concerned about the Viscount's predicament to ponder over what lay behind the personable gentlemen's wry expressions.

'Really?' Sir Philip's brows rose markedly as he accepted Isabel's invitation to seat himself. 'At the risk of appearing obtuse, I do not immediately perceive how I can be of assistance to you, my dear Miss Mortimer, given that until quite recently his lordship and I were, at best, acquaintances only.'

'And given that he attempted to win the woman who is now your wife,' she parried, 'begs the question, does it not, of whether you'd wish to help.'

Once again the gentlemanly Baronet showed his appreciation of her ready wit by a bark of laughter. 'Charles, old fellow, I think we can both appreciate just why our mutual friend chose Miss Mortimer as his—er—accomplice. A keen intellect, coupled with outstanding physical attributes, is a combination gentlemen of discernment find most appealing.

'But let me assure you, my dear young woman,' Sir Philip continued on a more serious note, 'that I bear Blackwood no ill will. In fact, had it not been for him, I might never have been the thoroughly contented man you see before you today. I owe him a debt of gratitude that if I could repay by being of any assistance I wouldn't hesitate. The only thing I can tell you is that when business took me to London quite recently, I never heard an ill word concerning our mutual friend. In fact, the opposite was true. Talk in the clubs was all about his exploits in Spain, which now have become common knowledge. And how dignified he has become during his years away.'

'But not so dignified that I won't attempt to kick you into the nearest midden if you continue to betray your darling wife's trust by flirting with other women the moment you're away from Staveley Court,' the Viscount jokingly threatened, as he arrived at the bench without being noticed.

'Come, Belle.' Reaching for her hand, he assisted her to rise to her feet. 'Let me remove you from these rogues' pernicious influence,' he added, above the appreciative masculine laughter, 'and return you to the safety of the drawing room, where my esteemed godmother can offer you her protection.'

Although she accompanied him willingly enough, Isabel couldn't resist saying, 'Do you think I need protecting from your friends? They seem very personable gentlemen to me. What's more, they're both very happily married.'

When she failed to elicit a response, she asked, 'Did you really ask Lady Staveley to marry you?'

'Told you that, did he…?' He smiled crookedly. 'Yes, I did, as it happens,' he freely admitted, little realising that he had caused a further searing pain to grip her, only to vanquish it completely a moment later by adding, 'Thank God she had the sense to refuse! She was no more in love with me than I was with her.'

It took a monumental effort to stop herself from gaping up at him. 'You were not in love with her…? Then why on earth did you ask her to marry you?' she demanded to know, not unreasonably.

'I'm not quite sure. But I do believe I was overwhelmed by a surge of chivalry,' he said matter-of-factly. 'Without going into details, we were obliged to spend the most confoundedly uncomfortable night in a barn, sheltering from a snowstorm. Afterwards I felt honour-bound to offer her the protection of my name, of course. But, as I've already mentioned, the darling girl refused. She was in love with Staveley, you see, and had been for a considerable time. And now,' he went on, as they crossed the drawing room, which had been gradually becoming more crowded with the steady arrival of new guests invited to the party, 'I'm going to leave you with Lady Pimm, who has expressly wished to speak with you, whilst I repair to the adjoining parlour and organise the commencement of the dancing.'

Isabel wasn't in the least unhappy to be left with the imposing matron, simply because it offered her the opportunity to thank her sincerely for the loan of the pearls.

Lady Pimm swiftly set her straight on the matter. 'But, my dear, it isn't I who you should thank. I merely brought them back to the Manor in order to restore them to the person I consider the rightful owner. The pearls belonged to Blackwood's mother. They were not from the family jewels, and so when she died Sebastian's father gave most all her personal belongings away to close friends and other members of the family.'

She shook her head. 'I cannot even begin to understand what possessed him to do such a thing! Cruel it was, an unfeeling thing to do. And all the more surprising because he was not innately a cruel person. But it was all of a piece with the rest where his attitude to his younger son was concerned.'

'Do you mean that he did not care for him at all, ma'am?' Isabel prompted when the font of knowledge beside her fell silent.

'I wouldn't go as far as to say that, my dear, no,' Lady Pimm responded, after staring thoughtfully at an imaginary spot on the carpet. 'The sixth Viscount Blackwood's first marriage had been, as so many are, an arranged affair. His wife Matilda was not a member of the aristocracy. None the less she came from good yeoman stock. And, more importantly, her wealthy father ensured that she came to the marriage with a generous dowry, a much-needed increment to the Blackwood family coffers. In return Matilda had her title. But, for all that, I believe it was a successful union, and of course the first Viscountess did her duty and presented her husband with an heir before she died.

'The Viscount's second marriage was somewhat different, however. Louise Carré was a member of the French aristocracy, accomplished and spirited, some might even say slightly haughty. Just like that son of hers can be on occasions when the mood takes him,' she went on, easily picking out the tall figure of the present holder of the title as he emerged from the adjoining parlour, from where strains of a favourite country dance could now be heard. 'When Louise's father died, her mother brought her over to England, where she caused no small interest during her first Season. Why she chose Blackwood among all the eligible gentlemen vying for her hand, the Lord alone knows! He was certainly infatuated with her, and she, young as she was, certainly graced the Manor, improving both the house and gardens.'

Lady Pimm stared about her in evident appreciation. 'And there's no denying Louise showed excellent taste. I'm so pleased Sebastian has restored this beautiful room to its former glory, selecting the very same colour scheme his beloved mother chose soon after she became mistress of the house.'

It took Isabel a moment or two to assimilate what she had been told, then it was as much as she could do to stop herself from gaping yet again that evening. 'So it was once green and cream?' she asked, wanting to be sure she had not misunderstood, and the dowager confirmed it with a nod.

'The wall covering might be a shade or two lighter than it once was, but no less tasteful for that.'

Wishing to know more about his lordship's mother, Isabel once again steered the conversation back to the late Viscountess by asking Lady Pimm how she had come to know her.

'When she and her mother came to London they rented the house next door to my late husband's town house. Although I was a few years older than Louise, we quickly became firm friends, and spent a deal of time in each other's company.' She sighed. 'I didn't wholeheartedly approve her choice of husband, and made my feelings known. But I am forced to admit that, at first, Louise seemed happy enough.'

'Evidently something happened to change that, ma'am,' Isabel prompted, when the dowager once again fell silent.

'Sebastian's birth, I should say,' Lady Pimm responded, surprising Isabel somewhat. 'Oh, I wouldn't go as far as to say the marriage crumpled. But there was no denying that Henry Blackwood was a possessive man, and very much resented the affection and time Louise lavished on their baby son. She and Sebastian became inseparable, and Henry understandably, I suppose, resented that bond of affection. Matters didn't improve when Louise's mother came to live permanently in England. After her daughter's marriage, she returned to her native France for a while. She was an extremely astute woman, and had the sense to flee the land of her birth before the Terror began in earnest. More importantly, I suppose, she managed to leave with her fortune intact...a fortune that she left to her grandson. He came into the inheritance when he attained the age of five-and-twenty. But, of course, he was in hiding at the time, and never touched so much as a penny. During the intervening years the legacy has been amassing quite some interest, I do not doubt. Sebastian is now a very wealthy man, a very desirable matrimonial prize. And thankfully he has the sense to know it, and remains wary.'

Isabel wasn't so much concerned about fortune-hunting débutantes and match-making mamas as she was about wealth being a motive for murder. If his lordship died without issue, who would benefit by his demise? she couldn't help wondering, and turned to the lady who had done so much to satisfy her curiosity thus far.

'Concerning my godson's private fortune, I couldn't say. But the title and the estate would go to his uncle, Horace Blackwood.' She gestured towards the sofa nearest the impressive fireplace. 'He's that great bloated lump sprawled over there. If his over-indulgence doesn't kill him, his indolence will,' she predicted, betraying no sympathy whatsoever. 'The poor, insipid creature beside him is his long-suffering wife. The twiddle-poop on the end of the sofa is their son. Although I suppose I shouldn't say that,' she went on, looking faintly conscience-stricken. 'He was a sickly child, never strong, and it's clear to me he isn't well now—so thin and pasty. He was in Italy until a few weeks ago, until Napoleon's escape became common knowledge. A warmer climate suits Clement better. He's not long for this world, I fear. Consumption,' she revealed in an undertone. 'The best thing he could do for the Blackwood clan as a whole would be to marry and produce a male child or two before it's too late.'

Sensible advice, if slightly callous, Isabel mused, increasingly warming to the outspoken matron beside her. 'And has his lordship no other close relatives present tonight?'

'Let me see.' Lady Pimm cast a look about the room,

her short-sighted eyes managing finally to pick out an impeccably attired young man of medium height, with a faintly haughty bearing. 'Yes, there's Francis Blackwood, over there,' she revealed, drawing Isabel's attention to the gentleman in question. 'He's the only son of the youngest brother, Hubert. Well, I say only son...' She gave vent to a wicked cackle. 'Who knows how many of Hubert's by-blows might litter the land? A rake-helly young fellow he was in his day. But, like his two elder brothers, he married well. In fact, he did rather better than both Henry and Horace, at least financially. He married a wealthy cit's daughter and acquired a fine property quite near here. Francis and Sebastian saw each other frequently as children, though I rather fancy Francis was closer to Giles, Sebastian's half-brother.'

'And is he married, ma'am?'

'No, surprisingly not,' Lady Pimm revealed. 'And I cannot for the life of me understand why not. He's an extremely personable gentleman, in my opinion. His features are good, his bearing is even better, and his manners are most polished. I do not believe he's averse to female company, although I've never heard his name seriously linked with any lady's.' She shrugged. 'Perhaps, like Sebastian, he's choosy.

'Unlike George Blackwood, over there,' she added, once again indicating a certain spot in the room where a tall gentleman with dark hair was conversing with none other than Isabel's cousin. 'He's a more distant cousin. Against his family's advice he married that flighty piece who, you may or may not have noticed, was sitting on Sebastian's right at dinner. I seem to remember my godson's name being linked with hers at some point or other in the dim and distant past, but I believe it was only rumour. Sebastian's fond of his cousin George. They're good friends. So he's hardly likely to snub George's wife, now is he?'

Indeed not, Isabel mused. All the same, given his lordship's past reputation where the fair sex was concerned, it was more than likely he'd made cuckolds of several men, and if George happened to number among them, he might still bear a grudge. Yes, revenge was certainly a strong motive for murder, as was the pursuit of wealth. But if either of those had been the inducement, then why had Sebastian's father and brother been slain and he had been effectively spared? No, there had to be something else behind it all; something that infuriatingly continued to elude her still.

Isabel was obliged to abandon her puzzling reflections when she and her companion were approached by a certain member of the Blackwood family, and she was introduced to Sebastian's cousin Francis who, she was silently forced to concede, lost none of his attractiveness when viewed from close quarters.

'Mortimer…?' he echoed, briefly retaining the hold he had on her hand. 'Now, where have I heard that name before, I wonder? Not one of the Devonshire Mortimers, by any chance?'

'It is more than likely, Francis, that you heard the name in connection with the tragic events that took place here some years ago. It was none other than Miss Mortimer's father who eventually made it possible for Sebastian to clear his name.'

Although his expression remained totally impassive, there was just for a moment a certain something about the intelligent grey eyes, when once again they rested upon her, that Isabel found hard to define, and which vaguely reminded her of someone else; only for the life of her she couldn't bring to mind who it might be.

'Yes, of course—the doctor's daughter, if I mistake not.

I did hear all about it. I can only suppose it must have been Sebastian who told me when I called to see him a few weeks ago. He will undoubtedly remain eternally in your debt.'

'Very likely,' Lady Pimm agreed, before changing the subject entirely by demanding to know why she hadn't seen him in the capital that year.

As it quickly became clear the two had many acquaintances in common, and therefore a quantity of gossip to exchange, Isabel excused herself the instant it was polite enough for her to do so, and made her way to the far side of the room in order to spend a little time with her cousin who was still being ably supported by the devoted Mr Johns. None the less, he remained only for the time it took to exchange a few pleasantries with Isabel, before tactfully moving away so that the cousins might converse in private.

'What an absolutely delightful party!' Clara enthused, fanning herself with the delicate ivory-and-chicken-skin present Isabel had given her for her birthday a few days before. 'Everyone has been so very kind to me, most especially his lordship, and Mr Johns too, of course. He has remained close by to support me throughout, should I become overawed by it all.'

Isabel rolled her eyes at this piece of naïve nonsense. Her cousin looked absolutely divine in the simple white-and-silver-thread gown she'd made. There couldn't possibly be a red-blooded male present who wasn't very well aware that she was by far the most lovely female in the room. His lordship's show of attention towards her might well have stemmed from purely altruistic motives. The same, however, could not be said for Mr Johns! She had seen him scowling heavily on two or three occasions, when one or two of the young blades present had made themselves known to Clara.

'Even though I am employed here as a governess, several gentlemen have secured a dance with me. Is that not kind?'

Resisting the temptation to tease her, Isabel merely nodded, before revealing that no gentlemen had requested her to dance. 'Well, except his lordship, that is,' she amended.

Clara frowned slightly. 'Yes, I think he has been keeping an eye on you, Isabel. I noticed him staring at you on several occasions during dinner, and a short time ago when you were conversing with Lady Pimm, though I can perfectly understand why. I hardly recognised you when you arrived, and walked into the room with his lordship. You look splendid in that dress. Mr Johns said that he had never seen you looking so well… And those pearls!'

'Why, yes, they are beautiful, aren't they,' Isabel responded, her mind working furiously. 'Lady Pimm brought them with her from London,' she revealed artfully, for some reason not wanting to disclose that they really belonged to the Viscount. 'And as for his lordship's behaviour…' She shrugged. 'I expect he's merely making sure I'm fulfilling my promise, that is all. I've pledged to behave with the utmost decorum throughout the evening and offend no one.'

'And also to dance with him,' a now very familiar, smooth velvety voice unexpectedly reminded her.

Chapter Ten

Although her cousin appeared slightly taken aback by the unexpected appearance of her employer, Isabel felt all at once so very gratified to be reminded of the promise she had made by none other than the host himself. For days she had experienced grave doubts about standing up and performing the *risqué* dance in public, and yet now, suddenly, she was spurred by a surge of heady recklessness. It mattered not a whit that her reputation might suffer. She'd never had any real standing in the community to lose, anyway. So why not enjoy to the full this one very special occasion to indulge in a little heady gaiety? After all, it was unlikely she would ever experience such intoxicating delights again, she told herself, as she willingly accompanied the Viscount into the adjoining room, where the master of ceremonies was announcing the commencement of the waltz.

Vaguely Isabel was aware of a few others taking to the floor. She thought she glimpsed Francis, accompanied by the wife of the distant Blackwood cousin, George, and Sir Philip Staveley too, partnering some lively young matron. Then she was conscious only of her partner, of the sensual warmth of his touch on her waist and hand as they took up their positions for the dance, of the warmth that instantly softened his eyes when they stared down into hers as they commenced to swirl about the room at the first strains of music.

'I do not need to ask whether you are enjoying yourself, *ma belle*,' he said, thereby revealing that he had no intention of performing the dance in stony silence. 'The radiance of your smile tells me all I need to know.'

Isabel was more than happy to follow his lead, and not only in the movements of the dance. 'Oh, sir, it's a wonderful party! You have some truly charming friends.'

'Yes, your outrageous flirting with Bathurst and Staveley didn't go unnoticed,' he returned, his dark brows snapping together. 'Lady Pimm was quite shocked to glimpse you holding two gentlemen whom you hardly know in conversation in the garden for such a long time. And two gentlemen who, might I remind you, are both happily married.'

'And I doubt I could do anything to alter that situation, even if I wished to try. Which I do not,' she parried, not fooled by this display of mock disapproval. 'I was merely endeavouring to fulfil the commission you placed upon me by speaking to as many guests as I can throughout the evening in the hope that one, at least, might be able to shed some light on those dreadful past happenings here at the Manor.'

This time when his brows snapped together his disapproval was not feigned. 'Then cease to do so forthwith. By all means continue circulating, and meeting as many of my friends and relations as you can. That is why you're here. And I shall certainly be interested to hear your views some time in the near future on several persons here present. But avoid asking direct questions about past events. You risk arousing suspicion if you do. Whoever murdered my father and brother is no fool, and he might well be among the guests here tonight, remember that.'

Although his lordship had no way of knowing for sure whether she heeded his advice, he kept a close watch on her throughout the remainder of the evening. She spent a deal of time on the dance floor with a number of different partners, as did her young cousin. This didn't surprise him in the least. They were without doubt in both face and form the two most well-favoured females present. Even so, whereas Clara Pentecost was possibly sought for her physical attributes alone, Isabel, judging by remarks made to him throughout the remainder of the evening, left a more favourable impression on her various partners.

He himself revealed a clear partiality for her company by selecting only her to dance with twice, besides escorting her in to supper. It had been his intention to show the more influential members of the local community that he looked upon her with complete approval, and by the time the evening had drawn to an end, he knew he had succeeded better than he could have hoped. It was only when he had seen the last of his guests safely away in their carriages that he began to doubt the wisdom of his action, and decided in the end to confide in the two of his houseguests in whom he had absolute trust.

Repairing to the comfort of his library, he dismissed the butler, ordering him to retire, before dispensing three large brandies himself. 'I hope you enjoyed the evening, gentlemen?'

'Wouldn't have missed it for the world,' Charles Bathurst assured him. 'I'm sure I speak for Staveley, too, when I say the only circumstance that would have improved the occasion is if we'd been able to bring our wives along.' He cast a conspiratorial wink in Sir Philip's direction. 'I'm sure they'd have wholeheartedly approved of the belle of the ball.'

The Viscount checked in the act of raising his glass to his lips. 'Yes, I must agree, the young woman I employ as governess is something quite out of the common way, is she not?'

Although both listeners uttered a shout of derisive laughter in unison, it was left to Sir Philip to prove that neither of them was fooled. 'Indeed she is. But is totally lacking her cousin's natural charm and captivating personality. It is your Belle who will long be remembered for attending the occasion.'

'That was my intention,' his lordship confessed, his sombre tone revealing he was not altogether pleased by his success. 'I wanted to make it clear to local society that Miss Isabel Mortimer had my full approval. But I cannot help feeling I made a terrible mistake in singling her out for particular attention. Evidently I revealed more than I had intended to do.'

Once again the two gentlemen seated in the comfortable chairs exchanged glances, only this time they were both clearly puzzled. 'I do not perfectly understand, Sebastian,' Bathurst admitted. 'If, for some reason, you wish to delay before declaring yourself, I cannot foresee a problem arising. I spoke to Miss Mortimer on several occasions throughout the evening, and not once did she give me any reason to suppose that she has the least notion of how deep your regard is for her.'

'No, Charles,' his lordship acknowledged, after giving vent to a strangely bitter laugh. 'I've taken very good care to ensure she doesn't know. She believes it is only gratitude I feel towards her. If you knew the trouble I had persuading her to come here tonight...' He shook his head, smiling as certain recent memories assailed him. 'But if you two were able to judge my true state of mind where Isabel is concerned, then it is reasonable to suppose that others might have succeeded in doing so too.'

'Evidently this troubles you, but I do not immediately perceive why it should,' Sir Philip admitted. 'I do not believe Miss Mortimer is indifferent towards you, Sebastian. In fact, I would go as far as to say I believe she holds you in high regard.'

'I can only hope she will continue to do so after what I must now do in order, if I can, to rectify matters,' his lordship revealed. All at once there was an unpleasant taste in his mouth, which he attempted to remove by swallowing a mouthful of brandy. 'I knew hers would be no ordinary wooing,' he added softly, staring down at what remained in his glass. 'I knew I would need to be patient and win her gently, and by degrees. Now, it seems, I must forgo even that pleasure for a while in order to ensure her continued safety.'

This time when his lordship's two friends exchanged glances there was an element of disquiet in both their expressions, a fact that was not overlooked by the Viscount, who continued to maintain his stance before the hearth. 'What would you do, gentlemen, to protect the women you love?'

'There is nothing we wouldn't do,' Sir Philip responded for them both. 'Do I infer correctly from that, that you believe Miss Mortimer might seriously be in some danger?'

'I can only pray not. In truth, though, I suspect much depends on what lay behind the murder of my father and brother. And that, gentlemen, I'm afraid, continues to elude me still.'

Charles Bathurst nodded. 'Yes, Miss Mortimer said much the same thing—uncover the motive, and one will discover the murderer.'

His lordship smiled softly, thereby erasing, in part, the troubled lines that continued to crease his high forehead. 'Yes, the perceptive little madam guided me down that path from the first, encouraging me to recall things that seemed totally unimportant at the time.'

'Such as what?' Sir Philip prompted, when the Viscount fell silent, after at last making himself comfortable in the chair nearest the hearth.

'Such as what led to the row that resulted in me storming out of the house that evening.'

Bathurst regarded the contents of his glass through narrowed eyes. 'Yes, I recall you mentioning that to me, after I had travelled from London to defend you all those years ago.' He smiled suddenly. 'When Sir Montague Cameron arrived tonight, I couldn't help thinking how relieved he must now feel that he didn't have you immediately clapped in irons and thrown into the local lock-up, after taking you into custody. At least he paid you the courtesy of confining you in reasonable comfort in those rooms overlooking the courthouse…under heavy guard, of course.'

'Patently not heavy enough,' Sir Philip countered sardonically, 'as you managed to effect his escape and spirit him away to the safety of the Colliers' home in Hampshire, without too much trouble, and without throwing any suspicion upon yourself.'

'It took some careful planning, especially getting him away to Ireland soon afterwards,' Bathurst admitted, looking very well pleased with himself it had to be said. 'And, of course, when I arrived the next day to discover the man I was to defend in court had escaped, I affected as much shocked dismay as would anyone in my respected profession. I even went so far as to assist Sir Montague in the search for the runaway by quite openly revealing those many haunts we frequented in our misspent youth—all to no avail, of course.

'But we digress,' Bathurst reminded his companions. 'If my memory serves me correctly, I believe you told me back then that the row with your father had something to do with a suggestion you made to improve the running of the estate.'

The Viscount was on his feet in an instant, and began to pace the floor, his mind racing back over the years. 'By heaven, Charles, I believe you're right! I'd been talking with the steward, Guy Fensham, all that afternoon, and he suggested it might be profitable to experiment with a different breed of sheep. I mentioned it to my father on my return. Initially he showed interest. Then Giles arrived home and, as usual, accused me of interfering in matters that were none of my concern. Father then took his part, and the inevitable row ensued.'

'Although it cannot be denied your previous steward's account of the events of that night did a deal to incriminate you, Sebastian,' Charles Bathurst reminded him, 'and the fact that he conveniently disappeared before your eventual return here is, undeniably, extremely suspicious. I cannot immediately perceive how Fensham could possibly have known for sure that a row would ensue between you and your father because of a suggestion he had made to you about sheep.'

'No, he couldn't be one hundred per cent certain, I'll concede,' his lordship readily agreed. 'But it would have been a fair bet. He would have been well aware that there was precious little sibling affection prevailing at the Manor. He would also have been aware of Giles's almost obsessive jealousy about the land he believed would one day be his, and that my brother bitterly resented any interest I showed in the running of the estate.'

'In which case, if his intention had been to cause disharmony, then you fell straight into the steward's hands by repeating what he said,' Sir Philip opined. 'But I do not immediately perceive how the death of your father and brother could benefit him… Unless, of course, he was working for two masters.'

'That possibility had occurred to me,' the Viscount admitted. 'It has also occurred to me that the person who would immediately benefit from my father and brother's deaths, and myself being hanged for the crime, is my uncle Horace. And I can also reveal that my father and his two brothers were not particularly close. That said, I have never once been given any reason to suppose that Horace Blackwood coveted the title, or disliked my father so intensely as to wish to plot his death. I have spoken with him at some length since his arrival here at the Manor, and nothing he has said has roused my suspicion. He is an indolent and self-indulgent individual who cares for nothing so much as his creature comforts, which he gets in abundance in his London home. He wouldn't wish to burden himself with the cares of maintaining a large estate at his age.'

'No, indeed,' Sir Philip readily concurred, having experienced for some years the grave responsibility it could be. 'Even if he did secretly have designs on the title at one time, he doesn't give the impression of having so now. And, if you'll forgive me saying so, Sebastian, your uncle's over-indulgence in many vices over the years has well and truly caught up with him. I do not believe he's destined to live to a very great age, or hold the title for very long should—God forbid!—it ever come to him now.'

'I couldn't agree more,' Bathurst announced. 'And neither would that son of his. Consumptive, unless I much mistake the matter.'

'You don't,' his lordship assured him. 'He spent some

time in Italy recently and his condition improved. Perhaps he'll return if Wellington and the allies can deal successfully with Napoleon this time.' He shrugged. 'Who can say. One thing I do know, though, is that my youngest cousin, Clement Blackwood, has even less ambition to inherit the title than his father. The only member of the family, according to Lady Pimm, who ever coveted the Viscountcy was Francis's father, Hubert Blackwood.

'He was the youngest of the three Blackwood brothers, and without doubt the most ambitious,' his lordship went on to reveal. 'In his youth he was purported to have been a little wild.' He threw back his head and barked with laughter. 'Must be a family failing! None the less, my uncle Hubert married a wealthy London merchant's daughter, and had a fine house built, some three or so miles east of here, and remained up until his death a frequent visitor to the ancestral home. He may well have been envious of my father's superior position in the family, but even so they rubbed along together reasonably well. Although, as I've already mentioned, the three brothers were not particularly close, my father did much prefer his youngest brother, Hubert.'

'Which all suggests, does it not,' Bathurst remarked, after digesting everything his friend the Viscount had revealed, 'that if it wasn't a member of the immediate family, then the murderer must surely be someone who had a grievance against your father, and possibly your brother too, and used you as a means to avoid suspicion falling upon him.'

'That seems the most logical alternative,' his lordship agreed. 'All I need to do is discover who, if anyone, hated my father so much as to murder him.' He sighed as he ran his fingers through his slightly waving black hair. 'Sadly, though, unless something unexpected comes to light, gentlemen, I believe my task will be nigh impossible.'

Unlike the Viscount, who retired in something of a sombre mood, Isabel felt elated by her undoubted success at the party, and woke the following morning experiencing a complete change of outlook, and a desire to do everything she could to maintain her unexpected and meteoric rise in local society.

For years she had been determined not to live beyond her means. When her father had become ill, and unable to work, she had been obliged to run the house on money he had saved throughout his life. He had not been a poor man by any means. Isabel clearly remembered how successful her father had been when he had had his practice in London. Unfortunately, financially he had not fared so well since moving to the country. It wasn't that his popularity had suddenly waned. Quite the opposite, in fact! His services had been sought by many, and he had given of his time equally between those who were quite able to pay, and those who could not.

None the less, they had lived well enough throughout the last years of her father's life, even if they had not enjoyed every creature comfort. In truth, though, Isabel had not known the full extent of her father's financial state until after his demise, when it had come to light that he had owned shares in several ventures. She had never so much as attempted to touch the interest that had been accumulating over the years. Knowing that she could not touch so much as a penny of the money left to her by her mother until she had attained the age of thirty, or married, Isabel had veered on the side of caution, and had continued to leave her father's little nest egg intact should some calamity arise where she had need of extra money at a moment's notice.

Viscount Blackwood's emergence into her life, or, rather, that of his wards, and the financial benefits she had managed to accrue from becoming a temporary guardian had ensured that she could well afford many things she had considered beyond her means. She couldn't deny she had enjoyed these extra luxuries during past months. Nevertheless, the enjoyment she had experienced was as nothing when compared to the pleasure she had attained from attending her very first significant social event.

Now Isabel could well understand why her father had always insisted that her mother continued to enjoy those privileges to which she had become accustomed before marriage. Fortunately Agnes Mortimer had been neither frivolous nor avaricious. Yes, she had enjoyed many of life's luxuries, such as owning her own carriage and attending social events. None the less, she had not squandered vast amounts on jewellery or very expensive clothes. Although she had experienced most every creature comfort before marriage, she had never selfishly attempted to persuade her husband to live beyond his means.

For perhaps the first time ever Isabel could appreciate just how much her mother had given up in order to marry the man she loved, and could only admire her for having done so. She would like to think she would have done precisely the same. Yet, at the same time, she could appreciate too why her mother had been determined to maintain certain standards, and still enjoy the finer things in life. She herself had sampled just that the evening before. She had experienced for the very first time what it was like to be socially acceptable, and she had no intention of relinquishing this new-found status if she could possibly avoid doing so.

Consequently she paid a visit to the notary in Merry-field who had dealt with her father's business arrangements for so many years in order to discover precisely how much she was worth.

Well pleased with the outcome of the visit, she then dragged Bessie along to the town's most fashionable dress-maker's and placed an order for several new gowns, including a riding habit, as well as certain other necessities, which immediately won her the personal attention of the owner of the establishment.

Even more delighted with the outcome of that visit, she then returned to the inn where she had left her one-horse gig, and ordered a light luncheon to celebrate what she privately considered was the beginning of a new era in her life.

'Well, I must say this is a rare treat,' Bessie declared, when the fare was brought to them in a private parlour by a young serving-wench.

'Yes, and one I hope we'll be experiencing a little more often from now on,' Isabel revealed, having already decided she'd need to travel to the local market town more often in the near future if her plans for herself were ever to be realised. 'Dear Papa's reliable cob is very capable, still, of pulling the gig. He was quite young when Papa acquired him, as you know. But I rather fancy taking up riding again. It's been too long since I enjoyed that form of exercise.'

Bessie was only partially successful in suppressing a little knowing smile. 'My, my, his lordship's return to the Manor has been no bad thing, I must say! At least not where you're concerned, at any rate.'

'Stop looking so smug!' Isabel ordered, not in the least amused by the assumption. 'I'll have you know, Bessie Wilmot, that my desire to take up riding again has nothing whatsoever to do with Lord Blackwood. If you must know there was a certain Major Radcliff and his wife at the party last night. They've recently moved into that large house on the outskirts of the village. I'd never met them before. Emily Radcliff and I rubbed along together remarkably well. It was she who suggested we might ride out together from time to time. Her husband is to rejoin his regiment almost immediately, and she said she'll need to find plenty to occupy herself whilst he's away. Not only that, I should very much like to accompany Josh from time to time, when he goes out… Satisfied?'

'If you say so,' Bessie responded, not looking whole-heartedly convinced.

'Well, if we're to talk about influences, Miss Wilmot,' Isabel returned in a flash, 'then I'd like to know who persuaded you to order that new bonnet. Scarlet feathers indeed!'

Although no response was forthcoming, Isabel was not deterred. 'Red wouldn't be the favourite colour of a certain bow-legged little coachman who finds any excuse to call in at the farmhouse when he's passing, by any chance?'

Bessie went quite pink with pleasure as she giggled like a schoolgirl. 'Oh, he's a downy one and no mistake, Miss Isabel! He's been getting me to teach him his letters a bit more. His wife started to teach him to read and write some years ago, before he joined the army. Right sad it was, miss. He came home from Spain to find his wife and son had died in poverty. Thrown out of their cottage they were. Poor Tom. Said he behaved badly for a time. Luckily the Viscount crossed his path, and offered him a position. Said it were the making of him.' She smiled smugly. 'The Viscount seems to have a good influence on a number of people, I'm thinking.'

Isabel wisely refrained from comment. So Bessie, seemingly realising her baiting would have no effect, turned to stare out of the window, and then gave a sudden start.

'Well, I'll be damned! I do believe that's the steward that used to be up at the Manor—the one you never cared for, miss. I always did wonder what became of him.'

'I believe you're right, Bessie. It is Guy Fensham,' Isabel agreed. Although she couldn't be absolutely sure, she strongly suspected he had emerged from the tavern across the street. She always avoided that particular hostelry, as it was often rowdy and frequented by drunkards.

'I wonder what he's doing here,' she went on, gathering her things together, and rising to her feet. 'Must have found employment locally, I can only suppose. I'll mention it to his lordship when next I see him. He might be interested.'

After paying their shot, Isabel turned, and was about to emerge from the inn, when she almost collided with none other than Francis Blackwood, who was on the point of entry.

Although he politely doffed his hat, Isabel had the feeling that he was slightly put out by the chance encounter for some reason, and yet he had been urbanity itself the evening before at the party. They had even danced together. 'I never expected to see you again so soon, sir,' she admitted, when he didn't attempt to speak. 'Do you often come to Merryfield? I can never recall seeing you here before.'

'Not so very frequently,' he admitted, all at once seeming to collect himself. 'A little matter of business brought me here today.'

'You too. What a coincidence! Fortunately I've finished mine, and am about to return home.'

He appeared disappointed. 'Can I not persuade you to remain a while longer and join me in some refreshment?'

Although she had no desire to be rude to one of the Viscount's relations, Isabel had no hesitation in declin-

ing, especially as she strongly believed the invitation had
stemmed merely from politeness, and no real desire for
her company.

'In that case, Miss Mortimer, I shall very much look
forward to seeing you again at the Camerons' dinner party
the week after next.'

'I haven't received an invitation, sir,' she didn't hesitate
to reveal, before detecting a strangely calculating look in
his eyes.

The smile he bestowed upon her before bowing over
her hand contained not an atom of warmth either. 'I, for
one, do not doubt for a moment that you shall, Miss Mortimer. Until then…'

The encounter left her feeling distinctly uneasy for
some reason. 'I do not think I can be quite normal, Bessie,' she remarked, heading towards the inn's stables in
order to collect the gig. 'The Viscount earned himself the
reputation of being a wild, unruly womaniser. His cousin
Francis, according to Lady Pimm, has never had even so
much as a breath of scandal attached to his name. Yet it is
his lordship in whom I would place my trust.'

Chapter Eleven

Although Isabel made a mental note to mention the unexpected encounter with Francis Blackwood to his lordship when next they spoke, it was thrust very much to the back of her mind even before she had reached home.

As she rounded the sharp bend leading to the village, she happened to catch sight of a tall, unmistakable figure on horseback, cantering across a meadow. Riding alongside his lordship was his ward Josh, and none other than the vivacious wife of his distant cousin.

All at once she experienced a rush of searing resentment, and no matter how hard she tried to tell herself that he was merely fulfilling his duties as host by entertaining his guests for the duration of their stay at the Manor, she was unable to suppress the swell of bitter disappointment at not having been invited to join the little riding party. After all, hadn't she and the Viscount spent quite some time in each other's company the evening before? Hadn't he shown his preference for her society by dancing with her twice, not to mention escorting her in to supper? He'd been granted ample opportunity to invite her out riding today. It was quite obvious, therefore, that he hadn't wished to do so. And that hurt.

Consequently, she didn't arrive back at her home in the happiest frame of mind, and her sombre mood didn't improve at all on finding her cousin, surprisingly, bent over the kitchen table, sobbing into a handkerchief.

'Why, whatever's wrong, Miss Clara?' Bessie asked before her mistress could do so. 'Has something happened up at the Manor?'

Clara shook her head. 'No, nothing like that. It's the Reverend Mr Walters. He passed away last night in his sleep.'

At this, Isabel exchanged a puzzled glance with Bessie. She knew well enough that her cousin possessed one of the kindest of hearts, but even so this show of grief seemed a trifle excessive, given that Clara had been barely acquainted with the elderly clergyman.

Having been blessed with a more down-to-earth approach to life, Isabel was quick to point out that, sad though it was, his death hadn't been unexpected. 'He's been ill for many weeks now, Clara,' she reminded her. 'Besides, I cannot help but feel the parish might benefit from the appointment of a much younger man. Mr Walters, as far back as I can remember, had always been sadly lax in his duties, even when he enjoyed reasonable health.'

If anything, Clara became more distraught by this common-sense approach. 'But that's just it!' she exclaimed between renewed sobs. 'If a new vicar arrives, he might wish to appoint his own curate. Then what shall I do? If Mr Johns is sent away, I might never see him again!'

Over her cousin's head Isabel exchanged yet another glance with the housekeeper. Clara might have admitted the true state of her heart at last, which was perhaps no bad thing. None the less, Isabel didn't immediately perceive what she could do to influence future events, and voiced her reservations aloud.

'Oh, but you can!' her cousin countered. 'You can approach Lord Blackwood. He'll listen to you, if you suggest Mr Johns should remain.'

An image of his lordship, the very last time she had seen him, flashed before her eyes. 'I'm not so very sure that's true,' Isabel returned dully, still rankled over being excluded from the little riding party. 'I believe his lordship has—er—other things on his mind at present.'

'Yes, yes, of course he has. I understand that,' Clara responded, a glimmer of hope glinting behind the unshed tears. 'But once all the guests have left the Manor, will you speak with him then? I'm sure Mr Johns mentioned once that his lordship's father had something to do with the living being offered to Mr Walters. So I'm sure Lord Blackwood has influence enough to ensure Mr Johns remains in the parish, if you persuaded him to.'

In truth, Isabel didn't wish to involve herself in matters that were none of her concern. All the same, she discovered she wasn't proof against the look of entreaty in her cousin's eyes and found herself relenting, at least up to a point. 'If an opportunity arises, then, yes, I'll put in a good word for Mr Johns. But I have no intention of approaching his lordship directly on the subject. It would do more harm than good if he was to view it as crass interference on my part.'

Although his lordship was not among the congregation on Sunday, he did attend the late vicar's funeral service held later that same week. He was accompanied by the Bishop who conducted the service, and who, according to Clara, had been staying at the Manor for several days. Although Lord Blackwood made not the least attempt to approach her, Sir Montague and Lady Cameron did make a point of doing so, and Isabel duly received that invitation to dine the following week foretold by Francis Blackwood.

For several days she remained in two minds, not knowing whether to accept or not. Her cousin's name had not been included on the invitation, which annoyed Isabel, but didn't seem to trouble Clara in the least. More irksome still was glimpsing the Viscount on two separate occasions riding through the village with none other than the Camerons' eldest daughter, Charlotte, who, for some reason, had cut short her stay with her grandmother in the metropolis. In the end it was none other than her new-found friend Mrs Emily Radcliff who managed to overcome the ever-increasing malcontent and persuade Isabel to accompany her to the dinner party at the end of the week.

It was only to be expected that his lordship would attend. Isabel spotted his tall figure the instant she entered the elegant Georgian mansion's impressive drawing room. In conversation with a small group of ladies, one of whom was, yet again, none other than Charlotte Cameron, he appeared wonderfully relaxed, and didn't so much as raise his eyes when the footman announced her arrival.

Fortunately her companion Emily Radcliff came to the rescue by preventing the maelstrom of negative emotions from taking complete control of Isabel by engaging the host and hostess in conversation, and directly afterwards their charming eldest son who, in turn, made to introduce them to the only other member of the Blackwood family present that evening.

'There's no need to make me known to these two charming ladies,' Francis assured him. 'I had the felicity of making their acquaintance at my cousin's house only the other week. And am so very glad that my prediction turned out to be true,' he added, drawing Isabel a little to one side, leaving Major Radcliff's young wife to converse with another guest.

'Yes, I'm beginning to think you might possess some special powers, sir,' Isabel said lightly, desperate not to allow increasing feelings of pique towards his kinsman to completely ruin her evening. 'I had no notion I was to receive an invitation. What other predictions about my future are you able to make, I wonder?'

Although he smiled readily enough, it contained an element of smugness. 'Ah, my dear Miss Mortimer, some things are so easily foretold. You were such an overwhelming success at my cousin's party that it was unlikely you would disappear from the social scene overnight. And as for your future…' All at once he seemed quite serious. 'Do you think it's entirely wise to know what Fate has in store for us?'

'The element of surprise would always add extra spice, I suppose,' she readily conceded.

'Yes, indeed,' he agreed. 'Besides, I think up to a point we are all architects of our own destiny, behaving in ways that ultimately have a bearing on future events.' Raising his eyes, he gazed across the room. 'Now, take my big cousin, for instance. Had he behaved with a little more— how shall I phrase it?—circumspection in his youth, he might so easily have avoided being accused of the murder of his father and brother. That said,' he added, when large grey-green eyes regarded him with keen interest, 'I, for one, never supposed the accusation was true.'

Because she didn't for a moment doubt the accuracy of what he had revealed, Isabel didn't hesitate to ask, 'Do you have any idea who might have been behind the murders?'

'One hesitates to raise doubts about a gentleman's integrity when one is a guest under his roof,' he whispered, wickedly smiling. 'None the less, it is common knowledge that Sir Montague and the late Viscount positively loathed each other, and never spoke for years, right up until my uncle's demise. Some dispute over the boundary between their respective properties, I seem to recall. Understandably, Sir Montague's dislike intensified when the dispute was resolved very much in my relative's favour.' He shrugged. 'But my uncle had altercations with numerous persons over the years. It's safe to assume, therefore, that some must surely have borne a grudge.'

It occurred to Isabel then that Francis Blackwood had been a deal more informed about the late Viscount's affairs than had the present holder of the title, and echoed this thought aloud. He merely shrugged again, however, before revealing that his cousin, after leaving Oxford, had been inclined to spend more time in the capital with his friends, well away from the comings and goings at the ancestral pile.

'And the truth of the matter is,' he went on, 'although I was closer to Sebastian in age, I had more in common with his older brother. My father died relatively young, you see, and so I came into my property before I had even left university. My home, like Blackwood Manor, boasts many acres of fine farmland, Miss Mortimer, so I often sought my uncle's advice, and Giles and I frequently discussed husbandry.'

This seemed reasonable enough, and yet a niggling doubt about this particular member of the Blackwood family had most definitely seeded itself and was growing rapidly. Francis clearly had been privy to much of what had gone on at the Manor, and therefore must have had an extensive knowledge of the general routines of the people who had resided there. Had this knowledge come merely from observations made during his frequent visits? Or had there been another revealing source? Hard on the heels of this puzzling question came the memory of certain remarks made by Lady Pimm on the night of the dinner party, which only served to increase her doubts about the trustworthiness of the man standing before her. Furthermore, a slightly more recent occurrence, that hadn't struck her in the least odd at the time, all at once began to acquire a more sinister significance.

Although she was aware that now was definitely not the occasion to voice suspicions, especially not to someone about whom she was beginning to harbour grave doubts, some reckless imp prompted her to dig a little deeper in an attempt to discover the inmost thoughts of her companion. 'So, who in your opinion was the intended victim?'

'Why, my uncle Henry, of course! Do you not agree?'

She shook her head, all the while scrutinising his attractive features for the slightest indication of what might be passing through his mind. She was increasingly beginning to feel he knew much more about what had occurred that night than he had thus far revealed, if her suspicion about his close association with a certain other person connected with the appalling events was correct.

'At first I thought your cousin Sebastian was likely to have been the real target. After all, his graceless behaviour in bygone years is legend. Now, though, I'm convinced it was the killer's intention all along to murder both the late Viscount and his elder son, and divert any suspicion from falling on himself by implicating your cousin. Which, of course, he succeeded in doing for a number of years. Had I not intervened, the killer would by this time possibly have been rid of a third member of the Blackwood family. How he must despise me for thwarting his ambitions.'

Although he frowned, appearing genuinely puzzled, his gaze was intense and unwavering. 'He must, indeed, if that had been his intention all along,' he agreed. 'But I do not immediately perceive why you should suppose it might have been.'

'Do you not?' Isabel raised one brow, betraying her scepticism at this response. He was an intelligent man. Surely he must have considered every possibility?

Undaunted by his lack of response she said, 'Well, let us look at the facts. Unlike yourself, I was never privy to the comings and goings up at the Manor in bygone years. All the same, even I can clearly recall observing the late Lord Blackwood and his son riding out alone on numerous occasions. It would have been a simple matter, surely, for someone with revenge in mind to lie in wait and take a pot shot at either the late Viscount or his son? But, no, the killer, at great risk of being discovered, gains entry by some means or other to the Manor and murders both his lordship and his heir and does his utmost to implicate the younger son. Either the murderer had a grievance against the Blackwood family as a whole, or he had a deal to gain by their deaths.'

'You perceive me positively agog with curiosity, Miss Mortimer! Who on earth would benefit by such a dreadful course of action?'

Isabel could only speculate on how much of his shocked amazement was assumed. 'Why, isn't it obvious…? Another member of the Blackwood family, of course! And I shall go even further by saying a member of the family who covets the title.'

Naturally enough he appeared affronted. 'I sincerely trust, Miss Mortimer, you do not include me in that offensive assumption. Might I remind you I am not next in line for the title.'

'No, indeed you are not. You are, however, a deal closer than you once were,' she pointed out, before wiser counsel at last prevailed and she decided that if he was as innocent as he appeared, then she was going beyond what was pleasing to suggest it might be otherwise. Although privately she might retain doubts about Mr Francis Blackwood's sincerity, she was obliged silently to acknowledge it would be wrong to accuse him of the least wrongdoing without some tangible proof.

So she merely shrugged her shoulders, feigning indifference in an attempt to make light of the whole matter. 'Thankfully my slight involvement in the sad business ceased a long time ago, sir. If his lordship wishes to attempt to discover the truth, then it is entirely up to him to do so, wouldn't you say?'

When he failed to respond yet again, and continued to stare at her intently, she allowed her own gaze to stray briefly to a certain spot across the room. 'And it doesn't appear as if your cousin is exerting himself unduly in an attempt to unearth the truth of what took place. It would seem he has other things on his mind at present.'

This time when she looked back at him his gaze seemed rather more speculative. 'Yes, he does, doesn't he—the delightful Miss Charlotte Cameron.' He reached for his quizzing glass and stared through it at the young lady in question. 'Certainly pleasing on the eye, but not, I wouldn't have thought, in my cousin's usual style. Which begs the question, does it not, is he merely being courteous by paying attention to the daughter of the house, or is there some other reason for this show of preference for her company this evening?'

'I wouldn't know, sir,' Isabel managed to respond, while manfully resisting the sudden urge to flee the room and return to the relative comfort of the farmhouse. She simply wasn't herself that evening, otherwise she would never have dreamt of voicing her suspicions about the murders at the Manor to a man who was, to all intents and purposes, a virtual stranger.

'But it is only to be expected,' she forced herself to add, in yet another attempt to convey she had no real interest in the matter under discussion, 'that he will one day marry, if only to beget an heir. And he will surely look for a wife among females of his own class.'

'Perhaps,' he agreed, turning that aid to vision on to her. 'But where my cousin is concerned one would be foolish to presume too much. He has the annoying habit of behaving quite out of character on occasions. That said, it would seem his tastes have changed over the years. Seemingly he is no longer attracted to the showy beauties of this world, as he once was.'

A servant in smart livery announcing dinner spared Isabel the necessity of formulating a response, for which she was extremely grateful. None the less, the subject of the conversation was never far from her thoughts. Throughout the meal she was conscious of the laughter and lighthearted banter emanating from further down the table where Lord Blackwood was seated, sandwiched between none other than the eldest daughter of the house and Emily Radcliff.

Lady Cameron had evidently given much thought to her table placements. No fool, she had known the happily married major's wife would prove no threat at all. Isabel began to appreciate other things too, as the meal wore on, with one excellently presented course being replaced by another. The reason for Charlotte Cameron's early return from the capital was quite obvious now, as was Sir Montague's surprising visit to the farmhouse a few weeks before, when he had done his utmost to highlight Lord Blackwood's less favourable traits. Clearly he had refrained from warning his own daughter to be wary of such a matrimonial prize!

Although she refused to allow her attention to stray from her own immediate dinner companions, Isabel found it no easy task to maintain a light-hearted conversation, or the pretence of pleasure in the evening. The truth of the matter was she had never felt less sociable. Consequently, the instant Lady Cameron rose from the table, inviting the ladies to return with her to the drawing room, Isabel took the opportunity to slip outside to be alone with her thoughts, and—yes—attempt to soothe her battered ego.

Locating a bench in a secluded corner of the neatly symmetrical formal garden, Isabel sought to make some sense out of her tangled feelings. The truth of the matter was she was jealous of the attention the Viscount was paying to Charlotte Cameron; resented the attention he paid to any woman except her. And it was madness to feel as she did! she told herself. He had more than repaid the assistance she had rendered him in order to clear his name. Why, if it hadn't been for his show of approval and support she wouldn't be here now, in this magnificent setting. And how she wished she were not here! Life had been so simple before his lordship had entered her world. She'd been happy with the simple pleasures in life… Would she ever find contentment again?

'You shouldn't be out here by yourself, *ma belle*.'

So wrapped had she been in her own private misery that her senses, normally so acute, hadn't even registered his approach. Nor had she any notion of just how long he'd been standing there in the shade of the tall yew hedge that bordered the shrubbery.

Very slowly she turned her head and forced herself to look up at him. With the best will in the world, though, she couldn't control the sudden surge of searing resentment at his total avoidance of her company since the night of his own splendid party. Did he suppose that she would be grateful for the smallest crumb of attention he was willing to bestow upon her now? If so, she would swiftly disabuse him! Although she might never inhabit the same privileged world as her more illustrious forebears, there was still a deal of pride coursing through her veins.

'Might I remind you, my lord, that I am my own mistress, and do as I please. I do not require advice, most especially from you.'

In one swift and lithe movement she rose to her feet and made to leave, only to have her left wrist captured and held fast in strong fingers. 'Unhand me at once, my lord!'

Even though she had managed to maintain remarkable control over her voice thus far, her right hand had instinctively curled into a neat little fist, ready to lash out should he risk importuning her further. Then she watched as strikingly blue eyes that could change in an instant from icy cool and disdainful to tenderly warm and approving travelled down the length of her arm, the look in them somewhere between the two extremes.

An unmistakable twitch at one corner of his mouth betrayed his thoughts, and only served to annoy her further. 'Might I remind you that I do not number among, nor ever shall for that matter, the doxies of your acquaintance who no doubt appreciate displays of masculine brutishness. Now kindly unhand me, my lord.'

His response was to give vent to a peal of laughter. 'My word, you can be a provoking little witch when the mood takes you, Belle!' he declared, before detecting the slight movement in her right arm. 'Ah, ah!' he warned, wagging a finger in front of her nose. 'You do not know me well enough yet to be sure just how I might respond to a cuff on the ears. So be sensible,' he advised, still wickedly smiling, 'and agree to meet with me tomorrow, and I shall release you. There are things we must discuss.'

Still miffed over his deliberate avoidance of her company in recent days, Isabel wasn't inclined to pander to his whims. 'I cannot imagine why you should suppose I might wish to discuss anything with you, my lord,' she responded, raising her chin slightly. 'Anything you have to say to me may be said now.'

'No it cannot,' he countered in a trice. 'For your own sake, Isabel, I must not be seen favouring you with my company.' He was all at once serious. 'Trust me and meet with me tomorrow.'

Although she didn't doubt he was earnestly troubled over something, and curiosity to discover just what was causing him such obvious disquiet had to a certain extent overcome her feelings of pique, she still felt unable to oblige him. 'I'm sorry I can't. I have an appointment near Merryfield tomorrow that I would prefer not to break. And I usually see Josh on Saturday afternoons, remember? We can hardly be private with him along.'

At first he looked suspiciously down at her, as though he thought she was merely making excuses, but then he nodded. 'Very well. Sunday, then, after church?' At her assent, he added, 'Where?'

'If you wish the meeting to be private, it cannot take place at the farmhouse or the Manor,' she pointed out, after a moment's thought. 'How about the home wood, at the spot where Jem Marsh was found?'

'Very well, midday in the home wood,' he agreed, before his acute hearing picked up a sound that Isabel had yet again quite failed to detect.

His lordship then released his hold on the slender wrist before addressing the new arrival with every evidence of pleasure. 'Why, Emily, you needn't have put yourself to the trouble of coming in search of her,' he declared, thereby instantly revealing his genuine fondness for his

friend Major Radcliff's young wife. 'As you see I've discovered the truant already and was on the point of escorting her back inside. My cousin Francis evinced a desire
to have Miss Mortimer partner him in a game or two of
whist, and I agreed to oppose him. Will you oblige me by
being my partner? I rather fancy administering a sound
trouncing this evening.'

Although Emily Radcliff laughingly agreed, Isabel
didn't find his last remark in the least amusing. The fact
that his shoulders shook slightly, when she cast him a suspicious look, before accepting his escort back inside the
mansion, only went to confirm her belief that his utter-
ance had little to do with a determination to win at cards.

None the less, she was resolved not to let her own partner down, and for the first few hands the honours were
evenly divided. Then Mrs Radcliff just happened to raise
a topic that had been very much on Isabel's mind in recent
days, and her concentration began to suffer as a result.

'Ah, yes!' Francis exclaimed. 'I did hear that old Cedric Walters had passed on.' Across the table he cast Isabel
a half-amused look. 'Natural causes, I sincerely trust?'

'There's no need to suspect otherwise,' his lordship assured him, studying the cards in his hand.

'I cannot tell you how relieved I am to hear you say that,
Sebastian!' Francis declared, before leaning in a conspiratorial way towards his cousin. 'I have it on the best authority, you see, that there is a suspicion abroad that someone
is attempting to decrease the members of our family.'

Not even by the slightest movement of his shapely dark
brows did the Viscount betray the least surprise at hearing
this, and his eyes remained steadfastly on the cards in his
hand as he said, 'May I be permitted to know from whom
you gained this pearl of wisdom, Cousin?'

It was then that Isabel appreciated fully for the first

time just how unbelievably imprudent, not to say down-right stupid, she had been even to broach the subject of the murders with Francis Blackwood. She knew next to nothing about the man, after all. From the first, instinct had warned her against him, that, unlike his cousin, he was not to be trusted. His openly revealing what was tan-tamount to a private conversation was surely proof that her instincts about him had been accurate? Or had he, per-haps, a very good reason of his own for having betrayed her to his cousin?

Once again ignoring the cards in her hand, Isabel raised her eyes to find her partner's fixed in her direction. More than assessing, they were fiercely penetrating in their re-gard, before they flickered briefly in his kinsman's direc-tion. 'It was a theory put forward by none other than my delightful partner, Sebastian.'

'Indeed?' his lordship responded so coolly that Isabel could almost feel the temperature in the surrounding air plummet by several degrees. 'And why should you sup-pose such a thing, Miss Mortimer?'

Seemingly he wasn't best pleased, and Isabel couldn't say she altogether blamed him. Whether or not his dis-pleasure stemmed from the suggestion that the perpetrator of the crimes might be a close relative, or for some other entirely private reason, she couldn't have said, for his ex-pression remained annoyingly unrevealing. None the less, she was determined to try to rectify her crass blunder of earlier in the evening if she could.

'I would be the first to admit, my lord, that I do not know your cousin at all well. But I am beginning to think, increasingly, that he can be wickedly provoking on occa-sions.'

Emily Radcliff at least appeared to find the response

amusing and her tinkling laugh went some way to dispel completely the hint of tension in the air.

'He knows full well it was a suggestion only, half-jokingly made. I was merely attempting to point out that the murderer might have been anyone, as the motive for the killings remains a mystery. Believe me, my lord, it wasn't my intention to cause offence.'

'Rest assured you haven't offended me, Miss Mortimer,' he responded, the warmth very much back in his eyes as they turned briefly in her direction. 'I'm sure there are some very unsavoury characters among the members of my family. You'd know, Francis,' he added, turning his attention to his cousin. 'Your knowledge of the family is far more extensive than mine. I'd even forgotten that the late vicar was related to us.'

'Only very distantly, Sebastian,' Francis assured him. 'Is the new incumbent to be selected from among the far-flung branches of our family tree, I wonder?'

'A replacement for our distant cousin, Francis, has already been decided upon. The good Bishop is to return on Sunday in order to reveal our new spiritual leader to the parish at large.'

Isabel could feel her own spirits plummet. Nothing she could say to his lordship now would make the least difference. The new vicar had been selected, and there was every chance he'd wish to appoint his own curate, if he hadn't already done so. She turned her attention back to the cards in her hand, but to little avail. She and her partner lost the game quite comprehensively, and thereafter failed to regain their winning position.

Chapter Twelve

By the time Isabel set out late on Sunday morning to keep that all-important prearranged appointment in the wood, her thoughts concerning the Viscount were in stark contrast to what they had been on the night of the Camerons' dinner party.

The previous day, not only had she become the proud owner of the most sweet-natured dapple-grey mare, she had also discovered the identity of the new incumbent from none other than her cousin. Like an excited child, Clara had come bursting into the kitchen at the farmhouse with the startling news that none other than Mr Benjamin Johns had been appointed the new vicar of St Matthew's.

Isabel had guessed at once who had exercised his influence and authority over the selection and greeted him with every evidence of pleasure, after she had drawn her mount to a halt a few feet from where he was seated on a sturdy tree stump.

She received no answering smile as he rose to his feet and assisted her to dismount. Beau fared rather better and at least received an affectionate pat.

'When and where did you acquire this creature, may I

ask?' he demanded to know, after running an expert hand down the mare's flanks.

Isabel was still experiencing far too much gratitude towards him to be in the least annoyed by his lofty manner. 'I told you I had an appointment near Merryfield yesterday. I bought her from a young farmer there. He assured me she was the best-natured animal on four legs. And he was speaking no less than the truth! There isn't an ounce of ill humour in her anywhere and she's so perfectly behaved!'

'Which is more than can be said for her owner!' he retorted. 'You should have known you might have use of any of the hacks at the Manor when you wished to ride. I could shake you for not consulting with me first,' he added harshly, though his expression told a very different story. 'And probably would, if I didn't adore you so very much.'

At this, she raised startled eyes. 'No, you didn't mishear me, *ma belle*,' he assured her, his voice, now, as soft as a caress. 'I've been in love with you almost from the first time I saw you.'

Stunned, it was as much as Isabel could do to gape up at him. The next moment she was in his arms, and was sampling for the first time the passion of a man of no little experience.

The suddenness of the embrace might have caught her completely unawares, and perhaps in some deep recess of her mind a tiny voice was advocating caution. Her body, however, was encouraging a far different response, and she raised her arms a moment before his slid about her, drawing her inexorably closer.

Then she was conscious only of him, of the taste of his mouth, of the power in the muscular frame pressed against her, of the increasing desire for these moments of exquisite physical pleasure never to end. It was only when he finally raised his head to bury his lips in her hair that a vestige of common sense began to return, but even so it was nowhere near strong enough to quell the need to cling to him and have him hold her protectively within the circle of his arms. She'd experienced nothing like it before. For the first time in her life she felt safe, protected and, yes, loved. No matter what his reputation had been in the past, she had never been given reason to doubt his integrity, and she didn't doubt him now, nor the depth of his feelings for her.

'I didn't intend for that to happen…at least, not for a while.' There was a huskiness in his voice that she'd never detected before, but certainly no suggestion of regret, as his next words blessedly proved. 'But do not expect me to apologise, Belle, because I cannot be sorry it happened. It's merely the result, I suppose, of stupidly depriving myself of your company during these past interminably long and tedious days.'

This admission did prompt her to raise her head from the comfort of his broad chest and move a little away from him so as to enable her to look up into his face. 'Ah, so you were deliberately avoiding me. Might I be permitted to know why?'

With a sigh, he released her at last, and then bent to retrieve her neat little beaver hat that had fallen to the ground at some point during their embrace. He then led her to the nearby tree stump so that she might sit, before making use of a nearby sturdy elm to rest his back.

'Until I can be sure that whoever murdered my father and brother will attempt nothing further, I intend to take every reasonable precaution. If revenge is foremost in his mind, then he could well attempt to punish me by doing harm to another.' He regarded her in silence for a moment. 'No greater hurt could he inflict upon me than to do mischief to you. I couldn't bear it, *ma belle*, if harm should befall you!'

In two giant strides he was before her again, drawing her to her feet and holding her protectively against him, as though to shield her from some hidden assailant.

'Believe me, nothing would give me greater satisfaction than to announce our betrothal to the world at large,' he assured her, after a further display of his sincere regard that left her satisfyingly breathless. 'I should derive such pleasure from parading my lovely future Viscountess before my friends.' Placing his hand beneath her chin, he very gently raised her head so that he might look down into eyes that clearly mirrored what was in her own heart. 'But for the time being our love must remain our secret. You must tell no one, my darling, no one, not even your trusty housekeeper. The world must continue to believe that I have a sincere regard for Miss Isabel Mortimer, based on respect and—yes, confound it!—gratitude, but nothing more.'

Although she quite understood his reasoning, and felt moved by the lengths to which he was prepared to go in order to protect her, she couldn't resist asking, 'But am I not to see you from time to time, my lord?'

A twitching smile was not the response she might have expected. 'Given your total compliance since your arrival in the wood, do you not think it is time you dispensed with formality, at least when we are private together?'

'Very well, Sebastian,' she returned, for the time being at least more than willing to remain agreeably submissive. 'But you haven't answered my question,' she reminded him.

All at once serious, he released her, and then took a step away. 'No, I do not wish to continue attempting to avoid you. I have found these past couple of weeks intolerable. But we must be careful, Belle—remain on our guard whenever we are together. Besides which,' he added with a rueful smile, 'my behaviour of late has not been altogether chivalrous, most especially where Charlotte Cameron is concerned. My heart belongs to you, Belle. It would be cruel to continue playing fast and loose with another young woman's feelings.'

Unexpectedly, he gave a shout of laughter. 'God, how damnably moral I sound! See what you've done to me, you witch!'

'I take no credit, sir. I have always thought you, innately, a good person.'

Once again he smiled ruefully. 'Well, I wouldn't go as far as to say that, my love. But I do believe I'm a deal better than some I could name.'

'I couldn't agree more,' she concurred softly, before her thoughts turned to their most besetting problem. 'Which makes the task before us very difficult, simply because I no longer believe you ever were the intended victim all those years ago… But you might well be now.

'Oh, no, Sebastian,' she added, cutting off the protest he had been about to utter. 'It's my future too now, remember. I intend to do all I can to uncover the truth. And I can begin by sharing certain matters that have been increasingly troubling me of late.'

As she seated herself once more on the tree stump, her expression was no less sombre than his own. 'I will begin by apologising to you for my stupid indiscretion at the Camerons' dinner party the other evening.' She could see at a glance she held his full attention. 'I discussed certain matters with your cousin Francis in an attempt to gauge his reaction. I cannot say I was even remotely successful. As you're probably aware yourself, he gives little of himself away. And that is perhaps why I instinctively do not trust him.'

The Viscount wasn't prepared to dismiss her doubts about his relative out of hand. All the same, he couldn't resist asking, 'Is this mistrust based purely on feminine intuition?'

'Not entirely, no. A little over two weeks ago, I bumped into him quite by chance in Merryfield.' She waved her hand in a dismissive gesture. 'Now, I fully accept there's no earthly reason why he shouldn't have been there. His home is situated a mere mile or two the other side of the town, after all. So I wouldn't have considered it in the least odd had I not happened to catch sight of none other than your ex-steward, Guy Fensham, coming out of the inn on the opposite side of the street a matter of a few minutes before the chance encounter with your cousin…an encounter that didn't appear to please him overmuch, though he tried his utmost to conceal the fact.

'I accept, too, their being in town on the same day might also be a coincidence, only,' she conceded, after winning no response. 'But, if not, and I'm inclined to believe a meeting between them had been arranged, it suggests an entirely different motive for the murders than has been considered before.'

'It is strange that you should mention the previous steward, Belle,' he said at length, 'because I have been going through my father's papers in recent days. He was meticulous—kept records in good order. Yet I can find nothing concerning Guy Fensham, not even a reference that might offer a clue as to where he came from, or who might have recommended him. Had I not been rather preoccupied with matters concerning the church during these past couple of weeks, I would have attempted to discover more about Fensham.'

At this her thoughts were instantly diverted, and she revealed how delighted she had been by Mr Johns's appointment. 'And my cousin Clara was doubly so. I know nothing official, but I wouldn't be in the least surprised if she wasn't the new vicar's wife within a twelvemonth.'

'I'm sure your cousin would prove to be an excellent helpmeet to a clergyman,' he responded in a trice. 'And now, my love, you must leave this place. I shall see you next Friday, if not before, for I too have been invited to dine at Emily Radcliff's home.'

After helping her to remount, his lordship watched her ride away, before turning and gazing for several minutes between the trees at the shady spot where Jem Marsh's remains had been found. Then he mounted and headed towards that area of the estate where a row of lime-washed cottages stood bathed in the early afternoon sunshine.

As had happened on the previous occasion the elderly ex-butler betrayed how honoured he felt by his master's unexpected visit, as he invited the Viscount to step inside his humble abode.

As had occurred on the previous occasion, too, his lordship didn't waste time, once initial pleasantries had been exchanged, in trying to discover what he wished to know.

Bunting stared silently down at the rug at his feet, appearing genuinely perplexed by the question asked of him. Yet, like so many of his advanced years, his memory of happenings long past was far more acute than his recall of recent events.

'I seem to remember that it was Mr Francis who recommended him to your father, my lord.' He scratched his head. 'Now, let me see… It was a year, maybe less, after Mr Francis's father died. He was a regular visitor to the Manor back then—two or three times a month. Came to ask about land management, and the like, and your father was always pleased to give advice. Seem to recall that Mr Giles weren't at all happy about the amount of time your father spent with your cousin, though.'

This came as no surprise to the Viscount. His brother had always been a selfish, possessive devil, resenting anything their father did that excluded him. This, the Viscount mused, must surely have been one of the main reasons why he and his father had never been close. Unlike his brother Giles, he had never attempted to vie for their father's attention or affection.

'And you're sure it was Francis who recommended Fensham to my father?'

'Positive, my lord. I remember particularly because it was one of the few times during my many years at the Manor when we were short-staffed. Three of the maids and two footmen had been struck down by the influenza that winter, and those of us who were well were having to cover. I was behind time with filling the decanters, sir, and so I was obliged to go in and out of the library on several occasions.' Bunting shrugged. 'His lordship quite understood. But I seem to recall Mr Francis wasn't too pleased by the interruptions.'

Lord Blackwood considered for a moment, before saying, 'And so as a result of my cousin's visit, Fensham was engaged.' He received a nod confirming this, before he remarked, more to himself, 'Then why was it, I wonder, I could find no written character references with regard to Fensham?'

'Because he never brought any with him, my lord,' Bunting surprisingly revealed. 'And that I do know. His lordship was impressed by Mr Fensham at the interview. I came into the library shortly afterwards, and I clearly remember your father standing by the window, saying that he thought Mr Fensham exactly right for the post. Then he muttered something about asking Master Francis for references when next he saw him. I can only suppose Master Francis had, maybe, seen the references himself, and retained them for some reason.'

'Perhaps,' his lordship agreed, staring thoughtfully down at his clasped hands. 'And there's no denying Fensham proved to be extremely conscientious during those first years. I clearly remember my father being most impressed with him, overall. "The best steward we've ever had at the Manor", he was wont to say. Yet, after his death, everything changed. By all accounts Fensham did the minimum of work, feathering his own nest for the most part from the estate's resources.'

Clearly saddened by the last years he'd been in service, Bunting nodded solemnly. 'That's true enough, my lord, so it's no good saying otherwise. Mr Francis did his best, though, sir. He was that concerned about the Manor. Was always so very fond of the old place, I seem to remember. He took it upon himself to contact your father's man in London. Mr Goodbody travelled up from London with your good friend Mr Bathurst. They saw to it that all the valuables were locked safely away, that the house was shut up and that all the servants were given references and paid off until the end of the year.' He shrugged. 'But I don't suppose there was much else they could do, sir, without your written permission.'

'I blame no one but myself for the state in which I found the Manor upon my eventual return. I should have left instructions with Goodbody.' His lordship's wry sense of humour came to the fore. 'My only excuse is that I had other more pressing concerns on my mind at the time— namely how to save my neck from the hangman's noose.'

He was serious again, as something else occurred to

him. 'How often during my years away did Francis visit the Manor, Bunting?'

'Oh, a fair few, sir—more often than not two or three times a year. Sometimes he even stayed overnight, when he would walk about the place, candelabra aloft, making sure himself, I suppose, that the ancestral home of the Blackwoods was in good order. He was the only member of the family who ever did concern himself, sir,' the old butler added, with a rare trace of censure in his voice. 'Your uncle never came near the place, after the day of the funeral, not once.'

'No, I know he didn't,' his lordship acknowledged. 'But let us concentrate on Francis again. As far as you know, did he ever consult with the steward, Fensham, during my years away? For instance, did he ever remonstrate with him for his tardiness?'

'He may have done, sir. Mr Francis always passes the steward's lodge house when he visits the Manor, his own home being in that direction. And I seem to recall one or two things about the estate receiving attention after his visits. But it never lasted long, you understand?'

Not doubting anything the old retainer had told him, but suspecting he'd learn little more, his lordship rose to his feet. 'Thank you, Bunting. You've been of immense help. Don't be surprised if you receive further impromptu visits from me. My curiosity these days is becoming insatiable.'

As a result of the interview with the old butler, his lordship paid a visit to his cousin the following day. He was lucky enough to find him at home, and more than willing to receive him, though he did betray a marked degree of surprise at the unexpected visit.

Given what Isabel had said about this particular member of the Blackwood family, his lordship was determined to remain very much on his guard. Although the reaction to the unexpected visit had seemed genuine enough, seeds of doubt about Francis had been sown in his lordship's mind. He was inclined to trust Isabel's judgement rather than his own. He was too close, had known Francis far too long to assess him in the way Isabel evidently could. To her Francis was virtually a stranger and, therefore, she could be entirely impartial.

'Why, Cousin!' Francis at last declared, rising from his chair, and nodding dismissal to the thin, rather stooped servant who had been employed as butler in the house for as long as the Viscount could remember. 'And to what do I owe the pleasure of this unexpected visit? Have you come to celebrate with me the wonderful news from across the Channel? Or is it merely a social call?'

'Naturally I am relieved at Wellington's success. But in truth it concerns me less than matters closer to home,' the Viscount revealed, before accepting the glass of refreshment held out to him, and making himself comfortable in one of the chairs. 'I'm here because I believe you are in a position to assist me, Francis.'

He waited only for his cousin to resume the seat opposite before, as was his custom, coming straight to the point of the visit, 'What can you tell me about the Manor's former steward, Guy Fensham?'

Light brows rose sharply in what appeared to be a further show of astonishment. 'Why, nothing, Sebastian! Why should you suppose that I know anything about the fellow?'

His lordship didn't allow his gaze to waver. 'Because I have it on the best authority that it was none other than your good self who recommended him to my father in the first place.'

Although the hand raising the glass to Francis's lips remained perfectly steady, it undoubtedly checked for an instant. 'Did I...?' Then, after a further moment or two, 'Why, yes, I believe I did, now you come to mention it! But it was well over a decade ago, Sebastian. You cannot possibly expect me to recall every last detail after all this time.'

'Allow me to refresh your memory, then,' his lordship responded, not wholly convinced by this declaration of poor recall. Francis, he clearly remembered, had always been as sharp as a tack. 'It was over fourteen years ago to be more exact. I had just gone up to Oxford, and you had by that time come into your inheritance. Seemingly, you must have discovered about the death of the steward who had looked after the Manor estate for decades, and visited my father recommending Fensham. Bunting is convinced Fensham came on your recommendation.'

'Ah! So your old butler is the informant.' Francis stared down into his glass, smiling crookedly 'Yes, butlers do have the uncanny knack of discovering everything that goes on in their domain, do they not? And dear old Bunting was a prince among butlers, I seem to recall.'

He raised a hand to his forehead and began to rub the skin, as though to stimulate memory. 'Now, let me see. I remember advertising for someone to help me get the most out of my own acres. Really I was after a good stockman, little more. Fensham applied, and I knew at once he was far too experienced for what I required, and came highly recommended.'

'Ah! So he was armed with references, then?' his lordship returned, having quickly digested this very interesting snippet. 'Can you recall from where he came? I could find no written information regarding previous employment among my father's papers.'

'How odd!' Francis took a moment to sample his wine. 'Fensham had excellent references, I do recall that. Surely he must have produced them during his interview. I cannot imagine your father employing him otherwise.'

'From what I have managed to discover, my sire seemed to suppose that you had retained Fensham's previous employer's written assurances of good character, and would forward them in due time.'

When Francis assured him this was not so, his lordship saw little profit in pressing the matter, and decided to adopt a different tack. 'Evidently you must have been satisfied of his good character, otherwise you wouldn't have recommended him to my father. Can you recall his previous employer's name or direction?'

Francis appeared to give this some thought. 'Not after all this time, no. It was no one I knew personally. For some reason the county of Shropshire springs to mind. Whether or not Fensham was born there or merely worked there for a time, I cannot be sure.'

'How very odd,' his lordship returned, smiling faintly. 'As you are aware, Francis, I wasn't overly concerned with the running of the estate during that period in my life. But, even so, I did engage Father's steward in conversation from time to time, and clearly recall the unmistakable trace of a local accent—not strong, it's true, but there, none the less.'

'Well, what of it?' Francis returned, raising a shoulder, and appearing completely unperturbed. 'It isn't unknown for people to adopt accents so as to be accepted by a local community.'

This, too, was reasonable enough, but his lordship was becoming increasingly less convinced by his cousin's show of unconcern over the matter. The old butler had been certain that Fensham had been engaged at the Manor on Francis's recommendation, and the Viscount was inclined to believe Bunting. After all, why should the old man lie…? But, there again, why should Francis? Whether Fensham turned out to be a good or bad steward shouldn't have mattered a whit to Francis. But had it? Once again he attempted to unravel the mystery from a slightly different angle.

Leaning back in his chair, he looked for all the world totally untroubled, and even managed to summon a half-cynical chuckle. 'Well, it just goes to show, Francis, that even the most careful of men can behave rashly on occasions. My father made it a rule never to employ anyone without good character references. Evidently he thought well enough of Fensham to do so. He even managed to hoodwink you, and you are one of the most astute men of my acquaintance. Left to his own devices, Fensham proved himself to be nothing more than a lying, conniving and manipulative rogue. How it must have pricked your conscience to see how your protégé neglected his duties after my father's demise!'

Again the hand raising the glass to Francis's lips checked for a moment; all the while his gaze never wavered from his lordship's face. 'Hardly my protégé, Sebastian,' he countered. 'I was barely acquainted with the fellow. Furthermore, you may be sure it gave me no pleasure whatsoever to see the ancestral home of the Blackwoods so shamefully neglected. I remonstrated with Fensham on numerous occasions. But sadly there was little I could do. You must appreciate I had no authority over him.'

Strangely enough the Viscount didn't doubt his cousin's sincerity over this at least. There had been a touch of bitterness and anger in his voice that had been unmistakable at mention of the Manor's neglect.

'No one blames you, Francis, over the state of the Manor, least of all me,' he assured him, striving to be fair, even though he was becoming increasingly mistrustful of his cousin's motives and actions. 'It was extremely remiss of me not to have left instructions with my man of business with regard to the family homes, before I left these shores.'

'But you have more than made up for the oversight since your return,' Francis pointed out graciously. 'The mansion has never looked so grand, not since your dear mother was mistress of the house.' A slight smile hovered round the perfectly shaped masculine mouth. 'Whose influence lies at the root of the sweeping changes, I cannot help asking myself?'

His lordship flatly refused to be drawn, and merely returned the compliment by pointing out the elegance of his present surroundings. 'You've always shown excellent taste, Francis, in dress, as in everything else. You really put the rest of us Blackwoods to shame!'

Although he appeared moderately pleased, and acknowledged the compliment graciously, Francis wasted no time in returning the conversation to the former topic by asking, 'Why this sudden interest in Fensham again? Given the evidence Miss Mortimer eventually put before the authorities, it's clear Fensham lied about your state of intoxication on that night, when he declared that, although still a trifle unsteady on your feet, you were quite capable of committing murder. It's also very clear now just why he did lie.'

'Not to me it isn't,' his lordship countered in a trice.

Francis did appear genuinely taken aback by this admission. 'But surely, Sebastian, it was in order to extract money, by whatever means he could, from the estate. The Lord alone knows how many deer were taken during your years away, not to mention numerous other game. He must have made a tidy little profit from his various illegal activities.'

'I'm very sure he did,' his lordship acknowledged, concealing his chagrin over this extremely well. 'Just as I'm also very sure that wasn't the real reason he lied. It merely turned out to be an added bonus, as it were. Unless I much mistake the matter, Fensham expected me to be hanged for the murders, and for my uncle to come into the title and acquire everything that went with it. I also suspect that he must have retained every hope of his services being retained by the new holder of the title. You see, I happen to know for a fact that our dear uncle Horace has absolutely no interest whatsoever in the land. He would have remained in London for the most part, merely enjoying all the benefits the estate brought him, and leaving the steward to do more or less as he pleased. None the less, I still do not believe that is why Fensham lied. Oh, no— there was much more to it all than a desire to make extra money from the estate.'

'Yes, yes, you might be right about that. Fensham certainly proved himself to be a rogue,' Francis agreed, after some moments. He raised his eyes and held his lordship's gaze levelly. 'But I do not immediately perceive what you could do in an attempt to retrieve past losses. Fensham must have fled the area months back.'

'Your judgement is normally so accurate, Cousin. But in this instant it is flawed. You see, I have it on the best authority that he was seen in Merryfield a little over two weeks ago,' his lordship quite deliberately revealed, while scrutinising his cousin's every facial movement. 'As we speak I have men scouring this section of the county for any word of him,' he lied. 'It is only a matter of time before he is found... Then, it will be only a matter of time before we discover the whole truth.'

'Needless to say, if I can be of assistance, you need only call upon me,' Francis returned, as his lordship rose to take his leave.

The master of the house made no attempt to accompany his cousin round to the stables, but moved across to the study window in time to watch the Viscount ride away. He watched until the head of the Blackwood family had ridden from view, and then went across to his desk to pen a hurried note.

Chapter Thirteen

After her meeting with Sebastian, Isabel felt as though she were living in an unreal world, floating in a bubble of happiness like some charmed character who had at last found and fallen in love with her perfect prince. Sadly, though, she was far too much of a realist to continue to believe in fairy stories, and within the space of twenty-four hours prickling little doubts had burst the bubble of euphoria that had surrounded her.

True to her word she had told no one, not even her faithful Bessie, of what had passed between Lord Black-wood and herself in the home wood. Which was perhaps just as well, she decided, as she took refuge in the sitting room early the following evening to be alone with her thoughts. Truth to tell she couldn't help wondering whether she might have imagined the whole thing, that her love for Lord Blackwood had somehow affected her hearing and understanding, and that the Viscount had never proposed marriage to her at all.

Her sense of humour managed to thrust aside momentarily the ever-increasing catalogue of doubts now plaguing her, allowing a rueful smile to touch her lips. The truth of the matter was, of course, he hadn't proposed at all! she reminded herself. Arrogant demon that he was, he had taken it for granted that she would automatically comply with his wishes, and accept him as a husband. He had been so self-confident that she could only suppose he had somehow known how much she loved him.

Again she smiled. There was no denying he was damnably astute. But this hardly made him the chivalrous knight in shining armour of her girlhood imaginings. Far from it, in fact, most especially if one were to believe every story concerning his supposed past indiscretions. But he was, none the less, a viscount, and a very heroic man. No one could dispute that. Moreover, he was a peer of the realm who was becoming increasingly respected for his sound judgement and fairness, whereas she...

The opening of the parlour door interrupted her depressing thoughts and she turned to see her cousin, dreamy-eyed and smiling softly, float into the room. If anyone appeared as though they had been well and truly pierced by Cupid's arrow, then it was Clara. Almost from the moment that she had discovered Mr Johns was the parish's new spiritual leader her eyes had held a faraway look, as though she were living in a perfect world that had nothing whatsoever to do with reality.

'You're home early,' Isabel remarked, after a quick glance at the mantel-clock. A rather disturbing possibility quickly followed. Lord Blackwood was universally liked and much respected by all those who worked for him. Nevertheless, he wasn't one to suffer fools gladly, and he expected all his employees to repay his generosity by providing good service in return. If Clara had spent her time up at the Manor mooning about like a lovesick fool, and neglecting her duties, why, anything might have happened!

'You haven't been dismissed, have you?' she queried gently.

Clara gurgled with mirth. 'Why, no, of course not! What on earth put such a foolish notion into your head?'

Brutal honesty prompted Isabel to respond. 'Well, you have been acting like a giddy schoolgirl for several days now. The sooner you and Mr Johns come to an understanding, the better it will be for all concerned.'

Clara blushed charmingly. 'Oh dear, and we've both been trying so hard to keep it a secret, at least for the time being.' All at once she brightened. 'But maybe we won't need to after today.'

Delving into the pocket of her gown, Clara drew out a letter and promptly handed it to her cousin, before settling herself beside her on the sofa. 'Lord Blackwood called in at the receiving office in Merryfield on his way home and discovered a letter there for me. You may read it if you wish.'

'Why, it's from Mr Goodbody!' Isabel declared, easily recognising the neat hand from the several communications she'd received from him when Josh and Alice had been in her charge. 'So, your stepmother wasn't speaking the whole truth when she came here. He makes no mention of her ever having been your legal guardian. Seemingly, the only provision your father made for you was a financial one—a neat little sum that you will inherit upon marriage, or when you attain the age of five-and-twenty. I wonder now…?'

Frowning suspiciously, Isabel handed back the letter. 'No doubt your stepmother hoped to come to some financial arrangement with your erstwhile suitor Mr Sloane upon your marriage to him.'

'It seems more than likely,' Clara agreed. 'Papa left Stepmama the house, which was only to be expected. According to Mr Goodbody, though, the greater part of Papa's money was left to me. He was not a wealthy man, by any means, but he was no pauper, either.'

'Indeed not,' Isabel agreed, wondering if this unexpected windfall might induce the well-matched pair to declare their intentions quite openly. 'Are you by any chance calling in at the vicarage this evening, Clara? I believe Bessie mentioned something earlier about Mr Johns having taken up residence there now.'

'No, he's coming round here tomorrow evening, as it happens. I invited him to dinner. I hope you don't mind.'

'Not in the least,' Isabel assured her. 'But you'd best check with Bessie first. You know how she hates not being prepared.'

Clara made to leave, but Isabel forestalled her by asking, as casually as she could, how the Viscount had spent his day. 'You mentioned he'd called in at the receiving office in Merryfield on his way home. Merely idle curiosity, of course, but I was just wondering whether you happened to know where he'd gone beforehand.'

'I do, as it happens,' Clara responded. 'Josh was disappointed not to be riding out with his guardian today. Apparently his lordship told the boy he would be calling on his cousin.'

'Did he, now,' Isabel murmured, when Clara left the room, closing the parlour door quietly behind her. She couldn't help wondering what, if anything, he might have discovered, or if his opinion of his cousin had altered as a result of the visit.

It might have surprised Isabel to discover to what extent his lordship's opinion of that particular member of the Blackwood family had changed in the space of twenty-four hours. The following afternoon, as he sat at his desk, the Viscount could only wonder at himself for never having noticed before certain rather unsavoury traits in his cousin's character. They had always rubbed along together reasonably well, even if they had never been particularly close. Their meetings in bygone years had always been genial enough, with Francis's home offering a welcome respite from the tensions always so prevalent at the Manor.

But now he couldn't help speculating on just how much of his cousin's affability had been feigned, a mere cover for sinister intentions. Much of it, if what he was increasingly coming to believe was indeed true, his lordship finally decided, after a further moment's consideration.

He'd been given ample time since his visit the previous day to cast his mind back over the years to several occasions when fierce quarrels had erupted between him and his father. On most every occasion an altercation had occurred during or shortly after one of Francis's frequent visits. What had seemed at the time innocent remarks made by Francis had lit the touch-paper of both his and his father's temper. But what had his cousin hoped to achieve by resorting to such stratagems?

Leaning back in his chair, his lordship gazed unseeingly at the wall opposite, recalling quite clearly that, more often than not, a quarrel had resulted in him storming from the house in high dudgeon, and not returning until he had vented his spleen in a breakneck gallop across the park. Had that been Francis's intent? he couldn't help wondering now. Had he hoped his uncle's younger son would suffer a fatal fall from his horse? His lordship was obliged to own that it might so easily have happened. He'd been a headstrong young man, with scant regard for his own safety.

But whatever Francis's intentions might have been, his lordship no longer trusted him. He had left his cousin's Georgian mansion the previous day firmly convinced his darling Belle had been oh, so right in her belief that his cousin was concealing something. Francis definitely knew far more about the ex-steward than he had been prepared to reveal. And he had certainly betrayed a flicker of disquiet when told that a search was now being undertaken to discover Fensham's whereabouts. This hadn't been the case then, of course, but Francis wasn't to know that. Today, however, four estate workers who knew Fensham by sight were indeed scouring Merryfield and its environs for any word or sighting of him.

The sound of an arrival successfully put an end to his lordship's reverie, and a moment later none other than the subject of his thoughts was being shown into the room. Although not unduly surprised to see his cousin again, he hadn't expected the return visit to take place quite so soon. Seemingly he had succeeded better than he could have hoped in stirring up the hornets' nest.

'Why, Francis! What brings you to the Manor?' Schooling his features so as not to betray his feeling of smug satisfaction, he rose to his feet, while dismissing the butler with a nod. 'Can I offer you some refreshment, or is this merely a flying visit?'

'It is, so I won't sample the fruits of the excellent Manor cellar, I thank you. I am here, Cousin, to request you return to my home with me.'

Very much on his guard, his lordship hadn't been deaf to the slight inflection in his kinsman's voice that had resulted in the request sounding more like a command. 'That is very gracious of you, Francis. But what makes you suppose I should wish to do such a thing?'

A sinister smile hovered around the visitor's well-shaped mouth. 'Because, Sebastian, if you do not you shall never see Miss Isabel Mortimer alive again.'

Not even by so much as a flicker of an eyelid did the Viscount betray the sudden eruption of combined rage and anxiety that consumed him. Even his voice remained remarkably composed when he said, 'If you have harmed her in any way, by the time I am finished with you, Francis, you will be unrecognisable…besides being very, very dead.'

'Oh, I'm well aware, my dear Cousin, that you are more than capable of carrying out such a barbaric feat.' Placing his hat and gloves down on the edge of the desk, Francis drew wide his perfectly tailored jacket to reveal what was beneath and, more especially, what was not concealed. 'And that is why you perceive me totally unarmed. Believe me, I have no desire to provoke you into rash action that we might both regret. You could, of course, easily overpower me,' he readily acknowledged. 'But be sure you would never reach Miss Mortimer in time to prevent her death.'

Francis took a moment to consult his fob-watch. 'If I am not seen leaving here, quite unharmed, and with you accompanying me, within the next fifteen minutes, the lady's fate will have been sealed.'

Although nothing would have given him greater pleasure than to reach across the desk and place his fingers round his cousin's throat and slowly squeeze the life out of him, the Viscount had no reason to doubt the threat would be carried out if he did so. There were a score of vantage points dotted about the estate from where someone might adequately conceal himself and watch the house without being observed in return. He dared not chance putting Belle's life at risk. Yet, if he did as asked…?

'And if I agree to come with you, what then?'

'Then you have my word that nothing will happen to Miss Mortimer until you have seen her again.' Francis waved his hand airily. 'I'm such a romantic! It would prey on my conscience if I permitted you to leave this world without saying a fond farewell to the great love of your life, Sebastian.'

All at once his sickly fawning smile faded. 'And do not attempt to insult my intelligence by trying to convince me otherwise. You gave far too much away on the night of your dinner party. I have never seen you look at a female the way you look at her.' He shrugged. 'Sadly, I cannot spare her. She, in turn, gave away too much the other evening at the Camerons' do. A pity in a way. She's an interesting girl, and I do not dislike her. But sadly she has already guessed too much.'

Once again he consulted his fob-watch. 'You now have ten minutes, Sebastian. Attempt to harm me and you will seal her fate…without the opportunity of one last fond farewell… The choice is yours.'

For perhaps the first time his lordship realised just how much he had changed in the past ten years. Once, he wouldn't have hesitated to overpower his cousin, and then attempt to rush to Belle's assistance. Age, however, had brought not only the gift of wisdom, but also circumspection. Most important of all it had brought him the gift of love. He could so easily attempt to save himself now, and would more than likely succeed, but in so doing he would destroy the most precious thing in the world. He couldn't live without Belle; he'd merely exist. And that was no life…

'So what do you expect of me now, Francis?'

'I'm so glad you've decided to be sensible, Sebastian.' His smile nowhere near touched his eyes. 'Firstly, you may reseat yourself and pen a letter to your lady love, which I shall dictate, of course, inviting her to dine this evening at my home.'

Lord Blackwood did as bidden whilst all the while his mind worked furiously. The letter might turn out to be a godsend, his one and only opportunity to alert Belle to the danger… But how?

'Come, come, Sebastian! You must think me a moon-ling!' Francis declared, after leaning over his cousin's broad shoulder to study every movement of the quill. 'Dear Miss Mortimer, indeed!' he scoffed. 'I'm certain you're not still on such formal terms, at least not in private.'

'Very well,' his lordship conceded, as he reached in the drawer for a further sheet of paper to begin the letter afresh with *My darling Isabel*.

'Ah, yes, that's a great deal better!' Francis approved, much to his lordship's intense satisfaction.

He then went on to write everything, word for word, dictated to him, until he had reached the end. Then he paused for a second or two only before signing his name with a flourish.

Frowning, Francis once again studied the finished letter. 'Your writing has changed, Sebastian. It is now quite legible. Yes, it has matured into a very stylish hand. But I do just wonder about the signature. Why just Blackwood?'

Raising his head, his lordship stared without so much as a blink up into his cousin's face. 'I thought you were more observant, Francis. Didn't you notice on the night we dined with Sir Montague and his family that Isabel continues to address me quite formally? She even does so in private,' he lied, without suffering the least pang of conscience. 'But I shall rewrite the letter if you wish, and sign it in whatever way you like.'

There was a moment or two's silence, then, 'No, it will do. Come, sand it down, and seal it with a wafer! We must not delay our departure further.' Once again he cast the Viscount an unpleasant, self-satisfied smile. 'Needless to say I have taken other precautions to ensure my continued safety. So I trust you will remain sensible and do my bidding throughout the journey to my home.'

It had become almost second nature to Isabel nowadays to take very great care over her appearance, most especially when in the house. That evening she took even more care over the dressing of her hair, and her choice of gown, for not only were they to have a guest dining with them, she also had a shrewd notion an announcement would be forthcoming. In this she was proved correct, which was most gratifying. What she hadn't expected, however, was that her consent to the match would be sought.

Pausing in the act of filling glasses for a celebratory toast, it was as much as Isabel could do not to stare open-mouthed at the happy couple, sitting side by side on the sofa. 'Good heavens! What have I to say to anything, pray? You don't need my approval. You are of an age to make up your own minds,' she declared, hoping she hadn't sounded ungracious, but very much fearing by her cousin's suddenly crestfallen expression that she had.

'Oh, but you are the only family I have left, Isabel…at least the only member I care about. You looked after me when there was no one else I could turn to. I do not look upon you as a mother, or anything like that. That would be foolish.' Colour rose in her cheeks, if possible making her look even lovelier. 'But I do think of you as a much older and wiser sister. I should like to think I have your blessing.'

Having invited Bessie into the parlour in order to join in a toast to the happy couple, Isabel felt she couldn't now order her housekeeper back into the kitchen to watch over her pots. All the same, it would have given her a deal of pleasure to box her faithful servant's ears when Bessie snickered at the backhanded compliment.

Much older, indeed! Isabel inwardly fumed. She was

only five years older, for heaven's sake! Anyone listening might be forgiven for supposing she was in her dotage!

Successfully concealing her chagrin, she finished dispensing the wine. 'Rest assured I couldn't be happier for you both. Although,' she added, eyes glinting wickedly, 'I once had high hopes for you, Clara. I knew a London Season was beyond my means to provide, but I thought my purse might just stretch to a week or two in Bath. I had every expectation of marrying you off to a duke, no less!'

'Oh, heavens, no!' Clara exclaimed, evidently having taken the teasing quite seriously. 'That wouldn't have suited me at all. I am a gentleman's daughter, and was reared to behave in a ladylike manner. But I have never had designs above my station. I think it a grave mistake to marry outside one's class. One could never be oneself.'

Isabel checked for just a second before handing Bessie her filled glass. Their gazes held briefly before Isabel lowered her own. None the less, she sensed that her faithful, wily companion hadn't missed the sudden feeling of despair mirrored in her eyes.

'I expect you are right, Clara,' she returned brightly, determined to shake off the moment of sheer despondency. 'But you two, on the other hand, are remarkably well suited.' She raised her glass. 'And I wish you every happiness.'

The toast was duly drunk, and not a moment too soon, for a loud rap on the kitchen door echoed down the passageway. 'Now, who can that be, do you suppose?' Bessie grumbled, leaving the parlour in order to answer the summons.

'I sincerely hope it isn't any visitors,' Isabel declared, seating herself opposite the happy couple. 'If there is one thing Bessie hates it's delaying dinner, especially when she's taken such care over its preparation. I'm looking forward to the feast. And to your wedding too,' she assured them. 'When is the happy day? Or haven't you decided on a date yet?'

'Ideally we'd both prefer a summer wedding,' Benjamin Johns revealed, looking adoringly at his future bride. 'But there's a deal to consider. My brother is putting up at the vicarage next week. If he is fortunate enough to attain employment at the Manor, he might need to stay with me until he's able to acquire lodgings elsewhere. Then, of course, I must accustom myself to all my duties in the parish.'

Isabel raised a sceptical brow at the latter declaration. 'You'll forgive my saying so, but I think you've been accustomed to most all of them for a considerable time now.'

Mr Johns, quite inured to the lady's plain speaking by this time, wasn't able to suppress a smile. 'Well, yes, perhaps I am. But I do take my responsibilities seriously, and shall always be willing to put the needs of my parishioners before my own.'

'I'm sure you shall. And needless to say, if I can be of assistance in any way, you have only to ask,' she assured him, before turning to Bessie, who had re-entered the parlour, with a letter in her hand.

'From the Manor, miss. Tom Clegg brought it over. He's waiting in the kitchen for a reply.'

'Oh, what a pity!' Isabel declared, after apprising herself of the contents. 'His lordship is dining over at his cousin's house, and invites me to join him there,' she added, revealing at least part of the missive's contents. 'But of course it's out of the question. I cannot possibly—'

'What is it, Miss Isabel?' Bessie's sharp eyes had detected her young mistress's sudden loss of colour. 'Is there something amiss?'

'I'm not altogether sure.' Rising to her feet, Isabel carried the letter across to the window, and read again, *My darling Isabel…* She immediately paused in her intense perusal and frowned as she raised her head to gaze sightlessly out at the front garden. He never called her Isabel, she reminded herself. Well, only rarely and then only when he was cross with her about something, she silently amended. She read on, wondering why he should desire her to join him at his cousin's house… *I have every expectation of discovering something of importance relating to the happenings at the Manor nine years ago, and should very much like you to be present to share the findings with me. My carriage is at your disposal…* On she read until finally she had reached the end, and her eyes became riveted upon the signature, most especially the formation of that all-important capital letter B, with its distinct and elaborate loop.

'Oh, my God,' she muttered, as the clear memory of the secret sign his lordship would have used to warn Wellington that the contents of a missive were fallacious suddenly came rushing back to the forefront of her mind. 'It's all a lie… He must be in danger.'

'Who's in danger, Miss Isabel?' Bessie, asked, after exchanging a startled glance with the couple on the sofa.

Without answering, Isabel brushed past in her headlong flight to reach the door. 'Did you say Clegg was in the kitchen?'

'Yes, but whatever's—'

Bessie broke off abruptly, deciding to save her breath in her attempt to keep pace with her young mistress, as Isabel rushed down the passageway.

'When did his lordship leave the house, Clegg?' she demanded to know the instant she burst into the kitchen to discover the groom appearing very much at home, as usual, seated at the table.

Although taken aback, he couldn't mistake the note of

anguish in her voice. 'Couldn't rightly say, miss. I were working in the stables at the time with young Toby. Seemingly the master left in Mr Francis Blackwood's carriage. Is there something amiss?'

'I very much fear there might be, yes. Here, Bessie,' she added, handing over the letter, just as the newly betrothed couple also entered the room. 'You may read it aloud.'

After the missive's contents had been revealed to all, several puzzled glances were exchanged, and it was left to Bessie herself to eventually voice what was clearly in most everyone's mind.

'But what's wrong with the letter, miss?' She received no response. 'I'll admit it do seem strange that his lordship didn't want me to accompany you. Mayhap, though, he thought you'd have protection enough with Tom, here, to care for you.' She shrugged. 'But it makes no never mind, anyway. You'll not be going, surely?'

'I have no choice. I must go,' Isabel surprised everyone by announcing before she began to pace up and down the large room, her mind working furiously. 'Lord Blackwood has done his best to warn me that something is wrong. It's my belief that letter was dictated. He never calls me Isabel, for a start.'

'Does he not?' Bessie queried, momentarily diverted by this very interesting snippet. 'What does he call you then, if you don't mind my asking?'

'Belle amongst…amongst other things, depending on his mood,' Isabel revealed, smiling in spite of the fact that she was deeply troubled. 'If my suspicions are correct, his lordship didn't go with his cousin willingly.' Her smile disappeared. 'Nor did he willingly write that letter.'

She turned to Clara. 'Didn't you say the Viscount visited his cousin only yesterday?' She received a nod in response. 'It seems strange to me that an invitation to dine wasn't issued then. Furthermore, if Francis Blackwood had any information to pass on, why on earth didn't he do so when he called to see his lordship this afternoon? No, it's all a pack of lies.' Isabel was firmly convinced she was right, as she took back the letter to read it again. 'This isn't an invitation to dine… Unless I'm very much mistaken, it's an invitation to meet my maker.'

'Oh, my gawd!' Bessie exclaimed, momentarily burying her face in her apron. 'What's to be done? You can't go, miss!'

'I have no choice, Bessie,' Isabel returned, sounding remarkably composed considering the most heart-rending possibility had already occurred to her. Her throat felt suddenly constricted as though encircled in a vicelike grasp, but even so she forced herself to say, 'The Viscount might already be dead, but if not, there's just a chance he might be saved.'

Clegg was on his feet in an instant. 'What do you want us to do, miss?'

This immediate vote of confidence was exactly what Isabel needed to concentrate her mind away from the heart-wrenching unthinkable and focus positively on what might be achieved.

She went across to the small window in the west wall of the farmhouse, which overlooked the yard, to see Toby Marsh in charge of his lordship's fine horses, and talking with the elderly man she still employed to do odd jobs about the place.

'I see you've brought young Toby with you, Clegg. That will prove useful.' She turned to her housekeeper. 'Go outside, Bessie, and instruct Troake to come in here. Try as best you can to appear quite normal. We do not know who may be watching the place.

'Mr Johns, I could do with your assistance too, if you are willing?'

'Of course. Anything I can do, you only need to ask.' The young vicar's handsome face betrayed his concern. 'I could never hope to repay the kindness his lordship has shown to me.'

'You might be able to go a long way in doing precisely that before this day is over,' Isabel responded. 'I want you to return to the vicarage now, and harness your gig. It shall not be thought strange if you leave your home at this time of day. It will be assumed you are merely paying a visit to a sick parishioner. I want you to pick up Toby Marsh, who'll be walking back to the Manor, and then go on to the steward's lodge and express my fears to him. Tell him to follow you and Toby with extra men.'

Isabel turned to Clegg as a further thought occurred to her. 'Do you and Toby both know the way to Mr Francis Blackwood's home?'

'That we do, miss. Took both his lordship and Lady Pimm out to visit when the lady were staying up at the Manor, back along.'

'Excellent, then Toby will be able to direct Mr Johns. Go out to him now, Clegg, and explain what has happened. Tell him to await Mr Johns at the Manor stables. And also tell him to arm himself.'

She broke off as her manservant followed Bessie into the room. She then learned from him that he had indeed glimpsed a stranger lurking in the spinney across the other side of the road earlier in the day. It was precisely what Isabel had feared—the house had been watched, and was possibly still being watched. Therefore it was imperative no one aroused suspicion.

After revealing more fully what she herself intended

to do, she retrieved her pistol from the top of the dresser, much to her housekeeper and cousin's alarm.

'Oh, Miss Isabel, you're never taking that thing!' Bessie wailed, having found her voice first.

'I'd be a damned fool to go without it,' she returned, practical as ever. 'The question is how on earth am I going to conceal it? If I were to wear a cloak on a balmy evening such as this, it would arouse suspicion at once. I shall just have to carry my shawl over my arm and hope that suffices. A knife I can strap to my leg.'

She glanced across at her trusty servant who was on the verge of tears. 'Come, Bessie, bustle about! You've never let me down before. Go find me the sharpest knife we have, and help me conceal it beneath my gown.'

Chapter Fourteen

In all the years he had spent out in the Peninsula, during those times he had come so close to losing his life, Lord Blackwood had never felt as he did now—almost beside himself with fear, only, not for himself.

Trussed up like a chicken, bound, gagged, and tied to a high-backed wooden chair, there was nothing he could do to warn the being who meant more to him than anyone or anything else in the world. Throughout the carriage ride he would willingly have given his own life if he thought there was the remotest possibility that Francis would spare Isabel. Yet he knew he would have been wasting his breath to try to plead for her life. Behind the refined and polished exterior there was a sinister bleakness in his cousin that, until recently, he had never realised existed. Almost from the first, Belle, bless her, had recognised something in Francis that she hadn't quite liked, hadn't quite trusted. One could only hope she had brought that innate feminine astuteness of hers to play when reading the letter, and would realise something was very wrong. It was a forlorn hope, perhaps. None the less, it was maybe their one and only chance of coming through this with their lives.

After once again straining ineffectually against his

bonds, his lordship abandoned his efforts and took a little time to catch his breath and attempt to restore some
feeling back into his hands, while using those moments
to stare about him. He'd been imprisoned in a room he'd
never entered before. Ordered at gunpoint to mount the
stairs, he had been escorted by two of Francis's henchmen
to the rear of the mansion. By the position of the sun at this
time of day, his lordship judged the room to be situated
in the west wing, and was clearly used to store artefacts
and items of furniture his cousin had evidently collected
over the years.

There was a fine Jacobean desk in the far corner. Dotted
about the chamber were several handsome walnut pieces of
furniture, upon which stood numerous vases, ornaments
and several elegant silver candelabras. There were half-a-
dozen finely made chairs, all in need of re-upholstering,
against one wall, whilst taking pride of place on the wall
opposite was a rather eye-catching painting of three young
men, all in their twenties.

His lordship frowned as he studied it more closely. One
very similar hung in the long gallery at the Manor. *The
Three Aitches*, his mother had been known irreverently to
call the picture, because it was a likeness of his father and
his two younger brothers, Horace and Hubert Blackwood.
There was one fundamental difference between the two
paintings, however. The one at the Manor had his father
taking pride of place in the centre of the canvas, flanked
by his two brothers, whereas in this copy Francis's father,
Hubert Blackwood, held centre stage.

'I'm sorry I have been obliged to neglect you for so long,
Cousin,' Francis apologised, having entered the room as
silently as a cat in time to catch his lordship's scrutiny of
the portrait. 'But I simply cannot abide being less than

well groomed at all times. And carriage journeys do so crease one's apparel.'

He then tutted, while beckoning to his butler, one of the two people responsible for making his lordship so uncomfortable. 'Really, Figg, there was no need to gag the poor fellow. Who's to hear him if he does shout? The rest of the servants will not return from the fair for some little time yet. Remove the gag at once!'

''Twere the groom gagged him, not me,' the butler grumbled while doing his master's bidding.

Francis ignored him, merely dismissing him with a nod when the servant had completed the task. 'Was that not kind of me, Sebastian, to allow most of the servants the afternoon off to enjoy the fair being held over Merryfield way?' Winning no response, he fixed his gaze on the object that had previously held his lordship's attention. 'My father had that painted. Wily demon that he was, he asked to borrow the original for a short period, soon after this house was built, and had an artist friend of his produce this splendid version.'

All at once he had the look of a rather satisfied cat. 'A far superior specimen to the one hanging back at the Manor! I might be faintly prejudiced, of course, but I always thought my sire the handsomest and most dignified of the brothers. Times without number he would bring me in here when I was a boy,' he continued, after once again winning no response. '"Look, Francis, my son," he would say, "were there any justice in the world, I would have been head of the family, not that short-necked, chinless eldest brother of mine whose lack of taste, grace and aristocratic bearing is quite lamentable!"'

Failing to elicit a response yet again, he stared across at the Viscount. 'I must say, though, he did approve of your mother. An elegant creature, with an abundance of style, he was wont to say about her. And I must say she did produce a Blackwood of some distinction. Werc it not for thee and me, Sebastian, the Blackwoods would be a very sorry lot indeed.'

'So it is your ambition to become head of the family, Francis.' His lordship made no attempt to hide the disgust he felt in either expression or voice. 'I would never have supposed for a moment that someone of no mean intelligence would have allowed his aspirations to spiral out of control, and prompt him to behave in a manner unworthy of the name he bears.'

Francis's look of smug satisfaction was all at once much less marked. 'That is one of the fundamental differences between us, Sebastian—you never had the least desire to hold the title, whereas I have dreamt of nothing else since those far-off days of my childhood.'

'But aren't you forgetting one very important fact— even if you are successful in removing me, you are still third in line,' his lordship pointed out.

Francis, however, merely waved one shapely hand in the air in a dismissive gesture, seemingly unperturbed. 'That is yet another area where we are vastly contrasting, Cousin. You were always intensely headstrong, wont to act on impulse for the most part, whereas I have always tended to consider most carefully, and am remarkably patient as a rule. Uncle Horace and poor Cousin Clement are not destined long for this world, I fear. If either of them continues to survive much above two years, I shall be very much surprised. Both are destined to die from natural causes, so no possible suspicion will fall upon me.'

'You may not be so lucky where I'm concerned,' his lordship pointed out with some satisfaction. 'Too many people know where I am.'

'True,' Francis readily concurred. 'But accidents do happen, most especially at night, and on lonely roads.'

'Indeed, they do,' his lordship agreed, having now some idea of his eventual fate, should his cousin have his way. 'But, even so, my unexpected death will not pass without an investigation being carried out. Then it is likely to be considered most odd that you invite persons to dine when you have given the majority of your staff leave to visit a local fair.'

'True,' Francis agreed again. 'But it seemed less of a risk than having a member of my household whom I do not trust implicitly witnessing what takes place here this evening. Besides which, I instructed my cook to leave ample fare prepared before she left the house. And, of course, she will attest to having done precisely that when questioned. Furthermore, your deaths on the road will not arouse too much suspicion. Not so many months ago there were quite a few incidents of highway robbery in the county, one or two even ending tragically in death.'

He had sounded so smugly sure of himself that his lordship once again experienced a desire to throttle the life out of him, should he be granted half a chance.

'Strangely enough, Cousin, I shall take no pleasure in removing you from the world,' Francis went on, when the Viscount continued to regard him with enmity clearly visible in his expression. 'For a very long time I clung to the hope that you would never return, that your headstrong ways of yesteryear would have induced you to commit some act of folly in some far-flung corner of the world that would have resulted in your demise.' He sighed, sounding genuinely remorseful. 'Unfortunately, it was not to be, and you did return. Nevertheless, for a while, I was prepared to allow you to linger. But then, sadly, an unforeseen and totally unexpected event took place—you, of all people, went and fell in love.'

Moving over to the desk in the corner, Francis poured himself a glass of wine before seating himself on the edge of the handsome piece of furniture, and then swinging one leg casually back and forth, appearing totally relaxed.

'I suspected it the instant I first caught sight of her at the party. By the time I left the Manor that night I was convinced I was right—yes, the unthinkable had happened. But even so, romantic that I am, I was more than happy to allow the course of true love to run smoothly for a time. Then, the foolish chit reveals rather too much on the night we dined with the Camerons. Even though she did her best to rectify the blunder, I knew she'd discovered something, but I knew not what until your visit here yesterday.' Once again he paused to sample his wine, before asking, 'Tell me, Cousin, would I be correct in thinking it was none other than Miss Mortimer herself who spotted Guy Fensham in Merryfield that day?'

Once again failing to elicit a response, Francis smiled. 'Of course it was! Foolishly I must have betrayed my unease when I bumped into her. I must say she's quite a sharp-witted little thing,' he continued, after staring meditatively down at a certain portion of the carpet. 'Which makes her behaviour at the Camerons' dinner party all the more difficult to comprehend.' He shrugged. 'But no matter. It was a grave error of judgement on her part, just as agreeing to meet Guy Fensham on that particular Saturday was mine... And speak of the devil!'

The door had opened, but it was a second or two before a man his lordship hadn't seen in nine long years entered his field of vision. He had changed a good deal. His hair now was liberally streaked with grey, there was a suspicion of a stoop about his shoulders, and his face was etched with many more lines. It wasn't any of these obvious changes that held his lordship transfixed for several seconds, however. It was something he'd unbelievably quite failed to detect until now, as the two men stood side by side, and the resemblance between them became so apparent.

'The carriage is about a mile away. I cut across the fields,' Fensham revealed, while all the while looking over at the Viscount in a distinctly hostile manner.

'I do believe, Guy, the son of your late employer has finally perceived the likeness between us,' Francis responded sagely. 'Yes, quite noticeable when we're standing together, is it not, Cousin? Brother Guy's features are somewhat coarser than mine. But then you and your half-brother didn't look so very alike, either—clearly the result of having different mothers. I cannot tell you what a shock it was when he appeared on my doorstep all those years ago looking for work, and claiming kinship.' He shrugged. 'Really, though, I shouldn't have been in the least surprised. Like your good self in your youth, dear Papa was a most shocking philanderer. The Lord alone knows how many of his other by-blows litter the land. Guy, my senior by some six years, is, however, the only one my father took the trouble to have educated, as far as I'm aware. Which shows, I think, how genuinely fond he must have been of his mother. He couldn't marry her, of course. It was quite out of the question as she came from the lower orders, besides having no money. But that is another story, and one that I shall not bore you with now.'

He raised his hand when he detected what had induced his lordship's heart to miss a beat. 'I do believe a carriage approaches. Now, Cousin, if I have your word that you will not call out, Guy, here, will not replace the gag. Break your word and Figg has instructions to dispense with the delightful Miss Mortimer at once, and you shall, by your own foolish actions, be denied the pleasure of seeing her again.'

'I shall not call out,' his lordship vowed.

As the carriage rounded the sweep of the drive and the handsome sandstone mansion came into view, Isabel picked up her lightweight shawl, and folded it several times very carefully, before draping it across her left wrist and hand in order to conceal the pistol. She was ready for whatever lay ahead. She could only pray that the others would be too, most especially Clegg. She didn't doubt that some attempt to overpower him would take place soon after their arrival. True enough, he was on the short side, but he was strong, and he had assured her he was ready for any attack.

As the carriage slowed, she peered out of the window and took some comfort from the fact that there was no one about. This state of affairs changed the instant the carriage drew to a halt before the impressive porticoed main entrance, for an ill-looking fellow emerged from the house to assist her from the carriage.

As much as she longed to do so, Isabel dared not so much as look back over her shoulder at Clegg, lest something in her expression betray her fears for his safety. Throughout the entire journey she had been plagued by heartrending concerns over Sebastian's well-being, and racked by remorse at having been instrumental in placing others' lives in jeopardy. Never would she forget the look on either Clara's face or Bessie's when she had been obliged to embroil men they cared so very much about in the affair. Her one small consolation was that she had been given little choice, and both men had offered their help most willingly.

'The master awaits you in one of the upstairs rooms, miss,' the stooped and faintly sinister-looking servant informed her, after closing the door against the outside world. 'Viscount Blackwood is with him. If you'd care to follow me?'

So far so good, Isabel mused, as she tamely did as bidden. Seemingly the high-ranking servant had detected nothing amiss with her demeanour. Nor, which was more heartening, had he thought to question the carrying of the silken wrap over her arm. Her only concern was whether he had lied. Was the Viscount truly there? More importantly, would she find him unharmed?

This agonising thought was successfully concealed behind the brightest of smiles as the servant threw wide a door and she saw Francis standing beside an elegant desk.

'Why, Mr Blackwood!' Tripping lightly forwards with every evidence of delight, she held out her right hand. 'How very gratified I was by your invitation to dine!' she managed to say, before stopping dead in her tracks. Unlike the assurance, her shock at finding a certain other person lurking a few yards away was not assumed.

'You are acquainted with Fensham, of course,' Francis remarked suavely, as Isabel stared from one to the other, easily perceiving the likeness between the two men now that she was seeing them close together for the first time.

For a moment or two she was undecided just how to proceed, whether or not to feign surprise at the association between the two men. Then her eyes strayed to the corner of the large room and her course was suddenly crystal-clear.

'Sebastian!' she cried, determined to reach him before anyone could stop her, and falling to her knees beside his chair.

Tears of joy filled her eyes at finding him alive, but she held them in check. Now was not the time to give way to emotion, she told herself, allowing the silk shawl to slip from her wrist to the floor, thereby continuing to conceal the pistol beneath.

'Have you been harmed in any way?'

He shook his head, while his gaze betrayed both sorrow and joy at seeing her there.

'How very touching, do you not think, Guy?' Francis declared, only to receive a snort of derision in response. 'Oh, but it is, dear fellow!' he persisted. 'I'm so pleased to have had my assumptions confirmed. They are clearly in love, and unless I am much mistaken my dear cousin's intentions with regard to this particular female are entirely honourable.'

Fensham seemed to debate for a moment, the look in his eyes not at all pleasant as they travelled over Isabel's trim, shapely figure. 'Honourable, eh…? Are you sure? She's hardly in the same class, after all.'

At this Sebastian shot a glance in Isabel's direction and couldn't mistake the fleeting look of raw despair that gripped her features the moment before Fensham began speaking again.

'I'll say this for the wench, though, she scrubs up well. Yes, I'll give her that. I wouldn't mind half an hour with her myself. If nought else it'd repay the interfering little baggage for meddling in matters that were none of her concern.'

'Loath though I am to refuse you anything, old fellow, after all the loyalty you've shown me over the years, but I'm afraid I cannot permit you to assuage your lust in that particular quarter. I gave my word as a gentleman that no harm would befall her until her—er—execution.'

Turning on his heels, Francis reached for the decanter on the desk once again. 'I think we might at least allow the condemned couple a final drink together. The reason I did not offer you one earlier, Sebastian, was simply because

I couldn't be sure that if I assisted you to a mouthful you wouldn't spit it right back into my face. But I'm sure you would not think of doing such a disgusting thing to the delightful Miss Mortimer, if she were to assist you. Perhaps you would be good enough to carry them over, Guy?'

With lightning speed, Isabel took full advantage of those precious seconds when both men's backs were turned. Swiftly removing the knife from where it had been safely concealed beneath her dress, she successfully cut through one of the cords that bound his lordship to the chair. His eyes widened in surprise, but apart from this he remained motionless until she had achieved equal success with the cords binding his wrists. Then he nodded to confirm he had felt the slight slackening of the bonds, and accepted the knife she left between his wrists with silent gratitude.

Even before Guy Fensham had turned to carry the glasses across to them, Isabel was on her feet, standing beside his lordship in order to conceal the one loose piece of rope that now dangled against the back leg of the chair. She could do nothing about the other end, and only hoped that the men wouldn't notice if it did show. She accepted the glasses and then turned to look down at Sebastian, surprising him again by winking conspiratorially at him, and then glancing down at her shawl.

He wasn't perfectly certain what she was attempting to convey, but he could hazard a fairly shrewd guess. His darling Belle was a damnably resourceful girl. Pray God their luck held!

As she made to place the glass to his lips, he gazed up at her. 'I'll risk it if you will, my darling. But you'd best be prepared for the wine to be drugged…or worse.'

'Do you know, Sebastian, I never considered that!' Francis declared, appearing faintly shamefaced. 'Very remiss of me, now I come to consider the matter. Truth to tell, dear boy, I've no desire to see either of you suffer unduly. I'm not a vindictive person. It shall remain on my conscience that I was kinder to your father and brother. It just so happens I did drug their wine.'

'A confession at last, my darling!' his lordship declared, much to his cousin's evident amusement.

'Not that it will do you much good, Sebastian,' he laughingly told him, before a noise from below, like that of breaking china, wiped the smile off his face. 'Now, what was that, do you suppose?'

'Figg knocking into something, I shouldn't wonder,' Fensham responded, betraying scant interest. 'You know how damnably clumsy he is. Why you continue to employ the idle buffoon, I'll never know.'

'Because he's avaricious. He'll do anything for money, and he can keep his mouth shut.' Francis sampled his wine, frowning. 'None the less, I do not intend to retain his services for very much longer, after tonight.'

'I find your complete lack of conscience quite astonishing, Mr Blackwood,' Isabel declared, her mind having woken up to a comforting possibility for the slight, unexpected noise that she too had detected. As the last thing she wanted was for Francis to insist on an investigation, she attempted to divert his thoughts immediately by saying, 'My besetting sin is morbid curiosity. Would you be gracious enough to satisfy it one last time and reveal how you managed to gain entry to the Manor on that certain spring night, all those years ago, in order to murder both your uncle and cousin?'

'I shall be only too delighted, my dear Miss Mortimer. After all, it's the least I can do in the circumstances,' he declared, executing an exaggerated bow. 'But first, I feel I must correct you over one small matter—I did not murder my uncle, only my cousin. Guy, here, must take full credit for his late master's demise.'

By the completely bland look on the ex-steward's face it didn't appear that he was plagued overmuch by a guilty conscience. It was also impossible to judge what was passing through the Viscount's mind, for his expression was totally impassive too. Isabel guessed, though, that he had more immediate concerns occupying his thoughts. By his slight arm movements she judged he was still attempting to work completely free of his wrist restraint, so his seeming lack of interest could be forgiven.

'Now, let me see…' Francis began. 'It was such a long time ago, I must needs take a moment or two to gather my thoughts… Ah, yes, I remember! I left the Manor some time before midnight. It was a clear night with a bright moon. Guy and I rendezvoused at the prearranged spot on the estate. He'd already dispatched his first victim by then, and concealed his body in the wood.'

Isabel chanced to look down at Sebastian. Then promptly wished she had not. The look in his eyes, the sheer, unadulterated hatred, was frightening to witness. The next moment it had faded, and she prayed she would never glimpse it again.

'You are speaking of Jem Marsh, I believe,' Isabel said softly. 'Was it necessary to murder him?'

From his jacket pocket Guy Fensham drew out a key. 'He didn't like the idea of me keeping this. He saw me return it to my pocket after leaving the house. Said I should have left it in the young master's bedchamber. I knew I couldn't trust him to keep his mouth shut, most especially concerning his young master's true drunken state.'

'I would have seen to everything,' Francis reminded him. 'You merely panicked.'

Fensham seemed unrepentant. 'But our plans changed

when he didn't spend the night with that woman he kept at the time over Merryfield way,' he responded, after nodding in the Viscount's direction.

'Yes, my getting inebriated in the local inn and being returned to the Manor must have caused some disquiet. But it also offered you a most convenient scapegoat did it not?' his lordship remarked drily, and then shrugged. 'Though I don't suppose it mattered much. Even if I had spent the whole night away from the Manor, the finger of suspicion would undoubtedly have been pointed squarely in my direction.'

'Undeniably!' Francis agreed. 'But really, Sebastian, you'd only yourself to blame. Even you must acknowledge you were wild to a fault in those far-off days, quite indifferent to what was said and thought about you at the time. You were a law unto yourself.'

'Very true,' his lordship agreed, at last freeing himself from the last constraint about his wrist. He had no real desire to bandy words with his kinsman, but he needed to play for time—time to consider how best to protect the wonderfully gallant lady at his side. Knowing full well she would be walking into a trap, she had, at even greater risk to herself, come armed.

His lordship had every expectation of dispatching one of them—his skill with a knife had been honed to a lethally accurate degree during his years in the Peninsula. But could he possibly free his ankles in time to protect Belle from the other? He recalled her gesture towards the silk shawl, lying just behind her on the floor. Even if she did indeed have an extra weapon concealed beneath, there were still Francis's faithful servants to contend with. Time was not on their side. Sooner or later he was going to be forced to act, but until then…

'Would I be right in supposing that it was none other than your good self, Francis, who risked discovery by mounting the stairs in order to daub my unconscious person with our relatives' blood?'

The bow was answer enough. 'Yes, I surmised as much. And would I also be correct in assuming that you didn't regain entry to the house by way of the side entrance, using the very key Fensham has retained all these years?'

'You would indeed, Cousin,' Francis confirmed. 'I gained entry by way of the French windows. I had asked to see the garden shortly after we'd dined, you see. For May it was a surprisingly chilly night, as I recall. Your father and brother chose not to accompany me for a breath of fresh air. Not surprising really, I'd already drugged their wine, and they were beginning to feel the effects. It was a simple matter for me to relock the door, and then pretend to throw the bolts before drawing the curtains.'

'And then much later you made good your escape by using, unless I much mistake the matter, that certain ill-fitting window in the same room?' This time his lordship received a nod of acquiescence in response. 'You made only a very few mistakes that night, Francis. The first was to leave the key in the lock of the French windows. It is always kept in the drawer of the bureau. The other foolish blunder was to attempt to implicate me by relying wholly on the evidence of your accomplice. In your eagerness to dispense with yet another member of the Blackwood family you conveniently forgot that there were others who witnessed my sorry state that night.'

Francis appeared to consider this criticism, and then nodded. 'Yes, I think it's fair to say that was an error of judgement on my part. From Guy I learned about the good doctor's involvement, of course, and feared all might be lost. Then I foolishly imagined all would turn out as planned again, when I discovered he had become ill. I never supposed for a moment that his written account lay forgotten in some drawer. Still…' he shrugged '…no real harm was done, after all. The four people who now know what really took place that night are in this room. Fensham won't talk, of course. To do so would be to place a noose about his neck. And as far as you two are concerned…'

He reached for his glass, and raised it as though in a silent toast. 'I'm sorry I cannot allow you a few minutes alone together. Time is pressing, and I fear my servants will not be too long delayed in returning from the fair. Besides which, I could not trust Miss Mortimer not to attempt to release you from your bonds, Cousin.'

His protracted sigh of regret was clearly audible, though whether it was genuine was a different matter entirely. 'A pity it must end this way, my dear,' he announced, fixing his gaze on Isabel. 'I truly believe you have many quite exceptional qualities, and would have made a fine Viscountess, just like your predecessor.'

'Let's get on with it, and put an end to this charade!' Fensham urged, though whether out of consideration for the prospective victims, or because he was heartily bored, was equally difficult to judge.

'Very well, Guy,' Francis obliged him. 'Which will you dispatch? The pistols are in the drawer, ready loaded.'

'I'll see to the—'

Guy Fensham had uttered his last. The knife used at the farmhouse for skinning rabbits was embedded in the ex-steward's chest, thrown by his lordship with lightning speed, and unerring accuracy. By the time his partner in crime had assimilated what had occurred, Isabel had extracted the pistol from beneath her shawl. A moment later Francis was slumped beside his half-brother on the floor.

The next moment the door had been thrown wide and to his lordship's astonishment several of his employees, not to mention his own recently appointed vicar, burst into the room.

Chapter Fifteen

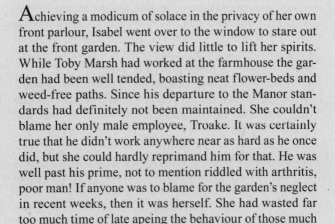

Achieving a modicum of solace in the privacy of her own front parlour, Isabel went over to the window to stare out at the front garden. The view did little to lift her spirits. While Toby Marsh had worked at the farmhouse the garden had been well tended, boasting neat flower-beds and weed-free paths. Since his departure to the Manor standards had definitely not been maintained. She couldn't blame her only male employee, Troake. It was certainly true that he didn't work anywhere near as hard as he once did, but she could hardly reprimand him for that. He was well past his prime, not to mention riddled with arthritis, poor man! If anyone was to blame for the garden's neglect in recent weeks, then it was herself. She had wasted far too much time of late apeing the behaviour of those much higher placed on the social ladder, attempting to be something she was not. And it had to stop!

Instantly her thoughts turned to the Viscount, as they all too often had in recent weeks. She had seen nothing of him whatsoever the previous day. Which had come as no very big surprise, it had to be said. He must have been fully occupied explaining to various interested parties details surrounding the deaths of his cousin and the Manor's former steward. No doubt he had done his utmost to shield her as much as he possibly could from further involvement, and having to answer a thousand-and-one unpleasant questions.

Benjamin Johns had called the previous day to see how she went on, however, and had confirmed that he had received a visit from both Sir Montague Cameron and a Justice of the Peace presiding in the locale where the late Francis Blackwood had resided.

On that never-to-be-forgotten evening his lordship had, she clearly remembered, voiced nothing but praise for the way she had attempted to organise his rescue, most especially involving the Reverend Mr Johns who, as luck would have it, had arrived in time to overhear the gist of what had been said in that upstairs chamber, and whose account of events had subsequently proved invaluable.

'A masterly example of forward thinking, my darling!' Sebastian had praised her before handing her into his carriage, where Mr Johns, designated the role of duenna, had sat awaiting her.

After a few further gentle words of farewell, he had ordered both Clegg and Toby, seated up on the box, to ensure her safe return home. That was the last time she had seen his lordship…

The next time, she felt certain, would not be long delayed, and she dreaded the encounter, for somehow she must find the strength to tell him she could not be his wife.

The parlour door opened, making her start, a circumstance that didn't escape Bessie's eagle-eyed gaze. 'Oh, Miss Isabel, you're as nervous as a kitten! Not that I'm surprised, not after what you've been through.'

Bessie had already received a reasonably detailed account of what had taken place at the late Francis Blackwood's home on that fateful evening, when Tom Clegg too had taken the trouble to pay a visit to the farmhouse the previous evening. She shuddered at the mere thought of it all; most especially harrowing was what her poor mistress had been obliged to do in order to save the Viscount. Putting a period to someone's existence was bound to cause any right-minded person a deal of remorse. All the same, it wasn't like the young mistress to brood over matters that couldn't be mended.

She regarded Isabel's wan expression keenly. Could there be something else distressing her? Bessie couldn't help wondering. If so, there was a certain someone sure to sort it out—someone who, unless she had misread all the signs in recent months, meant a great deal to her mistress.

She raised her head as her ears detected a certain unmistakable sound. 'I do believe that were a carriage just drew up in the yard. I'd best go see who's a-visiting.'

Isabel didn't respond. There seemed little point in doing so. She had a fairly shrewd idea of the identity of the caller, just as Bessie had done. What was the point in saying she didn't wish to receive visitors? Like as not his lordship would merely brush past and demand an audience. Besides which, what could be gained by delaying the inevitable encounter?

She knew it was he who had entered the parlour unannounced even before he declared, 'I've had the most exhausting day thus far, my darling! Been up since daybreak, and not a drop of liquid passing my lips since breakfast. I'm absolutely parched!'

Without awaiting a response Sebastian helped himself to a glass of wine, and was on the point of pouring a second glass when he checked, noting for the first time the droop of slender shoulders, and registering, too, the fact that she had made no attempt to turn from the window in order to look in his direction.

Picking up the filled glass, he sipped the contents meditatively, while moving slowly across the room. 'I'm sorry I've been unable to see you before now, my darling,' he said, assuming this must surely be what had given rise to this negative reaction to his visit. 'But, as I'm sure you can imagine, I've had the very devil of a time explaining everything to the authorities. Not only that, I'm having to deal with all Francis's affairs. I was obliged to speak to my cousin's lawyers in Merryfield, only to discover whilst there that he's only gone and named me as the main beneficiary in his will, would you believe?'

This brought her head round, as he had suspected it might, and there was nothing artificial in the astonished look she cast him. 'Why on earth should he have done that, do you suppose? I genuinely believe he didn't dislike you, but he couldn't possibly have thought that much of you, otherwise he wouldn't have planned what he did.'

'And there you have it in a nutshell, my darling,' he returned, his sharp eyes not missing the slight wince at his endearment. 'I'm not in full possession of all the details as yet. In fact the only reason I had for calling on the notaries was to apprise them of Francis's demise. It was then I discovered certain aspects of the will. Quite naturally, while enquiries are ongoing regarding the details surrounding my cousin's demise, the lawyers are being cautious. But what they did reveal is that Francis made major adjustments to his will sometime last autumn, when he discovered I'd returned to England.'

'That's all very well, but I still fail to understand why he should have done such a thing, in view of the fact that he intended to dispose of you,' Isabel pointed out, having set her own heartfelt concerns aside for the present.

'I suspect he was merely taking extra precautions for when he did arrange my demise,' his lordship responded, ever the realist. 'After all, who would suspect him of the dastardly deed when he had named me beneficiary in his will. Given that he had no wife and children to support, he was merely striving to convey the impression he was a loyal member of the Blackwood clan, sincerely attached to the head of such a noble family.'

Isabel shook her head, still finding it difficult coming to terms with what had taken place during the past days, and to what depths some people would sink in order to attain their ends.

'I wonder how long he had been obsessed with the idea of being head of the family, of owning the ancestral home and having the title?'

Sebastian shrugged. 'From a very young age, I strongly suspect. What little he did reveal suggested the burning ambition was instilled in him by his father.'

Finishing off his wine, he placed the glass on the sill behind her, and then stared down intently, easily detecting the suddenly wary look before she lowered her eyes.

'I dare say that for a few days to come I shall be engaged far too much in dealing with matters relating to my late cousin, not least of which will be organising some kind of funeral. But for the rest of this day, I'm entirely at your disposal, my darling. So tell me what kind of a day you've had thus far. More importantly, tell me what you're planning to wear this evening at Emily's do?'

Given the trauma of recent days, it was hardly surprising that her expected presence at Mrs Radcliff's proposed dinner party had escaped her memory entirely. Isabel clasped her face in her hands, a clear indication of her genuine distress.

'Oh, Lord, I'd forgotten all about it! I must send a note at once, begging to be excused. In the circumstances I'm sure Emily will understand.'

'She might, but I most certainly shall not,' he responded, easily preventing her headlong dash across the room to the bureau by the simple expedient of momentarily grasping her elbow. 'I have no intention of playing the hypocrite by going into mourning for someone who did his level best to cut short our allotted time on this earth. Furthermore, it will be considered extremely odd if I announce our betrothal to the world at an event where my fiancée isn't present.'

There was no mistaking the heartfelt distress in the large grey-green eyes before delicate lids lowered and she swung round to face the window again. 'You don't understand, I—'

'Oh, I think I understand perfectly well,' he countered, cutting her off mid-sentence without suffering the least pang of conscience. He recalled seeing that selfsame look not so many days before, and knew precisely what was causing the anxiety. 'I suspected at the time that you had paid too much heed to Fensham's idiotic notion that our stations in life are vastly contrasting. Undoubtedly it has grown out of all proportion, resulting in your firm belief that you are unsuitable to be my Viscountess. Well, I don't want to hear anything further about it!' he continued, the annoyance and resolve in his voice unmistakable. 'It is utter nonsense, anyway! Even Francis—devil take him!— could appreciate your suitability to be my wife.'

Astute man that he was, he had calculated her misgivings in a trice, and had dismissed them as swiftly. None the less, Isabel couldn't so easily forget what Fensham and, more especially, what her cousin had said. Clara had not touched briefly on the subject of marrying out of one's class for any ulterior motive. She had merely remarked on something that she truly felt…what the vast majority of people would feel. Although Isabel had no intention of betraying her cousin as being partially responsible for her present anxiety, she felt no compunction whatsoever in using his late cousin in an attempt to try to make him see reason.

'I never supposed for a moment Francis was in earnest when he said what he did. I believe he was merely making sport of me.'

'You are utterly wrong in that assessment,' he returned, with such conviction that she instantly began to doubt her own judgement in the matter. 'Francis was ambitious, lethally so as things turned out. But one thing he was never guilty of and that was insincere flattery. From the first he recognised you for what you are—a lady of quality, a lady of integrity and sound judgement. He knew you posed a real threat because, unlike Fensham, he instantly recognised your suitability to be my wife.' He smiled ruefully. 'Ashamed though I am to admit as much, I was a trifle slower in my appreciation of your exceptional qualities. I had been in your company on several occasions before I knew you'd make me the perfect wife, *ma belle*.'

'Please do not call me that,' she managed faintly, her resolve slowly ebbing away, as he moved a step closer and she could feel the warmth of his breath fanning the nape of her neck. 'My command of the French tongue is nowhere near equal to yours, but even I know what that means. And I am no beauty, sir. Your friends would not call me so.'

A moment's silence only, then, 'Ah, but you see, *ma belle*, they are not blessed to see you through my eyes.'

This was just too much for Isabel's rapidly weakening resolve. She felt her knees buckle and would have been powerless to stop herself sinking to the floor if strong arms hadn't encircled her. The next moment she was being carried across to the sofa, where she received further corroboration, had she needed any, of the depth of Sebastian's feelings for her.

Emerging breathless from the masterly display, Isabel rested her head upon his shoulder. She didn't doubt the depth of his regard. How could she? None the less, niggling doubts about her suitability to become his Viscountess remained.

'Of course you are bound to feel some anxiety with regard to your future role in life, my darling,' he said, once again reading her thoughts with uncanny accuracy, after raising her chin and staring long and hard into her eyes. 'It would be strange if you did not. But, remember, I shall always be there, should you need advice.'

She couldn't help smiling at this. He had clearly made up his mind that he would take her to wife, and seemingly nothing she could say would detract him from this objective. And, truth to tell, she no longer wished to try. 'It would seem, my Lord Blackwood, you are determined to have your way.'

There was a hint of smug satisfaction in the smile he cast down on her. 'Not so very long ago an astute young woman said to me that if I ever proposed marriage to a lady I truly loved, I would never take no for an answer. And how right she was! The only reason I would accept my *congé* from you, my darling girl, is if you were to say that you truly did not love me.' The self-satisfied look was all at once more pronounced. 'And that you could never do… No girl could do what you did not so many days ago and not be in love. So…'

Delving into his jacket pocket, he produced a small, square box, and after briefly displaying its magnificent contents before a pair of astonished eyes, he slipped the diamond ring on to her finger.

For several seconds it was as much as Isabel could do

to stare at the exquisite gem. 'It's so beautiful,' she murmured, holding her hand up towards the window so that the large stone reflected the light in a myriad of colours. 'Is it part of the family jewels?'

'Certainly not!' He sounded affronted, but she was not fooled. 'I purchased it in London when I was there a few weeks ago,' he then happily revealed, knowing as he did so that she would realise his regard had not suddenly manifested overnight, but had been steadily growing over many weeks. 'Mention of the family jewels is a timely reminder, none the less. One of the reasons I came over was to ask if you wished to wear again tonight that pearl set you wore at my dinner party, and very thoughtfully returned to the Manor?'

The mere thought of doing so made her smile, but then she thought better of it. 'No, no, I do not think so. It's only a small affair, after all, and I do not wish to appear vulgarly overdressed,' she said, proving that she was already considering behaviour and how she would appear to the world at large. 'I think Mama's single string will suffice, most especially as I shall be wearing this beautiful adornment,' she continued, once again staring down at her hand. 'Besides, apart from our announcement, I would imagine the evening will be slightly muted. No matter how much of a brave face Emily Radcliff puts on at the present time, she must be so deeply worried about her husband across the Channel.'

His smile was distinctly crooked. 'Evidently you haven't yet heard, my dear. In truth, I only learned earlier this week that Wellington and the allies won a great victory at a hitherto inconsequential place called Waterloo. Emily has already received word that her husband came through the battle virtually unscathed, and will be returning within a few weeks. Apart from which, she has a further reason to celebrate. As you might be aware, she didn't accompany her husband because she thought there was just a chance she might be increasing. Now she knows for sure she is.'

Isabel was delighted with the news. Before she could voice her joy, Bessie returned to the room, wanting to know whether Lord Blackwood wished his groom to return to the Manor for any reason.

'No, Bessie, you may tell him his future mistress has wisely decided not to wear the pearls this evening, and that I shall be returning there myself presently.'

'Very good, my—' Bessie broke off, gazing in awe-struck silence for a moment or two at the couple sitting rather informally close on the sofa, before adding, 'Oh, my word, you don't say!'

'I do,' the Viscount returned with simple pride. 'So you may be the first to congratulate me on my great good fortune in becoming betrothed to your mistress.'

'Oh, I do, sir. Indeed I do!' Bessie declared, wiping a suspicion of tears on the corner of her apron.

'Of course it will mean your removal to the Manor in the very near future. My present housekeeper will be returning to London to look after the town house, leaving the position of housekeeper at the Manor vacant. Which I sincerely trust you will fill.'

Clearly overcome, it was much as much as Bessie could do to nod dumbly before Isabel dismissed her and turned to her future husband with a half-reproachful look. 'You are taking a deal for granted, my lord. What do you suppose I am to do when Bessie goes up to the Manor?'

'Do…?' He was slightly taken aback for a second. 'Why, you'll be there with her, of course. No,' he added, holding up a hand at the protest he knew was about to be uttered. 'I refuse to have a needlessly long engagement. London, of course, will be positively swarming with people wanting to celebrate Wellington's victory. I flatly refuse to attempt to organise our wedding there with all that going on. So, what I propose is a quiet wedding, here in the parish, with the good Mr Benjamin Johns officiating.'

Isabel was not in the least unhappy with that suggestion. In fact, she rather thought she would prefer it to a great society affair, held in the metropolis, where she would know so few people. Those occasions were definitely for the future, when she had acquired a little know-how. All the same, she could foresee just one slight problem.

'Well, naturally, I'm delighted to hear that your cousin and Mr Johns are betrothed. They are admirably well suited, as I've remarked before,' he responded, when she had revealed the news. 'But I tell you plainly, my darling, I have no intention on awaiting their nuptials before we tie the knot ourselves. I shall call at the vicarage in a day or two, and organise the banns. I intend we should marry within a month. Then we shall, maybe, visit Bath. I have a desire, you see, to make a return trip to the West Country to visit one or two friends.'

Isabel knew precisely who he meant, and was not averse to the idea in the least. She would like to renew her acquaintance with both Charles Bathurst and Sir Philip Staveley, and meet their wives. But she still felt unable to go off willy-nilly on her honeymoon and ignore her responsibilities.

'But what about Clara? I can't go and leave her here on her own to fend for herself,' she pointed out.

'No one is expecting you to do any such thing,' he calmly assured her. 'Once we're married, it will be perfectly in order for her to move into the Manor, where Bessie will be in a position to look after her until your return.'

Isabel settled herself again in the crook of his arm, wondering whether all her future worries would be smoothed out so adroitly. It would be nice to think so. Undoubtedly becoming Viscountess Blackwood would bring its own responsibilities. None the less, she had the feeling she would cope very well with such a loving tower of strength to guide and protect her.

* * * * *

Betrayed And Betrothed

Prologue

1812

Although engaged in securing the pack to his saddle, Major Bartholomew Cavanagh's attention was fixed on the column of soldiers leaving the camp. His expression was sombre, but as he wasn't a gentleman given to smiling much it was sometimes difficult to assess his mood. All the same, his friend, approaching unobserved, was somewhat surprised not to detect at least a flicker of animation in the ruggedly masculine face.

'Good gad, Bart!' Captain Fergusson exclaimed. 'Anyone might suppose you were about to set off on a skirmish, instead of returning to England on a spot of long-overdue leave.'

This succeeded in igniting a flicker of amusement in Bart's dark eyes, as he turned them briefly in the direction of the young officer whose cavalry uniform made him look rather conspicuous in this section of the camp. 'You want to be careful, Giles,' he warned. 'You know your lot don't appreciate one of their own fraternising with lowly infantrymen.'

Although both had earned the reputation of being level-headed, conscientious officers, whenever together the camaraderie they had enjoyed since boyhood was never far from the surface.

'Got little choice but to mix with the scaff and raff if I want to see you,' Giles returned, having taken his friend's banter in good part as always. 'Though why the deuce a horseman of your excellence chose to become a foot-soldier defeats me.'

As this singularly failed to elicit a response, Captain Fergusson knew better than to attempt to probe further. 'Received any more news about your father?' he asked, with an abrupt change of subject.

Bart shook his head. 'As you know, I've never rated my stepmother's intelligence above average. One thing I will say for Eugenie, though—she isn't prone to exaggeration. If she says my father's health is causing concern, you may be sure he isn't well. But even if this were not the case, I should still have spent this leave at home. It's high time I made my peace with my family.'

Raising his eyes, Bart once again focused his attention on the line of soldiers marching towards the range of hills in the distance. 'These past years out here in the Peninsula have certainly changed my outlook on life. Things that once were vastly important no longer seem so.' He shrugged, straining the cloth of his rifleman-green jacket. 'Experience of war affects most of us in one way or another, I suppose. Brings out the best in some; the worst in others.'

Nodding in agreement, Giles followed the direction of his friend's gaze. 'Wellesley evidently means business. I see he's sent the Provost out with the column.'

'After the casualties suffered in recent months, he cannot stand by and do nothing when men are deserting in such numbers,' Bart commented. 'There's rumoured to be around a hundred hiding out in those hills. If they can find enough to eat, they'll possibly do well enough for now. When winter sets in it'll be a different matter.'

'I hear Wellesley's prepared to be lenient, and offer free pardons to those willing to give themselves up. But he won't hesitate to hang those who don't.'

His eyes hardening, Bart's gaze slid once again to the distant hills. 'I must confess there's one out there I'd give much to see dangling from the end of a rope. Wellesley calls the common soldier the scum of the earth. And in Septimus Searle's case he couldn't be more right. A more black-hearted devil you'd be hard pressed to find. And I was unfortunate enough to have him in my company. It's a pity I shan't be here to witness him receiving his just deserts, because I'm certain he'll never give himself up voluntarily. He wouldn't choose to be under my command again. He knows I'd make his life hell.'

Captain Fergusson betrayed surprise, for his friend had the reputation of being considerate and fair, and was well respected by the men in the ranks. 'It isn't like you to be so vindictive.'

Totally unrepentant, Bart mounted his horse. 'Searle's committed most crimes from rape to murder. My sympathies lie with his victims. But for the next few weeks I intend to put my experiences of the Peninsula, both good and bad, behind me, and enjoy more pleasurable activities, while I become reconciled with my family.'

Chapter One

1816

Only the steady ticking of the mantel-clock disturbed the silence now pervading the parlour at Foxhunter Grange. Miss Abigail Graham, resolutely staring through the window, her eyes carefully avoiding that area of garden beyond the shrubbery where she no longer ventured, was finally coming to terms with the fact that she simply could not, would not, continue with her present lifestyle.

'Well, child? Have you nothing to say?' the master of what was generally held to be a very fine country residence at last demanded, his voice noticeably harsher than it had been a short time before, when he had calmly revealed the arrangements made for her immediate future. 'Can you not find it within yourself to offer a mere word of thanks for the trouble I've taken to ensure you will be suitably entertained during my absence? Am I not to receive the smallest token of gratitude?'

'Gratitude?' Abbie echoed, finally abandoning her silent contemplation of the late spring blooms in the largest of the flower-beds, and turning to look at him.

No one could have failed to perceive the strong resem-

blance between them. Although thankfully having been
spared the strong, hawklike nose that characterised most
male and several unfortunate female members of the family down the generations, Abbie had inherited the striking Graham colouring of violet-blue eyes and silky black
hair. At a glance no one could fail to appreciate too that
Mother Nature had seen fit to bless her still further with
an elegant carriage, and a slim, shapely figure that even
the plainness of her grey gown, more suitable for a governess, could not disguise. Nor could her hair, swept severely
back and arranged in a simple chignon, detract from the
loveliness and perfect symmetry of features set in a flawless complexion.

'If I thought for a moment the arrangements you have
undertaken to ensure that I do not remain here at the
Grange during your absence stemmed from a wish to offer
me the opportunity to enjoy the company of the godmother
I haven't seen for almost sixteen years, I would be exceedingly grateful.' Only the pulsating vein at her temple,
clearly visible beneath the fairness of her skin, betrayed
the fact that Abbie was perilously close to losing her admirable self-control for the very first time, and giving way
to years of pent-up frustrations in an explosion of wrath.
'But I know you too well. The only reason you desire to
see me safely packed off to Bath is merely an attempt on
your part to prevent a closer friendship developing between
me and our new practitioner.'

Only briefly did Colonel Augustus Graham betray a
flicker of unease, as he studied the surprisingly hard set
to his granddaughter's features.

'You are talking nonsense, child!' he announced, as
he reached for the glass of fine brandy at his elbow with
a hand that for once was not perfectly steady. 'You are
clearly ailing for something. Perhaps it would be wise to

delay your departure for a few days, until you are more yourself.'

'Oh, no, Grandfather,' she countered. 'Ailing or no, I shall leave early tomorrow, as arranged. If the female my godmother is kindly sending to bear me company does indeed arrive as planned later today, she should feel sufficiently restored to commence the return journey first thing in the morning.'

The note of determination clearly came as a further surprise to the gentleman whose granddaughter had always been wont to show him the utmost respect. He rose at once to his feet to rest an arm along the mantel-shelf, before once again regarding her from beneath bushy, grey brows. 'Evidently you are piqued because I chose not to disclose until today the arrangements I had made with Lady Penrose for your sojourn in Bath.'

'I should like to have been consulted, certainly,' Abbie admitted, still somehow managing to maintain her admirable self-control. 'And although I'm positive it wasn't your intention, in point of fact you've served me a good turn, sir. Living with my godmother during the next few weeks will grant me ample opportunity to take stock and decide where and, more importantly, by what means I shall support myself until I attain the age of five and twenty, and inherit the money left to me by my mother.'

'What on earth are you talking about, child?' the Colonel demanded, making no attempt whatsoever to conceal his increasing displeasure. 'Quite naturally, you will return here. The inheritance your mother left you is a mere pittance when compared to what you'll receive from me. You'll be a wealthy woman once I'm gone, with money enough to live comfortably throughout your life…providing, of course, you give me no reason to alter my will.'

It needed only that totally unnecessary and unsubtle

threat to sever the rein she had maintained on her temper. 'Change it and be damned to you, sir!'

Abbie was well aware that few men, let alone a woman, would dare to speak to her grandfather in such a fashion, but she was beyond caring now. The fact that his own eyes were glinting ominously and his mouth was set in a grim straight line, evidence of his own ill humour, could not deter her from at last revealing her strong sense of ill usage, and the unhappiness she had suffered at being treated with cool indifference by the gentleman who, throughout her childhood, couldn't have been more loving or considerate towards her.

'You are not the same man who brought me here fifteen years ago, Grandfather. You couldn't have been kinder to me then, more gentle or understanding.' She thought she detected a muscle contracting along the line of his jaw before he turned briefly to glance at the portrait of his late wife, taking pride of place above the grate. 'But all that changed, did it not, the moment I dared to go against your wishes by refusing to marry that precious godson of yours?'

'The manner of your refusal was inexcusable,' he reminded her, his voice harsh, unbending.

'It was ill done of me, yes,' innate honesty obliged her to concede. 'I should have been more gracious in my refusal. But I had only just turned seventeen. And you offered me no opportunity to discuss the matter with you in private first.'

There was no response forthcoming, and Abbie, easily discerning the taut, uncompromising set of his features, realised he was in no mood to unbend towards her even now, and faced the fact there and then that, in all probability, he never would.

'I cannot alter what has happened in the past, Grandfather. And, given the opportunity, I tell you plainly, I wouldn't attempt to try. I could never bring myself to marry a man I did not both love and respect.'

This claimed his full attention, and once again Abbie found herself on the receiving end of that hard, uncompromising gaze to which she had grown all too accustomed in recent years. 'How can you say so? You were fond enough of Bart when you were a child,' he reminded her.

'Yes, perhaps I was, a little,' she acknowledged, after giving the matter a moment's thought. 'But children grow up, Grandfather. We simply wouldn't have suited.'

He dismissed this with an impatient wave of his hand. 'And how you can say you do not respect a gentleman who has served his country so courageously during the recent conflict with France, earning a commendation from the Regent himself no less, is beyond my understanding.'

'His bravery on or off the field of battle is not the issue here,' she pointed out. 'His principles, however, are a different matter entirely.'

'Principles!' he barked. 'Let me tell you, my girl, his principles are above reproach. If it hadn't been for Bart's intervention, I would have gone after you that day and administered the thrashing you so richly deserved!'

If he had expected this admission to endear her to the godson he had always so admired, Abbie wasn't slow to disabuse him. 'Then he served me an ill turn by interfering, for I would far rather have suffered a beating than the cool indifference I've been forced to endure since that day. And if you imagine for a moment,' she went on, not granting him the opportunity to respond, 'that, after attaining my majority, the reason I continued to tolerate being treated little better than a servant was because I feared finding some means by which I might support myself, you couldn't be more wrong. I did so because I hoped that one day you'd find it within you to forgive me, and we might enjoy the wonderful companionship we once shared. But I refuse to delude myself any longer.'

Abbie could see by the contemptuous curl on his thin lips that he considered her resolve no longer to be dependent upon him an empty threat, a mere passing whim, even before he snapped, 'Don't be ridiculous, child! How on earth do you suppose you could support yourself?'

Steadfastly refusing to be disheartened by the belittling tone, Abbie returned his openly scathing look with one of her own. 'At the very least I could attain a post as a housekeeper. After all, I've been running this establishment for nigh on six years. A governess is not out of the question, either. I've been given ample time to improve my mind during those numerous occasions when you've done your utmost to ignore my very existence, and have left me to my own devices, while you've been out and about enjoying the company of your friends.'

Abbie attained a modicum of satisfaction in seeing the curl fade from his lips, and a flicker of uncertainty appear in his eyes, before she transferred her gaze to the portrait above the grate. 'And there is always the possibility that I might be able to make good use of the gift I seem to have inherited from Grandmama, a gift which only you have failed to acknowledge I possess. Then, of course, I don't rule out marriage entirely. But if and when I am ever tempted to take the matrimonial plunge, it will not be to our local practitioner, even though I value his friendship highly. And it will most certainly never be to that precious godson of yours, whom I hold in utter contempt.'

The fist he brought down hard on the mantel-shelf came perilously close to sending several ornaments toppling to the floor. 'Damn it, child, why? What did Bart ever do to give you such a disgust of him?'

The disdainful curl on her lips was a masterly repro-
duction of the one he had perfected only a short time before. 'It is a little late to ask that of me now, Grandfather.
Besides which, I am no talebearer. If you're so keen to
discover just what turned me against Bartholomew Cavanagh, then ask the man himself what took place in the
summerhouse six years ago on the very day he proposed
marriage to me.'

Not prepared to discuss further an incident she would
far rather forget, Abbie went across to the door. 'I shall not
be joining you for dinner this evening,' she announced,
'I have my packing to organise. So I shall take my leave
of you now, and wish you a pleasant sojourn with your
friend in Scotland.'

Abbie did not look back before she left the room, and
so omitted to see the thoughtful expression coming into
her grandfather's eyes a moment before he went over to
take up her former stance before the window. Raising his
head, he stared across the vast south lawn at the corner
of the garden, where that ornamental wooden structure
stood, hardly visible now behind shrubs and trees. The
summerhouse, he well remembered, had once been a favourite haunt of his granddaughter's, just as it had been a
favoured retreat with both his wife and his son. It was true
that for some considerable time Abbie had never ventured
into that area of the garden. Why had he never appreciated that fact before?

Then he shook his head, dismissing it from his mind.

The hired post-chaise, conveying Abbie and her godmother's personal maid, reached the outskirts of Bath just
after noon, three days later. They had made the journey in
easy stages, and in weather that had been kind to them by

remaining clement; but even if this had not been the case, Abbie would still have enjoyed the experience.

It had been many years since she had travelled any great distance from her grandfather's home, set in the heart of Leicestershire's famed hunting country, and she had discovered much on the journey to capture her interest. Most of all, it had been the companionship of her godmother's personal maid that had made the journey so vastly enjoyable.

Miss Evelina Felcham was unlike any other maid Abbie had known before. All the servants at Foxhunter Grange, wary of the Colonel's uncertain temper, were wont to treat their master with the utmost respect at all times. It had quickly become clear that Felcham wasn't in the least in awe of her mistress; nor was she reticent to voice her opinions, whether or not she had been called upon to do so.

'I do hope Godmama isn't worried because we didn't arrive earlier in the day. But I do not get to travel about the country, and I didn't wish to hurry the journey,' Abbie remarked, peering interestedly through the window as the post-chaise progressed along the busy streets in the centre of the city, and, in consequence, didn't notice she was being regarded keenly.

'Lord bless you, miss! Don't you fret none over that,' Felcham advised. 'Lady Hetta don't concern herself nowadays over much at all, leastways, not as you'd notice. Grown dreadfully indolent since the master died, so she has. Might have been otherwise had she been blessed with children of her own. But it wasn't to be. Your visit will do her the world of good, I'm sure.'

Abbie withdrew her attention from the activity in the streets, as a slightly worrying thought occurred to her. 'I hope Godmama isn't offended if I don't recognise her. I doubt I shall, you know. I didn't recognise you.'

'That's not surprising, miss. You were no more than seven or eight when your parents brought you on that visit. But I would have known you anywhere,' Felcham assured her. 'You're blessed with your father's colouring, right enough, but you do bear a strong resemblance to your lovely mama.'

'Do I?' Abbie felt inordinately pleased to hear this. Over the years she had frequently studied the only likeness she possessed of her mother, a watercolour miniature set in a silver frame, and thought she could perceive a resemblance, even though she had frequently been told that she favoured the Grahams.

She sighed. 'I do not remember either of my parents at all well, Felcham,' she admitted. 'It was shortly after we paid that visit to Lord and Lady Penrose's home in Surrey that they went off to Italy.'

'Yes, miss, I well remember,' Felcham responded softly. 'Tragic, it was—both of them succumbing to the typhoid.' She favoured Abbie with yet another of those penetrating stares. 'But you've been happy enough in your grandfather's care, so I was told. The mistress always said as how your letters were always so cheerful.'

'Yes…yes, I have,' Abbie answered, quickly turning her head to stare out of the window once more, but not before she had noticed the contemplative expression take possession of her companion's sharp features this time.

Fortunately she wasn't forced to endure those dark eyes steadfastly turned in her direction for very long. Within a matter of a few minutes only, the post-chaise had pulled up outside a fashionable residence in Upper Camden Place, and she was soon afterwards being shown upstairs by an elderly housekeeper to a charming salon on the first floor.

The room's sole occupant, whose hand hovered over a box of chocolates, conveniently positioned on the table by her elbow, turned a pair of deceptively dreamy blue eyes in the direction of the door. A flicker of recognition swiftly followed, before she rose from the chair and moved with surprising agility for someone of ample proportions to clasp Abbie in a welcoming embrace.

'Here, let me look at you!' Lady Henrietta Penrose held her goddaughter at arm's length, the better to study the delicate features beneath the poke of what was undeniably a plain, unfashionable bonnet. 'Oh, yes! I would have recognised you anywhere, my dear.'

Having been starved of displays of affection for some considerable time, Abbie felt both moved and faintly embarrassed by the warmth of the welcome she was receiving from a lady who to all intents and purposes was a complete stranger.

'It was so kind of you to have me to stay, ma'am,' she said, after docilely allowing her godmother to draw her over to a chair. 'I'm very much looking forward to exploring the city.'

'And enjoying the entertainments Bath has to offer, too, I hope,' Lady Penrose responded, while she studied the equally unfashionable attire beneath the unprepossessing head wear. 'I wouldn't dream of trying to suggest, my dear, that we can compete with the pleasures to be found in the capital, but I'm sure we'll find plenty to amuse you while you're here.'

Abbie very much suspected that her godmother certainly enjoyed the easy pace of life in this once very fashionable watering place. Already she had detected a definite aura of lazy contentment about Lady Penrose, which gave her every reason to suppose that Felcham had been brutally honest when she had divulged that her mistress had become sublimely indolent in recent years. Yet, at the same time, Abbie felt equally certain that, although her god-

mother might eschew unnecessary physical exertion, her
brain was rarely inactive. Unless she was much mistaken,
behind that tranquil façade lurked a keen mind.

'I'm certain I'll have a lovely time, ma'am. But you
mustn't put yourself out on my account. I'm quite accustomed to living a quiet life, you know?'

The feigned look of surprise failed to disguise the resurgence of that perceptive gleam. 'Has hunting begun
to wane in popularity, then? You do surprise me! I had
foolishly supposed the Shires continued to attract those
sporting-mad young gentlemen in society.'

'They do, ma'am,' Abbie didn't hesitate to assure her.
'Grandpapa frequently entertains at Foxhunter Grange.
More often than not we have one or two of his wide circle
of friends staying at the house.'

'Indeed? Then you are accustomed to company and entertaining.' Once again Lady Penrose subjected her goddaughter to a gaze that was calmly assessing before her
attention turned to the young maidservant who had entered
the room, bearing a tray of refreshments.

After dispensing tea and encouraging her goddaughter
to sample the several delicacies provided, Lady Penrose
admitted that, although surprised to receive Colonel Graham's letter proposing the visit, she had been very much
looking forward to having her goddaughter residing under
her roof, and would be very reluctant to see her leave.

The speculative gleam that instantly sprang into violet
eyes immediately following this pronouncement did not
go unobserved. Consequently, the instant the servant returned to collect the tea tray, Lady Penrose instructed the
maid to show Abbie to her bedchamber and then to inform
Felcham that her mistress wished to see her without delay.

The instant her goddaughter had departed, she rose
from the chair and went across to the escritoire to take

out a certain letter. She had only just reminded herself of its contents when her personal maid entered.

'What's to do, Felchie?' she demanded without preamble.

If the loyal maid was surprised by the blunt enquiry, she certainly betrayed no sign of it as she quietly closed the door and moved further into the room. 'A mystery, my lady, wouldn't you say?'

Lady Penrose shook her head. 'It is quite beyond my understanding how such a lovely young woman, who is both charming and well mannered, should have attained the age of three-and-twenty and remained unmarried.'

'Perhaps she's content living with her grandfather,' Felcham suggested, but the lack of conviction with which she spoke was not lost on her mistress.

'But you didn't gain that impression.'

'No, my lady,' Felcham admitted. 'It's my belief that Miss Graham and her grandfather are not upon the best of terms at the present time. Naturally I didn't attempt to pry. But what I can tell you is that on the morning of our departure Colonel Graham left the house early, and Miss Abbie showed no inclination to await his return so that she might take her leave of him.'

'Could it be, perhaps, that she was reluctant to visit Bath, do you suppose?'

'I wouldn't have thought so, no,' Felcham assured her.

'No,' Lady Penrose agreed, 'and neither would I. She showed a deal of enthusiasm for the entertainments I have planned for her, and yet at the same time...'

She turned her attention once more to the letter. 'The Colonel writes that, if I should feel it necessary, I may undertake to purchase some new gowns for his granddaughter and forward any bills to him.' A pained expression took possession of her plump features. 'Her attire is positively

dowdy, more suitable for a servant. Are all her gowns so
plain and unfashionable? If so, it will not be a bill for one
or two dresses he'll be receiving.'

There was a suspicion of a twitch at one corner of Felcham's mouth. She knew well enough that her mistress,
although middle-aged, and sadly growing steadily more
portly with every passing year, still had an eye for fashion. 'Apart from one or two evening gowns, m'lady, there
wasn't much in her trunk of which you'd approve, although
it has to be said that her linen is of the finest.'

'Well, that's something, I suppose,' Lady Penrose was
obliged to concede, before she began to brush the Colonel's
letter meditatively back and forth across one of her chins.
'All the same, a trip to the fashionable shops in Milsom
Street tomorrow morning might prove beneficial.'

Surprisingly enough not only the weather, which overnight heralded the change from over a week of pleasantly
dry days to rain, made very much worse by a blustery
south-westerly breeze, but also her goddaughter's surprising lack of enthusiasm forced Lady Penrose to postpone
her shopping spree at least for the time being. Naturally
she was disappointed by Abbie's seeming indifference to
the idea of replenishing her wardrobe, and not just mildly
troubled too when her goddaughter declared that she had
no intention of turning herself into an advertisement for
the *Ladies Journal*, and that she had brought sufficient
clothing for her stay in Bath.

Yet that evening, when Abbie joined her in the hall,
just prior to their leaving for what Lady Penrose was hoping would be the first of many parties they would enjoy
together, she could find no fault with her goddaughter's
appearance. The dark-blue silk gown, though plain, was
clearly the creation of an excellent seamstress. Felcham had

been permitted to arrange the dusky locks in a more elaborate style for the occasion, and the string of pearls adorn-
ing the slender neck, with matching ear-drops, definitely
added to the overall air of refinement that her goddaughter
exuded. All in all, Lady Penrose was not displeased with
the display of quiet elegance, but wasn't prepared to admit
defeat quite yet in her desire to hear her goddaughter pro-
claimed one of the most fashionable young ladies in Bath.

'Thank heavens the rain has stopped!' she remarked
with relief, as they stepped outside to the waiting carriage.
'With luck we shall be able to visit the Pump Room tomorrow. I'm eager to make you known to all my friends,
though I expect there will be a good many at Agnes Fergusson's little do tonight.'

Abbie couldn't help smiling to herself. Already she had
discovered that her godmother was a sociable animal, enjoying the company of the wide circle of friends she had
made during the ten years she had resided in the city. As
most residents made visits on foot, and no one had been
willing, seemingly, to brave the elements, Lady Penrose
had appeared at a loss to know how to pass the time. Abbie,
on the other hand, hadn't allowed the lack of company to
detract from the enjoyment of her first full day in Bath. She
had grown accustomed over the years to filling her days,
and had found it no difficult matter to entertain herself.

'Do not concern yourself on my account, ma'am. I do not
grow bored with my own company, and am never at a loss
to keep myself occupied,' Abbie didn't hesitate to assure
her, and once again found herself receiving yet another of
those thoughtful glances to which she had been subjected
from time to time since her arrival in Bath. She couldn't
help wondering what was passing through her godmother's
fertile mind, and was not left pondering for long.

'I gain the distinct impression that you're accustomed

to being on your own a good deal. Do you not have many friends of your own?'

'I suppose I have suffered in recent years from a lack of female companionship, ma'am,' Abbie admitted, seeing no reason to conceal the truth. 'Most all the friends of my own age I made during the years I've lived with Grandpapa are either married now or have moved away from the area. But I'm upon good terms with the wives of Grandpapa's neighbours.'

'All of whom, I suspect, are somewhat older than yourself.'

'Yes, Godmama,' Abbie confirmed. 'But I must confess, in general, I prefer the company of older women.'

'Yes, I suppose you must, my dear. But then by your own admission you are accustomed to little else.' Lady Penrose was silent for a moment, before asking, 'And are there no eligible young gentlemen living in Leicestershire these days?'

Having little doubt now in which direction the conversation was heading, Abbie couldn't forbear a further smile. Surprisingly, she didn't resent her godmother's questions in the least. In fact, she would have been amazed if the matter of her continued single state hadn't been raised at some point during her stay. She couldn't help feeling, therefore, that making her own views clear on the subject of matrimony at this early stage would avoid misunderstandings in the future.

'We certainly see very many visiting the area, ma'am, and there are one or two eligible young gentlemen living nearby, including the local practitioner, who has become a particular friend of mine. But I have yet to meet a man with whom I could happily spend the rest of my life.'

'But then you've hardly been given the opportunity to do so, have you, my dear?' Lady Penrose wasn't slow to point out, shaking her head and appearing genuinely bewildered. 'I quite fail to understand why your grandfather waited until now before permitting you to stay with me. Since you attained the age of seventeen, I have written on numerous occasions, suggesting that you visit me in Bath.'

'I must confess I didn't know that you had, ma'am,' Abbie disclosed. 'You never mentioned anything in the letters you wrote to me.'

'No, child. I considered it only right and proper to attain your grandfather's consent first before broaching the subject with you. Needless to say, I wasn't successful.'

'No, you wouldn't have been,' Abbie acknowledged, having no difficulty in appreciating the reason why. 'Your revelations come as no real surprise to me, ma'am. Grandpapa would never risk my forming an attachment.'

Lady Penrose's expression changed from puzzlement to annoyance in a matter of seconds. 'You are not suggesting, I trust, that he is selfishly determined to keep you at Foxhunter Grange in order to bear him company in his declining years?'

'Oh, no, ma'am,' Abbie assured her. 'But he remains doggedly determined I shall marry the man he has always intended I should wed. Which, now I come to think about it, makes his acceptance of your kind invitation this time most strange.'

'Oh, no, my dear. It wasn't I who wrote to the Colonel,' Lady Penrose hastily revealed, 'but he who wrote to me, asking if I would kindly have you to stay for a few weeks. His letter came as something of a surprise, I must admit. Although, needless to say,' she added, noticing her goddaughter's frown of consternation, 'I was delighted to comply with his request. He was certain, you see, that you would far rather visit Bath than accompany him to the Scottish Highlands.'

Well, he wasn't wrong there, Abbie mused, before a puzzling thought suddenly occurred to her. Why, though, she wondered, had her grandfather gone to such trouble? If his intention had been merely to try to prevent a deeper friendship developing between her and the young doctor, then why hadn't he simply dragged her off to Scotland with him? No, something else had prompted his actions, she felt sure. But what?

The carriage drawing to a halt outside a fashionable dwelling on the outskirts of the city granted Abbie insufficient time to dwell on the conundrum, and she successfully thrust it to the back of her mind as she accompanied her godmother inside the house. Their hostess, stationed at the entrance to a large, tastefully decorated drawing-room, greeted her with real warmth, putting her instantly at her ease.

'Your friend is a charming woman,' Abbie remarked, as they moved away to allow some new arrivals to greet the hostess. 'She puts me in mind of one of Grandpapa's neighbours.'

'Yes, Agnes Fergusson is a dear soul. We've been friends for years. But you mustn't be offended if she makes a point throughout the evening of introducing you to eligible young men,' Lady Penrose warned. 'She enjoys playing the matchmaker. Understandable enough when you consider she successfully married off her five daughters without any trouble whatsoever.'

'I shan't be offended,' Abbie assured her, as they managed to find themselves two vacant chairs by the wall. 'But I hope she isn't upset when I prove to be her first failure.'

She gazed about the crowded room with interest, thereby missing the lines of concern momentarily creasing her godmother's forehead. 'Clearly your friend is a popular hostess, ma'am. If you consider this merely a small party, I should dearly like to know what—'

Curious to know what on earth could have induced her goddaughter to break off mid-sentence and her delicate features to freeze in an expression of stunned disbelief, Lady Penrose turned her head to discover a tall gentleman, accompanied by a woman of middle age and a girl of about seventeen, greeting her friend Agnes Fergusson.

She then turned back to her goddaughter, and was astonished to discover her delicate cheeks now drained of every vestige of colour. 'Why, my dear! Whatever is the matter? You've grown quite dreadfully pale.'

There was an ominous click as slender fingers tightened about a delicately painted chicken-skin fan.

'Damn him…! Damn him…! Damn him!'

Chapter Two

Only her godmother's voice, distinctly betraying concern, checked the progress of what amazingly might have become an all-consuming anger, and stopped Abbie from storming from the room. Even so, it was several moments before she could drag her gaze away from the source of her fury, and several more before she dared trust herself to ask the burning question at the forefront of her mind.

'Are you by any chance acquainted with the gentleman who is presently holding our hostess in conversation, ma'am?'

It was sufficient for Lady Penrose to cast a second brief glance only in the direction of the door. 'No, why do you ask? Do you know him?'

The response had been so prompt that Abbie didn't doubt the truth of the denial, and the suspicion that Lady Penrose might have been party to Colonel Augustus Graham's devious stratagems swiftly began to dwindle.

'Yes, ma'am, I know him,' she admitted, after watching the object of her displeasure steer his two female companions across the room towards a sandy-haired gentleman who, only moments before, had hailed him cheerfully.

'That is none other than my grandfather's godson, the man he is determined I should marry.'

Lady Penrose regarded the gentleman with far more interest this time, noting the easy grace of the long-striding gait, the superb breadth of shoulder, and that telltale aristocratic line of his profile. 'And you, my dear…? Is that your wish also?' she asked gently, and was surprised to witness an expression of hard determination take possession of Abbie's delicate features.

'Believe me when I tell you that the sun would rise in the west before I'd ever agree to wed Bartholomew Cavanagh.'

A moment's silence, then, 'Oh, I see.'

The murmured response drew a catlike smile to Abbie's lips. 'Yes, and I too begin to see just why my grandfather went to so much trouble to ensure that I would be safely ensconced in Bath at this time. He must have known Cavanagh would be here, and was therefore confident that we would run into each other at some point.'

That deceptively dreamy haze had disappeared completely from Lady Penrose's eyes. 'I sincerely trust you do not suspect that I am in your grandfather's confidence, and knew his intention from the first?'

Abbie's smile turned to one of warmth. 'No, ma'am, I do not think it,' she assured her. 'But I'm certain you must appreciate that it does make my remaining here a little awkward. I'm not so foolish as to suppose I can succeed in avoiding him entirely.'

'And you would, understandably, prefer to leave,' Lady Penrose responded, without attempting to argue the point, and was about to attract the attention of a passing footman in order to arrange for her carriage to be brought round to the door, when she felt the touch of a gently restraining hand on her arm.

In the years to come Abbie was to look back and appreciate fully that the decision made in that fraction of a second was to determine the course of her life. Naturally, at the time, she was blissfully unaware of the fact. All she was conscious of was a sense of shame. Her godmother had misunderstood, had surmised quite wrongly that she merely wished to leave the party, when in fact Abbie's real desire was to flee the city. Suddenly, though, she knew she could not, would not, run away like a frightened child from either the party or the city. She wouldn't allow her grandfather's obsession dictate the way she lived her life one moment longer!

'No, ma'am,' she countered, 'I do not wish to leave. I flatly refuse to allow Mr Cavanagh's presence to influence my behaviour in the least. I fully intend to enjoy all the pleasures Bath has to offer during my stay with you.'

'That's the spirit, child!' Lady Penrose positively beamed with approval before her expression once again grew thoughtful. 'Do you suppose your grandfather informed his godson of your proposed stay in Bath, and the reason for his presence in the city is to seek you out?'

Until that moment Abbie hadn't considered this as a possibility. 'I honestly couldn't say. But I strongly suspect that Grandfather must have known Bart intended visiting this place, and that was precisely why he made contact with you. I haven't set eyes upon Bart in six years, ma'am, not since the last time he visited Foxhunter Grange, just prior to his joining the army. We've never corresponded either, not a word, but he does write to Grandfather from time to time.'

Discovering this, Lady Penrose grew more pensive, and for a full minute stared in silence at the subject under discussion, her gaze once again revealing that behind the mantle of lazy good humour lurked a keenly perceptive mind, before voicing the opinion that his actions were hardly those of a gentleman whose interests were engaged. 'His years in the army, quite naturally, would necessitate long periods of separation. But there was nothing to prevent him writing to you. You might well discover he's experienced a change of heart, and that you are worrying for no purpose.'

Abbie's spontaneous shout of laughter induced several of those nearby to glance interestedly in her direction. 'Oh, I never supposed for a moment that that delicate organ was ever involved, my dear ma'am. No, he merely agreed to marry me to please Grandpapa.'

Lady Penrose looked far from convinced. 'Well, you might be right. But I must confess that to my mind he doesn't bear the appearance of a gentleman who would be easily coerced into actions of which he didn't approve. And who, by the by, are the two females in his party?'

Abbie had been wondering about this herself. 'I've never set eyes upon either of them before, so I cannot be certain. But I suspect the girl, who does bear a resemblance to Bart, at least in colouring, might well be his half-sister, and the older female his stepmother.'

'If you are right, then I should imagine he's here as their escort, and not for the purpose of seeking you out. Furthermore, the gentleman who is at present engaging the party in conversation is Agnes Fergusson's son, Giles. He too was in the army, and injured at Waterloo, which has left the poor boy with a sad limp. Evidently they are friends. So it is not unreasonable to suppose that Mr Cavanagh is here at Giles's invitation.'

Abbie was given no time to dwell on this very real possibility, for the musicians hired for the evening struck up a chord to announce the commencement of dancing, and a

young gentleman suddenly appeared before her, requesting her as his partner.

It was on the tip of her tongue to utter a polite refusal,
but when it became clear that the young man was none
other than a son of another of her godmother's closest
friends Abbie, not wishing to cause offence, thought better of it, even though she knew that by joining the set she
was in the gravest danger of drawing attention to herself
by crossing a certain tall gentleman's field of vision.

The prediction turned out to be all too accurate. The
steps of the dance took her and her partner past the spot
where Bartholomew Cavanagh and his party remained in
conversation with Giles Fergusson, and all at once Abbie
sensed she was being regarded with keen interest. She
succeeded in concentrating on the steps of the dance and
her partner for a further full half-minute before curiosity
overcame common sense, and she turned her head to discover a pair of intelligent dark eyes, set in a ruggedly attractive face, firmly fixed in her direction.

Prompted by some imp of mischief, she chose to acknowledge him by the merest nod of her head, the result of
which sent dark, masculine brows rising sharply in combined recognition and surprise, a definite indication that
he hadn't expected to discover her in Bath.

Consequently she was not unduly astonished, when the
set had drawn to a close, and her partner had returned her
to her godmother's side, to discover Bart making his way
purposefully across the room towards her. Nor was she
unduly taken aback when he at last stood before her and
the first words she had heard him utter in six long years
was his surprise at discovering her here.

'Yes, I must admit to having been—er—somewhat astonished to see you enter the room, Mr Cavanagh,' she
divulged, before introducing him to her godmother who,

if the mischievous glint in her eyes was any indication, had derived no little amusement out of the gross understatement.

How Abbie wished she too could experience just a modicum of the same! The truth of the matter was, though, she very much resented having to acknowledge a person whom she had held in utter contempt for half a decade and more, and could only hope she could somehow manage to conceal the fact for the time good manners forced her to converse with him.

'The Colonel didn't mention you'd be in this part of the world when he wrote to me a few weeks ago, Abbie,' he openly admitted, turning back to her, his dark eyes narrowing slightly as he detected the slight stiffening in her perfectly proportioned slender frame at his free use of her given name.

'He failed to mention you would be, come to that, Mr Cavanagh,' she returned with icy politeness.

'No?' Those expressive dark brows rose again. 'How very odd! I feel sure I informed him I would be unable to join him in Scotland as I would be escorting my sister here this spring.' He studied her in silence for a moment, his gaze penetrating, as though striving to read her inmost thoughts. 'Would you be so kind as to allow me to make you known to my sister and stepmother, Miss Graham? They have heard me speak of you often in the past, and would dearly like to make your acquaintance.'

As she considered it would have been exceedingly churlish to refuse, she acquiesced, and within a short space of time was very glad she had, for Miss Kitty Cavanagh proved to be a very likeable and vivacious seventeen-year-old girl, whose unaffected manner Abbie found refreshingly candid, even if some of her remarks were a little disconcerting.

'I suppose, Miss Graham, at your age you must have enjoyed lots and lots of Seasons,' Kitty commented, after Abbie, graciously offering her chair to Mrs Cavanagh, came to stand beside her.

'Which is tantamount to suggesting that you consider Miss Graham at her last prayers, you outrageous little baggage!' her brother scolded, thereby earning himself a speaking glance from eyes of as dark a hue as his own. 'When will you learn to put a guard on that unruly tongue of yours?'

He turned to Abbie who, not in the least offended, was doing her utmost not to laugh. 'You must allow me to apologise on my tactless sister's behalf. One of her many faults, I'm afraid, is a tendency to speak without thinking.'

'I wasn't meaning to be rude,' his sister assured him defensively. 'I think Miss Graham is very pretty, don't you?'

Abbie hardly knew where to look. She could feel the heat stealing into her cheeks, and suspected the tall man beside her was deriving no little enjoyment out of her embarrassment.

'Exceedingly,' he agreed, with a suspicion of a twitch at one corner of his shapely mouth. 'But then I have always considered her so.' He smiled in earnest as deep blue eyes favoured him with a look of mingled suspicion and astonishment. 'Her manners too, as I recall, were always above reproach. Which, I fear, is more than I shall ever be able to say about yours.'

Pulling herself together with an effort, Abbie decided that it was time to intervene before Miss Kitty Cavanagh's feathers were totally ruffled by her elder brother's strictures. Evidently the siblings had more in common than their colouring. Even so, she didn't suppose for a moment that either would find it in the least flattering to be informed that there was a certain similarity in their characters too.

'I have never been privileged to enjoy a Season in town, Miss Cavanagh. Indeed, this is the first time I've ever travelled any real distance from my grandfather's home in a very long time.'

Receiving no response, Abbie gazed from brother to sister, unsure which of them seemed more surprised by the admission. She thought she also detected what might well have been a hint of concern in Bart's expression before he asked bluntly, 'Was that entirely through choice, Miss Graham?'

Although having already decided that he too did not boggle at plain speaking, Abbie was somewhat taken aback by the directness of the question, and unsure just how to answer.

The truth of the matter was, of course, that her grandfather had never encouraged her to travel far from home, nor indeed socialise to any great extent, simply because he had feared she just might cross the path of a gentleman whom she would desire to marry. But she could hardly reveal to Bart that his godfather had done everything humanly possible to shield her from the attentions of eligible bachelors in the belief that one day she would fulfil his fondest hope. The last thing in the world she wanted was for Bart to misunderstand, to suppose that she had been happy to comply with her grandfather's wishes. Worse still, she would hate for him to think that she regretted her decision not to become engaged six years before, and had remained single in the hope he might repeat his offer of marriage.

'I have been content enough, sir.' Uncertain whether he believed her, she added, 'And as I've never evinced the least desire to relinquish my single state, a Season in town would have been a needless expense. However, no longer being in my first flush of youth, as it were, I think it highly unlikely I'd be considered a suitable choice for any young bachelor set on matrimony, and so experienced no reluctance whatsoever in visiting Bath.'

'If you suppose that, my girl,' Bart countered bluntly, 'you must be all about in your head!'

It wasn't so much the irritation easily discernible in the deep voice that surprised Abbie as the look of annoyance she couldn't fail to perceive before he turned away to converse with Lady Penrose. Seemingly, Kitty noticed it too, for she stared thoughtfully at her brother's broad back for several moments before her dark eyes, brightened by a speculative gleam, once again turned in Abbie's direction. Her lips parted, but whatever remark she had been about to utter was held in check, and she merely continued to regard Abbie in a considering way.

Fortunately Abbie was not forced to endure having both her features and figure scrutinised for any slight flaw for very long. Mrs Cavanagh, evidently feeling that it was time to circulate, attracted her daughter's attention, and soon afterwards they slipped quietly away to mingle with the other guests. Which, thankfully, induced their escort to accompany them, and left Abbie free to enjoy the remainder of what turned out to be, surprisingly enough, a most pleasurable evening.

The following morning, as she bore her godmother company for the first meal of the day, Abbie was once again plagued not so much by misgivings over her stay in Bath as a resurgence of resentment towards her grandsire over the devious methods he had adopted to attain his ends.

At least, though, she mused, she couldn't lay any blame squarely on Bartholomew Cavanagh's broad shoulders. She might not hold him in the highest esteem, and she could never envisage her opinion of him changing to any significant degree, but she was forced to own that he was no dissembler. There wasn't the remotest doubt in her mind that he had been as much surprised by her presence at the Fergussons' party as she had been by his. Furthermore, to do him justice, apart from that one occasion when he had taken the trouble to come across to speak with her, and make her known to his female relations, he had paid her no attention whatsoever, not even once asking her to dance.

Lady Penrose, reaching for a third buttered roll, cast her silent companion a furtive glance. Although she would have been the first to acknowledge that she didn't know her goddaughter at all well, she wouldn't have supposed for a moment that she was a young woman prone to fits of the sullens. Yet this morning Abbie certainly seemed slightly subdued, and there was definitely a marked degree of dissatisfaction in her expression. What could be troubling her? she wondered. Surely she wasn't worrying unnecessarily over Mr Cavanagh's presence in Bath? There was only one way to find out for certain.

Striking dark blue eyes met hers across the table a moment after she had voiced her query. 'And really, my dear, I do not feel you need concern yourself unduly,' Lady Penrose went on, striving to reassure. 'You are three-and-twenty, after all. No one can force you to form an alliance with a gentleman, if you have no wish to do so.'

'True. But my grandfather retains the hope that he can. We didn't part upon the best of terms,' Abbie at last revealed, an unmistakable note of regret in her voice. 'Also, he could not have made it clearer to me that, if I married against his wishes, he would disinherit me.'

Lady Penrose sat quietly digesting what she had learned, experiencing a swell of varying emotions. Colonel Graham, a gentleman she had met on two occasions only in the past, was swiftly figuring in her thoughts as a cold-hearted brute who betrayed scant concern for the feelings of others, least of all his granddaughter's. Alongside this ever-swelling animosity, and a strong determination to thwart the Colonel, was a sense of shame and deep regret for never having taken the trouble to visit the daughter of the woman who had once been her closest friend. It was true that she had not wished to interfere in Abbie's upbringing, and had believed that her goddaughter had been happy living with her grandfather. Sadly, she was fast coming to the conclusion that this had not been the case, and was determined to make amends for her neglect in the past in any way she could.

But first there was much she needed to discover, not least of which was why her goddaughter was so set against marrying Bartholomew Cavanagh, for she was forced silently to own that he had left her with a very favourable impression after their first meeting.

'And are you prepared to allow your grandfather's threat to influence you in any way?' she asked gently.

'Certainly not!' The conviction in Abbie's voice was unequivocal, as was the determined set to the softly rounded chin. 'If ever I do marry, it will be to a man of my own choosing.'

Secretly impressed by this display of fortitude, Lady Penrose didn't hesitate to voice the desire to help in any way she could, but was a little surprised by the prompt acceptance of the offer.

'You see, ma'am, I had already decided, before I left Foxhunter Grange, that it would be a mistake to return to live with Grandfather,' Abbie went on to confess. 'If I thought for a moment he might relent…might accept that I have no desire to marry his godson…' She shook her head. 'His arranging for me to visit you at a time when he knew Bart would be here is proof enough that he is as determined as ever.'

Lady Penrose reached across the table. 'Have you been so very unhappy, my child?'

Abbie stared down at the plump fingers covering her hand. 'I haven't been wholly content in recent years, no,' she admitted with total honesty, and was surprised to hear her godmother give vent to a very unladylike snort.

'I'm beginning to take that grandfather of yours in strong dislike.'

'Oh, no. You mustn't do that, ma'am,' Abbie countered, surprising herself somewhat by so quickly coming to his defence. 'Believe me when I tell you that he couldn't have been kinder to me when first I went to live with him.'

Her expression grew markedly softer as her mind's eye conjured up images from the past. 'He went out of his way to spend a deal of time with me, even though he went to the expense of engaging a governess to educate and take care of me. He taught me to ride, to fish, and even took the trouble to teach me how to handle a pistol. I spent many, many happy hours in his company. It was only after I refused to marry Bart that his attitude towards me changed, and he grew remote. And to a certain extent I can understand his behaviour, and make allowances,' she went on to admit, betraying a depth of tolerance and understanding in her nature that Lady Penrose could not help but admire. 'You see, Bart possesses many characteristics Grandpapa most respects in a man. The fact that he's a bruising rider and chose to join our brave men out in the Peninsula would have been enough for the Colonel to place him on a pedestal. But his admiration was won long before Bart joined the army. In his eyes Bart can do no wrong.'

'But you, my dear, evidently do not hold him in such high regard?' Lady Penrose prompted, and saw at once a shuttered look take possession of her goddaughter's features before Abbie rose to her feet and went to stand by the window.

'No, ma'am I do not,' she admitted, her voice cold and uncompromising, a clear indication to Lady Penrose that to probe further in an attempt to uncover what lay at the root of the dislike would be a grave mistake at this juncture, but even so she could not resist asking.

'Was there ever anything official between you, or an understanding that you would one day wed?'

'Not as far as I was concerned,' Abbie answered, after a lengthy silence, 'although it wouldn't surprise me to discover that Grandpapa had considered the possibility from when we were children.'

'Have you always held Mr Cavanagh in dislike, child?' Lady Penrose asked, after a further lengthy silence.

'Dislike?' Abbie echoed, frowning slightly as she gave the matter some thought. 'No, I cannot say that I ever disliked him. To be honest, though, I did resent his presence. Grandfather always paid me far less attention whenever Bart was staying with us. And, of course, the seven years' difference in our ages meant that we had little in common. So, as you can imagine, the suggestion that we should marry came as…as something of a shock.'

'Yes, I can appreciate that it must have done,' Lady Penrose murmured, while thinking, But that most definitely wasn't the reason why you refused him.

Intrigued though she was, she once again succeeded in curbing her curiosity for the time being, and merely said, 'That, however, is all in the past, and it is your future that must concern us.'

'Yes, yes,' Abbie readily agreed, the shadow of an unpleasant memory fading from her mind. 'And you could be of immeasurable help by assisting me to acquire a position as a governess or companion, whereby I'll be able to support myself until I attain the age of five-and-twenty and come into the inheritance left to me by my mother.'

In stunned silence Lady Penrose watched her goddaughter return to the table. 'You must be all about in your head, child, if you imagine I'd contemplate ever doing such a thing,' she managed at last. 'I appreciate why you've no desire to return to your grandfather's house. Very understandable, if I may say so. But the solution to your problem is before you! You will remain here with me.'

'Oh, but—'

'Save your breath, child,' Lady Penrose interrupted, thereby revealing a surprisingly stubborn side to her nature. 'I refuse to be deprived of this golden opportunity to salve my conscience and make amends for my shocking neglect over the years. No, no,' she added, when Abbie attempted to protest again. 'My mind is made up. And what pleasure I shall derive too in making you the toast of Bath!'

Although she experienced no desire whatsoever to turn herself into a fashion plate, Abbie made no attempt to swim against the tide of her godmother's enthusiasm when, later that morning, they visited the premises of the female who was generally considered Bath's foremost modiste.

Believing there would be far less competition, Madame Dupont, alias Molly Blunt, had chosen Bath in preference to London to set herself up in business. Her judgement had not proved faulty, and she had swiftly earned a reputation for fine workmanship and attention to detail.

Lady Penrose had been one of her first customers, and had remained loyal. Consequently Madame was only too happy to set aside current orders to oblige such a valued client; and doubly so when she set eyes on the perfect figure and wonderful colouring of the young woman whom she was being asked to dress in style, even going so far as to offer a walking dress with matching accessories, which had been ordered by a customer who had been annoyingly slow in settling her bills.

The outfit proved to be almost a perfect fit, and by the time Abbie and her godmother had pored over fashion plates and selected materials for new gowns, the slight adjustments had been completed by one of Madame's employees, and Abbie was able to leave the shop dressed, for the first time in her life, in the height of fashion.

'One can always rely on Molly's judgement,' Lady Penrose remarked, after informing her coachman to return to Upper Camden Place, as she intended to continue to the Pump Room on foot. 'That outfit is most becoming. And the colour's so right for you!'

Although she had always paid more attention to neatness than style, Abbie was secretly pleased with her new attire, but could not resist commenting on the shocking price.

'Don't give it another thought, child,' Lady Penrose adjured her. 'I most certainly shan't. And I'll derive a deal of satisfaction in forwarding the bills to your grandfather. My one regret is that I shan't be there to see his expression when he is obliged to dig deep into his pockets not for just one or two dresses, but for a whole new wardrobe of clothes. Serves the old curmudgeon right!'

Abbie, unable to suppress a gurgle of laughter at this wicked sentiment, entered the famous Pump Room in her godmother's wake. Several pairs of eyes, betraying either admiration or envy, or a mixture of both, were turned in her direction, including a pair of alert brown ones, which Lady Penrose at least had noticed had been firmly fixed in her goddaughter's direction on several occasions throughout the previous evening.

Abbie, however, remained as ignorant of Bart's presence as she had been over his watchfulness at the party, until she took her first sip of the famous waters, and a deep masculine rumble swiftly followed her shuddering grimace.

'I would have expected you to have had more sense than to sample the wretched stuff, my girl,' he told her bluntly, his dark eyes warmed by amusement.

'Why, Mr Cavanagh, you turn up in the most unlikely places!' she returned, hoping she had sounded more composed than she was in fact feeling at his unexpected appearance. 'I would have thought a good gallop across the Downs would have been more to your taste than hobnobbing here in what I'm reliably informed is a veritable hotbed of gossip.'

'You're right. I would much prefer to be anywhere but in this insipid place,' he freely acknowledged. 'But needs must when the devil drives.'

She took a moment to study him closely, and could detect no fault with his appearance. Clearly his apparel had been chosen for comfort rather than style. Although undoubtedly some would consider his neckcloth too plainly arranged, his waistcoat downright unimaginative and his coat too loosely fitting to display a pair of fine shoulders to advantage, no one could fail to appreciate that he was a wealthy country gentleman whose healthy tan and muscular physique betrayed a predilection for outdoor pursuits.

So what on earth had induced him to visit Bath, where sedate strolls, polite conversation and quiet dinner parties were the preferred pastimes? Surely a sporting-mad gentleman, who thought nothing of riding at a neck-or-nothing pace, would find little to amuse him in Bath's genteel society?

'I wouldn't imagine your health has prompted your visit to this city, sir,' she remarked, drawing his attention away from the blue ribbon tied in a coquettish bow beneath her chin. 'So I cannot help wondering what particular devil has been the driving force bringing you here?'

His expression, which had betrayed mild approval, changed in an instant as he cast an exasperated glance at some spot over his right shoulder. 'My pestilential young sister is the demon that prompted my actions, ma'am. My father saw fit to burden me with shared guardianship with Eugenie, who is far too indulgent where her daughter is concerned.'

'Oh, dear,' Abbie responded unsteadily, finding the mere thought that Bartholomew Cavanagh found his sister something of a trial wickedly satisfying. 'She is somewhat troublesome on occasions then, sir?'

'Not if she knows what's good for her,' he returned, with a certain grim satisfaction.

'My, my! How fearsome you sound!' She peered up at him through what he considered extraordinary long black lashes. 'I'm very glad you're not my brother.'

'Believe me, Miss Graham, you couldn't possibly be more pleased than I that I am not,' he purred silkily, a spontaneous smile instantly softening the harsh contours of his face, and bringing a rush of colour to her own.

Fortunately she was spared the necessity of formulating some response by the unexpected arrival of his particular demon, who appeared before them with the information that Giles Fergusson had arrived with his mother, and was wishful for a quiet word.

Bart might not have been best pleased to have what Abbie considered had degenerated into a rather embarrassing tête-à-tête brought to an abrupt end, but she most definitely was and bestowed a dazzling smile upon her unwitting rescuer.

'I'm so glad to see you here this morning,' Kitty an-

nounced by way of a greeting. 'You see, I'm in desperate
need of help, and could think of no one else to turn to, and
have been racking my brains to think of some way of seeing you in private.'

Although the crowded Pump Room was hardly the ideal
place to achieve this objective, Abbie, intrigued, obliged
her young companion by moving over to one of the windows, where fewer persons were congregating.

'And how may I be of service to you, Miss Cavanagh?'
she prompted, when Kitty regarded her much as she had
done the previous night: assessingly, with head on one side.

'Oh, might we not be friends? I do so hate unnecessary formality, don't you? May I not address you by your
given name?' Kitty asked, looking so ridiculously young
and hopeful that Abbie found herself automatically com-
plying with the request. 'Oh, I'm so glad,' Kitty went on
in a rush. 'I really wouldn't feel at all comfortable asking
for your help otherwise.'

Abbie began to experience misgivings. 'I should dearly
like for you to look upon me as a friend,' she reiterated.
'But if something is genuinely troubling you, wouldn't it
be better to confide in your mother or brother?'

'Good heavens, no!' Kitty looked appalled at the mere
thought. 'Mama defers to Bart's judgement in most everything. And as he's the very one causing me so much
bother, I can hardly approach him, now can I?'

Abbie was forced to agree with this, but steadfastly refused to concede more until she knew the precise nature
of the problem besetting this engaging young woman, and
just why Kitty might suppose that she could be of assistance. She was not left in ignorance for long.

'I want you to help me find Bart a wife.'

Abbie received this intelligence in stunned silence, cer-

tain that she must surely have misheard. 'I…beg…your…
pardon?'

Something in her tone must have alerted Kitty to the
very real possibility that she was on the point of losing a
worthy ally, for her expression changed dramatically from
eager anticipation to that of a half-starved waif pleading
for a crust.

'You will help me, won't you?'

'Assuredly not!' Abbie answered, completely unmoved
by the look of helpless appeal. 'I would never serve one
of my sex such a bad turn by bringing her to the notice of
your brother!'

It was out before she realised what she was saying and,
more importantly, what she was revealing. Sadly, it was already too late, for Kitty, after a moment's stunned silence,
was already asking that all-important question.

'No, of course I don't dislike him.' Even to her own ears
the assurance sounded highly unconvincing, so Abbie felt
obliged to add, 'But we're hardly what one might term
close friends.'

'But you've known each other for years,' Kitty pointed
out. 'And I know Bart thinks highly of you.'

Although the disclosure came as something of a shock,
Abbie recovered in an instant. 'Be that as it may, I feel
certain he wouldn't welcome interference from me, most
especially in such a delicate matter. Besides, your brother
is more than capable of making his own choice of a suitable wife.'

'He already has,' Kitty astounded her by divulging. 'At
least, he's well and truly smitten. I can tell.'

'In that case, Kitty, I do not perfectly understand why
you should feel the need of my help,' Abbie responded,
unable to suppress a frown of disapproval over her companion's indelicate choice of language.

'Because I want to make sure he comes up to scratch. We are here only until the middle of July. It might be some time before Bart can see her again, and anything might happen in the meantime. She might meet someone else.'

Abbie's frowned again at this. 'Are you sure the girl's feelings are engaged? Who, by the way, is the unfortunate… I mean, who is the young lady who has found favour with your brother?'

For several seconds Kitty appeared to find the toes of her shoes of immense interest, before she raised her head to stare rather sheepishly in the direction of the door. Then her eyes widened in excitement, as though she had been assailed by a brilliant idea.

'Why, she has just this moment walked in. And look, Bart is approaching her!'

Abbie turned her head in time to see Kitty's brother bow with lazy grace over a dainty hand. 'Was I not introduced to that young woman at the party last night?'

'Very possibly, as she was there,' Kitty confirmed. 'Her name is Caroline Whitham. She's with her brother Stephen. She's terribly shy. I wager she's blushing to the roots of her hair at this very moment, poor thing.'

She turned back to discover Abbie still studying the object of Bart's attentions. 'Oh, you will assist me, won't you? We cannot talk here, but if you could meet me in Sydney Gardens this afternoon, I'm sure we could come up with some schemes to bring them together as much as possible. I'm certain Miss Whitham mentioned that she too walks in the gardens most every afternoon, weather permitting, so it would be a simple matter to approach her if we should hit upon some idea.'

She received no response and, undeterred, added, 'You cannot know what it's like to have a brother like Bart who always thinks he knows best. I love him dearly, but he can be so overbearing on occasions, forever correcting and scolding and telling one what one may or may not do. But if Bart were to marry, all my troubles would be over. He'd be far too busy looking after his wife to pay much attention to me.'

With an arresting look in her eyes, Abbie turned to stare sightlessly out of the window. If Bart were to marry all my troubles would be over, she echoed silently.

Chapter Three

'Whitham's sister is a pretty little thing,' Giles Fergusson commented as his friend rejoined him.

Nodding in agreement, Bart watched the young officer who had served under him out in the Peninsula escorting his sibling to that area where glasses of the famous waters were being dispensed. 'Young Whitham is to be envied. His sister's behaviour, from what I've observed, is above reproach. Which,' he added, his brow darkening, as he transferred his gaze to a certain spot by the windows, 'is more than I'll ever be able to say about my own.'

Following the direction of his friend's disapproving gaze, Giles smiled indulgently. 'To some extent she reminds me of my youngest sister. Kitty's merely high-spirited. She'll calm down in a year or two.'

This assurance did little to console Bart. 'Perhaps. But she's more than capable of wreaking a deal of havoc before then.' His brow lifted slightly. 'Although I've absolutely no objection to her forming a friendship in that quarter.'

Once again Giles glanced across the room, only this time to study Kitty's companion. 'Ah, yes! I recall you mentioning last night that you're acquainted with Miss Graham. I spoke with her briefly myself at the party.

Struck me as a very sensible young woman, as well as being immensely pleasing on the eye. If her reason for visiting Bath is to form a suitable alliance, I cannot envisage there'll be much difficulty.'

Receiving no response, Giles returned his attention to his friend to discover dark brows drawn together in a severer frown than before. 'Evidently you don't agree.'

'Oh, no, it isn't that,' Bart assured him. 'I'm not altogether sure, though, just why she's retained her single state for so long.'

'Perhaps the thought of marriage doesn't appeal to her.'

If possible, Bart's frown grew more pronounced. 'The thought of marrying me certainly did not.'

Giles was astonished, and made no attempt to conceal the fact. 'Good gad! I thought I knew most everything about you, old fellow, but I never knew you'd been tempted into parson's mousetrap.'

'My godfather suggested the match. Thank the Lord Abbie had the good sense to refuse! We were both far too young.'

'And now?' Giles prompted when Bart seemed about to relapse into a thoughtful silence.

'Now…? Well, let us just say I've sown my wild oats. I feel ready to settle down.'

Giles pursed his lips together in a silent whistle. 'Well, well, well! Sits the wind in that quarter, eh?'

Bart chose not to comment and merely watched his sister's progress as she came across the room towards them, with what he considered to be a wickedly satisfied expression on her face. He was instantly on his guard.

'What mischief are you brewing, brat?' he demanded, when at last she reached his side. 'I know that look of old.'

She favoured him with an angry scowl, equal to his own, before transferring her attention to his far more personable companion, a gentleman whom she had adored since childhood. 'I cannot imagine why Bart should always suppose I'm plotting mischief. Anyone would imagine I was still seven years old.'

'I wish you were, I'd know how to deal with you,' was her brother's muttered response, the result of which earned him a further darkling look.

'I wager Giles was never so beastly to his sisters as you are to me.'

Bart wisely refrained from teasing her further, and merely suggested that, as he had one or two letters he wished to write before nuncheon, they find her mother and return to the house. Kitty's obliging him without demur surprised him somewhat, for she was a sociable little creature who, in general, much preferred to be in company than sit quietly indoors occupying herself. The uneasy feeling that she was being accommodating for a very good reason crossed his mind.

'You appear in remarkably good spirits today, Kitty,' he said, when she began humming a popular tune as they set off on foot in the direction of the house that he had rented for the duration of their stay.

'I'm enjoying myself here,' she admitted. 'I know I wished for a Season in London and was upset when you flatly refused to countenance such a venture in your usual highhanded fashion. But I've decided that Bath isn't so dull, after all. I'm beginning to get to know some very interesting people.'

'Yes, I noticed you speaking with Miss Graham, Kitty,' her mother put in. 'A very charming young woman, I thought. I wonder…do you think it's too late to send her and Lady Penrose invitations to our party next week, Bart?' she added. 'You wouldn't object, I trust?'

'I cannot imagine why you might suppose I'd not approve, Eugenie,' he returned, hoping he hadn't sounded impatient, but very much fearing from her suddenly crest-fallen expression that he had.

Falling back a pace in order to allow mother and daughter to walk together, he took himself silently to task over his unnecessary brusqueness. It couldn't be denied, though, that he found himself becoming increasingly irritated by his stepmother's insistence on seeking his approval over the most trivial matters. All the same, he was forced to acknowledge that perhaps his own behaviour over the years had been much to blame for this.

He had been close to his own mother, touchingly so, and her death, when he had been eleven years old, had been a bitter blow from which it had taken him considerable time to recover. His relationship with his father had been reasonably good too until his sire, without warning, had upped and married the local vicar's eldest daughter.

Kitty's arrival the following year hadn't improved the situation one iota. Instead of one interloper with whom he must share his father's affections, there had been two. Consequently he hadn't hesitated to seek the attention he had so selfishly desired by spending many of his school holidays with his godfather, a gentleman who had been only too happy to indulge him in his preference for outdoor pursuits.

Undeniably he had grown into a self-seeking young man who had cared for naught but the pursuit of his own pleasures. After leaving Cambridge, he had spent much of his time in London, enjoying the many pleasures the capital had to offer. With hindsight he now realised he may well have continued down that ruinous path, where gambling, drinking and womanising occupied much of his time, if a sudden whim, fostered by his godfather, to join his many friends fighting out in the Peninsula, had not overtaken him.

His years in the army had, he believed, improved his nature. He would never attempt to suggest that he hadn't now a flaw in his character. Far from it, in fact! But at least he'd learned to consider the feelings of others and not attempt to shirk his responsibilities.

He focused his gaze once again on the elder female walking just a few feet ahead. It was far too late now for him to forge a closer relationship with his stepmother, though God only knew the poor woman had done everything within her power over the years to create a bond between them by showing a depth of understanding towards him which he ill deserved. Nor had he any intention of becoming a hypocrite by attempting to display a deep affection that he had never felt towards her. But it wouldn't hurt to acknowledge that she had maintained high standards in the running of the household that was now legally his, and ensure she knew that he no longer selfishly resented her presence under his roof.

'I'm very much looking forward to our party next week, Eugenie,' he assured her, as they arrived at their rented accommodation. 'Apart from those few guests I've insisted upon inviting, I'm happy to leave all the arrangements to you. You're an excellent hostess, and I've every confidence the evening will be a resounding success.'

Leaving his stepmother glowing quite pink with pleasure at the unexpected praise, and his half-sister looking a mite surprised too, he parted company with them in the hall, taking himself into the library, with every intention of responding to the letters he'd received earlier in the day. He had made excellent inroads into his correspondence, when he was interrupted in his task by the unexpected arrival of his sister.

For once in her life she betrayed slight diffidence as she approached the desk. 'I'm sorry to disturb you, Bart, only I was wondering whether I might ask a favour of you?'

As he had never observed the least shyness in her character before, he was immediately on his guard. 'You can always ask, Kitty.'

'Well, I was just wondering, if you're not otherwise engaged, that is, whether you would accompany me out for a walk after nuncheon?'

Had she not seemed reluctant to meet his gaze, as she repositioned, quite unnecessarily in his opinion, the bottles in the standish, he might not have considered the request in any way out of the ordinary. 'Why this sudden desire for my company, minx? Why not take the air with your mother?'

'Oh, Bart! You know Mama is no great walker. Besides, she prefers to rest in the afternoons. It is such a nice day, I thought we might visit Sydney Gardens. I've been told by several people that it's very pretty there, and I don't want to take my maid. She dawdles so.'

'Very well,' he relented, albeit against his better judgement. 'Providing you leave me in peace for the time being, I'll escort you.'

His prompt acquiescence earned him a sisterly peck on one cheek and a brief, spontaneous hug. His eyes narrowed as he watched her skip from the room, looking very well pleased with herself. Yes, she was definitely up to something, he decided, already regretting pandering to her whims.

Abbie herself was of a similar mind when she entered the popular gardens midway through the afternoon. Before the suggestion had been made, she had never once considered that Bart's marrying might be the solution to all her own problems. She couldn't deny she still felt extremely angry over her grandfather's devious schemes in getting her safely established in Bath at a time when he was aware his godson would be there. She couldn't deny either that she remained deeply hurt over the Colonel's attitude towards her in recent years. Even so, that didn't alter the fact that she still loved him dearly, still treasured those wonderful memories of their early years together, when he couldn't possibly have done more to make her happy, after the loss of her parents.

She glanced at the young parlourmaid who had been willing to accompany her out on such a fine afternoon. Given the choice, she was forced to own she would far rather return to Foxhunter Grange than remain in Bath, where she felt sure that, once the charm of novelty had begun to wane, the city's petty restrictions where young, unmarried females were concerned would soon begin to irk her unbearably, and she would then crave those extra freedoms to be had by living in the country.

Yet, was she prepared to abandon her principles and interfere in someone else's life in an attempt to attain her own ends? Misgivings once again began to assail her. She might not know Bart very well, but even so she felt certain he wouldn't appreciate anyone meddling in his personal concerns. Furthermore, would she ever be able to reconcile it with her conscience if she was to aid Kitty in her determination to see her brother safely wedded? Was she really capable of condemning some poor, unfortunate girl to a life tied to that dissolute rake?

'Why, what a delightful surprise running in to you again, Miss Graham!'

Startled out of her guilty musings by that familiar, deep voice, Abbie stopped dead in her tracks. Had she observed Bart and his sister approaching, she wouldn't have hesitated to take immediate action in order to avoid the encounter. As it was, she had little choice but to appear pleased to see them. Which was no difficult task where Kitty was concerned, even though she had almost made up her mind not to become involved in the girl's match-making stratagems.

'Indeed, it is a surprise, sir,' she was able to say with total sincerity, for she hadn't expected Kitty to be escorted by her brother. 'Of course I've been aware of your penchant for outdoor activities for some considerable time, but I hadn't realised that strolling in pleasure gardens numbered among them.'

A distinctly challenging gleam brightened his eyes. 'Ahh, but, Miss Graham, you must remember that you do not know me very well…at least, not yet. But that can easily be remedied. I left Eugenie in the process of sending you and your godmother belated invitations to our party next week. I hope you'll delight us all by accepting.'

'Oh, do say you'll come!' Kitty put in, when Abbie hesitated, unwilling to commit herself. 'I'm sure you'll enjoy it enormously.'

'I'm certain I should too,' Abbie agreed. 'But I simply cannot accept without first consulting Lady Penrose. She may have made prior arrangements.'

'Naturally you cannot obligate yourself now, Miss Graham,' Bart readily concurred, before his precocious sister could attempt to force the issue. 'But at least you can delight us both by remaining with us to enjoy these gardens on such a pleasant afternoon.'

Abbie glanced at the young maid who had accompanied her out, wondering whether she could possibly make her presence the excuse to decline the invitation by insisting the servant return to the house in order to fulfil her other duties.

Bart, however, proved too perceptive, reading her thoughts with uncanny accuracy. 'Be assured my sister and I shall see you safely returned to Lady Penrose, so you no longer require the services of the maid.'

The challenging look was back in his eyes, daring her to argue the point, but she refused to give him the impression that his presence in any way disturbed her. Polite indifference was the attitude she must always strive to adopt whenever her and Bartholomew Cavanagh's paths crossed in the days and weeks ahead. Besides which, his presence today might turn out to be a blessing in disguise. At least Kitty would be unlikely to broach the subject of her plans for his future within his hearing, thereby granting Abbie a little more time to decide whether she wished to become involved or not.

As things turned out, she swiftly discovered she had grossly underestimated her young friend's resourcefulness, for no sooner had she dismissed the maid, and fallen into step beside them, than Kitty instantly raised the topic of things they might do to keep themselves entertained during their stay in Bath.

'I think it would be a splendid notion to organise a picnic, don't you?' she asked, appearing the picture of innocence as she glanced up at her brother. 'We could ask some of our friends. You'd come, wouldn't you, Abbie?'

Her tongue suddenly decided to attach itself to the roof of her mouth as two pairs of brown eyes fixed themselves in her direction: one pair flashing a look of entreaty; the other glinting with unholy amusement. 'Well, I… I…do not think that I…'

'Perhaps Miss Graham feels she has too many years in her dish to indulge in such pastimes, Kitty,' her brother suggested, much to Abbie's intense annoyance. She favoured him with a dagger look, the result of which had him straining to control his mirth. 'It has been my experience that, in general, when females reach a certain age,' he added, lips twitching, 'they tend to spurn outdoor activities, preferring instead the more genteel occupations, such as needle-craft, reading and preserve making, nothing too strenuous.'

'She isn't that old, for heaven's sake!' Kitty exclaimed in all seriousness.

'Indeed, no,' Abbie put in, before Bart could utter any ribald response to his sister's backhanded compliment. 'And a picnic will make a pleasant change from all the cap-making occupying so much of my time of late.'

Unlike her brother, whose shoulders were once again shaking in silent, appreciative laughter, Kitty looked appalled. 'You haven't taken to wearing caps already, have you, Abbie?'

'Only after nuncheon, dear, when I feel the need to rest for an hour or so.'

'She's but jesting, Kitty,' Bart assured her, deciding to bring the badinage to an end. 'Although it might be wise, if you are seriously contemplating eating alfresco, to organise the outing for one morning, if you were also thinking of including your mother and Lady Penrose in the party, that is. Which I think you must do. Miss Graham might not be a schoolroom miss, but she still requires a chaperon.'

Astonished that a person of such dubious morals would consider the proprieties, Abbie shot a glance in his direction, half suspecting him of mockery. Something in her expression must have betrayed her scepticism, for his eyes narrowed and grew increasingly probing. All at once the disgraceful episode that she had witnessed taking place in her grandfather's summerhouse sprang into her mind's eye with embarrassing clarity. Powerless to prevent the sudden surge of heat rising from beneath the neckline of her gown, she could only hope that her heightened colour might be attributed to the combined effects of exercise and the warmth of the day.

His sister, at least, seemed oblivious to her increasing discomfiture. Stopping dead in her tracks, Kitty uttered a shriek of delight. 'Why, only look, Bart!' she cried, unwittingly drawing his thoughtful attention away from Abbie. 'I do believe that is none other than Mr Whitham and his sister, sitting over there. How fortunate that we should have chanced upon them again today! I'll run on ahead and invite them to join the picnic, should I?'

Without waiting for a response, she sped away, leaving Abbie experiencing both a twinge of resentment and a pang of envy. Naturally she could not quite like being left alone, if only for a short time, in the sole company of a gentleman whom she didn't hold in the highest esteem, while at the same time she couldn't help but admire Kitty's innate ability to dissimulate. The girl belonged on the Drury Lane stage! No one would have supposed for a moment that she hadn't been genuinely surprised to come upon the Whithams. Yet, how could this possibly be so, when only that very morning she had assured Abbie the siblings would be in the gardens later in the day?

'Do not feel obliged to involve yourself in my incorrigible sister's schemes if you truly do not wish to do so, Miss Graham.'

Startled, Abbie scanned the rugged profile, wondering if he had guessed his sister's intent. 'I'm sorry, sir. I do not perfectly understand what you mean.'

'The picnic, Miss Graham. Do not feel obliged to join the outing if it is not to your taste.'

Unwittingly he had offered her the golden opportunity to decline if she chose. Yet, perversely, she experienced no desire to do so. To date she had done nothing to aid and abet his sister, so no blame could be laid at her door should he uncover Kitty's underlying purpose. Furthermore, a visit to a local beauty spot would be most pleasant. Why should she deny herself the treat? She had enjoyed precious few diversions in recent years.

'I cannot imagine why you might suppose I do not wish to join the excursion, Mr Cavanagh. I think it a splendid notion.'

The element of doubt that continued to linger in his eyes for several moments was vanquished by a smile of such warmth that the harsh lines of his features were instantly softened. 'I cannot tell you how relieved I am to hear you say so, Miss Graham. It will require the combined efforts of two sober-minded persons of advanced years, such as ourselves, to ensure the occasion doesn't deteriorate into a sad romp.'

Against all the odds Abbie found herself enjoying his surprisingly teasing manner. 'In that case, sir, I'd best play the part to the full and don one of my fetching caps.'

'Don't you dare!' he hissed for her ears only, as they approached the bench where Kitty, looking very well pleased with herself, sat beside the shy young female whom she was seemingly intent on calling sister in the not too distant future.

It was swiftly borne in upon Abbie that this goal was not beyond Kitty's reach, for no sooner had a few pleasantries been exchanged than the Whithams declared their delight in joining the proposed picnic, and the excursion was arranged to take place two days hence, at a place to be decided upon later.

'Would you mind very much, Bart, if Caroline and her brother escorted me back to the house?' Kitty asked. 'It's on their way, so I shan't be putting them out. It would grant us the opportunity to consider where would be an ideal place to enjoy the picnic. After all, they reside in Bath and so ought to know all the best spots.'

As the Whithams appeared only too happy to oblige, Bart raised no objection. Abbie, on the other hand, was less enthusiastic at having only Kitty's brother to escort her home, though she somehow managed to conceal the fact very well when she and Bart parted company with the others at the entrance to the gardens.

Amazingly enough, however, by the time they had arrived at Upper Camden Place, she had begun to revise her opinion of her escort. Although she abhorred his manners and morals, and doubted she could ever be brought to overlook these defects, she was forced to own that he was an intelligent man, well read and knowledgeable on a wide range of subjects, and had proved to be surprisingly good company.

'Would you care to step inside for some refreshments, Mr Cavanagh?' she enquired, after debating for several moments whether to issue the invitation, and then deciding that common courtesy dictated she must after he had put himself to the trouble of escorting her safely home.

As she couldn't imagine that sipping tea in an elegant drawing-room was his preferred way of spending an afternoon, she confidently expected him to utter a polite refusal. Consequently she was surprised when he accepted with alacrity, declaring that it would grant him the opportunity to invite Lady Penrose to his forthcoming party in person.

This, as things turned out, he was obliged to postpone, for they entered the drawing-room to discover Lady Penrose, for once appearing distinctly ruffled, in earnest conversation with her head groom.

'Oh, my dear, thank heavens you're back!' Lady Penrose declared, sounding genuinely relieved. 'The most dreadful thing has—' She broke off when she observed the tall figure standing behind Abbie in the doorway. 'Oh, and you have brought Mr Cavanagh with you. How very nice!'

'What has occurred to overset you, ma'am?' Abbie didn't hesitate to ask the instant her godmother had exchanged a further polite greeting with her unexpected visitor.

'Oh, it is too provoking!' she declared, relapsing once again into a perturbed state. 'The stable-lad has suffered an injury! Jenkins, here, has just this moment informed me. And it really is most inconvenient! Why must he break his leg now, of all times!'

'I cannot imagine he did so on purpose, ma'am,' Abbie pointed out gently, before turning her attention to the groom. 'Has the doctor been summoned?'

'Aye, miss,' Jenkins responded. 'Not that there were any need. T'other lad did a proper job. Doctor said as how he couldn't 'ave set it better 'imself.'

'Oh, do explain things properly, Jenkins,' Lady Penrose ordered, after seeing Abbie frown in puzzlement, 'otherwise my goddaughter will not understand the dilemma.'

'Well, it were this way, miss,' he began, when three pairs of eyes had turned in his direction. 'I sends young Jem out earlier to the blacksmith's to get one on the 'orses shod. While he were waiting he wandered out into the street. Now he swears he were pushed. But I reckon that's all nonsense, m'self—reckon he thought to save 'imself a right ticking off.' He tutted. 'Jem be a right dozy nodcock! It's my belief he weren't looking where he were going, and walks straight out in front of a carriage.

'Now the blacksmith, and the lad that were wi' him at the time, seemingly looking for work, goes out to see what all the to-do's about. They carries young Jem back into smithy, and the lad sets the leg there and then, no trouble. Then the blacksmith brings Jem back 'ere in his cart, while this 'ere lad takes care o' mistress's horse. So when I 'ears the lad's looking for work, I comes up 'ere to see the mistress.'

He paused to cast an imploring glance in Mr Cavanagh's direction, as though expecting one of his own sex more likely to sympathise. 'I can't manage by m'self, not with all the extra duties. And all I can say is this 'ere lad seems to know what's what. But it ain't my place to take men on, 'specially not strangers.'

'So you can understand my predicament,' Lady Penrose announced the instant her groom fell silent, but Abbie, at a complete loss, didn't hesitate to shake her head.

'My dear, I know nothing whatsoever about engaging grooms,' her godmother explained. 'My dear husband always saw to that sort of thing. I only ever concerned myself with household staff. It is true what Jenkins says, though. We do need to engage someone. Jenkins cannot be expected to drive me about and take care of you when you go out for your rides.'

'Oh, but, ma'am, there's no need to concern yourself about me,' Abbie assured her. 'I didn't come to Bath expecting to ride too often, if at all.'

'Oh, but you must, my dear!' Lady Penrose countered swiftly. 'As soon as I knew you were coming to stay, I asked Jenkins to arrange for the hire of a suitable mount for you. And your new riding habit will be delivered within a very few days, so you will be able to go out whenever you choose. I've long since known of your fondness for riding, and I do not wish you to give up any of your favourite pastimes on my account, especially as you are considering taking up residence with me permanently.'

Abbie could almost feel those dark brown orbs boring into her back, but steadfastly refused to look at the gentleman standing directly behind her, until he said,

'Ma'am, if I may be of service?' Bart transferred his gaze to Lady Penrose. 'Unlike yourself, I'm accustomed to hiring outdoor workers, although I think Miss Graham ought to be present during the interview. It is, after all, primarily for her benefit that you require the services of a groom.'

'Oh, Mr Cavanagh, that is most kind!' Lady Penrose declared, clearly delighted by the offer of assistance. 'If you would care to conduct the interview in the downstairs parlour, I shall arrange for refreshments to be brought here in readiness for your return.'

Although not altogether unhappy about having Bart there to offer support, Abbie might have wished no mention had been made of the possibility of her taking up permanent residence in Bath. She felt sure he must have experienced a degree of puzzlement, not to say shock.

Yet, surprisingly enough, he made no attempt to allude to the matter when they had attained the privacy of the downstairs parlour. He merely took up a stance before the window to stare out into the street, declaring as he did so that he was deriving far more enjoyment out of his first sojourn in Bath than he might have supposed.

Abbie wasn't permitted to speculate for long on whether there had been some underlying meaning in the admission, for she detected the sound of a heavy tread in the passageway, and a moment later a tall figure was filling the open doorway.

In height and build there was little to choose between the stranger and the man who immediately abandoned his position by the window to come to stand beside her. There, however, all similarities ended. The new arrival was much younger than Bart, no more than two-and-twenty, Abbie guessed. A crop of bright blond hair tumbled untidily over a bronzed forehead, beneath which a pair of clear blue eyes, betraying a marked degree of diffidence, stared solemnly into the room.

'Well, don't just stand there like a stock, lad! Come in and close the door!'

Bart's brusque command had the desired effect. Accustomed to taking orders, the young man immediately responded to the voice of authority, and came forward, turning his misshapen hat nervously in his work-roughened hands.

'Now, I understand you're looking for work?'

'Aye, sir, that's reet.'

'By your accent I deduce you're not from around these parts,' Bart said, remarking on something that had instantly occurred to Abbie too.

'Born and bred in Yorkshire, not far from Kexby, sir.'

'Kexby...?' Abbie echoed. 'What a coincidence! There's a relative of mine living near there... Sir Montague Graham.'

'Why, bless you, miss!' A boyish grin tugged at the stranger's mouth. 'That do be strange! I were born on the Graham estate. My pa were a labourer there up until he died a few year back.'

'And were you employed by Sir Montague?' she asked.

'No, miss. Since I were eight year old I've worked for Mr Remington, a close neighbour.'

'And why have you chosen to leave Remington's employ, and find work in this neck of the woods?' Bart asked, thinking it strange. In his experience country people rarely strayed far from their roots, unless it was to find work in the local towns and cities.

'Well, it be this way, sir... Mr Remington's been ill for some time. He ain't got no children. When he dies his property will be sold. Mr Remington's always been good to me, sir, very fair, and he told me straight he couldn't guarantee I'd be given work when the new owner arrives.'

'That's understandable enough,' Bart remarked, before belatedly enquiring the young man's name.

'Arkwright, sir. Josh Arkwright.'

'So, what brought you down to the West Country, Josh?' Abigail enquired, having already decided that she liked him, and would be happy to have him for her personal groom.

'Mr Remington had a favourite brood mare. He wanted to be sure she'd go to a good home. So he ask me to bring her down to an old friend of 'is who lives a few miles south of 'ere.'

'Who is…?' Bart put in.

'A Mr Diggory, sir. My master wrote asking Mr Diggory if he could offer me work at his place, but Mr Diggory couldn't, sir. Said as times were 'ard, and he couldn't afford to take on more men. Said I might try my luck in the larger towns 'ere abouts—Bath or Bristol, if I didn't 'ave no hankering to return to Yorkshire.'

'And is there any reason in particular why you don't wish to return?' Bart was not slow to enquire.

Josh shrugged. 'There's nowt there for me now, sir. All my family's dead, excepting a sister who's married to a mill worker and lives in Halifax. And for all I know, Mr Remington might have passed on by now. He gave me a quarter's wages in advance, sir, and money enough to get back should I 'ave a mind, but…' he shrugged '…don't see that there's much point iffen I can find work 'ere.'

'You do realise the position is only temporary, until the stable-lad is up and about again,' Bart wasn't slow to point out.

'Aye, sir, I knows that reet enough. But at least it'll give me a chance to look about for something more settled, if I do decide to stay down here.'

Bart acknowledged this with a nod before asking Josh if he had retained the letter his former employer had written to Mr Diggory, and received an immediate shake of the head in response. Abbie, however, was not unduly concerned that he had no references, for she had already made up her mind to offer employment, and instructed him to return to the stables, and take up his duties immediately.

'I hope you don't come to regret that altruistic gesture, my girl,' Bart warned the instant Josh, appearing far more cheerful, had departed.

'Why should I? He's explained just why he's in need of work. He seemed open and honest. Besides which, I rather liked him. I think he deserves a chance.'

Bart smiled grimly. 'One can sometimes come to regret charitable acts. One should never judge at face value. People are not always quite what they seem.'

'Believe me, Mr Cavanagh, I'm not as naïve as you seem to suppose. I'm fully aware that genial outward trappings can conceal someone capable of the most despicable acts,' she responded softly, and then turned to leave, but not before she had glimpsed a speculative gleam in those dark brown eyes of his.

Chapter Four

It was with decidedly mixed feelings that Abbie surveyed the unblemished June sky the instant she awoke on the morning of the proposed picnic. On the one hand, she was looking forward to her first venture out of the city to explore the surrounding countryside on what promised to be a perfect late spring day; on the other, she would far rather not have been destined to spend several hours within close proximity to someone whom she had been happy to stigmatise as nothing more than a callous philanderer; someone who, moreover, had begun to infiltrate her thoughts of late rather more than was comfortable.

She couldn't deny that she'd been grateful for Bart's support during the interview with Josh. Furthermore, she considered the fact that he had made no attempt to influence her decision to any significant degree very much to his credit. But was that reason enough to begin to question her former opinion of him, to begin to wonder whether she had been too severe in her judgement of his character? She knew the base behaviour of which he was capable. Dear Lord! Hadn't she witnessed it with her own eyes?

The arrival of her godmother's personal maid, and not the young servant girl who usually waited upon her each morning, succeeded in gaining her immediate attention, and she demanded to know if ought were amiss.

'Absolutely nothing, miss,' Felcham assured her. 'It was just that I thought I'd see to you myself, as I've already dealt with the mistress.'

'Good heavens!' Abbie found it impossible to conceal her astonishment. 'Do you mean to tell me Godmama is up and about already?'

'Yes, and downstairs at this very moment breaking her fast. She's as excited as a child, Miss Abbie. You're a wonderful influence on her, to be sure! Since your arrival here, more often than not, she's been up betimes to join you at breakfast. And I've noticed she's more inclined to walk these days rather than order the carriage. And today she's off on a picnic, of all things!'

'Yes, I was surprised myself when she accepted Mr Cavanagh's invitation,' Abbie admitted, recalling the speculative gleam in her godmother's eyes when she had learned of the proposed outing. 'She accepted the invitation to his party too.'

'Well, between you and me, miss,' Felcham said, depositing the pitcher on the washstand, 'her ladyship has a soft spot for the strong-willed type. And that Mr Cavanagh doesn't strike me as a gentleman who'd stand any nonsense—knows what's what, I'd say.'

'He's certainly nobody's fool,' honesty obliged Abbie to concede. 'And, of course, he just happened to be about at a time when Godmama felt in need of a little masculine support.'

Felcham tutted. 'Don't know why Jenkins couldn't have sorted the business out himself, instead of coming to the house, troubling her ladyship. He'd know well enough that the mistress wouldn't object to him having someone else to help out until young Jem is up and about again. Though,

I have to say,' she added, collecting the new muslin dress and burgundy-striped spencer from the wardrobe, and laying them carefully upon the bed, 'that it's a pity Josh isn't to stay on permanent. He seems a nice young fellow to me, polite and hard working. And with a deal more in his garret than both Jenkins and Jem put together.'

'I shall reserve judgement until I've witnessed him tooling Godmama's carriage. Which, I believe, Jenkins has instructed him to do today,' Abbie responded, as she began her toilette.

Felcham, being vastly more experienced, was a good deal quicker than the young housemaid who usually helped Abbie to dress and to arrange her hair. Consequently Abbie was soon making her way downstairs to discover her godmother happily perusing the newspaper.

'Good morning, dear. Looking forward to the outing today, I trust?' Lady Penrose said by way of a greeting, and without raising her eyes from the printed sheets. 'Great heavens! The man must have grown weak in the attic even to contemplate taking such a strumpet to wife!'

Having by now grown accustomed to Lady Penrose's quaint habit of thinking aloud, this sudden pronouncement in no way astonished Abbie. 'Perusing the gossip columns again, Godmama?' she quizzed her. 'What juicy morsel has captured your interest, I wonder?'

'Lord Soames, the crass fool, has only gone and proposed marriage to the Dowager Lady Fitzpatrick! She's half his age, and the most flighty baggage who ever drew breath.'

The knife Abbie had been holding fell from her fingers to land on her plate with a clatter, instantly drawing her godmother's attention. 'Why, my dear! You're looking very pale. Are you not feeling quite the thing?'

Regaining her composure with an effort, Abbie managed a semblance of a smile. 'I'm fine.' She saw at once that her godmother wasn't convinced, and couldn't say that she was altogether surprised. She was no expert at dissembling, and there had been precious little conviction in her voice. 'It just so happens that I'm acquainted with the lady,' she thought it prudent to admit. 'The Fitzpatricks are Grandpapa's nearest neighbours.'

'Why, yes, of course! I'd forgotten the family estate is in Leicestershire. You would know then that the late Sir Oswald Fitzpatrick hasn't been in his grave much above a year.' Lady Penrose shrugged. 'Still, it's in keeping with the rest of her behaviour, I suppose. Ever a flighty piece, she was. Married Oswald Fitzpatrick, a man old enough to be her father, when she'd just turned eighteen. His son by his first marriage was only a year younger than Sophia. Clearly she favours husbands in their dotage and lovers much younger than herself. She's had scores of admirers over the years, if what the gossips say is true.'

Abbie had only listened with half an ear, as images she would far rather forget began flashing before her mind's eye, memories of a day that had effectively changed her life: that ill-fated afternoon visit to the summerhouse, followed a mere few hours later by the unexpected proposal of marriage. Even now, after all this time, she well remembered the humiliation and disgust she'd felt when Bart had proposed, or, rather, wholly supported his godfather's desire for a union between them; recalled too the way she had recoiled when he had come forward, hands outstretched to grasp hers; how she had fled the room in a state of near hysteria, declaring that Bartholomew Cavanagh was the very last man in the world she would marry.

'Oh, do forgive me, my dear.' Lady Penrose's abject apology blessedly drew Abbie back to the present. 'I shouldn't be discussing such matters in front of you,' she added, mistakenly supposing that embarrassment had been responsible for the bright crimson hue now suffusing Abbie's high cheekbones.

'I'm not a child, ma'am,' Abbie reminded her, having managed to suppress the surge of anger that never failed to assail her whenever she thought back to that fateful day. 'Believe me, Sophia Fitzpatrick's reputation comes as no great surprise to me.'

'Given that she used to be a close neighbour of yours, I don't suppose it does,' Lady Penrose commented. 'She's had a score of lovers over the years. Not that I blame the gentlemen, of course. There's no denying Sophia Fitzpatrick is attractively packaged. It would be a rare man indeed who would refuse what was so enticingly offered.'

Abbie failed to suppress a contemptuous smile. 'There is much in what you say, ma'am. That is perhaps why it is best that I never marry. I should never willingly accept a husband in my arms who reeked of another female's perfume.'

Lady Penrose moved her hand in a dismissive gesture. 'I do not think you need harbour any fears, my dear. I wouldn't attempt to suggest there are not those who actively seek their pleasures elsewhere after they are married. But many gentlemen remain faithful to their wives, and sensibly sow their wild oats before contemplating matrimony.'

Although Lady Penrose noticed a sudden, arresting look in violet eyes, she received no response, and decided to change the subject by revealing that Giles Fergusson and his mother were to join the picnic. 'So it looks as if it will turn out to be a very jolly outing, don't you agree?' she said, but was no more successful in attaining a response than she had been moments before.

* * *

Having experienced grave doubts about spending several hours in the company of her grandfather's godson, it was perhaps unfortunate that Abbie had been forcibly reminded about one of Bart's less commendable traits, the result of which had ultimately resulted in the unfortunate estrangement between her and her grandfather. Although she suspected Bart himself was completely ignorant of this fact, this in no way lessened his guilt in her eyes.

Hence, it was as much as she could do to acknowledge his greeting when, later that morning, she emerged from the house in time to see him draw a smart racing curricle to a halt directly in front Lady Penrose's waiting carriage.

She experienced no similar reluctance in greeting his companion, who jumped nimbly to the ground, looking every inch the excited child.

'Giles will be along with his mother directly,' Kitty informed Lady Penrose, who had emerged from the house in Abbie's wake. 'It was very good of you to offer her a seat in your carriage, ma'am. Mrs Whitham was persuaded to come, and Mama is travelling with her. I don't think we could have brought anyone else along, with all the food baskets in our carriage.'

'It's likely to be cramped in ours too,' Abbie wasn't slow to reveal. 'Godmama saw fit to bring along extra provisions.'

'A picnic isn't a picnic without champagne, and a variety of delicacies to tempt every palate' Lady Penrose announced. 'I'm certain we'll all manage to squeeze in somehow.'

Kitty cast Abbie a surprised glance. 'But surely you don't propose to make the journey in a closed carriage? Giles is driving himself in his phaeton. It will be much more fun travelling in the open air.'

Abbie was much struck by the suggestion, until Kitty added that she would bear Mr Fergusson company and Abbie was welcome to take her seat in her brother's carriage.'

'Perhaps Miss Graham would prefer not to spend time in my sole company,' a smooth voice from above drawled, and Abbie raised her head to see Bart regarding her steadily, his gaze both accusing and challenging at one and the same time.

'I don't know why you might suppose that, Bart,' his sister responded, before Abbie had a chance even to begin to think of some reason to refuse. 'You've known each other for years and years. Quite ancient bosom friends, in fact!'

In face of this piece of gross impertinence, it was as much as Abbie could do to gape in astonished outrage as Kitty hurried away to greet Giles and his mother, who had just arrived.

'How old does she imagine I am?' she managed at last to utter in a falsetto voice, the result of which had Bart striving to preserve his countenance.

Even though the poke of the charming bonnet hid most of her face from view, he had little difficulty in imagining those lovely features slightly marred by an indignant frown. 'May I apologise on my thoughtless sister's behalf. What I believe she meant to convey was that she understood us to be friends of long standing. But are we, do you think?'

This drew her attention, as he had suspected it might, and it was no difficult matter for him to detect the wariness in her expression, before he glanced over his shoulder in time to see Kitty taking Mrs Fergusson's place in Giles's phaeton. 'It would appear my sister has had her way. Not that I'm unduly surprised. Giles is far too indulgent.'

He turned his attention back to the vision, strikingly

attired today in white and burgundy, now standing alone on the pavement. 'Are you willing to be equally generous in spirit and indulge me by bearing me company on the journey?'

There was only a moment's hesitation on her part before she proceeded to clamber up beside him, though she blatantly ignored the hand he held out to assist her.

Smiling to himself, Bart glanced once again over his shoulder to ensure that Mrs Fergusson was safely ensconced in Lady Penrose's carriage, and then gave his horses the office to start, leading the small cavalcade along the street.

'Tell me, Miss Graham,' he remarked, after they had driven along in silence for perhaps five minutes, 'is it out of consideration for me that you sit in stony silence? If so, your thoughtfulness is entirely misplaced. I'm capable of handling a team and conversing at one and the same time.' He waited in vain for a response before adding, 'Or is it that you are attempting to formulate some uncontroversial answer to the question I asked a short time ago?'

If the truth were known, Abbie had been endeavouring, without much success, to ignore the contact with the muscular thigh that persisted in brushing against her skirts. She didn't even attempt, however, to ignore his last comment. 'I'm sorry, Mr Cavanagh, I cannot recall your asking any question.'

As she appeared genuinely puzzled, Bart was inclined to believe her. 'Then allow me to refresh your memory— I asked if you considered us friends?'

Although she didn't precisely stiffen, he sensed the withdrawal behind that barrier she had mentally erected between them since the very start of their renewed acquaintance in Bath. She was definitely wary of him, though why this should be was a complete mystery. As far as he could recall, he had never done or said anything to her detriment. In his youth he might not actively have sought her company, something that he found himself wishing to do increasingly of late. But was that reason enough for these frequent displays of aloofness on her part? Why was she so determined to keep him at a distance? Was it the male sex in general she mistrusted, or just him?

'I cannot in truth say that I've ever considered you a friend, sir, merely an acquaintance.'

The answer came as no real surprise, and served to increase his determination to break down that barrier she seemed intent on maintaining between them. 'But would you not agree that we have been acquainted long enough to dispense with the unnecessary formality you have chosen to adopt since our first meeting? After all, Abbie, you don't appear to object to my sister, who has known you a short time only, making free with your given name.'

He had successfully spiked her guns over this matter. Moreover, he knew by the slight smile suddenly appearing round that delectable mouth that she had already silently acknowledged this fact. True, it might be just a small victory, but at least it was a step in the right direction. All the same, he sensed that it was too soon yet to attempt building a closer relationship between them; sensed too that he must attempt to win her trust, otherwise that almost tangible barrier would undoubtedly widen and she would become increasingly remote.

Consequently he sensibly refrained from plying her with questions, even though he was determined to discover just what it was about him that she didn't quite like, didn't quite trust. Instead, he maintained a flow of conversation, touching upon nothing that might cause her unease.

By the time they had met up with the Whithams and his stepmother at the prearranged location, and were heading out of the city, his companion was at least voicing an opinion on the various topics he raised. More rewarding still was that, by the time they arrived at the place where the picnic was to be held, Bart truly believed he was making excellent progress towards a better understanding between them, for although he wouldn't have dreamt of suggesting that they were upon friendly terms precisely, at least much of her former reserve had thawed.

Nevertheless, once the rugs had been spread on the ground, and the food baskets had been removed from the carriages, she didn't hesitate to seek the company of her godmother.

'Well, I must say this is most pleasant,' Lady Penrose remarked, contentedly sipping her way through a second glass of champagne, while nibbling a savoury tart. 'I'm so very glad I came—a perfect day. One cannot help but feel at peace with oneself in such a glorious setting.'

Abbie, gazing across the grassy-covered slope, strewn with an array of wildflowers, to where the sparkling water of a gurgling stream meandered its way across the landscape, might have wholeheartedly agreed, had she not felt slightly uneasy about the real purpose behind the outing.

Turning her head slightly, she transferred her gaze to the object of her thoughts, sitting among the younger members of the party.

From the moment they had been introduced, Abbie had been favourably impressed by the Whitham family, and with Miss Caroline Whitham in particular, whom she considered a charming young woman, if a trifle shy. But whether she would make a suitable wife for Bartholomew Cavanagh was highly doubtful. In her opinion they would make a mismatched pair. Bart was the strong, domineering type who, she clearly remembered from years before, liked his own way in all things. Poor little Caroline would soon find her spirits crushed.

But it had nothing whatsoever to do with her, Abbie reminded herself. If Bart chose to marry the kind of female who would always defer to him, and Caroline was happy to play the submissive little wife, then so be it! Such an arrangement certainly wouldn't do for her. She had spent the last six years attempting to live companionably with an overbearing, irascible gentleman. Bart and her grandfather had been fashioned in the same mould. The best way of dealing with such persons was to stand up to them, she decided before her gaze slid to another member of the group.

Although she would have been the first to admit she didn't know Giles Fergusson at all well, she had been favourably impressed thus far. He could by no stretch of the imagination be considered remotely handsome, but an abundance of charm and a natural, unaffected manner, which couldn't fail to please, more than compensated for his lack of good looks. Moreover, he was the type of person who, she very much suspected, would always consider the feelings of others before his own, an admirable trait that she could never recall Bart revealing years before.

Unconsciously her gaze had shifted, and she realised with a start that a pair of almond-shaped eyes, amusement clearly visible in their dark brown depths, were staring directly back at her from beneath raised brows.

For one embarrassing moment, as he suddenly rose to his feet, she thought he was about to come over and demand to know why he had become the object of her interest. Mercifully he did not; he merely strolled up the grassy bank in the direction of the carriages, and went directly to his own light travelling carriage, extracting a small barrel from inside, and what appeared to be four pewter tankards. With the exception of Josh, who appeared more interested in examining Bart's fine bays, the various grooms were soon gathered about him, gratefully sampling the ale.

'How very thoughtful of Mr Cavanagh!' Lady Penrose announced, after following the direction of Abbie's gaze. 'Not many would be so considerate to their employees as to ensure that they too enjoyed the day.'

'No, they would not,' honesty obliged Abbie to concede. She was forced silently to acknowledge too that she might not have been totally accurate in her assessment of Bart's character. Just because she had never witnessed any acts of thoughtfulness on his part years ago did not necessarily mean he was devoid of the finer feelings. The truth of the matter was she well remembered the boy; she had yet to know the man.

Kitty caused a diversion when she suddenly jumped to her feet, and suggested a game of battledore and shuttlecock. The younger Whithams were eager to challenge her and her brother, and soon the game was underway.

While watching the energetic game, Abbie was content to sit with her godmother until Lady Penrose, at last succumbing to the warmth of the day, and the effects of the champagne, began happily dozing.

Picking up her sketch pad, which she had had the forethought to bring with her, and a spare rug, Abbie repositioned herself several yards away, and began to scan the picturesque setting beyond the babbling stream. The outing had turned out to be far more enjoyable than she could have imagined, and she intended to capture on paper just one view that would always remind her of her first venture into the Somerset countryside.

'May I join you, Miss Graham? Mrs Whittham and my mother too are now happily lying in the arms of Morpheus.'

'Of course, Mr Fergusson.' She watched him lower himself awkwardly. 'I have yet to hear you complain, but I believe the injury you sustained at Waterloo continues to cause discomfort.'

He didn't attempt to deny it. 'Compared with many, I came through relatively unscathed. But, yes, Miss Graham, I still suffer, some days more than others. After the battle I was patched up pretty well. At least I didn't lose my leg, but the army surgeon failed to notice the piece of shattered bone embedded in my knee. I had it successfully removed earlier this year by a top London surgeon, who assured me that eventually I would be able to walk again without the aid of a stick. Although,' he added, smiling, 'it will be a while yet before I'm prepared to indulge in anything so energetic as that.'

She followed the direction of his gaze, her eyes automatically focusing on the tallest member of the quartet. 'Your friend Mr Cavanagh appears to have been one of the more fortunate ones who came through the conflict without suffering severe injury.'

'As you probably know, he was obliged to leave the army in '14, when his father died, and so wasn't at Waterloo. But you are wrong, Miss Graham. Bart sustained several injuries during the Peninsular Campaign. A French cavalryman wielding a sabre nearly cost him an arm, when he went to the aid of a wounded senior officer. His bravery earned him his Majority. And deservedly so!'

Evidently he thought much of his friend, and Abbie didn't suppose for a moment that Giles Fergusson's respect was easily won. 'I recall years ago that Bart never betrayed any nerves on the hunting field. It surprised me somewhat when he didn't choose a cavalry regiment when he decided to join the army. There's no denying he's a fine horseman.'

Giles's smile was crooked. 'His decision to become an infantryman surprised a good many people, Miss Graham, myself included,' he freely admitted. 'The truth of the matter is, I suspect, though you will never persuade him to admit as much, that Bart didn't go out to the Peninsula to exhibit his prowess in the saddle, but to fight for his country.'

For the second time in the space of half an hour Abbie was forced silently to acknowledge that she didn't know Bartholomew Cavanagh, the man. Once again she found her gaze automatically lingering in his direction, until she realised that Giles's grey eyes were regarding her keenly, and swiftly returned her thoughts to the present. 'Now, of course, you both must find life vastly different—quite tame, in fact, from what you endured during these past years.'

'Well, mine certainly is. I have few responsibilities, at least at the present time. It will be a different matter when I inherit my uncle's property. Bart, on the other hand, now manages a place far larger than the one I'm destined to own one day.' There was a suspicion of a boyish grin about his mouth as he added, 'And I think he finds his sister something of a handful on occasions.'

'There's naught amiss with Kitty,' Abbie said, coming to the girl's defence without a second thought. 'She's young and full of life, that is all. She'll calm down in a year or two.'

'Precisely what I've told him myself, Miss Graham, and I should know, having had vastly more experience of younger sisters.'

Abbie watched as he transferred his attention to the four taking part in the game, and noticed his gaze growing increasingly tender as he continued to study one player in particular, clad in a pretty primrose-coloured gown. She pursed her lips together in a silent whistle when something she had never considered before sprang into her mind. Interesting, she mused. Yes, most interesting.

She was denied the opportunity to ponder long on her startling discovery, for the game ended and Kitty came across, happily taking Giles's place when he moved away to talk to Bart.

'Exhausted, Kitty?' Abbie enquired, as the girl lay down on the rug beside her.

'Yes. But very well pleased. We won.' She appeared smugly satisfied. 'I like to win.'

Stretching out her hand, Abbie reached for the sketch pad and box of pencils, and began to draw the animated little face, swiftly capturing the mischievous glint in sparkling brown eyes, and the playful smile pulling at the perfect bow of Kitty's mouth. 'No, don't move!' she ordered, when her subject made to sit up straight. 'You say you like to win, Kitty,' she added, quickly capturing the outline of the soft, feminine jaw, 'but I think you should be prepared to lose on occasions. I might be wrong, but I suspect you're doomed to disappointment if you suppose your brother might propose marriage to Miss Whitham.'

Abbie wasn't certain what had prompted her to say what she had. Yet, all at once she knew it was true. She had noticed Bart talking with Caroline earlier. Obviously he liked the girl, but his eyes had lacked that certain look that Abbie had glimpsed in Giles Fergusson's when he had been gazing at the subject of her sketch only minutes before.

'Oh, but he admires her,' Kitty argued, her expression suddenly guarded. 'He's always saying how charmingly she behaves.'

'That's possibly quite true. Whether or not he admires her enough to propose marriage is an entirely different matter, however,' Abbie pointed out. 'Furthermore, do you think they're suited? Your brother, as you know, has something of a strong, autocratic streak in his nature. What is more, he isn't afraid to speak his mind. Miss Whitham, I rather fancy, is the type of female who would quickly wilt beneath too many harshly spoken words.'

Kitty appeared to consider this for all of ten seconds, before suddenly jumping to her feet. 'Oh, were you still sketching me? I'm sorry, Abbie, but I cannot sit still for long. Besides, it looks as if they're ready for another game. You can take my place. I'll bear Giles company for a while, and watch.'

Having been given little choice in the matter, Abbie abandoned her drawing for the time being, and followed Kitty across the grass. Stephen Whitham suggested a change of partners, an idea that seemed to appeal to everyone except Bart, who frowned slightly when Caroline shyly joined him.

As Caroline quickly proved to be the weakest player by far, Abbie thought she understood the reason behind Bart's slightly disgruntled look. She and her partner very quickly took a commanding lead, the game ending with Abbie gently tapping the shuttlecock just over the rope, a deft little shot that had Bart flying through the air in an attempt to retrieve it, and ending flat on his face on the ground.

Abbie dissolved into chuckles, laughing so much she ended with a painful stitch in her side, and was forced to take refuge on her rug once again.

'You little baggage!' Bart muttered, dropping down beside her, and ineffectually attempting to remove the grass stains from his tight-fitting breeches.

She knew at once he wasn't really angry, and was forced silently to own that he was a good sport. 'Never in my wildest dreams did I ever imagine I would see you scrabbling about in the dirt!' she announced, still unable to control her mirth. 'I wouldn't have missed it for the world!'

For answer he cast her a look of exasperation, before lying flat on his back and closing his eyes. Abbie automatically reached for her sketch pad again, and for a while continued to work on the drawing she had begun of Kitty, until the girl herself called across, asking if she would care to join the others in a walk down to the stream. Abbie declined, preferring to continue with her sketching. She half expected Bart might go, but when he didn't offer to move, and continued to lie beside her, head resting in his hands, she couldn't resist doing a wicked caricature of him, emphasising the long, hawklike nose, the cleft in his strong chin, and mischievously adding a mulish look to the powerful jaw.

The scratching of pencil on paper eventually induced him to open one eye in time to see her adding the finishing touches to beetle-black brows.

His own instantly drew together as he eased himself up into a sitting position, the better to view the finished result. 'So that's how you see me, is it?' The scowl grew more pronounced. 'Not a very flattering likeness, if I may say so. I resemble nothing so much as a buffle-headed pugilist whose nose has been broken on several occasions.'

'It's a caricature, Bart,' she assured him, holding the pad at arm's length. 'Even if I do say so myself, I've definitely captured that stubborn set to the chin.'

Reaching out, he easily wrested the pad from her, and in so doing flicked over the page to the likeness of his sister. The expression of exasperation faded from his features and was replaced by one of dawning wonder. 'This is really good, Abbie… Excellent, in fact! You've captured exactly that look she has when she's plotting mischief.'

The thought evidently disturbed him, for he frowned again. 'What were you discussing at the time?'

She had never made a convincing liar, so didn't attempt to deceive him. 'Er—you, I believe.'

'Were you, by gad!' He was on his feet in an instant. 'I'd best make sure she's behaving herself.' He began to stride away in the direction of the stream, but turned back to add, 'I'd like to see that again when you've finished it.'

It had sounded as if he genuinely meant it, and Abbie was immensely touched by the compliment, possibly because it was so unexpected. Unfortunately she was unable to do very much more to the sketch, because the older members of the party, suitably refreshed after their repose, were keen to return to their homes.

Abbie helped to pack up the picnic baskets and fold up the rugs, so that by the time the others had returned from their walk, most everything had been carried back to the coaches.

'Can I not persuade you to bear me company on the return journey?' Bart asked, when Abbie was on the point of joining Mrs Fergusson and Lady Penrose in the carriage.

She took a moment only to consider. 'Why, yes! I rather think I'd prefer to travel in the open air.'

He bent a look of mock reproach upon her, as he helped her into his curricle. 'You certainly know how to deflate a man's ego, Miss Abigail Graham. I was hoping that it was the prospect of enjoying my company that might persuade you.'

Yet again she knew well enough that he was teasing her, and was about to respond in kind, when she realised she had left her sketch pad behind. She wasted no time in hurrying back to collect it, but even so the other carriages had moved off and were already out of sight by the time she had resumed her seat beside him.

'Don't concern yourself. It won't take many minutes to catch them up,' Bart assured her, easily interpreting the slightly troubled look. 'There's no need for you to feel the least nervous in my company, Abbie. I do not make a practice of seducing innocent damsels.'

For a moment he felt certain she had stiffened, but then decided he must have been mistaken, and that she had merely settled herself more comfortably, after placing the sketch pad beneath the seat.

In the event that she was genuinely uneasy at being left alone with him, he wasted no time in setting off to catch up with the rest of the party, and they were soon bowling along at a sensible pace, conducive to the conditions of the road.

Consequently, when it happened it took them both completely unawares. One moment they had both been enjoying the splendid views in the unfamiliar landscape; the next the carriage had come to rest in a ditch at a very peculiar angle. Hat askew, Abbie found herself sitting in a hedge, while Bart endeavoured to soothe his frightened horses.

He swiftly had them quietened sufficiently enough to turn his attention to the main object of his concern. 'Are you all right, girl?'

Anxiety had added a harsh edge to his voice, but thankfully she appeared not to notice, as she accepted his helping hand to rise, and his aid in freeing her skirts from the clutches of a particularly troublesome bramble.

'Yes, I think so...ouch!'

Before she knew what was happening, Bart had lifted her quite off her feet and, ignoring her demands to be put down at once, carried her out of the ditch, eventually settling her on the grassy bank, where he proceeded to examine the injured limb.

'Really, there's no need to fuss so,' she assured him, endeavouring to brush down her skirts, and receiving a smart slap on the wrist for her pains.

Once he had satisfied himself that the injury was nothing more serious than a slight sprain, he raised himself off his haunches, while suggesting she straighten her bonnet as it made her appear a simpleton. The resulting fulminating glance he received was sufficient to assure him that she was none the worse for her ordeal.

'With any luck, one of the others will return to see where we've got to before too long. In the meantime you sit there and rest that ankle, while I unhitch the team.'

Although he received a further speaking glance, brimful of resentment this time, she made no demur and Bart was able to turn his attention to his horses once more. He had just accomplished the task when what he had predicted happily turned out to be true. A phaeton came bowling round the bend towards them. More satisfying still was the sight of his own trusty head groom bearing his friend company.

'Hackman, here, thought you must be in a spot of bother when you didn't catch up,' Giles disclosed, as he brought his team to a halt. He spotted the wheel lying in the road almost at once. 'Not to worry. I noticed a smithy in the village where we waited for you. It's no more than a mile or so up the road. I'll go back and get help.'

'Be good enough to take Miss Graham with you, Giles, and see her safely restored to Lady Penrose,' Bart said, helping Abbie, who thankfully appeared hardly to limp at all, up into the carriage. 'There's no need for the others to linger, but I'd be grateful if you remained, just in case the wheel can't be repaired today.'

'Are you sure you'll be all right?'

The anxious note in Abbie's voice was not lost on him. Nor could he mistake the reluctance to leave in her expression. Bart didn't doubt for a moment that she would have stayed if she thought she could have been of some help. Being an immensely sensible young woman, however, she had accepted she would have been more of a hindrance than anything else.

'Don't concern yourself, Miss Graham. Any man who can face a French column ain't going to trouble himself over a simple accident like this,' Giles assured her, before giving his horses the office to start.

'Aye. But was it?' Hackman muttered, having overheard the remark. 'I checked the carriages myself this morning, just as I always do afore we set out on a journey. And it were as sound as a nut, I'd stake my life on it.'

Bart regarded the older man in silence. Hackman had worked for the Cavanagh family all his life. There was no man he would trust more, and he would certainly never doubt his word.

'Lynch pins can work loose, Hackman.'

'Aye, sir, that they can, 'specially if they're helped.'

'Are you suggesting someone deliberately tampered with the curricle?'

'Ain't saying that at all, sir,' Hackman eventually answered, after he'd satisfied himself that neither of the bays had suffered harm. 'All I'm saying is I checked the carriage over myself, as I wouldn't trust that useless, rat-eyed Dodd to do it.'

Bart smiled wryly at this. 'You really don't care for your new underling, do you, Hack?'

'Ain't a case o' liking or not, sir,' Hackman answered, running a hand through his grizzled hair. 'I knows well enough you gave the lad a job on account of thinking so well of his father. But Amos Dodd was a mite different from his son... If the work-shy young slug is his son, which I doubt. He's got no love for beasts, sir, not like that young groom o' Lady Penrose's. Now, he's another sort altogether! Knows a thing or two about 'orses, he do.

Had a good long look at this turnout o' yourn back along at the picnic.'

Eyes narrowing, Bart glanced at his wheel lying in the road. 'Did he now?' he murmured.

Chapter Five

The following day Kitty and her mother paid a visit to
Lady Penrose's house. Abbie felt a complete and utter
fraud receiving them in the drawing-room, reclining on
the *chaise longue*, rug over her knees, like some feeble in-
valid, when she had sustained nothing more serious than a
twisted ankle. And a slight twist at that! Yet she couldn't
deny that after years of being ordered by a brusque, ex-
army Colonel not to make a fuss over a few aches and
pains whenever she'd taken a tumble from a horse, Lady
Penrose's cosseting had come as a pleasant change, though
Abbie had drawn the line at having the doctor summoned
over such a trifling injury.

During the visit Kitty disclosed that her brother had returned to the house well before dinner the previous evening, and that he had surprisingly left the city again earlier
that morning, after receiving an unexpected express from
their nearest neighbour, Lord Warren. What might have
induced him to return to their country home in Glouces-
tershire, she had no way of knowing. Bart, seemingly,
had chosen not to confide in her, though the twinkle in
her dark eyes strongly suggested that she fully intended

to enjoy this period of unexpected freedom from her sibling's strict control.

Initially, Abbie too felt a sense of relief, knowing that she could go about the city without running the risk of crossing Bart's path. Yet, surprisingly enough, the period of contentment was short-lived. Before too many days had passed, instead of experiencing pleasure each time she saw Kitty and her mother without their tall escort, she suffered an acute stab of disappointment, with the result that it became increasingly difficult to dismiss the possibility that she just might have grown to like the immoral, infuriating creature. She did not, however, permit this disturbing likelihood to detract from the pleasure she continued to attain from residing in Bath, especially not when she took to riding about the city with her blond-haired groom every day.

At first Josh would always remain deferentially those few feet behind, speaking only when spoken to, and then only briefly. This state of affairs thankfully didn't last for long. Within a few days they would ride along companionably together, unless Abbie happened to speak to an acquaintance, in which case the groom would keep a discreet distance.

Josh's cheerful outlook and unfailing politeness was in stark contrast to the demeanour of the dour, middle-aged groom whose company she had been obliged to suffer whenever she had wished to explore the countryside surrounding her grandfather's home. The more she was with Josh the more she grew to like him, and inevitably the concern she felt over his future increased too.

But what could she do? She wasn't in a position to offer him a permanent situation; and it was hardly fair to expect her godmother to go to the expense of paying for the services of a groom she didn't require, once her own servant was fully recovered. Nor was it right to expect Josh to remain with her for the next few weeks if the opportunity arose for him to acquire a situation elsewhere. On the other hand, though, she very much resented the mere thought of having to lose his services before it became absolutely necessary.

After a deal of soul searching, she decided to broach the subject, when they rode out together on the day before the Cavanaghs' party was due to take place, by suggesting to Josh that it might be wise to begin looking about for another post.

His expression was all at once a mixture of surprise and disappointment. 'But why, Miss Abbie? Have I displeased you in some way? If I've been too forward, like, I'm reet sorry. Thing is, I've never been a lady's personal groom afore.'

If anything, this frank admission made Abbie feel more disgruntled than before. She doubted she would ever find another groom to suit her half so well. 'No, Josh, that isn't it at all,' she assured him. 'If I could keep you, I would. Sadly I cannot. As you know, at present I'm a guest in my godmother's home, but my future is uncertain. There's just the faintest chance I might return to live with my grandfather. But he wouldn't require your services. He has staff enough. And Lady Penrose will not retain you once her own stable-lad has recovered.'

'Aye, I know that, miss.' He gave her one of those boyish grins that made him appear much younger than his twenty-two years. 'You were straight with me from the first. But until Jem's up and about you'll want me, won't you?'

'Not if, in the meantime, you can find yourself something more permanent. What I'm trying to say, Josh, is if you do happen to hear of something you think will suit, don't stay with me through some misguided sense of loyalty, and let the opportunity slip through your fingers.'

A thought occurred to her. 'Perhaps I can be of help too. I've become acquainted with several persons here in Bath, I shall ask on your behalf if they know of anyone requiring the services of a groom. Mr Fergusson and Mr Whitham have lived in the city for some time and their acquaintance is large. There's also the possibility that Mr Cavanagh might be able to help.'

'Now, there's a man, if you don't mind my saying, miss, that I wouldn't mind working for. Knows a thing or two about horses, does Mr Cavanagh. I had a look at those bays of his, and I can tell you I ain't seen no finer.'

Honesty forced Abbie to agree with this. 'Yes, he's certainly a good judge of horseflesh.'

'I remember both the bays and his carriage horses whinnying when he came over to give us grooms a drop of ale at the picnic. My old pa use to say that if creatures takes to a man, then there ain't a deal wrong wi' 'im.'

Abbie couldn't help smiling at this quaint philosophy, even though she would never dream of adopting it herself. And with good reason where Mr Bartholomew Cavanagh was concerned! His treatment of horses might well be above reproach. He might well possess the ability to win their trust and affection with little difficulty. Even so, members of her own sex would do well to remain a deal more cautious in their dealings with him.

She chose, however, to keep these reflections to herself, especially as they had just arrived back at Upper Camden Place. After handing the reins to Josh, she went directly into the house, and was at once informed that her presence was required in the upstairs drawing-room as soon as possible.

Delaying only for the time it took to change out of her habit, Abbie went along to the drawing-room to discover none other than the gentleman who had infiltrated her thoughts far too frequently of late seated beside his sister on the sofa. He rose at once to his feet, one dark brow arching at the smile of delighted surprise Abbie singularly failed to suppress.

'What a relief it is to see you, sir,' she announced, striving to ignore the tingling sensation in her fingers as he held them briefly in his own. 'Kitty was only saying yesterday, when we met in the Pump Room, that she very much feared you wouldn't return in time for the party.'

The arch of one masculine brow grew more pronounced. 'Hoped I wouldn't be returning in time, I think you mean.'

'No, such thing, sir!' Lady Penrose countered, noting with satisfaction the becoming colour in her goddaughter's cheeks as Abbie joined her on the sofa. She smiled to herself before revealing, 'I do believe you have been greatly missed.'

Masculine eyes strayed momentarily to the young woman seated beside her. 'Indeed, ma'am? By whom?'

'By me, for one,' Lady Penrose admitted. 'I was denied the opportunity to thank you for arranging that delightful picnic. It was most enjoyable!'

'A pity it didn't pass without mishap.' He turned his attention fully on Abbie. 'I trust you're suffering no lasting effects from the injury.'

'No, sir, I am not,' she assured him. 'Far too much was made of a trifling ailment.'

'If that is so, ma'am, then you cannot possibly refuse to stand up with me at the party tomorrow night.'

Abbie didn't miss the triumphant gleam in his dark eyes, clearly betraying his delight at her foolishly walking into his well-baited trap. Aid, however, came from an unexpected quarter.

'But you never dance, Bart,' Kitty reminded him. 'Or rarely so.'

'True,' he acknowledged. 'But I've decided our party will be one of those rare occasions when I exert myself to waltz.'

'In that case, sir,' Abbie announced, not without experiencing a degree of smug satisfaction, 'I'm afraid I must decline. I do not waltz.'

'Why ever not, child?' Lady Penrose appeared genuinely surprised. 'Surely you're not one of those who still disapprove? Why, it has been danced even here in this staid old place for quite some time at private functions!'

'Oh, it isn't that. It's merely that I've never learned how,' Abbie hurriedly explained.

'Oh, well, that is easily remedied,' her godmother returned, rising to her feet as nimbly as any seventeen-year-old girl. 'Providing Mr Cavanagh is willing to remain to offer assistance, that is?'

'I am completely at your disposal, ma'am,' he assured her promptly. Which left Abbie wondering what irritated her more: her godmother's satisfied smirk or the look of unholy amusement on Bart's face for having comprehensively spiked her guns.

Admitting defeat with as much grace as she could muster, she helped clear an area for dancing, while her godmother, seating herself at the fine instrument in the corner of the room, selected various pieces of music, with Kitty's assistance.

The embarrassing moment when she and Bart took up their positions could not be long delayed, and Abbie braced herself for that bodily contact the dance demanded. What she was totally unprepared for was her instant reaction to the gentle masculine clasp on her waist and fingers. What she ought to have felt was revulsion, not a pleasantly warm sensation slowly spreading across every inch of her skin. She risked a glance up at him through her lashes, and then promptly wished she had not, for the slight twitch she detected at one corner of his mouth was proof positive that he was very aware that she wasn't as indifferent to his touch as she was striving so hard to appear.

As dancing had always been one of her favourite pastimes, Abbie swiftly managed to channel her thoughts once the tuition was underway. She mastered the steps with relative ease, though she was forced grudgingly to admit that, for someone who by his own admission danced only rarely, Bart was an extremely adroit teacher. Consequently within a relatively short space of time they were swirling about the room together in complete harmony, as though they had danced together on scores of occasions before.

'That was excellent,' Lady Penrose announced, clapping hands that only moments before had moved expertly over the keys. 'Would you like me to select another tune so that you may practise a little more?'

'Oh, no,' Abbie answered promptly, thereby denying Bart the opportunity to decide. She became aware that he still retained a hold on her hand and withdrew it. 'There's nothing further Mr Cavanagh can teach me.'

'Certainly not about the waltz,' he murmured for her ears only, and then chuckled as she took a few hurried steps away from his side. 'I believe we must be on our way too, Lady Penrose,' he added, turning his attention to her. 'Otherwise Kitty's fond mama will imagine the worse— that I've strangled her daughter in a fit of rage.'

'You have my deepest sympathy, Kitty,' Abbie told her, even though the girl appeared to have taken her brother's teasing in good part. 'If Bart is a prime example of how brothers treat their sisters, I'm heartily glad that I was never cursed with one.'

'Husbands can be as bad,' Bart warned, 'if not a good deal worse.'

'In that case, I'm equally glad I have decided to eschew matrimony.'

Abbie had meant it in jest, but it was clear from the reactions of her listeners that not one of them was amused by the untruthful declaration. Lady Penrose seemed shocked, Kitty ridiculously disappointed and Bart looked nothing so much as downright angry. Then his expression changed, and he merely appeared thoughtful while he helped return the pieces of furniture to their former positions.

'Well, that was a most—er—fortuitous visit, wouldn't you agree?' Lady Penrose remarked, the instant her guests had taken their leave.

'Unexpected, certainly,' Abbie answered, before she turned to find her godmother regarding her keenly.

'Were you surprised by it? How strange!' Smiling at some private thought, Lady Penrose sought refuge in her favourite chair. 'I, on the other hand, would have been amazed had Mr Cavanagh not made a visit soon after his return.'

The following evening, as she accompanied her godmother into the house the Cavanaghs had rented for the duration of their stay in Bath, Abbie experienced a degree of trepidation at the ordeal ahead of her. And an ordeal was precisely how she had come to view that promised dance with Bart!

Although she had seen nothing of him since his visit the day before, he had continued to intrude into her thoughts, if anything, more than ever. More disturbing still was the uneasy suspicion that Bart himself now strongly suspected that she wasn't as impervious to his masculinity as she might wish to appear.

The warmth that immediately sprang into his eyes the instant he caught sight of her approaching strongly sug-

gested that he wasn't indifferent to her either. She couldn't
recall him ever looking at her in quite that way years ago,
and found herself experiencing a flutter of mingled excitement and satisfaction knowing that he found her very much
to his taste. Yet at the same time she felt that it would be
foolish beyond measure not to keep a firm control on her
emotions where he was concerned. She must never forget that his dealings with her sex could not withstand too
close a scrutiny. Yet, surely it could do no harm for them
to become…just friends?

'Has something occurred to disturb you?' he asked
softly, the instant Lady Penrose had turned from him to
exchange a few words with his stepmother.

Abbie looked up to discover warmth still lingering in
eyes that had become searching. He had evidently detected
something in her expression to betray her slightly troubled
state. If anything, it was increasing with every passing second he retained that gentle hold on her fingers.

'If I appear a little concerned, it is only the prospect
of having to perform the waltz in public for the very first
time,' she said, with a flash of inspiration.

'There's no need for you to feel anxious' he assured her,
his gaze straying from her face to take in every detail of
her appearance.

She knew she was looking her best in a new gown of
spider gauze over pale blue silk, with matching accessories. Her hair had been beautifully arranged by Felcham in
a mass of bouncy curls into which the skilled abigail had
fastened a tiny spray of artificial forget-me-nots. To complete the ensemble Lady Penrose had kindly loaned her a
pair of sapphire earrings and a sapphire pendant, the end
of which almost reached the cleft between her breasts. His
gaze was like a soft caress as it lingered there momentarily,

bringing an extra glow to her cheeks which she could only hope he would attribute to the contents of a rouge pot.

'I'm no monster, Abbie, no matter what you might think,' he added, when at last he raised his eyes again to hers. 'I'll not roar at you if you should happen to step on my toes. In point of fact, I would consider it a small price to pay to have you partner me in a waltz.'

For some obscure reason Abbie was finding it a little difficult to breathe, and nigh on impossible to control her suddenly erratic pulse. It wasn't as if she was unused to receiving admiring glances from the opposite sex. Somehow, though, this man's regard was both unnerving and exciting at one and the same time.

'Why, sir, I do believe you are attempting to flirt with me,' she responded archly, in a valiant attempt to conceal her increasing confusion.

'I never flirt,' he countered, his voice little more than a husky whisper. 'And if I were ever tempted to try, be assured it would never be with you.'

Fortunately the arrival of more guests made it possible for Abbie to move on, but not before she had glimpsed the twitch at one corner of that far too attractive masculine mouth, which suggested strongly that he had detected her faint sigh of relief.

No sooner had she and her godmother found themselves two vacant chairs by the wall, than Kitty surprisingly joined them, looking bright-eyed and excited, and very pretty in a new gown of ivory silk.

'Bart said I might leave him and Mama to greet the rest of the guests, as the dancing will commence soon.' She gazed in a vague way about the crowded salon, decorated for the occasion with vases of flowers and several graceful potted palms. 'I must say Mama is very clever at organising this sort of thing. Even Bart admits that she's an extremely good hostess. And he isn't one to pass too many compliments, especially where our sex is concerned.'

Kitty then seemed to recall to whom she was speaking, and favoured Abbie with a furtive glance. 'I don't think he holds females in general in very high esteem, except the odd one or two. And you, definitely, number among those exceptions.'

Unfortunately Abbie, who at that moment had just happened to take an unwary sip from a glass of fruit punch, pressed upon her by a passing footman, dissolved into a fit of coughing.

'What rot!' she exclaimed when she was able.

'Oh, no, my dear,' Lady Penrose surprisingly countered. 'Kitty is absolutely right. Assuredly, her brother does admire you. From the first, I suspected that he was one of those gentlemen who have little patience for megrims and vapours. And for all that you are intensely feminine, you have inherited your grandfather's strength of character, as well as, I strongly suspect, a certain degree of his stubbornness too.'

Abbie wasn't certain whether this was intended as a compliment or not. From odd things Lady Penrose had let fall in recent days, she had gained the distinct impression that her godmother didn't hold Colonel Augustus Graham in the highest esteem. Which wasn't unduly surprising in the circumstances, she decided. She and her godmother had formed a close bond in a short time. It was perhaps understandable, therefore, that, given the Colonel's behaviour towards his granddaughter in recent years, Lady Penrose would have taken him in dislike.

Rudely brought out of these reflections by an unexpected squeal of delight from Kitty, Abbie turned her head to see what had induced her young friend to become so animated. Two young gentlemen had just entered the room, both dressed in the height of fashion: one startlingly so in primrose and lavender; the other more soberly in a black long-tailed coat and buff-coloured breeches. By the dour expression on Bart's face she considered it reasonable to suppose that he wasn't altogether pleased by the appearance of one, or perhaps both, of them.

'Why, it is! It's Cousin Cedric!' Kitty exclaimed, clapping her hands delightedly. 'I wonder what could have brought him to Bath? Do excuse me, I must go across and welcome him.'

'Now, which of them is Cousin Cedric, do you suppose?' Abbie murmured, having found it impossible from that distance to detect any similarity between the cousins. 'Is it the dandy who seems unable to move his head because of the ridiculous height of his shirt points, or the faultlessly groomed gentleman beside him?'

'I suspect it is the overdressed young sprig,' Lady Penrose answered bluntly, thereby betraying her opinion of his attire. 'The Adonis, unless I much mistake the matter, is none other than Charles Asquith, the Dowager Lady Marchbank's nephew. From what Hermione Marchbank tells me, her young ne'er-do-well of a nephew is frequently in dun territory. He only ever pays her a visit when payment of debts becomes pressing. The foolish creature usually bails him out eventually.'

Abbie could not help but smile at this frank disclosure. There wasn't a great deal Lady Penrose didn't know about the comings and goings that went on in Bath. Evidently she didn't hold the Dowager Lady Marchbank's nephew in the highest esteem. There was no denying, however, that he was very pleasing on the eye. Definitely the most handsome man in the room, Abbie swiftly decided, as Kitty steered the gentlemen towards them and she was able to study his perfectly chiselled features and the expert arrangement of guinea-gold curls more closely.

'So what brings you to Bath, Ceddie?' Kitty asked, after making the introductions, and surprisingly focusing her attention on her cousin, rather than his striking companion.

'My friend Charles, here, fancied a change of air, so I agreed to bear him company while he paid a visit to his favourite aunt.'

'Definitely in dun territory. The young care-for-nobody!' Lady Penrose muttered.

Fortunately no one except Abbie appeared to have heard, as Cedric Cavanagh had at that moment been admitting to having been a trifle bored with life in the capital of late. 'The same old round of balls and parties, and Mama parading every new debutante before me,' he went on, stifling a yawn. 'Really, it was becoming quite tedious.'

'Oh, I know I shan't find it dull at all,' Kitty responded. 'I'm looking forward to my come-out next year. I would have liked a Season this spring, but Bart flatly refused to entertain the notion. Said I needed practice in how to comport myself in polite society.'

Cedric drew an ornate snuffbox from the pocket of his nip-waisted jacket, and with a very affected air extracted a pinch of its contents. 'Loath though I am to agree with my big cousin on anything, I do believe he has a point there. Hoydenish behaviour ain't tolerated in town, especially among the debs. And I shouldn't like for you to disgrace the proud name we bear.'

Abbie, exerting masterly self-control, managed not to laugh. She didn't quite know what amused her more—her godmother's expression of comical dismay, or the darkling glance Kitty bestowed upon her dandified cousin.

She raised her own eyes in time to catch a touch of merriment flitting over handsome features, and decided that, although Lady Penrose might well have his measure, and he was possibly little more than the pleasure-seeking wastrel she considered him to be, Mr Asquith at least possessed a sense of humour.

'Ceddie, old boy, I'm surprised at your lack of *savoir-faire*,' he said. 'I shall certainly have to think seriously about excluding you from my circle of friends if you show signs of becoming boorish.'

Cedric's look of outrage was almost Abbie's undoing. 'I shall take leave to inform you, Charles, that my conduct and manners are held to be above reproach. Which is more than can be said for certain other members of my family. If Kitty's behaviour on occasions gives rise for concern in certain quarters, I for one could appreciate why, and never blame her. Her brother could hardly be considered a suitable role model. A positive brute!' A shudder ran through his wiry frame. 'I cannot tell you how it grieves me to think that Bart will one day become head of our family.'

'Taking my name in vain again, Cedric?'

Bart, having approached them completely unnoticed, had a wry grin on his face too. Abbie could only assume that, far from being annoyed, he had attained a deal of unholy amusement from overhearing his dandified cousin's strictures on his behaviour. Amazingly enough, Cedric made no attempt to deny it. More surprising still, he returned his much taller cousin's sardonic look without so much as a blink.

'I have never made any secret of the fact that I think you totally unsuitable for the role, Bartholomew,' he reiterated, withdrawing his gaze momentarily to remove an infinitesimal speck from his sleeve.

'No, not unsuitable,' Bart corrected, 'merely lacking the ambition to inherit the title. Unlike you, who covet nothing more. And in case it has escaped your memory,' he went on, not offering Cedric the opportunity to deny the accusation. 'our esteemed uncle took a second wife not two years ago.'

Cedric's lip curled, but it was a poor imitation of the look of contempt on Bart's face. 'It is unlikely at his advanced age that the marriage will ever prove fruitful.'

'He isn't so decrepit as you evidently imagine, Cedric, and is still able to perform all the duties of a husband,' Bart assured him. 'In his most recent letter I was delighted to read that he's very much looking forward to the autumn, when he expects Lady Cavanagh to present him with a pledge of her affection.'

Although Cedric appeared genuinely stunned by this intelligence for a moment, he recovered quickly enough, and shrugged. 'There's no guarantee it will be a boy.'

'True,' Bart agreed, looking suddenly grave. 'But I for one do hope it is the son he desires, even though, in my eyes, the child could never replace our cousin Philip, whose demise was a great shock to us all.'

It occurred to Abbie then how ignorant she was about the Cavanagh lineage. She experienced a surprising desire to learn more. Unfortunately an awkward silence followed Bart's admission, and she was not unduly sorry to hear the musicians hired for the evening strike up a chord to announce the commencement of dancing, and willingly acquiesced to Mr Asquith's request to partner him.

'Have you just recently removed to Bath, Miss Graham?' he enquired, as they took up their positions in the set.

'I have been here almost a month, sir, as a guest of my godmother, Lady Penrose.'

'You are not related to the Cavanaghs in any way?'

All at once Abbie became aware that several young ladies were darting envious looks in her direction. And little wonder! Charles Asquith was without a doubt the most striking gentleman present.

'No, sir, although I have been acquainted with Bartholomew Cavanagh for very many years. He is my grandfather's godson.'

'Ah, I see! So it is unlikely that you are able to satisfy my curiosity by divulging why there is a suggestion of antipathy between Cedric and Miss Cavanagh's brother?'

As they parted in the dance Abbie took the opportunity to glance at Bart, who was still bearing Lady Penrose company, and was surprised to discover him staring fixedly at the area set aside for dancing, his brow darkly forbidding. She had noticed Kitty and her cousin join the set, but she couldn't imagine either Cedric or Kitty was responsible for the highly disgruntled expression. In point of fact, had she been a fanciful female, she might have supposed that she was the object of his evident displeasure.

'No, sir, I'm afraid I cannot.' She risked a quick look over her shoulder, and smiled to herself. Cedric Cavanagh was as light on his feet as his partner. 'I cannot imagine the cousins have very much in common, though, can you?'

As the steps of the dance separated them again at that moment, he was unable to comment, and when they came together again, he voiced the hope that their arriving without invitations hadn't been responsible for giving rise to any ill feeling.

'I should think that highly unlikely, sir,' she assured him. 'I would be the first to admit that I do not know Bartholomew Cavanagh very well, but I wouldn't imagine he'd concern himself over such trifles.'

It was a timely reminder, and the instant the dance came to an end Abbie, surprisingly experiencing no reluctance whatsoever to relinquish her position as possibly the most envied female in the room to another, returned to Lady Penrose's side.

As luck would have it, Bart had by that time moved back across to the door to welcome some late arrivals, so she didn't hesitate to discover if her knowledgeable god-mother could satisfy her curiosity over Bart's genealogy.

'Oh, yes. I met all three Cavanagh brothers during my very first Season. Henry, the eldest and holder of the title, was by that time married, and so too was George, to Bart's mother. The youngest brother Frederick married his wife during my second Season, if my memory serves me cor-rectly. Each of the brothers produced one son. Again, if my memory serves me correctly, Lord Cavanagh's sole offspring, Philip, died three, or maybe four years ago in a riding accident. All very sad. As you heard Bart mention, his uncle remarried—a widow, I believe, and quite some years his junior.'

Abbie gazed across the room at their host, who at that moment happened to be conversing with a lively young matron who put Abbie forcibly in mind of a certain other female of Bart's acquaintance. She felt an uncomfortable feeling in the pit of her stomach, as though her insides were attempting to twist into knots.

'I gained the distinct impression that Bart was fond of his late cousin,' she said, in an attempt to force her thoughts in a new direction, 'though not so enamoured of Cedric. It's clear that Cedric is resentful of Bart's superior position in the family. I suspect, though, there's more to his obvious resentment than just that.'

Kitty, rejoining them a moment later, a little breathless after the dance, was able to enlighten them. 'Oh, Cedric has never quite forgiven Bart for laying about him with a riding crop,' she disclosed, grinning wickedly. 'Not that I blame Bart for doing so,' she added in her brother's defence, when her interested listeners looked appalled. 'Bart may have his faults, but no one could ever accuse him of not caring for his horses. He made it clear to Cedric that he wasn't to ride the prized hunter, but Cedric took no notice. I'm afraid when Bart discovered what Cedric had done he lost his temper.'

Kitty turned her head to find her brother heading in their direction once again. 'I must say, though, Bart's a lot more tolerant now than he used to be, but he can still become out of all reason cross on occasions.'

'Still talking about me behind my back, minx?' he quizzed her, as she twinkled wickedly up at him, and for the first time Abbie appreciated that there was a genuine bond of affection between brother and sister. He didn't wait for a response, but turned to her, reminding her that she had promised him the next dance.

'Having just discovered how brutal you can be on occasions, I'm not at all sure that I'm being altogether sensible in placing myself in your hands, even on a dance floor,' she teased, as they took up their positions in readiness for the first waltz.

He favoured her with one of his lopsided grins, which she was beginning to find most endearing, before glancing briefly across at his sister, still happily conversing with Lady Penrose. 'What has the little minx been saying to my detriment?'

'Merely that you beat your younger and much smaller cousin black and blue,' she enlightened him, surprisingly finding it no difficult matter to concentrate on the dance and converse at the same time.

'Damnable little idiot!' he growled, then smiled as perfectly arched brows rose. 'Cedric, not Kitty. No doubt you've learned why he earned my disapprobation? At best, he is merely a competent horseman. He might easily have broken his fool neck. Or worse, he might have injured my prized hunter! The trouble with Cedric is that he's too damned fond of getting his own way.'

Abbie smiled up at him in some amusement. 'That, if I may say so, seems to be a family failing.'

His bark of appreciative laughter induced several heads to turn in their direction. 'Yes, you're right. I could never tolerate being thwarted, still can't for that matter. On that occasion my father surprisingly took Cedric's part; said that I shouldn't have set about someone half my size. The black looks I kept getting from my aunt and uncle for having had the temerity to take a riding crop to their precious son didn't make the situation any easier. So I took off and inflicted myself upon you and your grandfather, something that I was inclined to do when things hadn't been going my way at home.'

Smiling ruefully, Bart shook his head, as if ashamed of past actions. 'That, as it happens, turned out to be the last time I stayed with your grandfather. If my memory serves me correctly, it was shortly after I paid that impromptu visit to your home that I decided to offer my services to King and Country and set sail for the Peninsula.'

Lowering her eyes, Abbie stared fixedly at the diamond pin nestling in the folds of his neckcloth. As though she would ever forget that particular visit! His life had changed afterwards and so too had hers. But in her case definitely not for the better!

As their dance drew to an end Abbie somehow managed to suppress the surge of resentment the memory of that particular visit never failed to evoke. She might well have succeeded in putting it from her mind entirely had it not been for the regard Bart subsequently received from the female guest who had paid him marked attention a little earlier.

Mrs Drusilla Herbert was not a total stranger. Since her arrival in the city, Abbie had seen her, accompanied by her dull, morose husband, at two or three fashionable parties. Up until that evening, however, she had never appreciated just how strong the resemblance was between Mrs Herbert and the late Sir Oswald Fitzpatrick's vivacious widow: the blonde hair, the blue eyes, the same full, pouting lips and curvaceous figures. Yes, they were strikingly similar. And possibly shared similar tastes in their lovers too, she thought bitterly, as she watched Bart look down, with a twisted half-smile, when full breasts were pressed invitingly against the sleeve of his jacket.

Resolutely turning her head away, she swallowed hard, but was given insufficient time to ponder on the disturbing possibility that the acrid taste which had suddenly invaded her mouth might have stemmed from something other than that old, lingering resentment, for a young gentleman was standing before her, requesting her hand for the next set of dances.

Thereafter a succession of different partners kept her on the dance floor for much of the time. Sadly, though, not one succeeded in holding her attention, at least not for long. Nor did any one of them manage to revive that tiny flutter of mingled excitement and pleasure that she had experienced when swirling round the room with Bart. This, and the fact that the host himself made no attempt to ask her to dance a second time, did little to combat her increasing ill humour. Consequently she didn't hesitate to slip quietly out of the French windows on to the terrace at the first available opportunity to be alone with her thoughts.

Considering that it was growing increasingly warm in the salon, Abbie was surprised to discover no one else taking advantage of the fresh air, and didn't hesitate to avail herself of one of the wicker chairs, tucked away in the shadowy corner of the terrace.

For a few moments she attempted to pierce the gloom and study the garden. She could just make out the outlines of various shrubs, and neatly clipped hedges, but could detect no movement, certainly nothing to suggest that she wasn't alone. Everyone else, it seemed, was happy to remain inside, enjoying the dancing and companionship of the other guests. So why wasn't she deriving much pleasure from the evening? It was so unlike her to fall prey to moods of despondency. Yet there was no denying she had, and deep down she knew precisely why.

She shook her head, wondering at herself, but refused not to face up to the truth. Unbelievably she had not attempted to prevent herself from becoming increasingly fond of a man whose manners and morals left much to be desired. She had believed…hoped, maybe, that he had changed, that he wasn't the same self-seeking, callous creature he had been in his youth. A forlorn hope, she thought bitterly. Any man who could flirt openly with another man's wife, in full view of the cream of Bath society and, worse still, with the lady's husband standing not six feet away, was past praying for! A debauched lecher he was and would remain. And it was utter madness to suppose he might ever change!

'Ah, Miss Graham,' a smooth voice drawled. 'So this is where you've been hiding yourself.'

Startled, Abbie swivelled round in her chair to discover Mr Asquith standing not three feet away. Evidently he had been looking for her, but the knowledge that her company was sought by the best-looking man at the party did little to revive her spirits, a fact that her smile quite failed to disguise.

'Has something occurred to upset you, ma'am?' he

asked, sounding a trifle aggrieved, as though accustomed to a more fulsome response from the objects of his attention. 'Would you prefer to be alone?'

'Not at all, sir,' she answered promptly, if not entirely truthfully. 'I merely wished for a breath of air, and became lost in thought.'

Perfectly moulded lips lifted into the most attractive masculine smile Abbie had ever seen, and yet surprisingly it did not even give rise to the slightest fluttering in her breast. 'Won't you sit down, Mr Asquith, and bear me company for a short while? Or did you seek me out at someone else's behest...my godmother's, perhaps?'

'It was entirely on my own account,' he admitted, seating himself, like the perfect gentleman, at a discreet distance so that not so much as a fold of her skirt brushed against his immaculate attire. 'I was hoping that you would favour me with the final dance before supper and allow me to bear you company during the meal afterwards, or are you promised to another?'

She could so easily have been, as numerous gentlemen had requested her company. But, foolish creature that she was, she had resolutely left that space on her dance card clear in the hope that Bart would wish to write his name there. What a bird-witted female she was to be sure!

Again she was forced to do battle with a surge of pique tinged with jealousy, before she could utter with any degree of conviction, 'I should be delighted to have you bear me company, sir, even though I know it shall make me the object of envy where most of the young ladies present are concerned.'

'Your appearance alone, my dear Miss Graham, would ensure that,' he murmured, before raising her hand and brushing his lips lightly across her fingers.

Although unaccustomed to such displays of gallantry,

Abbie didn't feel in the least embarrassed, or even shocked. In fact, if anything, the handsome Mr Asquith's behaviour rather amused her. All the same, she thought it might be prudent not to offer further encouragement to a person who was undoubtedly a master of the art of dalliance, and was on the point of uttering a mild reproof, when she caught a sudden movement. A moment later their host was emerging from the shadows, and in no good humour, if his deeply furrowed brow was any indication.

'I trust I do not intrude.' Bart's voice, though level, distinctly betrayed the fact that he didn't care a whit if he were *de trop*. He moved slowly towards them, as stealthily as a predatory beast, his gaze no less menacing either as it remained fixed on Abbie's companion. 'I believe you are engaged for the next dance, Asquith. Do not let us detain you.'

For several unnerving seconds Abbie feared a confrontation. Mr Asquith's admiring expression had faded and he appeared as grim now as their host. 'May I escort you back to the protection of Lady Penrose's side, Miss Graham?'

As Abbie had no intention of becoming involved in an unpleasant scene, she made up her mind to intervene the instant she observed the muscles along Bart's jaw tighten still further.

'There's no need for you to trouble yourself on my account, sir,' she answered, rising swiftly and placing herself between the two. 'Be assured I shall return in time for our dance.'

'What the devil do you mean by skulking out here with a man of his stamp, my girl?' Bart demanded, the instant Mr Asquith had sauntered back into the salon.

Abbie swung round to face him, the guard on her own temper weakening with every passing second. 'Where I go, and with whom, is entirely my own concern, Mr Cavanagh. Kindly remember that I am not Kitty, and therefore not obliged to defer to your dictates.'

Lips curled back into a smile that bore little resemblance to Mr Asquith's charming offering of minutes before. 'Had you been my sister, Miss Graham, you wouldn't be standing there with that expression of childish defiance, but would have been locked in your room by now, nursing a sore rear.'

By the glint in his eyes, Abbie was under no illusion that he would have derived immense satisfaction from carrying out the humiliating punishment, and was obliged to use every ounce of self-control she possessed not to take a hasty step away, and to school her features into an expression of unalloyed contempt.

'No doubt such brutish, cavalier antics appeal to the type of female on whom you choose to dispense your favours, Mr Cavanagh. Let me assure you that I, on the other hand, am completely unimpressed by such behaviour.'

'Is that so?' he husked. 'Perhaps a display of raw masculinity is precisely what would do you the most good, Miss Abigail Graham.'

The threatening gleam in his dark eyes intensified, a distinct warning that she foolishly chose not to heed. The next moment her arms were imprisoned behind her back, both wrists held captive in long fingers, while her chin was thrust up and held fast in his other shapely hand. There was a flash of white teeth as his gaze, softening noticeably, focused on her mouth.

Swiftly accepting that it would be futile to struggle, Abbie refused to demean herself by engaging in an undignified attempt to free herself. His face drew ever nearer, his intent clear, and she braced herself for the penance he was determined to exact.

For several moments shock held her rigid. Instead of the

hard, punishing kiss that she had anticipated, his lips were gently arousing, skilfully so, exerting only sufficient pressure to force hers to part and mould themselves perfectly to his. Instead of revulsion, she experienced a wave of tactile pleasure, a wealth of unfamiliar sensations that left no part of her immune. Never would she have believed it possible to experience such delight in the mere contact with a masculine mouth. Now she wanted him to free her, but not to run away. Quite the opposite, in fact. She longed to place her arms around him, to experience more than just contact with his lips.

As though he were able to read her every thought, he released her chin to run his hand down the length of her neck to the fine bones of her shoulder, his feather-light touch arousing a further surge of foreign sensations that had rapidly achieved precedence over conscious thought. In those few blissful seconds, when his lips followed the burning trail of his exploring fingers, and she heard the guttural sound rising in his throat, she was aware only of him and of the desire for this man alone to satisfy a rapidly increasing need.

Then, unbidden, that humiliating memory returned with a vengeance—Bart's ardent fondling of naked breasts before fumbling beneath skirts. She could even hear those same low moans of pleasure as clearly now as she had six years before, when his all but naked companion had slid her fingers beneath his breeches' flap.

Never would Abbie have believed it possible for shame to replace pleasure or disgust crush desire so comprehensively, or so swiftly, had she not experienced it for herself in those next wholly degrading moments when reality returned with a vengeance.

Easily escaping from the hold on her wrists, she stepped back, a surge of anger filling the void that disbelief had left in its wake. Before she realised what she was doing, her arm had swung in a wide arc, and her hand had made contact with a resounding slap. She saw the resulting flash of anger in Bart's dark eyes, but didn't remain long enough to witness the mingled bewilderment and sadness that swiftly replaced it.

Chapter Six

Gazing longingly at the lace-edged box on the table beside her chair, Lady Penrose once again summoned up sufficient will-power not to remove the lid and sample the delicacies within. To be sure, her goddaughter was proving a marvellous influence, she decided. Undeniably she was more inclined to take exercise, and she consumed far fewer glasses of her favourite tipple, port, these days. Furthermore, she had substantially reduced her daily intake of chocolates and sweet biscuits, with the result that she had lost several pounds in weight and was feeling a good deal better for having done so. She just wished that Abbie was deriving as much benefit and pleasure from her sojourn in Bath, as she herself was in having her as a guest under her roof.

Oh, undoubtedly the girl was contented enough, Lady Penrose reflected, resting her head against the chair and gazing absently up at the plaster-work ceiling. But contentment was far short of real happiness, and dear Abbie deserved her share of that after what she had endured in recent years.

She felt again that stab of resentment towards Colonel Graham for treating his granddaughter so unfairly, for not taking account of her wishes and feelings. Yet, at the same time, she was forced to own that she was increasingly taking the view that the Colonel's godson might indeed be the very one for Abbie. When the girl set aside her understandable resentment, she and Bartholomew Cavanagh rubbed along together very well. They were remarkably well suited and had, she very much suspected, more in common than either of them as yet realised. One thing was certain, though—Abbie, not in the least in awe of him, wasn't afraid to speak her mind, and Mr Cavanagh, Lady Penrose suspected also, rather admired her for it.

Unless she was very much mistaken too, their relationship had taken something of a turn for the worse the previous evening. Smiling to herself, she recalled the thunderous expression on Bart's face when he had spotted that handsome ne'er-do-well, Mr Asquith, heading for the terrace shortly after Abbie herself had taken refuge out there. She hadn't been best pleased herself, for although she was sure that her goddaughter was far too discerning to be beguiled by a handsome face, she had no intention of allowing her to become the butt of malicious gossip, and had been about to go after her, when Mr Cavanagh had gone striding past, heading purposefully towards the French window.

Just what had taken place outside after Mr Asquith's return to the salon was anybody's guess. All the same, their host's subdued mood, and her goddaughter's forced gaiety during the latter part of the evening, gave one every reason to suppose that something untoward had occurred.

A light tap on the door, quickly followed by the housekeeper's entrance, succeeded in restoring Lady Penrose to the present. Vaguely she recalled having heard the sound of the door-knocker, and assumed this must be the reason for the interruption.

'It's a gentleman wishing to see Miss Abbie, my lady. I wasn't certain whether she'd returned. Shall I inform Mr Cavanagh that she's not at home?'

'No, don't do that,' Lady Penrose countered, her mind working rapidly. 'Just show him up… Oh, and, Mrs Bates,' she added, checking the housekeeper's immediate departure, 'when my goddaughter returns, just ask her to come straight up here to me. There'll be no need to mention we have a visitor.'

Lady Penrose had every faith in her loyal housekeeper to carry out the instructions to the letter. Which was perhaps just as well, she decided, for it was highly likely that Abbie would avoid the drawing-room like the plague if she discovered the visitor's identity. And that would serve no useful purpose at all, especially if Mr Cavanagh's sole reason for calling was to attempt a reconciliation.

In point of fact, Lady Penrose's assumption was only partially correct. Bart had indeed decided to call with the intention of offering the olive branch, but he was also determined to discover just what it was that made Abbie decidedly wary of him.

He had spent the majority of the night staring blindly at the canopy above his bed, turning over in his mind certain aspects of their association since her arrival in Bath, most especially the events of the previous evening.

Once he had mastered his annoyance at being dealt a sound box round the ear, he had swiftly acknowledged he'd been at fault in presuming to criticise her behaviour, even though he still felt it incumbent upon him to stand her protector in the absence of her grandfather.

As far as the rest of the interlude on the terrace was concerned, he couldn't find it within himself to regret what had taken place between them. What had come as a complete surprise, however, was the feeling of overwhelming tenderness that had gripped him from the moment his lips had touched hers. Abbie too had not been indifferent to their very first embrace either; of that he felt sure. The rigidity had soon left her and her response had been sweetly satisfying. He had loosened his grasp and she had made not the least attempt to break free. Then, perversely, she had chosen to do so.

So what had happened? What had wrought the drastic change? He shook his head, at a loss to understand. If he had attempted to take his lovemaking a good deal further, he could have understood her becoming fearful or resentful. Only it was neither fear nor resentment her expression had betrayed the instant before she had lashed out at him like an avenging virago. No, it had been revulsion and anger.

The housekeeper's reappearance had the same effect upon him as it had had on her employer minutes before. Half-expecting to be denied an interview, he was pleasantly surprised when he was invited to follow her up the stairs. All the same, he couldn't quite disguise his disappointment when he entered the drawing-room to find only Lady Penrose present.

Her eyes twinkled at him, a clear indication that she hadn't failed to note his fleeting look of dissatisfaction. 'Mr Cavanagh, how nice to see you!' she greeted him, holding out her hand for him to bow over, which he did with remarkable grace for a man of his size. 'I do realise that it was my goddaughter whom you really wished to see. However, I am more than happy to entertain you until her return.'

After nodding dismissal to the housekeeper, she turned her attention to Bart again. 'Do help yourself to a glass of something, Mr Cavanagh. There's a particularly fine burgundy in the tall decanter over there. And whilst you're

about it, perhaps you'd be good enough to pour me a glass
of port. I've been remarkably good of late, but it cannot
hurt to suffer a little relapse now and then. After all, life
would be very dull if we didn't indulge in the odd little
vice, would it not?'

His fleeting disappointment having now receded completely, Bart couldn't help smiling to himself as he went
over to the decanters. He rather liked Lady Penrose, a
roguish matron of great charm and character, who was
certainly not lacking intelligence.

'You do not appear surprised by my visit, my lady,' he
remarked, after handing her her chosen tipple, and seating himself in the chair directly opposite.

'After your—er—disagreement with my goddaughter,
I would have been astonished had you not called, Mr Cavanagh,' she divulged, startling him somewhat.

He regarded her in silence for a moment over the rim
of his glass. 'Should I infer from that that Abbie has confided in you, ma'am?'

'You would be grossly mistaken if you did. Should you
be fortunate enough to come to know my goddaughter a
good deal better, sir, you will discover that she's one to
keep her own counsel for the most part. And she's most
definitely no talebearer.'

Lady Penrose took a moment to sample the contents
of her glass and to place the delicate vessel down on the
table beside her elbow, before favouring him with her full
attention once more.

'I, for one, am very grateful to you for your prompt
intervention last night. Abbie understandably would not
have been, however.'

He was suddenly alert. 'Then she does resent me for
some reason, ma'am… I suspected as much.'

Lady Penrose didn't attempt to deny it. 'I have no intention, Mr Cavanagh, of betraying my goddaughter's trust by repeating what she has told me. But I shall tell you this much… It is my belief that she has not confided in me fully, and that the real cause of her resentment…mistrust, call it what you will…lies very much deeper. If your intentions towards her are in any way serious, then you'd do well to discover what has fuelled those negative feelings towards you.'

Although intensely puzzled, Bart couldn't suppress a rueful smile. Up until that moment he hadn't fully appreciated the depths of his own feelings. Lady Penrose, on the other hand, had been a deal more discerning, and had suspected that his regard had been rapidly increasing. All the same, given that for some reason Abbie did bear him a grudge, was it possible to win her love?

Lady Penrose caught his attention by raising a warning finger. Then he heard it too: the light tread along the passageway. The next moment the door opened, and Abbie swept into the room, her sweet smile disappearing the instant her eyes fell upon him.

Lady Penrose was not slow to fill the breach. 'Ah, so there you are, dear! Did you manage to get everything you wanted in the library?'

With only the merest inclination of her head to acknowledge Bart's presence, Abbie came forward to give the two books she was carrying to her godmother. 'All except the Jane Austen novel you wanted, which I've been assured will be available for collection tomorrow.'

Bart, who had risen to his feet, was about to request a few minutes' private conversation with Abbie, when he detected the hint of warning in Lady Penrose's expression. Evidently she didn't think he would meet with much success, and undoubtedly she was right. Abbie, who had not attempted to sit down, looked as if she had every intention of departing at the first opportunity.

Lady Penrose managed to forestall her by saying, 'I'm so very pleased Mr Cavanagh has called, aren't you, dear? It grants us the opportunity to thank him for a most pleasurable evening.'

It was as much as Bart could do to maintain his countenance when a pair of violet eyes pierced him with a dagger look. There was a suspicion of a twitch, too, about Lady Penrose's mouth, before she added, 'And we are destined to enjoy many more pleasurable evenings during the forthcoming weeks. I received several invitations this morning.' She paused to look about her in a vague manner. 'I must have left the cards in the downstairs parlour. What a scatterbrain I am! Do be a dear and fetch them for me. I really ought to respond to one or two without delay.'

Abbie seemingly needed no further persuasion. She had reached the door before her godmother had finished speaking, and departed without uttering another word.

'Well…?' Lady Penrose smiled roguishly up at Bart. 'What are you waiting for? It will not take her long to discover the invitation cards are not in the parlour.'

Requiring no further prompting, he departed after the swiftest of farewells. As he descended the stairs he saw Abbie entering the room where they had conducted the interview with the groom a couple of weeks before, and didn't hesitate to follow.

She swung round as she detected the click of the door, her eyes hardening as she saw his hand still grasping the handle. 'What are you doing here? Surely even you are not so insensitive as to suppose that I've any desire to converse with you?'

'No, I don't suppose you have. But I've an earnest wish

to speak to you. If only to say how very sorry I am for my behaviour yesterday evening.'

Bart could see at a glance that he had taken the wind out of her sails. The implacable look was replaced by one of surprise, before she turned to stare out of the window. Clearly she hadn't expected an apology. Had she thought him incapable of making one, too high in the instep ever to consider himself in the wrong? His objective would be hard indeed to attain if she thought so poorly of him.

'You are not entirely to blame,' she said softly. 'My own behaviour left much to be desired. I should never have lashed out at you that way.'

Truth to tell, at the time he had not been best pleased, but now he could appreciate the amusing aspect of it. Not many men would successfully have broken through his guard. 'You pack a powerful wallop, ma'am. My ear stung for a considerable time afterwards.'

Although a watery chuckle greeted this sally, she looked genuinely repentant as she turned back to face him. 'Even so I shouldn't have done it, not after you had come out to the terrace merely to offer protection.'

Evidently he wasn't the only one to have passed a restless night. The interlude had obviously preyed on her mind also, and she was gracious enough to accept her share of the blame. He could not help but admire too the way she had remained at the party, and not feigned some trifling ailment in order to escape, like a frightened child, as most females of his acquaintance would undoubtedly have done.

'But there was no need for you to put yourself to the trouble,' she added, her tone marginally harsher. 'Lady Penrose had already put me on my guard concerning Mr Asquith. And be assured I'm no green girl to be beguiled by a handsome face. Besides which, it's rumoured that he's on the look out for an heiress, so he's hardly likely to concern himself with me.'

'Don't be ridiculous, girl!' Bart snapped, momentarily forgetting his resolve to keep a tight rein on his temper. Fortunately she didn't seem unduly put out by the reprimand. If anything, she appeared faintly amused by it. Nevertheless he decided it might be wise to try to choose his words with more care from this point in time.

'He could easily have discovered last night that you are closely related to Colonel Augustus Graham. Although your grandfather might not have gone into society too often in recent years, the fact that he's well-heeled is common knowledge.'

The amused glint in blue eyes intensified. 'But what isn't common knowledge, and what I shall not hesitate to make clear if Mr Asquith proves a nuisance by singling me out for particular attention, is that my grandfather has as good as told me that he intends to disinherit me.'

If Abbie had needed further proof that Bart was in complete ignorance of the situation which had existed between her and her grandfather for the past six years, she was being given it now. His expression was a mixture of astonished disbelief and anger.

'The devil he has!' he barked. 'I don't believe a word of it. The Colonel absolutely dotes upon you.'

She shrugged, before turning again to stare sightlessly through the window. 'Believe it or not, as you will. It is true, all the same. We have become estranged, Bart. And I cannot foresee that situation changing.'

'But why, Abbie?' He could not have sounded more genuinely puzzled, or troubled by what he was hearing, had he tried. 'What caused this rift between you? You used to be so very close.'

'Yes, we were,' she agreed, after several moments of

doing battle with her conscience, debating whether or not to tell him, and finally deciding that he would discover the truth eventually anyway. 'Unfortunately, though, my grandfather could never find it within himself to forgive me for refusing to marry you.'

When no response was forthcoming, Abbie turned to discover him staring fixedly at the carpet, his expression difficult to read, until finally he raised his eyes and she noticed that normally alert gleam shadowed by an emotion bordering on despair.

'So, that's it,' he surprised her by murmuring. 'That's why you bear me a grudge, harbour resentment. Yes, it is reason enough to dislike me.'

She experienced a strong impulse to rush over and place her arms about him, but curbed it. 'I do not dislike you, Bart,' she assured him softly. 'In fact, there have been times in recent weeks when I've liked you very well. But I cannot deny there have been many occasions when I've felt very embittered. As a girl, I resented my grandfather's obvious affection for you. And I very much resented the fact that he never attempted to take account of my feelings when he proposed that ridiculous union between us.'

Brown eyes narrowed at this, but, whatever had crossed Bart's mind, he chose not to share it with her, and merely asked, 'So what do you intend to do now? Remain with your godmother until he comes to his senses and sees reason?'

Her shout of laughter contained precious little mirth. 'For six years I hoped, prayed he would do just that, would come to acknowledge that my feelings should be taken into account. But I refuse to delude myself any longer. His attitude won't change. And I refuse to live in a house where I'm virtually ignored for the most part, and treated with no more respect than a servant. No…' she shook her head '…he'll not change. His arranging my visit to Bath at a time when he knew for certain you'd be here is proof enough of that.'

His sigh was audible. 'So, will you remain with your godmother? She's clearly very fond of you.'

'Yes, she's wonderful company, and I like her very well, only…'

'Only what?' he prompted.

'I do not wish to become her pensioner. Ideally I would like to set up an establishment of my own, be independent. Unfortunately that cannot happen until I'm five-and-twenty, and receive the inheritance left to me by my mother. I suppose I could repay Lady Penrose's kindness by becoming her companion. Only I do not think she would agree to it. And I know she would be hurt, not to say insulted, if I engaged in some genteel occupation in order to pay my way. The only other possibility is for me to take up painting in earnest, and hope to earn a little money that way.'

Without realising it, Abbie had spoken of an idea she had been nurturing for quite some time, and was surprised when she discovered Bart regarding her thoughtfully, disquiet etched in every contour of his face.

'Do not concern yourself on my account, sir. I shall come about. At least I now reside in a house where I'm treated with affection and respect, and am made to feel welcome.'

'Confound the Colonel!' Bart exploded, his temper having got the better of him again. 'How long does he intend to remain away?'

'I'm not altogether sure. It all depends on how long he remained in Yorkshire. He intended to spend some time with his nephew, Sir Montague Graham. Why?' She looked suspiciously across at him. 'You do not propose to pay him an impromptu visit, surely, because of what I've just told you?'

'Damned right, I do!' he answered, not attempting to moderate his language. 'And he'll find a missive, clearly stating my own views on the matter, awaiting him on his return.'

Abbie was beside him in an instant and, without conscious thought, placed her fingers on his arm. 'Don't, Bart…please don't do anything you might one day come to regret. I've no desire to be the cause of an estrangement between you. The matter is none of your making, none of your concern.'

'On the contrary.' If possible, he looked more doggedly determined than before as he stared at the tapering fingers resting lightly upon his sleeve. 'It is very much my concern. I owe you a debt of gratitude I could never hope to repay,' he astounded her by admitting. 'But for you I would have undoubtedly remained that wholly selfish care-for-nobody I was in my youth. I truly believe your refusing to marry me was the making of me, Abbie. I wouldn't attempt to suggest that I am now without fault, but at least I've learned to consider the feelings of others during these past years. Whilst I benefited, you were made to suffer. To me that's intolerable!'

Although moved by the stance he had adopted, she couldn't help but feel saddened that she might easily be the cause of a rift between two gentlemen who had been as close as father and son.

'If you make contact with my grandfather, Bart, then do so on your own account, for it shall not benefit me,' she said, in a last attempt to sway him. 'Believe me when I tell you that I'm content enough here, and have no desire to return to Foxhunter Grange.'

She half expected him to suggest that she might think

differently in time. What she did not anticipate was the blunt question he did ask. 'Why did you refuse to marry me, Abbie?'

Unable to return that penetrating gaze, she lowered her eyes, before taking refuge before the window once more. The silence lengthened between them, forcing her to give him an answer. 'We were too young… We would not have suited.'

'I agree with you, at least in part,' he responded, moving slowly across to the door. 'Your godmother will be wondering what has become of you, so I'd best take my leave.'

A few moments later, Abbie heard the front door close and saw him emerge from the house, appearing lost in thought, in a world of his own. Had he believed her? she wondered. Or had he suspected that she'd not been totally honest? And why hadn't she told him the complete truth? She shook her head, uncertain in her own mind just why she hadn't done so. She only knew that, for some reason, it didn't seem so important any more. What she had witnessed on that certain afternoon six years ago belonged to the past. Yes, Bart had changed. Why had it taken her so long to appreciate the fact?

The following day saw Abbie in the lending library again. She had accompanied her godmother almost to the Pump Room, when she had remembered the book, and had slipped away before Lady Penrose could voice any protest.

As promised, the librarian had the novel already wrapped, awaiting collection. She placed it into her reticule for safety's sake, and was about to retrace her steps, when her way was blocked by a tall figure looming in the doorway.

'Good heavens, Bart!' She smiled up at him a little tentatively, as he wasn't looking best pleased about something. 'I'm about to visit the Pump Room. I didn't expect to see you here.'

'And I didn't expect to come upon you without so much as a maid to bear you company,' he responded tersely. 'What's Lady Penrose about, permitting you to go about the city unescorted? I'll have a thing or two to say about that when next I see her.'

Inclined to be more amused than anything else by this blatant interference in her affairs, Abbie merely suggested that they remove themselves, as they were beginning to attract attention, not to mention succeeding in preventing others from entering the premises.

'Really, you are the outside of enough on occasions, Bart!' she told him, as they set off in the direction of the Pump Room. 'It will be all over Bath by tomorrow that you're taking an uncommon interest in my welfare. That was none other than Lady Crowe attempting to gain entry to the library. She's reputed to be one of the city's most notorious gossips.'

The broad shoulder that rose in a shrug of indifference was proof enough that he wasn't unduly troubled, even before he said, 'Well, what of it? It's no less than the truth. I do take an interest in you… Damnation!'

Abbie wasn't sure which surprised her more: the admission itself, or the forceful expletive that swiftly followed. The next moment her arm was taken in a vicelike grip and she was thrust none too gently down a side road, and into a doorway.

'What on earth are you about, Bart? This isn't the way I wish to go at all.'

'I know. But it's the only way to avoid meeting that confounded Herbert creature!' he snapped. 'That's the one big fault with residing in this confounded place—you cannot avoid bumping into those people you least wish to see! And

I cannot abide clinging females. The wretched woman has been casting out lures since the day we first met.'

Bart watched Abbie's blue eyes widen in astonishment. 'What...? Don't tell me she's a particular friend of yours?'

'No. But I thought she was one of yours,' Abbie admitted, after she had recovered sufficiently from the shock. 'You appeared to be enjoying her company the other evening, at any rate.'

'If you are referring to our party,' he responded, not slow to follow her train of thought, 'then let me remind you that, as host, I was obliged to make all my guests welcome. Had I had my way, she wouldn't have been invited in the first place, only I left all that side of things to Eugenie.'

He risked a glance over his shoulder. Then, deciding it was safe enough to do so, guided Abbie back towards the main street. 'Now what were we talking about...? Ah, yes, I remember! Your welfare.'

Again he received that startled wide-eyed look, and smiled. 'I've been giving a deal of thought to what you were saying yesterday, Abbie,' he admitted, 'and am pleased to say that I'm in a position to help.'

She merely looked suspicious now. 'What do you mean?'

'I should like to commission you to paint a portrait.'

'Whose?'

'Mine.' His shout of laughter induced several passers-by to stare in their direction. 'I cannot imagine why you're regarding me as though I've just sprouted a second head. Why shouldn't I have my portrait painted? I'm a man of means. It's high time I had my likeness done again.'

For several moments all she did was to gape up at him. 'Are you in earnest?'

'Completely,' he assured her. 'It would mean, of course, your returning to Cavanagh Court with us next week. For reasons which I'll not go into, I've been forced to shorten our stay in Bath. Lady Penrose is most welcome to bear you company, if she chooses to do so, but her presence is not essential. My stepmother will be happy enough to act as chaperon in your godmother's stead.'

When she made no attempt to respond, Bart looked down to discover her staring thoughtfully ahead, evidently willing to give the suggestion some consideration. 'Take a few days to think it over, and let me know your decision at the end of the week.'

Chapter Seven

It was midway through the afternoon, when the carriage turned off the road and into a tree-lined driveway, that Abbie caught her first sight of Cavanagh Court. Built in the mellow Cotswold stone, the leaded glass in its mullioned windows glinting in the sunlight, the Tudor manor house was, as she had frequently heard her grandfather remark, the most delightfully situated country residence for a gentleman of means.

As she followed Kitty and her mother into the entrance porch, Abbie had a brief glimpse of well-tended gardens, before her attention was again claimed by the house itself. As though by some intangible force, it drew her into the entrance hall. Its atmosphere, warm and friendly, wrapped itself around her, making her feel instantly at home, though it was left to the master himself, who, travelling in his curricle, had arrived a short time before, to utter the verbal welcome.

'I trust you will be very happy here, Abbie. If there's anything you require, do not hesitate to ask. I insist you treat my home as your own.'

The warmth in his eyes fading marginally, he turned his attention to his stepmother. 'I'll leave you to ensure that our guest is made comfortable, Eugenie. There are one or two matters requiring my immediate attention.'

Abbie was instantly aware of the change in Mrs Cavanagh's demeanour. All at once she seemed a little unsure of herself, nothing like the calm, sensible companion she had proven to be throughout the entire journey from Bath.

'Oh, yes, of course…but… Oh, where to put her? Are you certain you have no preference?'

'Oh, for heaven's sake!' Bart snapped, experiencing the usual stab of annoyance whenever his stepmother fell into one of her twittering moods. Then he noticed a perfect brow marred by a frown of staunch disapproval, and amazingly found his irritation waning. 'Why not put her in the blue bedchamber?' he suggested, before he bethought him of something else, and turned to his aged butler who had remained, awaiting possible instructions. 'Is the back bedchamber in the east wing still empty of furnishings?'

'Indeed, yes, sir. No decision has yet been made on a possible new colour scheme.'

'In that case, Eugenie, I would definitely suggest the blue bedchamber. That adjoining room can then function as a studio for Abbie.' The warmth instantly returned to his eyes as he fixed them on his guest. 'I shall leave you in Eugenie's capable hands, and look forward to seeing you at dinner, if not before.'

'I must say you have a wonderfully soothing effect on my brother, Abbie,' Kitty murmured, having studied his recent behaviour with interest. 'I thought Bart and Mama were reaching a better understanding whilst we were in Bath, but it seems I was wrong, and things really haven't improved at all.'

As it happened, Abbie wasn't left to puzzle over the surprising disclosure for long, for Mrs Cavanagh, after issuing instructions to her maid, took it upon herself to escort

Abbie to the allotted bedchamber, a light, airy room, the furnishings of which were in varying shades of blue, and which boasted a commanding view of an ornamental lake.

'Oh, this is charming!' Abbie declared, casting her eyes over the powder-blue bed hangings and matching drapes. 'How lucky you are to be mistress of such a delightful house!'

She took a moment to cast a glance across at the door that she assumed led to the adjoining chamber, which was to function as her studio, before turning in time to catch a wistful expression flitting over her companion's face.

'Yes, you're right. This is a pleasant house,' Eugenie Cavanagh agreed at length. 'Yet, I must confess that, although I've been very happy living here, most especially when Bart's father was alive, I've never felt wholly mistress of Cavanagh Court.'

She gave an uncertain little laugh as she went over to study the view from the window. 'That must seem strange to you, my dear. This has been my home for eighteen years, and still I find it difficult to issue instructions to the servants, most especially to those who were here when Bart's mother was alive. And I've never attempted to effect many changes. I realise now the mistake I made—I shouldn't have striven so hard to become a second mother to Bart, but ought to have concentrated my efforts on becoming mistress of this fine house.'

Abbie wasn't at all sure just why she had been designated the role of confidante. It was true that, from the start of their journey from Bath, Eugenie had suggested that all needless formality should cease between them and they had rubbed along together very well. All the same, it did not automatically follow that they were ever likely to become close friends.

Perhaps, though, Abbie mused, seating herself on the

edge of the bed, Eugenie felt some explanation was due for her show of diffidence in the hall a short time earlier. Abbie had to admit she had been surprised by the uncharacteristic behaviour, and more so by Bart's unfortunate reaction to it. She knew well enough that he could be quite abrupt on occasions, and wasn't the sort to suffer fools gladly, but even so, from what she'd witnessed while in Bath, Bart had always treated Eugenie with the utmost respect.

Not quite knowing what to think, she asked, 'Are you trying to suggest that Bart resents your being here?'

'Oh, good heavens, no!' Eugenie didn't hesitate to assure her. 'At least,' she amended, 'I do not believe he does so any longer.'

'Which means that he did at one time,' Abbie prompted, when Eugenie came to sit beside her on the bed.

'Well, that was only to be expected, wasn't it?' Eugenie responded, betraying a wealth of sympathy and understanding. 'Poor Bart was still a boy when his mother died. They were very close, sadly much closer than he and his father were ever destined to become. Within twelve months his father had married me, which I think Bart took as a kind of betrayal, an insult to his mother's memory. Kitty's birth the following year certainly did nothing to improve matters. Relations between Bart and his father went from bad to worse during that period. He was punished regularly for his rudeness to me, which I considered made the situation so very much worse.' A sigh escaped her. 'Ashamed though I am to admit to it, I felt enormous relief whenever he went to stay with you and your grandfather. I'm sure Bart was much happier there.'

Perhaps he was, Abbie mused, smiling to herself. But she most certainly was not! She could recall how much she resented his visits, so it wasn't too difficult to appreciate the resentment Bart harboured towards his stepmother, even if the poor woman had done little to merit it.

'But Bart's attitude did change, surely, as he grew older?'

'Oh, yes,' Eugenie didn't hesitate to confirm. 'He certainly became more tolerant of the situation here. And whenever he came home on leave during his years in the army, he couldn't have been kinder to me, and openly admitted how glad he was that I had married his father and made him happy during his declining years. Yes, he has mellowed in many ways. Yet he remains a strong-willed man who continues to find my displays of hesitancy a little trying.'

The wistful expression once again fluttered over Eugenie's kindly face. 'One of my dearest wishes is to see him happily married. I sincerely hope his future bride possesses the strength of character, which I sadly lacked, to make this house her home, and not maintain it as a shrine to his mother, which I foolishly always did.'

Abbie was at a loss to understand just why Eugenie should wish to share her concerns, unless it was because, misguidedly, Eugenie believed that she could influence Bart to make changes to his house and lands so that his future bride wouldn't feel, as clearly Eugenie had always done, as though she were living in the shadow of the late Elizabeth Cavanagh. If so, Eugenie was destined to be disappointed, for although Abbie felt she and Bart had developed a better understanding and had, against all the odds, become friends during their weeks together in Bath, she wouldn't dream of attempting to interfere in matters that were none of her concern. She was here to paint a portrait, not involve herself in the personal concerns of the various members of the Cavanagh family.

A housemaid entering with a pitcher of warm water

spared Abbie the necessity of having to formulate some non-committal response. Eugenie immediately left her in the capable hands of the young maid who, after ably assisting her out of her travel-creased garments and into a lightweight muslin gown, was in the process of repairing the damage the journey had wreaked on the silky black hair, when the bedchamber door opened yet again, and Kitty came skipping lightly into the room, appearing none the worse for having spent several hours in a closed carriage.

'Well, I must say, Kitty, you look wonderfully restored after the journey.'

'Oh, travelling never tires me. Mama said you would want to rest for an hour or so before dinner. But I said that was fudge, that you weren't in your dotage, and would enjoy a tour of the house.'

Once again Abbie found herself at a loss to know quite how to respond. If the truth were known, she would have welcomed an hour's rest, but rather than be considered an ancient, she refrained from admitting as much, and merely instructed her seemingly tireless young friend to lead the way.

The tour commenced with an inspection of the bedchambers in the east wing, all of which, though tastefully furnished, were betraying varying signs of wear. Wallpapers and curtains in several rooms were sadly faded, proof that little had been changed over the years.

They then proceeded to the west wing, and even though she was assured that the master of the house was still ensconced in his library, Abbie was reluctant to view the main apartments. She was certainly not disposed to linger either when she found her eyes returning again and again to the room's most imposing feature: a huge four-poster bed, adorned with claret-coloured hangings. Consequently she had no hesitation in agreeing to Kitty's suggestion of viewing the kitchens next.

'It will give you the opportunity to meet Cook,' Kitty added, as she led the way out of the room and along the passageway. 'Figg is a dear. She'll prepare anything you fancy, providing she thinks the lord and master will enjoy it too. Like all the older servants, she's a soft spot for Bart. His preferences always come first with them.

'We'll use the back stairs. It will be quicker,' she added, opening a door at the end of the passageway, which led on to a stairwell.

'I assume this leads to the servants' quarters,' Abbie said, gazing up at the flight of stone steps.

Kitty nodded. 'And out on to the roof. This part of the house is newer than the rest. Bart's grandfather enlarged the property about forty years ago. You can gain access to a limited part of the roof only, but there's a tremendous view of the surrounding countryside. Would you like to see?'

Abbie needed no second prompting, and as she followed up the stone steps, and out on to the leads, she was forced to acknowledge just how ignorant she still was about Bart's family history. 'You see, Kitty, I assume, from what you were just saying, that the house and lands once belonged to his maternal grandfather?'

'Yes, that's right—the Bellinghams. Bart was named after his grandfather. Mama remembers old Bartholomew Bellingham. She says Bart resembles his grandfather in character.'

Abbie's eyes began to twinkle. 'Ahh, I see! So he was an irascible gentleman too, was he?'

Kitty gurgled appreciatively. 'Oh, Bart isn't so bad. And at least he's fair. There isn't a person working in the house or on the land, as far as I'm aware, who doesn't have the utmost respect for him. He's really looked after this place since Papa died. The love of the land is in his blood, I suppose. He adores it here.'

While Kitty had been speaking, Abbie had been admiring the glorious landscape. Except for the moderate-sized park surrounding the property, the farmland stretched out as far as the eye could see. 'Yes, I can well understand why he does,' she said, drawing her attention away from the tremendous view to gaze absently down at one or two cracks in the masonry near her hand. 'And do you enjoy living here too?'

'Oh, yes,' Kitty didn't hesitate to assure her. 'Mama's youngest sister married a clergyman and still lives in the local parsonage, which was Mama's home before she married, so I've always had my cousins for company. I very much enjoyed our stay in Bath, but I'm not sorry to be back.'

Abbie frowned at this. It had occurred to her during the journey that Kitty had seemed surprisingly cheerful considering her visit to Bath had been shorter than planned. 'I must confess your attitude surprises me a little. After all, returning here has meant that you've been forced, for the time being at least, to relinquish any hope of a speedy engagement between Miss Whitham and your brother.'

All at once Kitty seemed to find it necessary to study the nails on her left hand. 'Oh, well, I can't be too disappointed about that. I was forced to come to the conclusion you were right all along. Caroline Whitham is pretty enough, but Bart would soon have tired of her. He needs someone who isn't afraid to stand up to him.'

Evidently mother and daughter thought alike where the master of the house was concerned, Abbie mused, smiling to herself as she accompanied Kitty back down the stairs to a stone passageway, by which one gained access to a sizeable courtyard at the back of the house and also the kitchen area.

After being introduced to most members of the household staff, Abbie was taken on a tour of the downstairs rooms, ending with a visit to the library, where they found Bart, seated behind his desk, reading through a pile of correspondence.

He looked up as they entered, and raised his hand, dismissing his sister's apology for disturbing him. 'I've dealt with everything I intend to do today.' He looked directly at Abbie. 'Did you manage to rest after the journey?'

'Good heavens, you're as bad as Mama!' Kitty scolded. 'Abbie isn't in her dotage quite yet. She doesn't need to rest.'

There was just a suspicion of a twitch at one corner of his mouth as Bart rose to his feet, and gathered together the letters. 'Dare I ask what you have been up to then since your arrival?'

'I've been showing Abbie round the house,' Kitty answered, her gaze straying beyond her brother's shoulders towards the window, where there remained clear evidence of a recent fire. 'How do you suppose it started, Bart? One of the servants being clumsy? Barryman is getting old, you know. It's high time he retired.'

'He's still more than capable of performing all his duties,' he countered, after watching Abbie's brow furrow as she examined the window. 'It was he, after all, who discovered the fire. He raised the alarm, and managed to have it put out before it had taken too firm a hold.'

He had tried to sound sublimely unconcerned, and was thankful when his sister didn't pursue the matter. 'If you're not too fatigued after your tour of the house, perhaps you'd both care to join me for a stroll in the garden? I could do with some fresh air.'

Kitty appeared to consider for a moment. 'Er—no, I think I'll bear Mama company for an hour before dinner. I know I can safely leave Abbie in your capable hands, brother dear,' she said, casting him a wickedly provocative grin before departing.

Bart couldn't help smiling too as he watched the door close behind her. His sister might be a confounded little minx on occasions, but she was no fool. Unless he was greatly mistaken, she already suspected that his reason for inviting Abbie to the Court had little to do with a desire to have his portrait painted.

He transferred his attention to the female who had come to occupy his thoughts far more than any other had succeeded in doing to find her still gazing avidly at that certain telltale spot on the window frame. It was obvious that she suspected something; suspected that the explanation given for the damage to the carpet, curtains and a sizeable section of wall covering was not the true one. He ought he supposed to feel aggrieved that she doubted his word, but he didn't. In fact, he was happy to confide in her, for he knew instinctively that she could be trusted.

'Is it your intention to study that window until it's time to go in to dinner? I'm sure you'd find a tour of the gardens a far more pleasant way of occupying yourself.'

'W-what?' She turned, that troubled frown still very much in evidence.

'What is it about my library window that causes you such concern?' He raised one dark brow in a quizzical arch. 'It could do with a coat of paint, I grant you.'

'It would benefit from some slight repair too. The wood around the catch has been gouged out. Recently, I suspect. The hallmark of an attempted break-in, I should say.'

When his only response was a crooked half-smile, Abbie guessed the truth at once. 'So none of the servants was to blame. It was an intruder. Have you discovered any valuables missing?'

Bart shook his head. 'No. Robbery, I do not believe, was the motive.'

She was not slow to understand. 'You mean the fire was started deliberately?'

Without responding, he came to stand so close beside her that the sleeve of his jacket brushed against her arm. Although his nearness brought vividly to mind that unforgettable interlude on a certain Bath terrace, Abbie experienced not the smallest qualm in being alone with him, and didn't attempt to put a seemly distance between them by taking a step away either.

Tall and strong, he could overpower her in a trice, just as he had done on that memorable evening not so long ago. Even so, some inner feminine wisdom assured her that, although he was certainly no saint, he would never force his attentions on an unwilling female, and would never take advantage of her vulnerability while she remained a guest under his roof.

Raising her eyes, she studied the line of his firm jaw. Yes, the rugged contours of his face undoubtedly betrayed his strength of character, intelligence and determination. Yet she could detect nothing to indicate that he was lacking compassion. If anything, the tiny lines about his eyes betrayed a sense of humour, and although there was nothing weak about the set of his mouth, the sensual curve to his bottom lip suggested a passionate nature rather than a cold-blooded one.

'Since the war there has been much unrest,' he began at last, and Abbie found it no difficult matter to concentrate on what he was saying. 'Hardly surprising when one considers that men who fought bravely for their country have come home to find themselves surplus to requirement. Without work they are unable to support their families. Discontent among the poor is widespread, and seems particularly prevalent hereabouts.'

He took a moment to stare across the park at the field where cows were grazing. 'I'm by no means the only one to have suffered loss of livestock and damage to property. Lord Warren, my nearest neighbour, has been a victim of the unrest too. But, for reasons which escape me completely, I seem to be the prime recipient of the surge of malcontent in this area that began earlier in the year. Which I find hard to understand, as I'm one of the few landowners hereabouts who have spoken out vociferously against the high corn prices. The torching of my library curtains and carpet was merely the latest in what I very much fear will turn out to be ever-increasing attacks.'

'So what do you intend to do?' she asked, sure in her own mind that he had already taken steps to protect his property. He did not disappoint her.

'As you heard Kitty mention a short while ago, our butler, Barryman, is no longer young, but remains conscientious. It's largely thanks to him the damage was minimal. All the same, a man of his advanced years cannot be expected to keep a constant vigil. That, in part, was the reason I shortened our stay in Bath, so that I could be on hand should anything else untoward occur. I have men now patrolling the grounds at night. Lord Warren is also arranging for a peacekeeping force to be sent to the area. Having a company of soldiers riding about the countryside will possibly deter many from engaging in unlawful acts, but it will prove no lasting solution to the problem of unrest.'

He drew his attention away from the view beyond the window to look down at her, and his features were instantly softened by the warmth of his smile. 'But all is far from doom and gloom. Besides which, the intruder, though it wasn't his intention, has served me a good turn. The library has been looking increasingly shabby for years. The fire has meant that I cannot postpone the redecorating any longer. So I should appreciate some advice on what new carpet and curtains to select.'

Abbie didn't attempt to hide her astonishment. 'It's Eugenie you ought to consult.'

He raised one brow in a sceptical arch. 'My stepmother has made few changes since she came to live in the house.'

'No, I know she hasn't.' Abbie didn't wish to be a tale-bearer by repeating what Eugenie had said to her in confidence. All the same she could not resist adding, 'Has it never crossed your mind to wonder why?'

Narrow-eyed, he regarded her in silence for a moment, then suggested they begin their tour of the garden, and said nothing further until they were outside, enjoying the warm, rose-scented air.

'I was not always kind to Eugenie,' he admitted, pausing to examine several particularly fine blooms. 'In fact, during those first years of her marriage to my father I was downright cruel, needlessly so, for she did nothing to warrant my antipathy. I very much resented her taking my mother's place, and made my feelings brutally clear. It's only in recent years that I have come to appreciate her fully, to acknowledge what a really fine person she is. But the damage, I'm afraid, was already done. She remains to this day a little nervous in my company, and her attacks of diffidence, her reluctance to make decisions, irritates me on occasions. If I did ask her to choose new furnishings for the library, I know she would be plaguing me constantly for assurances that I approve her choice.' He smiled wryly. 'And I'm not a man renowned for his limitless patience.'

He was nothing if not brutally honest, and Abbie couldn't help admiring him for this. 'You do not, if what

I have been told is true, resemble your late father in character. I seem to remember someone, possibly my grandfather, saying he was a restrained, tolerant gentleman.'

'He was,' Bart concurred, that wry smile in evidence again. 'But I tried his patience to the limits on more than one occasion over my attitude towards Eugenie. No one regrets that more than I. And not only for the beatings I justly received.' He shook his head, as though at some private thought. 'Eugenie proved to be his ideal mate. She suited my father very well, more so, I suspect, than my mother ever did. Like myself, my mother inherited that determined Bellingham streak. Yet she had a gentler side too, especially where I was concerned. It was she who planted the rose gardens here.'

'She certainly favoured the colour pink,' Abbie said, then realised when he frowned that he might possibly have taken the simple observation as criticism.

'You're right,' he agreed after a moment. 'There isn't much variation in colour. What would you do to improve it?'

'Maybe alternating squares of deep red and pink would look striking. And beyond the box hedge the same arrangement with white and yellow, perhaps.'

Bart caught sight of a slightly stooped figure, busily removing the dead flower heads, just beyond one of the dividing hedges. 'Figg,' he called, 'I want some changes made to the rose garden.'

By the deep lines of disapproval etched in the weather-beaten face, Abbie suspected the good Mr Figg didn't approve of change. As he came along the path towards them, he favoured her with a rather hard, suspicious look before touching his forelock and gazing up at his master.

'It be true, sir, that one or two of the bushes be getting old, but they still produce fine blooms, as you can see.'

'It's neither the quality nor the quantity of blooms that is at fault, Figg, merely the lack of variation in colour. So you will make yourself available tomorrow morning to discuss some alterations with Miss Graham, here. She has offered some splendid suggestions that I wish you to put into effect as soon as possible.'

Abbie wasn't certain which annoyed her more—Bart's lofty assumption that she would be happy to redesign his garden, or the openly hostile look the head gardener darted in her direction before he acknowledged his master's instructions and trudged away.

'I cannot imagine why you might suppose, Mr Cavanagh, that I should wish to involve myself in improvements to your gardens during my time here at the Court? Moreover, that I have the least desire to work hand in hand with such a surly, unpleasant fellow as your head groundsman?'

The haughty tone was completely wasted on him. 'Oh, you'll not be able to start the portrait until all the materials you require have arrived, which won't be for several days. In the meantime you'll not wish to be idle. And I have no intention of allowing you to become bored. Or slaving over a red-hot palette from dawn till dusk, for that matter. And as far as Figg is concerned, you'll have him eating out of your hand in no time.'

Abbie wasn't so sure, but decided not to pursue the matter and merely asked, as he calmly entwined her arm through his and they set off down a different path, whether the gardener was any relation to the cook.

'Brother and sister. Although neither is married, Cook is addressed as though she were. Both of them are unfailingly loyal.' His lips twitched. 'That is why I'm prepared to overlook my head gardener's—er—surliness. And the fact that he's good at his job, as are all those in my employ…with perhaps one exception.'

They had by this time arrived at the courtyard at the back of the house, from which one gained access to the stabling block and several large barns. There seemed a surprising lack of activity, the reason for which was soon explained when Bart's head groom emerged from the stable, leading a handsome chestnut stallion.

'The lads be over at the 'ouse, sir, sampling Mrs Figg's plum cake. Young Josh has joined 'em too, miss, if you were wanting a word wi' 'im,' Hackman added, smiling in approval at the way Abbie came fearlessly forward to make the acquaintance of his master's prized mount. 'He can be a mite skittish on occasions, miss. But you seem to 'ave a way wi' beasts.'

'And so she should, Hackman,' Bart remarked. 'She's lived round horses most all her life.' He detected a certain wistful expression flitting over her delicate features. 'But that doesn't mean I'll permit her to ride this one. You are at liberty to saddle up any mount in my stable for Miss Graham, except for Samson.'

'Understood, sir,' Hackman acknowledged, but Abbie merely smiled, a wickedly provocative smile that lent an added sparkle to her most striking feature.

'Don't you dare even think about it,' Bart warned in a voice that was all the more threatening because of its softness. 'I know well enough that you are a fine horsewoman. But Samson is headstrong, and no mount for a lady.'

Abbie thought it prudent not to tease him further, but could not resist saying, 'And what makes you suppose that I'll avail myself of any of your hacks? With all the other tasks you've set me, there will be little time for riding.'

'There'll be ample opportunity,' he countered, once again entwining her arm through his, as he guided her back across the courtyard. 'I've every intention of showing you round the whole estate.' The troubled frown returned. 'Just promise me, Abbie, that you won't attempt to go off on your own.'

She had thought it strange when he had insisted on bringing her groom to the Court. Now, however, she understood, and didn't hesitate to assure him. 'Yes, with the unfortunate happenings hereabouts, it's quite understandable why you wanted Josh along.'

'It's not just the unrest, Abbie,' he admitted. 'I could trust Hackman to take excellent care of you. But he'll not always be available, and I haven't much faith in that lad I employed a few months back. His father worked on the estate, and was trustworthy, and hardworking. I cannot say the same for his son. Hackman isn't happy with him, and I trust his judgement.'

They had by this time reached the path that led to the front of the house. Abbie paused to admire a fine wisteria that covered a substantial area of the side wall, thereby forcing Bart to stop also. The next moment a sizeable piece of masonry hit the ground with a resounding thud, a mere few yards away from where they both stood, causing Abbie to gasp in alarm, and Bart to frown heavily as he gazed above his head.

'My God!' he muttered. 'If you hadn't stopped when you did, Abbie… I'd better send someone up there tomorrow to effect necessary repairs.'

Chapter Eight

Thankfully, during the following days no further unnerving incidents occurred, and once the materials required to undertake Bart's portrait had arrived at the Court, Abbie quickly settled into a pleasurable routine.

Taking full advantage of Bart's kind offer, she availed herself of one of his horses. Most mornings, weather permitting, would see her riding out across the estate on the lovely dapple mare that had quickly become her favourite mount. Bart himself, more often than not, would bear her company, and whenever he was unavailable, Kitty was always more than ready to enjoy the exercise and fresh air, though she never once attempted to do so when she knew her brother was free.

Unfortunately he seemed less eager to make himself available in the afternoons, when Abbie would retreat to the makeshift studio to work on his portrait. After he had condescended to turn up for the first few sittings, during which she managed to complete a few preliminary sketches, he began to show a disinclination to remain for more than twenty minutes or so. And sometimes didn't concern himself to turn up at all!

When eventually she had felt it incumbent upon her to

draw his attention to the fact that his seeming reluctance to sit for his portrait would result in her remaining at the Court longer than had been anticipated, he had merely shrugged those broad shoulders of his and had said, 'Well, what of it? There's no urgency for you to return to Bath, is there?' To which she had had no answer, for if the truth had been known, she had swiftly grown to enjoy the comfortable life at Cavanagh Court.

From the very first the servants had treated her with the utmost respect, making life so very agreeable that she had been forced to give herself an inward shake more than once, to remind herself that the Court wasn't her home and that she would be returning to Bath long before summer had given way to autumn. Even Figg, after an initial display of resentment, had done a great deal to make her feel welcome whenever she had ventured into his domain. In general, after having listened intently to any schemes she had put forward to improve certain areas, he had shown genuine enthusiasm, and on one or two occasions had even gone so far as to voice ideas of his own. Which he had felt sure would meet with approval, providing Miss Graham would be willing to put the suggestions before the master herself.

Figg's sister too had proved no less accommodating, and had sent regular messages via the maids, assuring Miss Graham that should there be any particular dishes she would like prepared, she had only to ask. As Abbie had found nothing wanting in the estimable Mrs Figg's culinary skills, the message she had continued to send back was that she had been very well pleased with what had been set before her at mealtimes.

Nevertheless, she was destined to discover one morning, after she had been at the Court almost three weeks, that her efforts not to cause any of the servants undue work had not met with universal approval.

'Cook's right put out,' Rose, the young housemaid, announced, as she entered early as usual with the pitcher of warm water. 'Taken it into her head that you don't think she's capable of preparing any fancy dishes just because she ain't employed by some titled gentleman, and don't work in some posh London house.'

In face of this alarming disclosure, Abbie thought it prudent to adopt a different tack and, the instant she had completed her toilette, made her way directly down to the kitchens in order to soothe any ruffled feathers.

Unfortunately she discovered that evening, when joined by Kitty and her mother, that it was impossible to please everyone.

'Oh, dear,' Eugenie muttered, clearly dismayed, after Abbie had disclosed that one of her favourite dishes, chicken in a delicious creamy sauce, would be on the menu. 'Bart isn't at all fond of rich food nowadays. I think it must be the result of those years of privation, when in the army and forced to go without. He now much prefers simple fare.'

Abbie had by this time come to the conclusion that Eugenie wasn't so much in awe of her stepson as determined to do all she could to avoid those unpleasant confrontations she had been forced to endure years before.

Never had Abbie known such a good-natured, unselfish soul. Yet she could understand now just what induced Bart's occasional bouts of impatience where his stepmother was concerned. She had come perilously close to losing her own temper when she had consulted with Eugenie over the new décor for the library. Eugenie would agree wholeheartedly in one breath, then shed doubt in the next; until

Abbie, having decided only firm action would serve, had taken it upon herself to make the final decision. Appearing harassed, she had marched resolutely into the library to attain Bart's signature on the order form, only to receive an 'I told you so' look from the master of the house.

'If he doesn't choose to sample the dish, no one is going to force him to do so,' Abbie responded, betraying her indifference with a shrug. 'Mrs Figg has cooked for him long enough to know his likes and dislikes. She'll have provided an alternative, I'm sure. Besides which,' she added, 'pandering to the whims of strong-willed gentlemen is highly inadvisable. Believe me, I know! You run the risk of turning them into totally selfish autocrats.'

Kitty gurgled with laughter. 'You're not in the least afraid of my brother, are you, Abbie?'

'And why should she be?' queried a smooth voice, and they all turned to discover Bart standing in the doorway, his eyes, like his sister's, twinkling with amusement. 'She is far too sensible to go out of her way to annoy me.'

'Don't be too sure of that,' Abbie herself countered. 'I was unable to avoid a lengthy encounter with your gardener this morning, and succumbed to an imp of pure mischief. You'll never guess what I've managed to persuade him to grow in the shelter of the walled garden.'

'Oh, do tell!' Eugenie prompted, after Abbie had given way to a wicked chuckle.

'Dahlias.'

Bart's brows rose. 'What...? Not that newfangled flower?'

'Strangely enough, that is more or less what Figg himself said,' Abbie revealed. 'But believe it or not, he now fully intends to grow a large bed of them. What a pity I shan't be here to view the results when all his plans have been put into effect! I guarantee you'll have flowers enough to fill every room!'

Only Bart didn't appear to find the prospect pleasing. Abbie watched the smile leaving his eyes the moment before he turned and headed across the room in the direction of the decanters.

It crossed her mind to wonder whether he might be annoyed because she had taken it upon herself to suggest rather more changes in the garden than he deemed necessary. If so, his irritation certainly didn't last very long, for during dinner he barked with laughter, when she called him a contrary so-and-so, after he had helped himself to a second substantial portion of her favourite chicken dish.

He was disposed not to linger over his port either that evening, once the meal was over, and rejoined the ladies in the drawing-room in time to sample a dish of tea.

'I've been wondering, Eugenie,' he said, after settling himself beside Abbie on the sofa, as had become his custom, 'whether you would care to spend some time with your sister Mildred in Brighton this summer, as our stay in Bath was shorter than originally planned?'

Eugenie's expression of delighted surprise faded when her gaze slid to the person seated beside him. 'I should dearly love to, Bart. But, in the circumstances, I do not think I should leave at this time.'

He was quick to appreciate the reason behind her reluctance. 'Do not concern yourself over the proprieties. Abbie will be suitably chaperoned. All I need do is write to Lady Penrose. She informed me before I left Bath that she would be only too delighted to join us here at the Court should Abbie's stay turn out to be longer than originally planned.'

Abbie flashed him a look of exasperation. 'Which I can safely promise will be the case, if you continue to find excuses not to sit for me in the afternoons. I've been here for three weeks and have barely made a start.'

Although he smiled, he refused to be drawn, and turned his attention once again to his stepmother. 'So you may spend time by the sea with a clear conscience, my dear. I'm sure you and Kitty will find the change of air beneficial.'

Eugenie was very taken with the idea. Surprisingly enough, though, Kitty betrayed little enthusiasm, the reason for which became clear the instant her mother had departed in order to dash off a quick note to the sister of whom she saw little.

'It isn't that I don't wish to go, Bart,' she assured him when he commented on her lack of interest. 'It's just that I thought we might hold a party here for Mama at the end of the month. It's her fiftieth birthday, and I thought she'd like to celebrate with her neighbours and friends. If you're agreeable, I thought perhaps Abbie and I might arrange it so that it would be a surprise.'

'I think it a splendid notion,' he didn't hesitate to assure her. 'There's absolutely no reason why you cannot delay your departure by a few days, and if your mother should question the delay, all you need say is that Lady Penrose is unable to leave Bath before the end of the month.'

Abbie wasn't proof against the entreaty in Kitty's eyes, and didn't hesitate to offer her help.

Later, however, when she retired to her bedchamber, she wasn't altogether sure that she had been wise to involve herself further in the Cavanagh family's affairs.

After changing into her nightwear, she padded across the room and settled herself on the window seat, where she could gaze across the park at the moonlit waters of the lake.

How she loved that view! How quickly she had grown to love the whole place: the gardens, the house; and most especially the company of its master. It was pointless not facing the fact that, incredible though it was, she had by imperceptible degrees grown excessively fond of Bartholomew Cavanagh.

Smiling, she shook her head, unable to believe that just two months ago she had viewed him as the bane of her life, the person responsible for causing her so much malcontent. Now, though, she was forced to acknowledge she had been sadly at fault to denounce him as the villain of the piece. What had he done, after all? Nothing, she decided, except make a cuckold of her grandfather's most influential neighbour. And as Lady Penrose had once sagely pointed out—one shouldn't blame a man for behaving like a man. There was no denying either that Lady Sophia Fitzpatrick had been a willing participant in the affair. What still rankled, though, what she still, after all these years, found hard to forgive or forget, was that not two hours after his rendezvous in the summerhouse, he was voicing his earnest desire to marry her.

She shook her head, finding it difficult to equate the master of Cavanagh Court, solid, reliable and considerate, to that unfeeling, care-for-nobody who had heartlessly proposed marriage to her, while still wearing the very clothes he had worn when he had set off earlier to keep that assignation with Lady Sophia.

Something moving among the clump of trees by the lake caught her attention, putting an end to the unsavoury reflections. For a few moments, as the moon emerged from behind the clouds, it was possible to see quite clearly, and yet nothing now stirred.

It must have been pure imagination, she decided, before clambering into bed.

The following afternoon she was favoured by a visit from the master of the house, who condescended to sit for his portrait. Whether or not she had managed to prick his conscience the evening before was anybody's guess, though she began to think it highly unlikely when he soon betrayed signs of unrest.

'No one could accuse you of being a restful gentleman, Bart,' she told him, when he cast a longing look over his shoulder in the direction of the window. 'I believe I must resign myself to sessions of no more than fifteen minutes. And be thankful for small mercies, I suppose!'

Her dry humour never failed to bring a smile to his lips. 'Oh, it's too nice a day to be stuck indoors, Abbie. Let's go for a walk. I promise I'll give you a further half-hour later, but if I don't move soon I'll be as stiff as a varnished eel.'

Abbie was in two minds. She knew she ought to work on the portrait. Yet, Bart was right, it was too fine a day to remain inside, and the grounds beckoned. Furthermore Figg, an accurate forecaster of no little renown, had predicted change in a day or two, so it seemed such a pity not to take advantage of the clement weather while she may.

'I've only to collect my parasol. I'll join you downstairs in a few minutes,' she assured him, her decision made.

As good as her word, she met up with him again in the hall, winning herself a smile of approval for not keeping him kicking his heels before they set off across the sloping front lawn down to the lake.

By this time, of course, Abbie had explored most every area of the estate, either on horseback, or on foot. Undoubtedly her favourite haunt was the neat, well-tended gardens, most especially the shrubbery, where she could hide herself among the foliage for half an hour or so, and gain the solitude to read a book.

The lake too was high on her list of preferred spots. On two or three occasions she had ventured down to the water's edge and surprised the odd frog lurking among the reeds. She had never, however, made use of the wooden bridge to gain access to the far side, and decided to do so now in order to admire the view across the park from the shelter of the folly nestling among the trees.

The footbridge was not sufficiently wide to allow two people to walk side by side without brushing against each other at frequent intervals, so Bart, permitting her to lead the way, paused to study the reed-bed, which yearly had been encroaching further into the lake.

'It's no good,' he announced, his frown betraying his displeasure as he studied the far bank. 'I'll need to arrange for some men to clear most of this lot out. I taught Kitty how to swim here. It would be downright dangerous to attempt to do so now, with this lot snaring at your feet.'

'Ahh! So there are some advantages in having an older brother,' Abbie declared, 'especially having one who's willing to give of his time to teach something useful.'

Observing that now familiar wickedly teasing sparkle before she turned and strolled away, Bart couldn't forbear a smile of his own. What an absolute darling she was! he mused, studying the graceful way she moved. Blessed with lovely, regular features, a trim, shapely figure and a ladylike air that was completely natural and blessedly free from those annoying affectations adopted by too many of her sex nowadays, she was for him the epitome of womanhood. It was no mere physical attraction either, he was forced to concede. He admired her ready wit; this coupled with an abundance of sound common sense made her the ideal companion.

Perhaps, though, he was just a besotted fool in thinking her so perfect, merely a hapless male trapped in the toils of an emotion that had been steadily increasing since the night of the Fergussons' party, where they had come face to face again after so many years? Well, if this were indeed the case, he was forced silently to own that he was highly satisfied with this imprisoned state, and experienced not the remotest desire ever to regain his freedom.

Smiling still, he eased his elbows off the wooden handrail, and set off in pursuit. He slowly increased his pace and was within yards of her when it happened. One moment Abbie was standing there, appearing as though she hadn't a care in the world as she stared across the park in the direction of the village church, where Eugenie's father had once conducted the services; the next there came the sound of splintering timber, and she was disappearing through a large hole.

Bart made a valiant dive to reach her, but only succeeded in saving the now torn and misshapen pink parasol from suffering a similar fate. Without pausing to remove even his coat, he vaulted over the wooden handrail to land only a matter of feet away from where Abbie, gasping and spluttering, was endeavouring to keep her head above water. He had her on her back in a trice, one hand securely under her chin keeping her afloat. Terrified though she undoubtedly was, she thankfully obeyed his command not to struggle. It was an easy matter then for him to get them both safely back to within a few yards of the bank.

Bart soon discovered that negotiating a safe passage across the reed bed was to prove more difficult. Half-dragging, half-carrying Abbie, he found it as much as he could do to keep them both from sinking knee deep in the mud each time he moved. In the end it was only by making use of the gnarled roots of an overhanging tree that he managed finally to get them both safely on the grassy bank.

Exhausted, Abbie dropped to her knees, and it was several minutes before she could find breath enough to thank him for saving her life, for she was in no doubt that he had. Even if by some miracle she had managed to flounder her way to the water's edge, she would never have negotiated a path through the area of stinking, slimy mud.

When he made no attempt to respond, she glanced up to find him staring down at her, his expression an impenetrable mask. Then he slipped off his sodden, mud-streaked jacket and placed it about her shoulders, insisting that she keep it on; the reason for which Rose wasn't slow to make embarrassingly clear a short time later, when Abbie had reached the sanctuary of her bedchamber.

'Cor blimey, miss! You can see clear through that gown o' yourn where there ain't no mud a-clinging!' the little housemaid declared, betraying a deal more honesty than tact.

One glance in the full-length mirror was sufficient to confirm this humiliating fact. Abbie, having allowed Bart's jacket to slip from her shoulders, could feel the heat glowing in her cheeks as she saw the clear outlines of breasts, hips and thighs. The fact that her hair resembled nothing so much as a collection of rats' tails, and that her face, like the veritable urchin's, was streaked with dirt, were as nothing when compared to the knowledge that her charms had been revealed, if only for a brief period, to Bart's experienced gaze.

Peeling off the soiled gown, she tossed it aside, with the fervent hope that it was ruined beyond repair so that she might be spared the mortification of seeing it hanging again in the wardrobe, a taunting reminder of a humiliating episode she would far rather forget.

Once the bath had arrived she wasted no time in restoring her appearance, and was sitting patiently whilst the maid pinned the last few strands of hair into place, when there was a light scratch on the door and Kitty entered, carrying a sheet of paper in her hand and an expression of real concern on her face.

'Bart's just told me what happened. I can hardly believe it!' she exclaimed, plumping herself down on the bed. 'I told him it might so easily have been me who received a soaking. I went for a walk the other morning, when you and Bart were out riding, and came back over the bridge.'

'You would have fared rather better than I did, Kitty,' Abbie wasn't slow to point out. 'You, I understand, can swim.'

'Well, yes,' Kitty was forced to concede. 'But it would have been no easy matter, hampered by petticoats, to reach the bank.'

An appalling possibility occurred to Abbie. 'Surely you were wearing clothes when your brother taught you?'

'Well, yes. But a deal less than I'm wearing now.' Kitty chuckled at Abbie's expression of prim disapproval. 'You forget he is my brother, after all.'

But he isn't mine! Abbie silently countered, instantly banishing the foolish notion of asking Bart to teach her to swim from her mind, and then promptly changed the subject by inquiring the whereabouts of Eugenie.

'Oh, she took it into her head to call and see her sister at the vicarage. She hasn't done so since our return from Bath, so it's more than likely that Aunt Clara will persuade her to remain for dinner. I didn't accompany her because I wanted to make a list of those we must invite to her party.' Kitty glanced across at the maid, who was busily picking up the soiled garments to take downstairs for laundering. 'Don't forget it's supposed to be a secret, Rose. So don't go saying anything in front of Mama.'

'I won't forget, miss,' the maid assured her. 'It'll be nice having a large party here again. Cook especially is looking forward to it, though I did hear her say the sooner you can spare time to discuss menus for both dinner and supper, the better.'

Kitty cast a look of earnest appeal in Abbie's direction. 'You'll help me do that, won't you?'

'Of course I shall,' Abbie readily confirmed, feeling slightly guilty because she'd done nothing to help thus far. 'But surely you don't want to consult with Cook now? We can do so tomorrow. You've been indoors most all the day. Wouldn't you prefer to go out for a ride?'

'Yes, I would,' Kitty admitted. 'Dinner's been put back an hour because Bart wants to examine the damage to the bridge, so there'd be time enough. Only he told me you were to rest until dinner, and I wasn't to trouble you.'

Torn between a feeling of gratitude for Bart's concern for her well-being, and annoyance over his dictatorial attitude, Abbie hovered for a moment before announcing that she was more than capable of deciding whether she felt able to go out or not. 'And a good canter across the park would do us both some good, so I'll meet you in the stable-yard in half an hour.'

As Abbie had only to slip off a robe to don her habit, she arrived before the appointed time. Josh, she quickly noticed, was occupied in saddling the dapple mare she always chose to ride, and the youngest member of Hackman's staff, Tom, was busily cleaning out one of the stalls, while Ben Dodd, unkempt as usual, his mouth twisted by an unpleasant smirk, just stood there, leaning on his broom.

This was by no means the first time Abbie had caught him shirking his duties. She knew too that Hackman didn't hold this particular underling in high esteem, and could fully appreciate why. Yet it was not so much Dodd's work-shy attitude that Abbie found objectionable as his surly manner.

Unfortunately she had been forced to tolerate his company on the odd occasion when she had gone out for a ride with Kitty, for Dodd had been employed as Kitty's personal groom. Just what Kitty's opinion of him was was difficult to judge, for the girl seemed oblivious to his presence most of the time. How Abbie wished she could say the same! Unfortunately, she had too frequently caught a lascivious gleam in that shifty gaze of his, and had gained the distinct impression that he had been attempting to judge what she and Kitty would look like without their shifts.

Today, however, she was determined not to put up with his presence, and was almost upon him before he realised she was there. 'As you're clearly fatigued today, Dodd, Josh shall deputise for you and accompany us out.'

For once his eyes met hers, albeit fleetingly, and there was no mistaking the resentment lurking there. He looked for a moment as though he might argue, then he shrugged. 'As you like, miss,' he muttered before slouching away.

Kitty, when they rode out of the stable-yard, didn't appear to notice that they were being attended by a different groom. Nor did it seem that she had any clear destination in mind. In this, however, Abbie swiftly realised that she had misjudged her companion, when Kitty announced her intention of calling upon the most influential family in the neighbourhood.

'Lord and Lady Warren are in residence, because I know for a fact that Bart has ridden over to see them since our return from Bath. Lady Warren happens to be my godmother. She's very kind and will help us arrange things for the party so Mama doesn't find out about it.'

In this Kitty was absolutely correct. Lady Warren was delighted by the impromptu visit and greeted her goddaughter warmly. 'Of course I shall do anything to help, my dear,' she assured her the instant she discovered the reason behind the visit. 'You leave the invitation cards with me and I'll ensure they're all delivered, and enclose a little note of my own to say that replies must be sent back here to me. Not that I think too many will refuse. It has been some considerable time since a party was held at the Court.'

She then turned her attention to Abbie, running an expert eye over the stylish habit. 'And you are a friend of Kitty's, Miss Graham? You must find time to dine with us one evening during your stay in the county.'

'Oh, Abbie isn't my friend, Godmama,' Kitty announced ingenuously, thereby denying Abbie the time to thank Lady Warren for the invitation. 'Well, she is now. But she was Bart's friend long before she was mine.'

Abbie couldn't mistake the speculative gleam in Lady Warren's kindly grey eyes, but before she could disclose that the master of Cavanagh Court was none other than her grandfather's godson, and that she had been acquainted with Bart since childhood, her attention was captured by three gentlemen who unexpectedly entered the drawing-room. It was not so much her first glimpse of the tall, distinguished master of the house, or the young man who resembled him too closely not to be his son and heir that had her very nearly gaping in astonishment as the unexpected sight of the exquisitely attired young sprig entering in their wake.

'Great heavens!' Kitty exclaimed, nowhere near as successful as Abbie at concealing her surprise. 'What in the world are you doing here, Cedric?'

Appearing far from offended by his cousin's less-than-gracious greeting, Cedric seemed delighted to be the cynosure of all eyes, and took a moment to remove a speck of something from his sleeve before revealing that he and Richard Warren had attended the same school.

'Bumped into each other quite by chance when Ricky was staying overnight in Bath, breaking his journey after escorting his maiden aunt back to Somerset. When I happened to mention that I was already quite weary of that devilish dull place, he kindly invited me to return with him here.'

'And has Mr Asquith accompanied you?' Abbie couldn't resist asking, knowing full well that Bart wouldn't be best pleased if he had. Cedric, however, shook his head.

'No, he was quite content to remain with his aunt.'

Abbie couldn't forbear a smile at this. It was much more likely that Mr Asquith was paying avid court to some heiress, and Cedric had grown heartily sick and tired of trailing after him. Bart's cousin might have had his faults, but he was certainly no fortune-hunter.

Cedric might well have remained basking in the sunshine of her approval if he had not a minute or two later, after discovering the reason behind her visit to the Court, allowed the lingering resentment he harboured to surface.

'My, my, having his likeness painted, is he?' Cedric's weak mouth was twisted by an unpleasant smirk. 'For all his protestations to the contrary, it would seem my cousin is preparing himself for the day when he might hold a higher position in the family.'

Not surprisingly Lord and Lady Warren exchanged puzzled glances, as did Kitty and their son. Abbie, however, was under no illusion to what Cedric was alluding, and found herself instantly coming to Bart's defence.

'You are labouring under a misapprehension, Mr Cavanagh,' she told him, her voice as level as her gaze. 'In this instance Bart's actions stemmed from altruism, not ambition.'

If anything, this pronouncement appeared to puzzle everyone even more, Cedric included. All the same, Abbie refused to elaborate, and changed the subject by enquiring whether he would be remaining long enough in the locale to attend Mrs Cavanagh's birthday celebration.

He appeared much struck by the notion. 'Do you know, Miss Graham, I rather think I shall. Needless to say a country party wouldn't be my first choice of entertainment,' he admitted with quaint snobbery. 'But even though I stayed at the Court on several occasions in the dim and distant past, I cannot recall ever attending a large party there. It might well prove to be amusing to see how well Bart succeeds in entertaining his neighbours.'

It needed only that to fire Abbie's determination to ensure that Eugenie's birthday party turned out to be a memorable occasion, not the tedious little affair that Cedric clearly expected it to be.

A short while later, when she and Kitty were returning to the Court, she began to suggest others who might be persuaded to attend.

'I'll write to my godmother as soon as we get back to the house, and inquire if it's possible for her to leave Bath in time to attend the party. She'll be of invaluable help in keeping your mother entertained whilst we organise things. I wonder too,' she added as the Court came into view, 'whether Giles Fergusson might be persuaded to come.'

'Oh, what a splendid notion!' Kitty exclaimed. 'He's stayed with us on numerous occasions in the past. I'll ask Bart to write to him.'

Kitty's evident delight at the prospect of having Giles to stay in no way amazed Abbie. She had observed them together often enough while she had been in Bath to be very certain that Kitty held Giles in the highest regard. What did come as something of a surprise, however, was the sudden, unmistakable glow in her young friend's dark eyes. She had watched her conversing with Richard Warren a short while before, and it was clear to see that they were easy in each other's company, but even so that certain look had been absent from Kitty's expression.

'You're very fond of Giles, aren't you, Kitty?'

'Oh, yes. I liked him from the first,' she unblushingly admitted. 'I prefer the company of older gentlemen. They're not silly as younger men sometimes are. And I especially like Giles. He's interesting to talk to. What's more, he doesn't treat me like a child, as Bart tends to do. Though he's been heaps better of late,' she added, casting Abbie a sidelong glance. 'He's not nearly so sharp, either. You're a marvellous influence on him, you know?'

Whether this was true or not, Abbie would have been hard pressed to say. She was forced silently to acknowledge, though, as they rode into the stable-yard to find him standing there, impatiently tapping his crop against the side of one boot, that if her presence did have a beneficial effect on his temper, it was in no way foolproof.

He swung round the instant he detected the sound of hoofs on cobblestones, his thunderous expression evidence of his frame of mind.

'Where the hell do you suppose you two have been!' he bellowed, uncaring that the youngest stable-lad was staring at him in open-mouthed astonishment.

Chapter Nine

Unlike Kitty, who appeared dismayed by her brother's angry outburst, Abbie felt the first stirring of her own temper. Having lived with a brusque ex-army colonel for most of her life, she was well used to a gentleman's bouts of ill humour. Nevertheless, for all that her grandfather could be an irascible so-and-so on occasions, and not one to mince words either, he had never once taken her to task in the presence of others.

Out of the corner of her eye she detected the satisfied smirk on Dodd's unpleasant, weasel-like face as he led Samson from the stable. Obviously he had overheard his master's outburst, and was undoubtedly hoping to witness the female who had dared to dispense with his services so summarily earlier being taken down a peg or two. Nothing could more surely have strengthened her resolve to thwart Bart's intention of venting his spleen in public.

Drawing the mare alongside the mounting block, Abbie slid nimbly from the saddle, and then immediately turned her attention to Kitty. 'If you hurry, you'll have time before dinner to add those few names to your list of guests.'

Seemingly needing no further prompting, Kitty departed the instant she had placed her mount in Josh's charge. Abbie too handed the reins over to her groom, before walking serenely away in the direction of the garden. Whether her calm handling of the situation had momentarily left Bart speechless, she had no way of knowing. All the same, she couldn't say she was unduly surprised to hear the sound of rapidly approaching footsteps directly behind her a few moments later. The sudden clasp on her shoulder, before she was spun round none too gently, came as no real surprise either. Nor, for that matter, did his expression of barely suppressed rage.

'How dare you walk away when you know full well that I wish to speak with you?'

Although nowhere near as composed as she was attempting to appear, Abbie was determined not to make matters worse by losing the grasp on her own temper. 'You did not wish to speak to me, Bart,' she countered, maintaining the praiseworthy control. 'What you wished to do was vent your ill humour by browbeating me. And worse, you were prepared to do so in the presence of others. Your sister and stepmother are accustomed to your boorish manners, and seem willing to overlook them. I, on the other hand, am not. You were born a gentleman. You would do well to remember that in future, especially in your dealings with me.'

At this he appeared, if anything, more murderous than before. The muscles along the powerful jaw tightened visibly, and she could almost hear him counting slowly up to ten under his breath. Yet to do him justice he made no attempt to grasp her again and shake her until her teeth rattled, an action which, she didn't doubt for a second, would have afforded him the utmost satisfaction.

Instead, he merely ran impatient fingers through his hair whilst he raised his eyes to the patch of azure sky directly above his head. 'If…if my forceful enquiry in the stable-yard offended your delicate sensibilities, then I apologise,' he began, now exercising commendable restraint himself. 'However, you would do well to remember, Abbie, that even gentlemen are apt to give way to their feelings on occasions, most especially when their sound advice has been imprudently ignored.'

She neither misunderstood, nor was she reticent to air her own views. 'I am neither headstrong, nor insensible to your concerns for my well-being,' she assured him softly. 'And neither am I a child, Bart. I am quite capable of deciding whether I feel able to go out for a ride. Good heavens! You must think me a poor creature indeed if you suppose that such a trifling accident, as happened earlier, would be likely to overset me to such an extent that I must take to my bed.'

His expression became guarded, markedly so, and all at once she knew that far more lay behind his show of ill humour than she had supposed. As had happened before, she reached out to place her fingers on his arm. 'What is it? What's wrong?'

'What happened at the lake was no accident, Abbie,' Bart admitted at length, after giving the matter of whether to confide in her or not a few moments' intense thought. 'I returned to the bridge with Hackman to check for further signs of wear. The timbers weren't rotten, as I had supposed. They had been sawed through quite deliberately.'

When no response was forthcoming, Bart raised his eyes to discover her staring fixedly at a fine specimen of a pink rose, and was immediately struck by her lack of reaction.

'You'll forgive me for saying so, Abbie, but you do not appear unduly surprised.'

This succeeded in briefly recapturing her attention, before she took advantage of the bench conveniently situated directly behind her. 'In truth, sir, I'm not,' she confessed. 'You've already disclosed that you have suffered more damage to your property than the other landowners hereabouts—hayricks burned, fences pulled down and the fire at your house. It would seem that since your return from Bath the miscreants have decided to increase the frequency of their unlawful acts against you.'

Bart considered this for a moment as he settled himself on the bench beside her. 'It would be wrong to conclude that on the evidence of what has happened today.'

One fine brow rose in a sceptical arch. 'You think so?'

'Yes, I do,' he affirmed. 'After all, we cannot be sure just when the damage to the bridge was effected.'

'Well, I can tell you this much—' Abbie didn't hesitate to enlighten him '—Kitty herself mentioned that she had walked over the bridge just the other day. Furthermore, last night, I thought I saw someone lurking in the clump of trees by the lake. At the time I dismissed it as a mere trick of the moonlight. Naturally, after what happened today, I'm inclined to believe my eyes had not deceived me.'

For the first time she betrayed deep concern by frowning heavily. 'I'm not at all sure that that chunk of masonry, which happened to fall just as we were walking down the path beside the house, was a mischance either.' She held his full attention. 'You see, shortly after our arrival at the Court, I was up on the leads with Kitty. I noticed sections of masonry were betraying signs of wear. But when I rested my hand against the stonework, I detected no movement whatsoever. And I remember quite clearly that there wasn't so much as a breath of wind that day.'

For several moments Bart sat quietly digesting what Abbie had revealed, and more importantly what he strongly suspected was occurring to her as a very real possibility, but before he could voice his own thoughts, the sounds of an altercation succeeded in capturing his full attention.

'What the deuce…?' he muttered, rising instantly to his feet.

Although it was impossible to keep pace with his long-striding gait, Abbie didn't hesitate to follow, and arrived in the stable-yard, only moments after Bart himself, in time to witness her groom plant a flush hit to Ben Dodd's jaw, the force of which sent him sprawling in the dirt.

It would have afforded her much gratification to have been able to carry out such a feat herself, for she couldn't deny she had taken the ill-favoured Dodd in dislike. All the same, she was forced to own it wasn't the behaviour she had come to expect from her groom, whose disposition she had always considered placid. Moreover, it was an unequal contest, her groom having the advantage of both height and build, though it was much to Josh's credit that he made no attempt to follow up his advantage while his opponent remained on the ground.

'What the devil's going on here?' Bart demanded, striding forward and thereby effectively putting an end to hostilities. 'Well?' he barked, after waiting in vain for an explanation.

As neither groom appeared willing, or able, to meet his disapproving gaze, and both continued to stare dumbly at some spot on the ground, Bart turned his attention to his youngest employee, whose snub-nosed face he at last perceived peering round the stable door. 'What's this all about, lad?'

Even from where she stood Abbie could see the boy was trembling, and thought for a moment that it must be the presence of his master which had quite overset him, until she caught the glance he directed at Dodd.

Seemingly Bart had not been oblivious to the look of

terror in the boy's eyes either, for in the next breath he assured him he had naught to fear if he told the truth.

'Them's bin brawling, sir.'

'Yes, I saw that for myself, lad. But why did they fight?'

Once again terrified eyes shot a fleeting look in Dodd's direction. Abbie at least could guess the reason why the boy was reluctant to speak: Tom was fearful of repercussions should he reveal what he knew. After all, Hackman was not always on hand to ensure that both his underlings toed the line, and she strongly suspected that the work-shy Dodd was not above resorting to bullying tactics in the head groom's absence.

Abbie had no wish to interfere in a matter that was essentially Bart's concern, even though her own groom was involved. Yet she knew only too well that there was a limit to his patience, and that he wouldn't wait indefinitely for an explanation. She cast a look in Josh's direction, and thankfully he wasn't slow to interpret the unspoken request in her eyes.

'I started the fight, Mr Cavanagh,' he admitted, thereby instantly gaining everyone's attention. It was clear, none the less, by his suddenly intense look that Bart, like Abbie, suspected far more lay behind the scuffle than a mere difference of opinion.

'Why? What did my groom do to incite your wrath?'

Amazingly enough not only did Tom understand the question, it was he who supplied the answer. 'Mr Dodd were setting about your 'orse, sir, wiv a crop.'

As Dodd scrambled to his feet, Tom sought the protection of Josh's side, an action that told its own tale and which instantly ignited a spark of understanding in the eyes of his master.

'It were nothing, sir,' Dodd muttered. 'You know 'ow

skittish Samson be when he don't get no exercise. It were a lick or two I give him, that were all.'

Either Bart did not believe a word, or the explanation had come too late, for his expression had grown darkly uncompromising. 'Go and collect your belongings. And don't set foot on my land again.'

There was a noticeable improvement in the atmosphere in and around the stable block after Dodd's departure. Abbie frequently detected the sound of Tom's gleeful chuckles during the following days, and Josh too whistled as he went about his work. Precisely what Kitty's views were on the loss of her personal groom Abbie found difficult to judge, for Kitty made no comment within her hearing. Hackman, on the other hand, was not at all reticent to air his views.

'Never could take to the lad, Miss Abbie, and that's a fact,' he openly admitted, one morning, when she was returning to the house by way of the yard, and had paused to pass the time of day with the iron ruler of the stables. 'The master liked old Dodd and was prepared to give his son a chance. A big mistake to be sure, and a rare one for the master to make, for in general he's a good judge o' men, so he is.

'Came as no surprise to me, neither, that the young wastrel were mistreating the stock,' he went on, pausing in his grooming of one of the carriage horses. 'I had my suspicions. Not that I ever caught him doing so myself, more's the pity. I'd 'ave enjoyed placing a well-aimed kick to the seat of his breeches. Aye, there's a definite mean streak in that little runt, and no mistake, and we're well rid of 'im.'

'Had Dodd worked here for long, Mr Hackman?' Abbie asked, as he seemed disposed to chatter.

He shook his head. 'I mind he started in early spring, a month or so after the old groom had passed on.'

'I doubt Dodd will find it easy to obtain another position, given that he left without a reference.'

'Well, I don't know about that, miss,' he surprised her by responding. 'I did 'ere tell he'd been taken on by that there stranger who bought the tavern on the Evesham road early in the year.' He tutted. 'Don't drink there no more, m'self. Don't care for the company. Rum lot you get in there nowadays, if you ask me. Should suit Dodd fine. Be in good company, I'm thinking.'

'Well, you certainly do not appear to be missing the extra pair of hands,' Abbie remarked, after gazing about the recently swept yard.

'That we ain't, miss,' Hackman agreed. 'The work still gets done, though the master will need to think about taking someone else on afore too long. I'll be off to take the mistress and Miss Kitty to Brighton in a few days, and no one can expect little Tom to cope on his own. That groom o' yourn be a fine lad, though. Taken to 'im in a big way, so I 'ave. I'd be happy enough to leave him in charge while I'm away. But I don't expect you'll be staying too much longer yourself, miss.'

Up until that moment Abbie hadn't looked ahead to the day when she would be leaving the Court. Eugenie's birthday was looming large on the horizon, Giles and her godmother were due to arrive at the end of the week, and it stood to reason that once Eugenie and Kitty had left for Brighton, her days at the Court would be numbered. At least they certainly would be if Bart had his way, she decided, entering the house and making her way upstairs to her makeshift studio.

Since the mishap at the bridge, Bart had undergone something of a change and had found time to sit most every afternoon, with the result that the portrait was all but finished. That, she now realised, as she removed the protective sheet to study the subject of the painting, had been his goal. Of course it had. And she had been a simpleton not to have realised before! He wanted her away from Cavanagh Court as soon as possible.

Smiling wryly, she went over to one of the windows to stare out at the lake, and the bridge, which had now been repaired. Undoubtedly she would have felt deeply hurt if she had supposed for a moment that it was her company of which he had grown tired, but she knew this was not so. Good relations between them having soon been fully restored after their little altercation on the day of Dodd's departure, Bart had continued to seek her company frequently. No, it was much more likely that he desired her swift departure for her own safety. But what of his own? Surely he must suspect, as she did herself, that maybe something very sinister, perhaps some very personal revenge, lay behind these malicious acts perpetrated against him?

Detecting the click of the door, Abbie turned, and was not unduly surprised to see the subject of her thoughts entering the room, on time yet again for the sitting. His smile as he stared across at her was as warm as ever. Yet, wasn't there just a touch of concern in his expression too? How she wished he would share his troubles with her. How she wished she could remain at the Court to help uncover the identities of those responsible for the malicious acts, but she knew Bart well enough by now to be sure that he would never entertain the notion.

'Now what, I wonder, could be responsible for bringing that wistful look to your pretty face, my sweet?' he asked, resorting to one of those endearments which he was wont to use with such frequency that she was hardly conscious of them any longer. Only this time she was very aware, and something inside lurched painfully.

'I was merely thinking that, with this magnificent show of enthusiasm on your part to see the portrait finished, my stay here will soon be at an end,' she admitted, seeing no reason to conceal the truth, and watched as he took up his usual stance before the far window so that the light played about his hair, highlighting the rich chestnut tones, something that she had attempted to bring out in her painting.

Something flickered too in the dark depths of his eyes, but so fleetingly that she was given insufficient time even to attempt to interpret what it might have been. 'And do you find the prospect of a return to Bath not wholly pleasing?'

Abbie was in two minds. Once again she saw no reason to lie, while at the same time she had no intention of revealing just how depressing she found the mere thought of leaving the Court. 'I wouldn't attempt to pretend that I do not prefer life in the country,' she disclosed at last, choosing her words with care. 'But I am resigned, and very sensible too of how kind my godmother is to offer me the opportunity of sharing her home.'

'Had you agreed to marry me, the Court would now be your home,' Bart reminded her, 'and there would be no need for you to return to Bath.'

Whatever Abbie might have expected him to say next, it certainly hadn't been that. He had taken her completely off guard, and it showed. Unable to meet his suddenly intense gaze, she sat herself before the easel. Unfortunately her hand shook so much that she dared not attempt to continue with the portrait, and very reluctantly raised her eyes to discover an odd, almost smugly satisfied smile playing about his mouth.

'For quite some time I have suspected that more lay behind your refusal to marry me,' he admitted at length, his eyes momentarily straying to the trembling fingers of her right hand. 'Now, I'm firmly convinced of it.'

'We—we were both too young,' she responded, her voice as unsteady as her hand, and knew by the quizzical lift of one dark brow that he would no longer be satisfied with that explanation, even before he said,

'Very true. But neither your grandfather nor I wished for the marriage to take place immediately. I was more than happy to wait a year or two before tying the knot. In fact, I would have insisted upon it, had you agreed.'

His gaze once again grew intense, and she found it impossible to draw hers away. 'But you didn't agree, did you? You wouldn't even entertain the notion. In fact, after increasingly thinking back to that time, I honestly believe the mere thought of marrying me was abhorrent to you. And I cannot help asking myself why? What did I ever do to gave you such a disgust of me?'

Why in the name of heaven was he alluding to that period in their lives now? she wondered, somehow managing to suppress a groan. Why now, when the reason she had been so set against marrying him had been increasingly diminishing in importance? It wasn't that she was prepared to overlook his past behaviour—far from it, in fact; but at least she was mature enough now to appreciate why it had taken place.

'Come, Abbie,' he continued, after waiting in vain for a response. 'I would like to think that we have become… friends, that we now have a better understanding of each other. If…if there can never be anything else between us, at least let there be total honesty.'

His words, though almost casually uttered, were a revelation, forcing her at last to acknowledge, if only to herself, that her decision not to entertain even the idea of marrying him years ago might yet prove to be a grave error of judgement on her part. Against all the odds she had come to look upon him as a friend, certainly one of the best, if not the best she'd ever had. She would always treasure his friendship, and had no intention of repaying the kindness he had shown towards her by evasion or lies.

'You asked me to marry you because my grandfather desired the match, did you not?' she said softly. 'You were no more in love with me than I was with you.'

Thankfully he made no attempt to deny it. Yet his honesty, if anything, only made what she knew she must reveal next far more of a difficult task. 'When I was a child I can recall my governess reminding me often that self-esteem was a sin. Evidently she was aware that I suffered from a surfeit of pride. Indeed, I did, and still do, for that matter. Even now I would find it immensely difficult to welcome a gentleman into my arms, when another woman's odour still clings to his person.'

She didn't allow his expression of complete bewilderment to discourage her. She had come thus far, and was now determined to confess all. 'Cast your mind back to that last visit you made to Foxhunter Grange, Bart,' she ordered softly. 'Can you not recall what you were doing just an hour or two before you made your oh, so very gallant proposal of marriage? Can you not recall precisely where you were, and with whom?

'No?' she added, when his expression merely grew thoughtful and she received no response. 'Well, I'm no expert in such matters, but I wouldn't have considered the floor of a summerhouse the ideal place for—er—tupping.'

Had she not witnessed it with her own eyes, Abbie would never have believed it possible for healthily tanned skin to lose every vestige of colour in a matter of seconds. Never had she seen a gentleman appear more stunned, so

completely devastated. Only minutes before she had believed that he had every right to know why she had rejected his suit so comprehensively; now she would have
given almost anything to be able to retract the confession.

The memory of what she had witnessed on that spring
afternoon so many years ago no longer had the power to
overset her, as it once had. Only before she could assure
him of this, Barryman entered with the intelligence that
Lord Warren and an officer of dragoons awaited him in
the library.

Bart appeared not to hesitate to grasp the excuse to
leave, legitimate though it was, and strode from the room
without uttering anything further.

Chapter Ten

When she discovered they were to be deprived of masculine company that evening, owing to the fact that Bart had accepted an invitation to dine with Lord Warren, Abbie didn't attach too much importance to his absence. When he didn't put in an appearance at the breakfast table the following morning, however, and she discovered he had broken his fast early and had already left the house, she couldn't help wondering whether he was deliberately attempting to avoid her as much as possible, and that her leaving the Court at the earliest opportunity might be the best course of action, given that he might well be feeling uncomfortable now with her continued presence under his roof.

In the meantime she at least would strive to behave as normally as possible, just as though she had never made that wretched confession. She had planned to visit the nearest town in order to purchase a birthday present for Eugenie, and had hoped that Bart might accompany her. As this was out of the question now, she had no choice but to secure the services of her groom.

Although the town was several miles away, they made good time on a morning that was both dry and pleasantly

warm. It didn't take Abbie long to discover the ideal gift
for Eugenie; even though her funds were limited, she had
sufficient in her purse to buy the matching set of three
crystal containers in which perfumes could be stored.

Well pleased with her purchase, for she felt certain Eugenie would appreciate the gift, Abbie returned to where
Josh was awaiting her with the horses. She would dearly
have liked to remain for a while in order to explore the narrow cobbled streets in the town, but didn't delay her return,
for there was something that she wished to discuss with
Bart, an ideal solution to a problem that she was amazed
had never occurred to her before.

She cast a fleeting glance at the tall figure riding alongside. Whistling a popular ditty, Josh looked very contented.
No one could ever accuse him of having a morose disposition. Even when they had been in Bath he had always
appeared very well pleased to accompany her about the
city. Yet he, like herself, seemed just that fraction more
relaxed in the country. He had certainly seemed at ease
during his time at the Court, more so since Dodd's departure. Hackman thought well of him too. So surely there
was no need for Bart to engage another groom when the
ideal person was at hand?

She turned to look at him again, about to suggest that
he might like to remain at the Court after her departure,
and was surprised to discover deep lines etched across his
forehead. The reason for the grim expression was not difficult to locate. Propped against the front wall of a poorly
maintained tavern just a short distance ahead, a straw dangling from between his lips, was a very familiar figure.

As he detected the sound of hoofbeats he turned his
head, the length of straw falling as his mouth curled into
a sneer. 'Glad to see they're keeping you hard at it, Arkwright,' he jeered, as they drew nearer. 'Keep in Cavana-

gh's good books and you might even get old Hackman's job
one o' these days. Being at some master's beck and call is
all you're fit for. But some of us were born for 'igher fings.'

Abbie had no intention whatsoever of even paying Dodd
the common courtesy of acknowledging his presence, and
would have ridden past without favouring him with so
much as a second glance, had she not detected what had
now become a very familiar accent.

The next moment a swarthy individual, whose appearance was as unkempt as his tavern, emerged from the doorway. At least Abbie assumed it must be the landlord, for
Dodd instantly set about moving the barrel that had stood
by the wall beside him.

'Ah've just bethowt missen—' Catching sight of Abbie,
the new arrival ceased speaking abruptly. Then dark eyes,
set in a thin, sallow face betraying a lifetime's dissipation, favoured her with a long, insulting stare as she drew
abreast of him.

'Good day to 'ee, ma'am,' he called, raising a decidedly
grubby hand to the matted black hair at his temple. 'And
a reet fine morning it be too.'

'Indeed, it is,' she felt obliged to acknowledge, even
though she had no intention of pausing to exchange further pleasantries.

'What a coincidence, Josh, to find someone hereabouts
from your neck of the woods,' she remarked, once they
had ridden on a few yards.

'Nay, Miss Abbie, he don't come from my part of Yorkshire. He be a West Riding man.'

'I stand corrected,' she acknowledged, prior to glancing
back over her shoulder to discover Dodd and his employer
deep in conversation, still standing at the front of the inn,
staring fixedly in their direction. Perhaps Dodd was re-

vealing precisely who they were. If so, his companion for some reason appeared very interested.

A shudder ran through her as she turned to look at the road ahead. There was something decidedly unpleasant about that stranger. It was not just his filthy, unkempt appearance that was distasteful. There was something in his expression that was ugly, menacing. Little wonder Hackman didn't patronise the inn, she mused. She couldn't imagine too many travellers would risk sampling mine host's hospitality either, if the state of the exterior was an indication of what one would discover within.

The chance encounter with Dodd ought to have kept Josh's future in the forefront of her mind. Strangely it did not. Once they had ridden round the bend in the road and the tavern was no longer visible, her thoughts immediately turned to the last-minute arrangements for Eugenie's party, and it wasn't until she had arrived back at the Court, and discovered from Barryman that the master of the house had also returned, that her mind once again began to dwell on her groom's future.

Only for a moment did she hesitate before knocking on the library door and entering to discover Bart seated behind his desk, staring fixedly through the window. If, indeed, he was feeling slightly awkward now with her presence in the house, at least she could prove that she was not similarly afflicted. She had carried the secret of his affair with Lady Sophia Fitzpatrick around with her for six long years, for heaven's sake, and it hadn't prevented her from finally coming to look upon Bart as a friend! And she had no intention of allowing a past indiscretion to thrust a wedge in their friendship if she could do anything to avoid it, either! she thought determinedly, closing the door, and moving further into the room.

It was a moment or two before he took the trouble to

discover who had entered. Then he was on his feet in an instant, his expression betraying mild surprise, but certainly no degree of embarrassment.

'Kitty told me you'd gone out to buy a present for Eugenie,' he said, after gesturing her to the chair on the opposite side of the desk, which she took as an indication that at least he was in no hurry for her to leave. 'Did you enjoy your visit?'

'Very much. I would have liked to explore for a while, but there are one or two matters I must attend to before the party on Friday, the main one being to beard the lion in his den and persuade him to part with some of his splendid blooms so that I have something with which to decorate the large salon, and the dining-room.'

'I don't suppose you'll have much trouble with Figg,' he assured her, smiling briefly before his expression grew sombre and he began to gather together the papers that littered his desk. 'Did you have a particular reason for wishing to see me?'

'Yes, I did,' she answered, refusing to be daunted by his abrupt change of tone. 'I wondered whether you'd already found a replacement for Dodd and, if not, whether you might consider Josh for the position?'

If anything, his expression grew more serious, but at least she had succeeded in regaining his full attention. 'I'd be the first to admit to making a mistake in taking on Dodd, and I have no intention of making another, Abbie, not at the present time when I need to be especially careful. What do we know about Josh Arkwright? Nothing,' he went on without waiting for an answer. ' I maintain that it's a mistake to employ people without references. Dodd's a prime example.'

'True,' she was forced to agree. 'But surely you don't imagine that Josh had anything to do with the damage to the bridge, or that masonry falling from the roof? Why, it's ridiculous! What possible motive could he have? He isn't even from around these parts, so he cannot hold a grievance against you.'

Bart found himself smiling despite the seriousness of the conversation. 'I agree it does seem unlikely. The lad couldn't have been responsible for starting the fire, either. But then neither could Dodd. They were both in Bath at the time.' A sigh escaped him. 'I'm afraid at the moment, though, I'm suspicious of most everyone, looking at people I've known for years and wondering.'

'I would be less than truthful if I didn't own to the fact that it had crossed my mind to suspect someone close to you, someone who can gain access to the house. Someone who, moreover, would not seem out of place wandering about the grounds.' She shook her head. 'But I couldn't begin to imagine who it might be. Most all those you employ have been with you for years. So why all this sudden ill feeling towards you now?'

Again he found himself smiling. 'So you, like the Major who was here yesterday, are inclined to believe that something quite personal is the motive for the recent incidents?'

Abbie moved uncomfortably in the chair. 'Well, yes... Don't you?'

'If I didn't before, I'm certainly considering the possibility now,' he freely admitted. 'I discovered from Major Wetherby that there are certain factions among the poor openly voicing malcontent. And who can blame them? Times are hard. Perhaps, more significantly, he also confirms that instances of damage to property are confined to this area alone, the vast majority perpetrated against me. Which, of course, we already knew. So he's proposing to station half his men in the vicinity. There are plenty in the area willing to take them in. Personally, though, I'm not altogether sure that it's the solution.'

Abbie had no difficulty in understanding his reservations. 'You suspect that whoever is responsible will merely postpone any future unlawful action until the soldiers have moved on.'

A hint of respect sprang into his dark eyes. 'Yes, that's precisely what I expect will happen. The Major will be unable to keep his men here indefinitely. As soon as their services are required elsewhere they will move on.'

Bart easily identified the lingering expression of concern, before Abbie rose to her feet, effectively bringing the brief tête-à-tête to an end by announcing that she simply couldn't offend Eugenie's sensibilities by going in to luncheon smelling of the stables, and must therefore hurry and change her attire.

'For the time being we should be safe enough, with the Major's men billeted close by,' he assured her, arresting her progress across to the door. 'So put it from your mind. You've enough to think about with the party. Oh, and, Abbie,' he added, as she was about to withdraw, 'be sure that I shall give some serious thought to offering Josh a permanent position here.'

Although they did not travel together, Lady Penrose and Giles arrived within a matter of minutes of each other the following afternoon, and instantly Abbie was conscious of a different atmosphere in the house. Her godmother's easy manners and lazy good humour made her a popular house guest no matter where she stayed, and Eugenie's welcome could not have been warmer. Quite naturally Bart was delighted to have Giles residing under his roof, if only for a few days, so that he could enjoy some masculine company for a change, and Kitty too didn't attempt to conceal her pleasure at seeing her brother's close friend again.

Although promising faithfully to look in on her god-mother later, Abbie had no intention of interfering in the duties of the hostess, and happily stepped aside so that Eugenie, ably assisted by her daughter, could fulfil her role in the household by ensuring her guests were comfortably settled in their respective bedchambers. Lady Penrose, Abbie felt sure, would appreciate a rest after the journey. She felt equally certain that Giles, once he had changed his attire, would wish to seek out Bart's company again in the library. Consequently Abbie wasn't slow to avail herself of the opportunity of slipping quietly away to the garden, where she could be alone with her thoughts.

It was all very well for Bart to suggest that she shouldn't concern herself with his troubles, she decided, once again availing herself of that conveniently positioned bench half-way along the path. But for heaven's sake, how could she not! When he had put in an appearance at luncheon the day before, she had known she had been fanciful in sup-posing that he had been attempting to avoid her. He had been excellent company throughout the remainder of the day, behaving just as he had always done. Well, almost, she amended silently. Kitty and her mother might suppose that he wasn't unduly troubled by the series of unfortunate occurrences. But she had detected that expression of con-cern, which had returned in unguarded moments.

Surely there must be something she could do during the time she remained at the Court? After all, one might have supposed that, as an outsider, she would be able to view things more objectively than Bart; except, when she had been checking over the menus for the party with Cook the previous afternoon, and had raised the subject of the recent happenings, she hadn't doubted for a moment that Mrs Figg's concern for her master's safety had been genuine.

Yes, indeed it was difficult to believe that any one of the servants could have been involved in the unfortunate happenings. Yet, at the same time, the person responsible for the most recent misdeeds must surely have been someone who hadn't aroused suspicion by his presence at the Court?

'Now, miss, what's all this?' a rough voice suddenly demanded to know, instantly drawing Abbie out of her brown study. 'You ain't a-fretting yourself on account of the flowers, now? I won't let you down, miss.'

'Oh, hello, Figgie,' she acknowledged, easily managing a smile. Of all Bart's people she had, amazingly enough, grown most fond of this occasionally irascible old man. 'No, I know I can rely on you. Sit down, won't you? I'd like to ask you something.'

He neither showed reluctance to comply, nor did he attempt to stop puffing on his pipe, as he knew she didn't object to his smoking. 'What's worrying you, miss?'

Abbie couldn't prevent a further smile. One of the old man's most endearing qualities was his bluntness. He always said precisely what was on his mind. 'What's your opinion of the recent happenings here, Figgie?'

'Rum goings on, and no mistake. Mind you, miss, the one who did the bridge must be a right knock-in-the-cradle, if t'were the master he were aiming to 'urt.' His shoulders shook as he gave vent to a wheezy laugh. 'The master can swim like a fish, so he can.'

'Now that is something I hadn't considered,' Abbie admitted, more to herself. 'Everyone who works for Mr Cavanagh must surely know that he can swim.'

'Those that 'ave worked 'ere for some time would, miss,' he agreed, 'and that's most everyone. 'Cepting that groom o' yourn. But 'ee's a good lad. Brings me round a barrow load o' the good stuff most every day and puts it on the pile, yonder.'

His approval of Josh came as no surprise. Everyone seemed to like him. Which, she sincerely hoped, would act in his favour if Bart was seriously to consider employing him.

'What about the people employed on the land, Figgie? Are they all content working for Mr Cavanagh?'

'You'll not find one who'd say a word against him, miss, and that's a fact. Like his father and grandfather afore 'im, he be well liked.'

'Not by everyone,' she countered.

'Well, miss, I don't reckon anyone born and bred in these parts would bear 'im a grudge. He's fair to his people, and he's always done business with local tradesmen. Now I ain't saying the master's ain't put a nose or two out of joint in his time. He ain't afeared to speak his mind. Bound to 'ave rubbed someone up the wrong way. But I reckon there be more to it than that. Besides…'

Abbie detected the sound of approaching footsteps too, and turned to see Bart, closely followed by his sister and Giles, entering the garden by way of the wicket gate.

Bart was not slow to observe her either, or his head gardener, for that matter, and raised his brows in exaggerated surprise. 'What's all this then, Figg? Resting on your spade again, I see. I shall seriously need to consider turning you off at the twelvemonth if you continue neglecting your duties in this shameful manner.'

Abbie could not help smiling at Figg's wicked chuckle, as he rose to his feet and hobbled away to continue with what he had been doing. He was a canny old man whose knowledge stretched a deal further than the confines of the garden he tended so well. Perhaps there was something in what he had said, she mused, and the answer to Bart's present troubles would not be found here at the Court, but somewhere in his past.

'Would you care to bear me company?' Bart invited, smiling crookedly as Kitty and Giles walked past them, chattering happily together and seemingly locked in a world of their own. 'Otherwise, I very much fear that I'm likely to be ignored for the most part.'

'I, for one, wouldn't be at all surprised if you were,' Abbie declared, rising to her feet and automatically allowing him to entwine her arm through his without giving the matter a second thought. 'You know Giles is in love with her, of course?' she added, successfully maintaining a slow pace and forcing Bart to do likewise so that a discreet distance was maintained between them and the couple in front.

Once again those dark brows rose, only this time his surprise seemed genuine. 'Evidently you didn't realise.' She was unable to suppress a wicked smile of satisfaction. 'And here I have been misguidedly thinking you omnipotent! Seemingly it is much easier to be objective when one is not closely involved.'

'Don't be smug, baggage! It doesn't suit you,' he scolded, trying his utmost to look severe, but failing quite miserably. 'What makes you suppose my friend's affections are engaged? Has he confided in you?'

'Good heavens, no! If Giles is likely to confide in anyone then it will be you, Bart. But I doubt he'll ever broach the subject himself. I strongly suspect he considers himself far too old for her, and therefore unlikely ever to be in the running, as it were.'

'There's no denying there's a disparity in age, though I've always known that he's dashed fond of her.' He stared intently at the couple under discussion, as though attempting to view them in a different light. 'Kitty has never once hinted that her feelings might be engaged.'

'I'm not altogether surprised,' Abbie returned. 'I don't believe she realises it herself yet. But she will in time. She's openly admitted to me that she prefers the company of older men.' Her lips twitched. 'Which is quite amazing, considering from whom she has gained the majority of her experience of the more mature male.'

Clearly he was under no illusion as to precisely whom she was referring, and his low growl in response very nearly sent her into whoops of laughter. 'And females, of course, mature more quickly,' she continued, maintaining her self-control. 'Kitty might still be young, but she's neither frivolous nor shallow. When she returns from Brighton, you will have a clearer indication. She'll be granted the opportunity to meet many young men there, and of course in London too when she goes in the spring. But I shall be very, very surprised if she betrays a partiality for any gentleman's company.'

Although he made no attempt to discuss the matter further, Abbie knew she had given him much to mull over, which she considered no bad thing in the circumstances. It could do him nothing but good to think about something other than the disturbing incidents at the Court.

Consequently Abbie returned to the house, feeling very well pleased with herself. Parting company with the others in the hall, she went directly upstairs to fulfil the promise she had made to her godmother, and discovered her reclining on the *chaise longue* in her bedchamber, a plate of sweet almond biscuits and a glass of ratafia at her elbow.

Swinging her feet to the floor so that Abbie could sit beside her, Lady Penrose noted with satisfaction the healthy bloom in her goddaughter's flawless complexion. 'A bucolic existence evidently agrees with you, my dear. You look quite disgustingly healthy.'

Up until that moment Abbie had not appreciated just how much she had missed her godmother's lively company and wry good humour. Eugenie Cavanagh was undoubtedly one of the most good-natured females one could ever wish to meet. Nevertheless, it could not be denied that her conversation sadly lacked that special stimulating sparkle. Only with Bart could she enjoy a joke and engage in a little harmless verbal fencing.

'All things considered, I have very much enjoyed my stay here at the Court,' Abbie wasn't reticent to admit. 'I felt very comfortable here from the first. It's a lovely old house. In need of a little refurbishment here and there, as you can see,' she added, gazing about at the faded soft furnishings in the bedchamber, 'but its slight imperfections seem only to enhance its character and charm.'

'Like its owner, perhaps?' Lady Penrose suggested, grinning wickedly, and Abbie didn't pretend to misunderstand.

'Very well… Yes, I have come to view Bart in a new light,' she freely acknowledged, though for some obscure reason she didn't seem able to meet her godmother's knowing gaze. For some reason too she had developed the sudden urge to pluck at the folds of her skirt, like a diffident child suddenly thrust into the presence of an imposing stranger. 'But that was only to be expected in the circumstances, given the kindness he has shown towards me in recent weeks.'

'Very true,' Lady Penrose agreed. 'Although I might have wished he'd refrained from encouraging you in the idiotic notion of becoming a professional artist. I'm not denying that you have a natural talent, Abbie,' she thought it tactful to add, after receiving a brief, reproachful look.

'But you must face facts, my dear. No one who can afford to pay generously for a portrait to be painted will seek the services of an unknown. Almost all would wish for an acknowledged master to undertake the work.'

No matter how much she might resent it, Abbie had silently to acknowledge that what her godmother had said was true. Bart too would have known this, would have known that she would find it nigh impossible to support herself as an artist, especially as she had received no professional training. So why on earth had he encouraged her?

'I expect Bart was just trying to be kind,' she murmured, 'and didn't wish to be the one to crush my foolish hopes.'

Although she smiled at this, Lady Penrose refrained from comment, and merely asked how his portrait was progressing.

'All but finished,' Abbie told her, wishing with all her heart that it was quite otherwise, for she had no valid reason now to delay her return to Bath, and she felt sure that Lady Penrose would not wish to remain for more than a week.

She suddenly felt very low, and was relieved to see Felcham enter the room in order to help her mistress dress for dinner, because it gave her the excuse she needed to seek the sanctuary of her own bedchamber.

Going immediately over to the window, Abbie stared out at the view she had swiftly grown to love. Why was it that she had been able to accept that in all probability she would never become a successful professional artist, when she simply couldn't bear to think about the day when she would leave Cavanagh Court…and its master?

Chapter Eleven

Fortunately for Abbie she was kept far too busy throughout the following day, ensuring that everything would run smoothly for the surprise party, to dwell too frequently on her return to Bath. Which was perhaps just as well, she reflected, adding the finishing touches to her toilette, because she hadn't been at all successful in shrugging off her mood of despondency throughout the previous evening and had caught Bart regarding her intently on two or three occasions.

'You look lovely, miss,' Rose announced, placing the lightweight silk shawl about Abbie's shoulders, while at the same time studying the arrangement of her silky black locks. 'I watched very closely to how Miss Felcham did your hair, miss. I'm sure I could do it myself next time.'

'I'm certain you could too,' Abbie agreed. From her first day at the Court she had been more than satisfied with the young housemaid's services. 'I'm afraid, though, it's unlikely you'll be granted the opportunity to try. There'll be no more large dinner parties before your mistress leaves for Brighton. And I shall be returning to Bath myself at the end of next week.'

Determined not to fall victim to a fit of the sullens again

this evening, Abbie did her best to ignore the return of that painful spasm beneath her ribcage. 'In the meantime, you could do no better than try to pick up a few tips from Felcham. She's an extremely competent lady's maid. Which I'm sure you will be one day.'

This brought a smile to Rose's face. 'That's what I'd really like to be, miss, though it ain't likely to happen unless the master marries. Still, I don't suppose he'll leave it too much longer before he takes a wife.'

A pain, far more acutely searing than anything she had suffered thus far, shot through Abbie, and for a moment she felt the need to grasp the back of a chair for support. It was bad enough having to come to terms with leaving the Court; Bart's marrying was something she simply didn't wish to contemplate, now or ever.

Only by tapping into that deep well of inner strength, which had been steadily increasing during recent years, did Abbie manage to restore sufficient composure to take herself downstairs to the drawing-room where everyone had congregated. Thankfully Kitty was enthusing over the lovely amethyst set Bart had presented to Eugenie for her birthday, and Abbie was able to slip into the chair beside her godmother before anyone noticed she was there.

She was further aided by the arrival of the first guests; by the time she had taken her seat in the dining-room, and had worked her way through several delicious courses, she was feeling a deal more composed. Even so, she could scarcely bring herself to peer up at the head of the table, where Bart sat happily conversing with Lady Warren and another close neighbour's middle-aged wife.

'You and Kitty must have worked very hard this afternoon to arrange all the flowers, Abbie,' Lady Penrose remarked, sidling up beside her goddaughter the instant they had returned to the drawing-room.

'Yes, I'm rather pleased with the way things have gone thus far,' Abbie freely admitted, glancing across at the door, where Eugenie was stationed beside her stepson in readiness to welcome the first of the guests who had been invited just to the party. 'Of course Kitty and I realised at the outset that we would be unable to keep the event a secret, so we merely informed Eugenie that Bart had suggested a few people should join us for dinner this evening by way of a celebration, though it was clear she hadn't been expecting quite so many at table. And the party, of course, has come as a complete surprise to her, for which we have you to thank. It was a marvellous idea of yours to take her out in the carriage, keeping her away from the Court for much of the day'

'I thoroughly enjoyed myself,' Lady Penrose declared. 'Although I reside permanently in Bath now, I do not know this part of the country at all well. It was most agreeable seeing the sights. There's some lovely countryside round here.'

'I've done a deal of exploring whilst I've been here,' Abbie disclosed. 'I've never been at a loss for something to do. Bart has seen to that.'

Lady Penrose subjected her goddaughter to a prolonged stare before her attention was captured by a familiar figure. 'Good heavens! Where did he spring from? I thought he'd returned to London.'

Abbie turned in time to see Eugenie's eyes widen as she greeted Bart's cousin, and couldn't say she was altogether surprised by the reaction. Cedric Cavanagh's attire could never be described as sober, and this evening he was more startlingly arrayed than usual in a primrose-coloured coat, with matching knee breeches. The preposterously large nosegay fixed in his lapel was no less dazzling than the emerald nestling between the folds of the most intricately tied cravat Abbie had ever seen.

'Oh, dear me,' she murmured unsteadily. 'Just look at Bart's face. I do hope he manages to refrain from saying something cutting to his cousin throughout the evening. But I wouldn't lay odds on it.'

'What an utter twiddle-poop the boy is!' Lady Penrose exclaimed, not mincing words. 'Little wonder Bart doesn't hold his cousin in high esteem.'

Abbie was forced to agree. 'Cedric has been a guest at the Hall for almost three weeks. But this is the first time he's visited the Court. Bart has shown no interest in seeking his cousin's company either. Although I was somewhat surprised to learn from Bart, after he had dined with the Warrens the other evening, that Cedric would not be dining with us this evening, owing to the fact that he was accompanying Richard Warren to watch a mill.'

Lady Penrose was amazed and did not attempt to hide the fact. 'Well, well, well! Who would have supposed a fribble like Cedric would have been interested in the manly sport of boxing?'

Abbie frowned at this. 'Yes, perhaps he isn't quite what he seems,' she responded, before giving her godmother's arm a warning squeeze. 'Have a care, ma'am. I do believe the popinjay is heading our way.'

'Why, Mr Cavanagh, this is a surprise!' Lady Penrose greeted him. 'Bath has quite lost its sparkle since your departure. And little wonder! You whisked it all away, I see, in the folds of your cravat.'

Abbie almost choked, but Cedric appeared very well pleased as he attempted to peer down at the glinting emerald. 'Yes, it's a splendid stone, is it not? Mama presented it to me on my last birthday.' He then turned his attention to Abbie in order to secure her promise for a dance, and then, much to her intense relief, sauntered away in order to pay his respects to his favourite cousin.

Lady Penrose frowned as she watched him present the nosegay to Kitty. 'Well, at any rate, he appears to have a genuine fondness for her. I sincerely trust it is no more than cousinly affection, though. I cannot envisage Bartholomew Cavanagh ever being persuaded to sanction a marriage in that quarter.'

Abbie smiled to herself. 'I cannot imagine he'll ever be called upon to do so. Unless I'm grossly mistaken, Kitty finds Cedric amusing, nothing more.'

She refused to divulge more than this by betraying Kitty's regard for a certain other gentleman, even though she half suspected there was no real need for her to do so, for her godmother was no fool, and noticed a deal more than most people imagined.

On another matter, however, she had come perilously close to attaining her godmother's opinion. Undoubtedly Lady Penrose would have been the ideal person with whom to share her concerns over Bart's future well-being. All the same she had refrained from doing so, simply because she could not envisage any further incidents occurring during the remainder of her stay at the Court, most especially not now, when there was a company of dragoons stationed in the locale.

It just so happened that Bart had invited several of the young officers to the party, their smart dark blue uniforms making a pleasing contrast to the more sober black coats worn by the majority of the gentlemen present. Most all the younger female guests were eyeing the officers with favour, and Abbie too was not slow to accept Major Wetherby's invitation to dance, although her eager acceptance had little to do with a preference for gentlemen sporting dashing regimentals.

The Major wasn't slow to divulge that he had made Bart's acquaintance whilst out in the Peninsula. Something in his tone strongly suggested that their association had not been altogether amicable, but Abbie tactfully refrained from attempting to discover if she was right, and merely asked if any progress had been made in uncovering the identities of those involved in damage to property.

'No, ma'am,' he answered. 'And I'm not particularly hopeful that we shall bring any to book.'

'Oh, and why not, Major?'

'Because our inquiries thus far have come to naught. A reward is usually inducement enough for someone to reveal what he knows. But in this instance we have drawn a blank, which has only served to strengthen my belief that the unrest is not so widespread in this area, but an isolated pocket of perhaps two or three troublemakers who have a particular target in mind.'

Before the steps of the dance separated them, Abbie noticed his head turn fleetingly in the direction of the door, where Bart, stoically maintaining his role as host, still bore Eugenie company. Had it not been for the slight tightening of the muscles she perceived about the Major's full-lipped mouth, his expression would have been difficult to read. As it was, she was now firmly convinced that there was no love lost between him and Bart, and didn't hesitate to pick up the threads of their conversation when the steps of the dance brought them together again.

'You were referring to Mr Cavanagh, Major, I believe. That someone bears him a grudge also occurred to me,' she freely admitted. 'Yet I also know that he is well respected in these parts.'

'That I also have discovered. He had a reputation for fairness when in the army, ma'am. But one still makes enemies, and Cavanagh is no exception. You, I understand, have known him for some years. Therefore you must be well aware that he isn't always diplomatic, and isn't afraid to speak his mind.'

'True,' she was forced to concede. 'But I hardly think that sufficient inducement to attempt to burn down his house, or make attempts on his life.'

As the dance came to an end the Major drew her aside. 'Clearly you are in Cavanagh's confidence, ma'am, so I shall speak freely. Knowing him as I do, it's my belief that the answer to the conundrum lies in some action of his in the past, something he did to someone at some point. And that someone is now bent on revenge. I suggested this to Cavanagh the other night, when we dined with Lord and Lady Warren. I wasn't altogether sure that he had taken the possibility seriously. If you value his friendship, ma'am, I would strongly suggest that you persuade him to think long and hard about the past and the enemies he might have made. I cannot remain in the locale indefinitely to offer protection.'

It was at this point that Bart, having maintained thus far an amiable resignation to his duties as host, began to grow a fraction weary of waiting for the last of the guests to arrive, and glanced about the room at those who had had the common courtesy not to force him to kick his heels by the door. He found it no difficult matter to locate Abbie among the throng. He was surprised to detect what appeared suspiciously like a look of concern on her delicate features, and couldn't help wondering what had been said to bring about the evident disquiet.

'Damned Provost,' he muttered darkly, as his glance strayed to the gentleman bearing her company, whom he had never held in high esteem, and didn't realise his voice had carried until he noticed his stepmother regarding him with a marked degree of uncertainty.

'You do not need to remain with me, Bart, if you would prefer to bear the gentlemen company. I'm quite happy to linger here to welcome the last of the guests.'

He found it no difficult task to summon up a smile. It had taken him too many years to recognise his stepmother's fine qualities. Her displays of diffidence would always irritate him, he supposed. At least, though, she wasn't totally lacking intelligence, and her kindness more than compensated for her slight faults.

'I wouldn't dream of deserting you, Eugenie, on such an occasion as this.'

She blushed becomingly, like a girl embarking on her first Season. 'It was so very thoughtful of you to organise this for me, Bart. We haven't held a large party here in such a long time. It's delightful having all our neighbours and so many friends about us.'

Bart was surprised how much enjoyment he was deriving from the occasion too. Apart from the few weeks they had spent in Bath, they had done little socialising since his father's demise.

'It's Kitty and Abbie you have to thank, Eugenie. All I did was agree to the party, which I did most willingly. One should celebrate such a milestone in one's life. Though looking at you tonight, my dear, no one would suppose for a moment that you'd blessed this earth for half a century.'

He noted the second becoming blush his gallantry had engendered, but his satisfaction was short-lived, for a moment later he caught sight of Abbie again, dancing this time with Cedric, her expression, if anything, more troubled than before.

'Perhaps it's time we both mingled with our guests,' he suggested. 'We can rely on Barryman to locate our whereabouts in the event of yet more late arrivals.'

As she seemed only too willing to comply, Bart escorted

her to the corner of the room, where several ladies of her own age had congregated. He then took himself off to the adjoining parlour, which had been set out for those wishing to play cards, and immediately joined his closest friend, avidly watching the play at one of the tables.

'The duties of amiable host are beginning to pall, are they, old fellow?' Giles quizzed him, as Bart reached his side.

'I'm resigned, dear boy. Besides which, I'm fully conscious that I owe it to Eugenie to ensure the evening is a pleasurable one, and shall therefore fulfil my role by entertaining the more mature matrons present. The younger guests, with my irrepressible sister's assistance, will undoubtedly succeed in entertaining themselves.'

Giles regarded him for a moment in silence. 'I notice a great change in you, my friend. You appear far more contented than I've ever known you.'

Bart couldn't forbear a rueful smile at this woefully inaccurate observation. 'Then it would seem I missed my vocation in life. I should have become an actor. No, I'm not wholly content,' he admitted. 'And in the circumstances it's hardly surprising just why I'm not.' He reached out to lay a hand briefly on Giles's shoulder. 'We'll talk again later. But for the time being I must leave you to your own devices as my presence, it would appear, is required to make up a fourth at whist.'

He was happy enough to join the three ladies whose fondness for gambling had proved something of a trial to their respective husbands in recent years. He was happier still to relinquish his place a short while later to yet another female neighbour whose fondness for the game of chance was well known in the locale.

He then returned to the salon where most of the younger guests were engaged in a set of lively country dances, and was somewhat surprised not to find Abbie enjoying the exercise, for he well knew that she rarely missed an opportunity to step out on to the dance floor.

He eventually discovered her amidst a group of younger matrons, not appearing, it had to be said, totally engrossed in the conversation taking place. A moment later she moved away, and although she paused from time to time to exchange a few words with several of those whose acquaintance she had made since her arrival in the county, her intention was clear.

Bart had deliberately refrained from seeking her company thus far, simply because he knew well enough that to single her out for particular attention would only give rise to further speculation. He was fully aware that her presence at the Court during the past weeks had already caused a deal of gossip among his neighbours. This in itself would not have troubled him unduly had it not been that her future role in his life was far from certain. He could not have been more sure of his own feelings; of hers he was not so confident.

All the same, he was not prepared to ignore the fact that the woman he loved, the only woman he had ever truly loved, was worrying over something, most especially if confiding in him could ease her troubled mind.

Hence, he didn't hesitate to follow her example by escaping from the crowd by way of the French windows, and caught sight of her almost at once, standing in one corner of the terrace, staring out at that part of the garden where lanterns had been hung from the branches of trees.

At the sound of his footfall she turned, that wonderful, spontaneous smile of hers instantly diminishing his fear that all was not as it should be with her, but not completely. 'Feeling a little unsociable this evening, are we?' he quizzed, deliberately keeping his tone light.

'Not at all,' she answered. 'Merely taking advantage of a little fresh air.'

He wasn't at all convinced, but thought better of pressing her further, especially as their conversation might easily be overheard by anyone strolling in the garden. Besides which, he was finding it a mite difficult to prevent his thoughts from turning to that one other time when they had been alone on a shadowed terrace, and he had allowed desire to take control. He had never been able to forget those moments of sweet response before his advances had been summarily rejected. Now, of course, he could understand the reason behind the eventual rebuff. The wonder of it was that she tolerated him at all. Yet she did, and against all the odds she had, he felt sure, grown to trust him and, yes, had come to look upon him as a friend.

'And what brings you out here? Not tired already of playing the host?'

'Not at all. I am enjoying this evening.' He bridged the distance between them, and experienced a degree of satisfaction, when at last he stood so closely beside her and their bodies almost touched, that she didn't attempt to draw away even so much as an inch. 'You and Kitty have worked so hard to make this an enjoyable occasion. When Kitty and her mother return from their Brighton trip, I'll suggest we entertain more often.'

He would have expected her to approve of this, and yet surprisingly she frowned. 'Is there some reason why you have refrained from doing so in the past? All your neighbours seem so personable.'

'They are,' he readily concurred. 'Although I'd be less than honest if I didn't admit to liking some a deal more than others.' He shrugged. 'I suppose I've been too involved in the running of the property to concern myself about much else, least of all socialising. I should have considered Eugenie and Kitty more. It was selfish of me, I suppose.'

'No, you're not selfish, Bart,' she countered softly. 'A little thoughtless on occasions, perhaps, but not selfish.'

Only the very real possibility that he might jeopardise that surprisingly sweet rapport which had sprung up between them prevented him from covering that provocatively smiling mouth with his own. Friendship was a poor substitute for what he really wanted. Yet it would be foolish not to accept the heartrending possibility that he might never be offered more.

'If you're sufficiently restored, perhaps you'd allow me to escort you back into the salon before our absence gives rise to comment,' he suggested, taking a hasty step away before his self-control was too severely tested.

Although she acquiesced readily enough, he thought he detected a look akin to disappointment flit over her features the moment before she turned and moved back across the terrace.

He shook his head, wondering at himself, as he followed her back into the salon. It was possibly complete madness on his part to suppose that one day her friendship might deepen. Even so, he found himself clinging to the faint hope. It somehow sustained him and made the remainder of the evening far more pleasurable than it might otherwise have been. Nevertheless he wasn't sorry to bid the last of his guests a fond farewell and seek the company of the one person in whom he was happy to confide his present troubles.

'Unless you wish to follow the ladies' example and retire, perhaps you'd care to join me in the library for a nightcap?' he suggested.

Giles was only too happy to oblige. 'You never cease to amaze me, old fellow,' he confessed, after accepting the goodly measure of brandy, and watching Bart make himself comfortable in the chair opposite. 'For someone who has always thought little of social graces, you're an accomplished host.'

Smiling to himself, Bart stared down into the contents of his glass. 'As you yourself remarked earlier this evening, age has undoubtedly mellowed me. I am far less intolerant of my fellow man.'

One sandy brow rose in a quizzical arch. 'And I do not think we need look far to find the beneficial influence.'

Bart refrained from comment, and with an abrupt change of subject voiced the wish that his friend could make a longer stay. 'Of course I fully appreciate why you must leave tomorrow. How long do you propose to remain with your uncle?'

Giles was suddenly grave. 'Until the end. Sadly he'll not be with us much longer, a matter of a few weeks only, and it's the least I can do. After all, I am his closest relative, and heir.'

Having enjoyed a close friendship with Giles since boyhood, Bart knew a deal about his background. Giles had never evinced a desire to follow in his father's footsteps by studying law, and had gone into the army, once his education was completed, in the full knowledge that one day he would inherit his uncle's sizeable property in Somerset. Throughout his life he had maintained strong ties with his uncle, with whom he had enjoyed a far closer relationship than he had with his own father.

'I do appreciate how much you'll miss the old man,' Bart said softly. 'I know also that you'll take great care of your inheritance. Of course,' he added, striving for a lighter note, 'coming into a property does have some disadvantages. One instantly becomes a matrimonial prize.'

The ploy worked, for Giles's smile returned. 'Oh, I believe I'm capable of taking a leaf out of your book, old fellow, and succeed in keeping all the little darlings at bay.'

'What, all of them?' Bart quizzed gently. 'Or am I right in thinking there is one with whom you would happily share your life?'

Although clearly taken aback, Giles didn't attempt to deny it. 'How on earth could you possibly have known? Not even my mother has ever guessed.'

'You certainly succeeded in concealing your feelings from me,' Bart admitted. 'It was someone far more discerning than I who brought it to my notice. Since then I have been observing your behaviour towards my sister, and realise that my confidante, perceptive little darling that she is, had spoken no less than the truth.'

'Abbie, of course,' Giles murmured, before a glimmer of hope flickered over his features. 'Do you suppose Kitty might possibly have said something to her?'

'Abbie is of the opinion that Kitty, as yet, does not appreciate the depths of her feelings towards you, and I'm inclined to agree with her. Needless to say it didn't go unnoticed by me that my sister ensured that you were placed beside her at dinner, and also that she chose you as her escort in to supper.'

Only for a moment longer did the glint in Giles's eyes remain, then he shook his head. 'I know she has a fondness for me, Bart. But I'm too old for her.'

'That was precisely my first thought, old fellow,' he admitted, his white teeth flashing in a sportive smile. 'Until, that is, Abbie remarked upon my sister's preference for the company of older men, and yours in particular.' He was suddenly serious. 'As Abbie was at pains to point out, Kitty is neither fickle nor flirtatious. But she's still young. I am therefore determined she should be granted the opportunity to meet other gentlemen. If, however, after her

Season in Brighton and her visit to the capital next year, she has formed no attachment, you have my blessing to pay your address.'

A hint of colour had appeared in Giles's cheeks, surprisingly making him appear much younger than his thirty years. 'Thank you. I could ask no more of you than that. Or is it perhaps Miss Graham I ought to thank for being so perceptive and bringing to your notice my sincere regard for your sister?' He took a moment to sample the contents of his glass, while all the time staring intently across at his friend. 'I cannot help wondering, though, whether she's as perceptive with regard to you.'

If Giles had been expecting a rueful grin in response to this gambit, he was doomed to disappointment, for Bart, after several moments of stony silence, merely tossed the contents of his glass down his throat, and stalked back across to the decanters for a refill. 'I'm sorry old fellow,' he added. 'I didn't mean to pry.'

'I'm not at all certain whether she does realise,' Bart revealed, when at last he returned to his chair. 'And the truth of the matter is that I'm too much of a damnable coward to leave her in no doubt, lest her decision to marry me remain the same as before.'

Giles was silent for a moment, then said, 'But as you remarked yourself, neither of you were ready for matrimony then.'

'The truth of the matter is, old fellow, I was foolish enough to make the proposal at my godfather's behest, and experienced nothing but relief when she turned me down flat,' Bart admitted. 'If I ever gave the matter any thought at all, and I cannot recall her refusal ever preyed on my mind to any significant degree, I assumed she at least had had the sense to realise that we were too young.'

Giles gazed sagely across at him. 'Evidently you have since discovered more lay behind the refusal.'

'Oh, yes, much more,' Bart confirmed, before disclosing everything that had occurred during the last fateful visit to his godfather's home.

'Oh, my God!' Giles muttered, surprisingly igniting a spark of merriment in Bart's eyes.

'I do believe that that was more or less what passed through my mind when Abbie finally confided in me.' He shook his head, all amusement gone. 'I couldn't have offered her a greater insult had I tried—enjoying the favours of a neighbour's wife one moment, and the next professing my devotion to her. The wonder of it is she ever spoke to me again!'

'But surely she must realise the affair meant nothing, merely a young man sowing his wild oats, as it were,' Giles suggested hopefully.

'Yes, perhaps she does,' Bart agreed, staring intently at a spot on the ceiling. 'At least I believe she has come to look upon me as a friend. And perhaps I should be satisfied with that.'

'No, you shouldn't,' Giles countered, without giving the matter a moment's thought. 'You should tell her precisely how you feel about her now. You may come to regret it if you don't.'

Bart didn't misunderstand. 'If I delay, then I run the risk of losing her to someone else. Yes,' he agreed. 'That is a very real possibility now that she is to reside with her godmother. But it's a risk I must take. I cannot attempt to woo her now, especially not here at the Court and at the present time. I'll not have her put at further risk. She must leave.'

Bart was surprised by his friend's lack of response, for Giles was well aware of what had been happening at the Court in recent weeks. 'You appear doubtful,' he prompted, when Giles continued to stare silently down at the empty hearth. 'Surely you can appreciate my reasoning?'

Clearly troubled, Giles nodded. 'But has it never occurred to you to consider that it might be Abbie, not you, who is the real target? And before you dismiss it out of hand,' he added, when Bart was about to do just that, 'remember one thing. She has been with you on both occasions—when the masonry fell from the roof, and at the bridge. Furthermore, she was with you on the occasion when your curricle just happened to lose a wheel a few weeks ago.'

Bart took a moment to consider, then shook his head. 'No, impossible! No one would ever wish to harm that darling girl!' he declared, and then promptly dismissed it from his mind until the following day, when he witnessed an incident that forced him to take the suggestion rather more seriously.

Chapter Twelve

Midway through the following morning, while making use of the stable-yard as a short cut, Abbie was surprised to discover her normally hardworking groom sitting outside the largest of the stables, whittling away on a piece of willow.

Far from looking guilt-ridden at being caught idling away his time, he appeared remarkably well pleased to see her, and rose at once to his feet. 'Can I give you a hand with them, Miss Abbie?'

'I didn't expect to find you here,' she remarked, gratefully handing over the rug, and the basket of food that Cook had insisted pressing upon her in the event that she should lose track of time and miss luncheon. 'I thought you'd have accompanied Miss Cavanagh and Mr Fergusson out on their ride.'

'No, Mr Hackman's done that, miss, seeing as Mrs Cavanagh went out in Lady Penrose's carriage and his services weren't required.'

Abbie had been invited to go with the ladies on a visit to several neighbours, but had declined, mainly because she had wished to do a few sketches of the Court and surrounding park land as a memento of her stay. She had also been invited to join Kitty and Giles on their ride, and had declined that invitation too, having decided they might appreciate some time alone together before Giles returned to Somerset later in the day.

As they set off across the park towards the group of stately elms adjacent to the folly, Abbie's thoughts once again turned to the future well-being of the person striding happily alongside.

Since her arrival at the Court, Lady Penrose had mentioned that, although he had not accompanied her on the journey, her young groom was now fully recovered and undertaking his duties. Which meant, of course, that Josh's services would no longer be required. Knowing of Bart's reluctance to employ strangers—and in the present climate no one could blame him for that—Abbie had refrained from raising the matter of the groom's future employment again. Josh himself hadn't made her situation any easier. He had seemed so wonderfully contented here at the Court that she had tended to shy away from broaching the subject again. Time, however, was fast running out, and she could no longer avoid doing so.'

'I do not know whether you're aware of it or not, Josh, but Lady Penrose's young groom is fully recovered,' she said, before she could change her mind.

'Happen her ladyship's head groom, Jenkins, did mention it, miss.'

As Josh was certainly no simpleton, Abbie found his seeming indifference a trifle disturbing. 'You do realise what it will mean, of course?' she persisted. 'Lady Penrose is unlikely to keep you on.'

'Aye, miss. Wouldn't expect her to neither.'

'But, Josh, aren't you in the least bit concerned?' She favoured him with a searching glance before shaking out the rug and spreading it on the ground. 'What will you do—try for some work round here, or return to Bath with Lady Penrose and myself on Friday?'

He raised his well-muscled shoulders in a shrug of complete unconcern. 'I hadn't given it much thought, miss. Happen summut'll turn up. It always does.'

Not knowing whether to admire this devil-may-care outlook or not, but deciding any attempt to discuss the issue further would be a complete waste of breath, Abbie settled herself on the rug, and began to sketch her favourite view of the Court. With her various drawing materials scattered about her within easy reach, she was very contented. She guessed Josh was too, for he had soon settled himself on the grass directly behind her, and hadn't been slow either to accept the invitation to avail himself of the contents of the food basket.

For a few minutes she was conscious of a steady munching sound, but certainly wasn't aware when it had suddenly stopped. She was as oblivious to the fact that a tall figure was approaching from the direction of the lake as she was of Josh, reaching for a stout stick, while stealthily rising to his feet. The distant warning cry caught her completely unawares, as did the sudden whoosh of air as the stick was brought down hard by her shoulder, narrowly missing the fingers of her outstretched left hand. She was hardly given time to assimilate the reason behind Josh's action before the sound of heavy running footsteps caught her attention. The next moment Bart, looking murderous, had Josh firmly held by his shirt front and was delivering a crushing blow to his jaw.

'Stop! Stop!'

Scrambling to her feet, Abbie clung to the sleeve of Bart's jacket for all she was worth in a valiant attempt to prevent him from following up his advantage by delivering a second punishing blow. 'Look! Look behind you!' she screamed.

For a few moments it seemed as if Bart was oblivious to her presence, or was intent on ignoring it. Then very slowly he turned his head to see the coiled, half-crushed serpent at the edge of the rug. 'Good Gad!' he muttered, releasing his hold on Josh and grasping Abbie's arms so tightly that she almost winced. 'Did it strike? Were you bitten?'

'No,' she assured him. 'Thanks to Josh. I didn't even realise it was there.'

It would have been a gross exaggeration to suggest that Bart's expression betrayed the least contrition. No one, however, could have doubted his sincerity when at last he apologised, and held out his hand to help Josh to his feet, least of all the groom himself who, if anything, appeared amused as he rubbed the swelling on his jaw.

'You've a powerful left hook there, Mr Cavanagh,' he declared, totally without rancour. 'Can tell you've done a bit of sparring afore now.'

For answer Bart smiled ruefully before turning his attention to Abbie to discover her looking distinctly pale. Instinctively he placed an arm about her shoulders and drew her close. She trembled slightly, but made not the least attempt to free herself from his gentle clasp.

'Be good enough to take your mistress's belongings back to the house, Josh, and I'll see you later,' Bart said, before entwining Abbie's arm through his and leading her gently away. 'I'm sorry about that. You must consider me a complete blockhead charging in upon you in that way.'

'No, not at all,' she hurriedly assured him. 'If there is one thing I cannot abide, though, it's snakes.' She shuddered again before something occurred to her, and she favoured him with a searching stare. 'But you hadn't seen the snake. It was Josh you attacked. You thought he was about to strike me with that stick. What on earth made you suppose he would wish me harm?'

Bart had the grace to look a little shamefaced. 'God knows, Abbie… I've not known what to think. And after what Giles said last night…'

'What did he say?' she prompted when his voice trailed away and he stopped to stare across the lake towards the house. 'Surely he didn't attempt to suggest that Josh might be responsible for the happenings of late?'

There was no mistaking the note of mocking disbelief in her voice, and he could only wonder at himself now for jumping to such a ludicrous assumption the very moment after he had seen the groom raising the stick high above Abbie's head.

'No, he didn't,' he admitted, once again fixing his attention upon her, his expression no less penetrating than hers had been a short time before. 'But what he did suggest was that I might not have been the target for these most recent attacks, and that it could possibly have been you.'

'What?' Abbie was stunned and it clearly showed. 'Giles must be all about in his head to suppose such a thing. Why, it is a ridiculous supposition! Who on earth would want to harm me…? And why?'

'That was precisely my initial reaction,' he admitted, guiding her towards the folly, where they could sit for a while, sheltered from the sun's harsh rays. 'But since then I've been giving it some thought.'

He led her across to the stone bench, and made no attempt to release the clasp on her hand as he sat down beside her. 'Since we met again in Bath,' he continued softly, 'you have done me the singular honour of confiding in me.' There was just a suspicion of tightening muscles along the length of his jaw. 'It's just possible that others might know that your grandfather has threatened to disinherit you. Could there be those with a vested interest, those who would be happy to see you disinherited, or worse—totally unable to fulfil your grandfather's dearest wish?'

Abbie did not misunderstand. 'By putting a period to my existence, you mean.' Although she felt moved by the touching concern he was betraying for her well-being, she couldn't prevent the mischievous side of her nature from coming to the fore. 'So what you are suggesting is that I must remain on my guard against the person who is most likely to benefit after my grandfather's demise?'

He regarded her steadily. 'To be blunt—yes.'

Somehow she managed to affect a look of wide-eyed innocence. 'But I'm certain *he* would never resort to such tactics.'

'One can never be sure,' Bart countered in all seriousness. 'Money is a strong inducement.'

It took a monumental effort, but somehow Abbie managed to control her mirth. As it had clearly never occurred to Bart to suppose that he might well be the main beneficiary in her grandfather's will, it would be grossly unfair, she decided, to make fun of him. Besides which, it really was no laughing matter. His actions of a short time earlier proved that he had grown concerned for her welfare, and it wasn't difficult to guess what might have given rise to his suspicions.

It was true that her grandfather had intended to break his journey to Scotland by remaining for a few days in Yorkshire with his nephew, Sir Montague Graham. It was likely, as her grandfather held his nephew in high esteem, that he might well have confided in him, revealing his dissatisfaction with his granddaughter's behaviour. Even so, she found it impossible to believe that Sir Montague, a gentleman of the highest principals, would ever attempt to turn the situation to his advantage by engaging the services of someone who would ensure that her days were numbered, and did not hesitate to give voice to this firm belief.

'Apart from his threat to disinherit me, Grandfather has never chosen to enlighten me as to the exact contents of his will. All the same, he has never given me any reason to suppose that he has any intention of leaving a substantial portion of his wealth to any member of the Graham family.'

'What…?' Bart made no more attempt to hide his surprise than Abbie had done a short time earlier. 'Not even to his nephew, Montague?'

Abbie gained a modicum of satisfaction from knowing that she had judged his thoughts correctly. 'My grandfather is very fond of his nephew, understandably so. Monty is the most level-headed, charming man. He is happily married and, as far as I'm aware, very plump in the pocket. He spends most of the year in Yorkshire with his wife and children. According to Grandfather, he rarely visits the capital, and has never been addicted to games of chance.'

He appeared so ludicrously disappointed that Abbie could not forbear a further smile. 'Let me assure you, Bart, that if Sir Monty's pockets were to let, he would approach Grandfather for a loan, not engage the services of Joshua Arkwright to dispose of me. Which, I assume, was precisely what you did think.' She shook her head, certain in her own mind that this could not be so. 'Besides which, even if it were true, and Monty did mean mischief, it would avail him nothing, for unless I'm very much mistaken, Grandfather has every intention now of leaving the bulk of his wealth to you.'

It was all of ten seconds before Bart found his voice. 'The devil he has!' His expression was all at once hard and uncompromising. 'My God! I shall have a deal to say to him when next we meet.'

Easily disengaging her hand from his, Abbie placed

her fingers on the sleeve of his jacket, slightly creased now after his totally unnecessary tussle with Josh. 'Please don't, Bart,' she pleaded softly. 'Unless I'm much mistaken, you've already gone against my wishes and written to Grandfather. Let that be enough.'

No denial was forthcoming, and when he continued staring broodingly at a certain spot on the ground, she knew he was unwilling to acquiesce to the request. She knew too that it would avail her nothing to force the issue, and so decided to return his thoughts to their former topic by asking what precisely had eventually persuaded him to suppose that she might be the intended victim.

'After all, Bart, these unfortunate happenings began weeks before I came to stay here,' she pointed out, 'and have all taken place solely on your property.'

'Not strictly true,' he corrected, rising to his feet. He paused to run a hand through his hair, clear evidence of his continuing troubled state of mind. 'Don't you remember that occasion when we experienced the mishap in the curricle?'

Although, in truth, she had never given the incident a second thought, she did so now, and had no difficulty in remembering just what had occurred. 'But surely that was just an accident, pure and simple? An unfortunate mischance?'

'Perhaps,' he acknowledged. 'But it's never happened to me before, at least not in one of my own carriages. Hackman is particularly conscientious and makes thorough checks himself before embarking on any journey. He swears the curricle was in good order before we set out from Bath.'

'So you believe the wheel was deliberately tampered with?' Abbie said, reading his thoughts accurately. 'And Josh accompanied us that day... Is that why you suspected him?'

Again he ran impatient fingers through his hair, wondering at himself for harbouring such a suspicion even for a moment. 'The lad's had plenty of opportunities to do you harm, had he chosen to do so. He's been your only escort on scores of occasions during your stay here, not to mention in Bath. And after what happened today, I'm certain he isn't responsible.'

'And I am equally certain that you're the one in danger, not I. Major Wetherby saw fit to confide in me last night. He firmly believes that those isolated incidents perpetrated against your neighbours during recent months were merely an attempt to divert attention from the real target, namely yourself.' Abbie waited in vain for some response. 'Surely it must have occurred to you that these happenings bear all the hallmarks of acts of revenge? Can you think of no one who might wish you ill in retaliation for…for something, perhaps, that you have done in the past?'

Although she had striven to keep her voice equable, devoid of the smallest hint of recrimination, Abbie knew by that penetrating, narrow-eyed regard that he hadn't been slow to appreciate her train of thought. Ashamed though she was, she couldn't deny that, after her conversation with Major Wetherby, she had found herself studying every attractive matron attending the party, assessing and wondering if, perhaps, Bart's intimate liaisons with married women had been confined to just one.

'Righteous I am not, and have never been,' Bart volunteered, thereby putting an end to her unsavoury reflections. 'But disabuse yourself of the notion that I ever embarked on a career of making cuckolds of friends and neighbours when their wives were willing to do so.'

It took a monumental effort, but Abbie continued to hold his reproachful stare. If there was one thing she had discovered about Bart in recent weeks, it was that he had scant regard for those who lacked the courage of their own convictions and did not stand their ground. 'I cannot deny that it crossed my mind as a distinct possibility. It crossed my mind also to wonder about your cousin.' She continued to maintain her steady gaze. 'I believe I did hear him mention that he has every intention of returning to London today. But did it never strike you as odd that he should suddenly take it into his head to visit the area in the first place?'

Although he raised one brow in a decidedly sceptical arch, he made no attempt to dismiss the idea out of hand, and paid her the common courtesy of considering the suggestion for a full minute before finally giving a decisive shake of his head.

'It's true enough that there's no love lost between us, and that he resents my more senior position in the family. It's also true that he, too, is sufficiently plump in the pocket to have paid someone to perpetrate these acts against me, without sullying his own hands. But one thing I will say for Cedric—he sets great store by family honour. He would never do anything to discredit the name he bears.'

Abbie had no reason to doubt the truth of this. Yet it left her at a loss to know what else to suggest. 'Then I suppose we shall be forced to look elsewhere for the answer, maybe further in the past for the motive… At least,' she amended, rising to her feet, and moving towards him, 'you must do so, Bart, for my time here at the Court is fast drawing to a close, and I have the uneasy feeling that your particular nemesis isn't satisfied quite yet.'

She stared up at him, half-expecting to discover a slightly mocking glint in his eyes, or that look of impatience which he bestowed upon his stepmother whenever Eugenie's nerves got the better of her. She detected neither. If anything he looked rather forlorn, though whether he had taken the warning seriously or not was impossible to judge, for the next moment he raised one broad shoulder in a dismissive shrug, as though bored with the topic, and was suggesting they return to the house to enjoy a final luncheon in Giles's company.

During the walk back, Bart deliberately kept the conversation on mundane matters in an attempt to prevent her dwelling on his troubles. He was much moved by her evident anxiety, and although he would never have admitted as much, the fears she had voiced had certainly crossed his mind.

His immediate concerns, however, were not for himself but for the being who had swiftly come to mean everything to him. Abbie was possibly correct in her assertion that no one would wish to harm her. After what she had revealed, it did seem highly unlikely that she had been the intended target, and perhaps he had been foolish ever to consider it as a possibility. All the same, he could not be easy in his mind until she was safely back in her godmother's home. In the meantime the very least he could do was try to ensure that she was placed in no danger because of some possible past action of his.

After seeing her safely back inside the house, Bart went directly to the stable-yard in search of the person whom he was now firmly convinced would ably assist him in his endeavours. He quickly located Josh's whereabouts in the largest of the stables and drew him outside, insisting that he sit beside him on the rough wooden bench.

'Firstly, I want to apologise again for my behaviour, earlier. Yes, Josh,' he added, raising a hand to silence the young groom's embarrassed protest. 'I hope I never become too proud to admit I have been at fault. My assessment of your character has been sadly flawed.' He smiled to himself. 'Miss Graham, seemingly, is far more discerning than I. She trusted you from the first.'

'Well, sir,' Josh said, looking puzzled, 'I hope I've given good service.'

'You may be at ease on that score,' Bart assured him. 'But I want you to be more conscientious still during the time your mistress remains here at the Court. I want you to ensure that she never goes off anywhere on her own, not even just to take a stroll in the garden. I am entrusting you to guard her with your life.'

The frown deepened. 'Why, sir? Is something queer going on?'

'Yes, lad…something queer is going on.' Bart debated within himself for a moment, then decided to take Josh into his confidence. 'You must have heard about the deliberate damage to the bridge?'

'Aye, sir,' Josh confirmed. 'And the fire at the house.'

'Those were by no means the only instances. There have been several others, one or two of which I hope you may be able to shed some light. Firstly, I want you to cast your mind back to that outing we enjoyed whilst we were in Bath. Can you recall seeing anyone lingering near my curricle?'

Leaning forward, Josh rested his elbows on his knees while he stared at a spot across the yard. 'Well, only the grooms, sir. I seem to remember Mr Hackman and Dodd tending to the horses. But then they would, wouldn't they?'

Bart chose not to respond to this. Instead he said, 'And do you recall, on the day you arrived here, going off to the kitchen with Dodd?'

'Aye, sir. And a reet fine plumb cake it were too,' he confirmed with a boyish grin. 'Mrs Figg gave me a second bit, as I remember.'

'And Dodd went with you to the kitchen, did he not?'

'Aye, sir. He showed me the way, but…'

'But what?' Bart prompted when Josh frowned again.

'I mind he said he'd forgotten something, and went back across the yard.'

'You saw him return to the stable?'

'No, sir. I went into the kitchen. Dodd came in a while later.'

Time enough, Bart considered, for Dodd to have slipped up on to the leads, and dislodge that piece of masonry. He frowned. But why should Dodd wish him harm? Gratitude was what he should have felt at the time, surely? After all, he'd been offered a place at the Court when he'd been looking for work. On the other hand, it couldn't be denied that, except for the fire, for which he couldn't possibly have been responsible, as he had been in Bath at the time, Dodd had been on hand to perpetrate the other malicious acts. And it was true that nothing untoward had occurred since his departure. It couldn't be denied either that Dodd was the type to do most anything for money. It was not inconceivable, therefore, that he'd been working for two masters.

He shook his head, deciding to ponder over the conundrum later, and easily concentrated his thoughts on something of more import at the moment. 'How have you liked working here with Hackman, Josh? He can be a hard taskmaster, I know.'

If Josh considered the question a little strange, he certainly betrayed no sign of it, and his reply was prompt enough. 'He likes to see the work get done, sir. And there's nowt wrong with that.'

'Then you wouldn't object to taking orders from him? Naturally it wouldn't be for ever. Hackman will retire in a few years, and I'm certain that, when he does, you'll be more than capable of taking his place.'

Bart smiled at the look of open astonishment he received. 'Yes, I'm offering you a permanent position here, Josh, if you wish to take it. I would want you to accompany Lady Penrose when she returns to Bath on Friday to ensure the ladies arrive safely. Then, if you choose to return here, you may be certain there'll be a place for you. I do realise, of course, that you might prefer to go back to your native Yorkshire.'

Josh shrugged. 'There's nowt there for me now, sir.' He took a moment to gaze across at the park land. 'Happen I could settle 'ere. Reet taken with the countryside, I am. And I ain't the only Yorkshireman to have taken a shine to this part of the world, neither.'

'Is that so?' Bart responded, more out of politeness than any real interest. 'So you've met a fellow countryman hereabouts?'

'Aye, sir, t'other day when I were out with Miss Abbie. Happen he be the one Dodd be working for now. Owns that tavern out on the Evesham road.' He shook his head. 'Didn't take to 'im, mind. Didn't like the look of 'im. West Riding man, not from my part.'

Having no real interest in learning about the divisions in Josh's native county, Bart hurriedly brought the discussion to an end and made his way back to the house. He had almost reached the front entrance before the young groom's disclosure struck him as odd, and he recalled something that had occurred to him before, when he had assisted Abbie in interviewing Josh—that it was not unheard of for people to move away from their county of birth in order to find work, but generally folk of Josh's station in life did not travel far from their roots, unless there happened to be a very good reason for doing so. So what had induced another native of Yorkshire to settle in this part of the world?

Chapter Thirteen

Even though he felt a sense relief as he watched his fine travelling carriage setting off on the first leg of its journey to Brighton, Bart accepted he wouldn't experience any real peace of mind until the young woman standing beside him had been removed by her godmother from his sphere also. That, of course, would not take place until Friday, just two days hence. In the meantime he could take some comfort in the knowledge that he had done all he could to ensure her continued safety whenever she left the house.

The thought jogged his memory. Nevertheless, he waited until Lady Penrose had returned indoors, before revealing to Abbie that he had something to impart. 'What with Giles's leaving, and all the hustle and bustle since, preparing for Eugenie and Kitty's departure this morning, it quite slipped my mind.'

The admission instantly captured her full attention. She gazed up at him enquiringly, her head slightly on one side, an expression that always put him in mind of an inquisitive kitten. 'No doubt you'll be relieved to know your young groom's future is secured. I offered him a position here, and he accepted.'

It was an impulsive action, brief and little more than a

featherlight brush of lips against his cheek. Yet it left him almost rocking on his heels and stuttering like many of those raw recruits who had been under his command out in the Peninsula. 'Well… I…er…um… I'm glad you're pleased.'

The hand that impulsively touched his sleeve did little to restore his equilibrium. 'Oh, Bart, I could never begin to express my gratitude.'

'Then please don't try,' he adjured, taking a hurried step away before the desire to imprison her in his arms overmastered the iron self-control that he had somehow managed to exert over himself in recent weeks. 'Now, if you'll excuse me, I must leave you to your own devices. There's someone I must see.'

Bart delayed no longer in heading for the stable. He could almost feel those gorgeous-coloured eyes staring after him. He shook his head, wondering at himself. Stiff-necked wasn't the word for it! Supposedly a man of the world, experienced and self-possessed, he had been completely bowled over by what had been nothing more than a prolonged peck. Yet he couldn't deny that it had shaken him, possibly because her reaction had been totally unexpected, so natural and unselfconscious.

After mounting the horse his latest employee had only moments before led from the stable, Bart set off across the park, striving to keep as firm a rein on his spirits as he held on the powerful stallion beneath him.

Yes, against all the odds Abbie had grown to care for him; her reaction of a few minutes before and the touching concern she had betrayed over his well-being in recent weeks was proof of this. Amazing though it was, she now looked upon him in a favourable light and, more importantly, had grown to trust him. It was immensely gratifying. But it wasn't enough. No, nowhere near enough. Yet he was still faced with the heartrending possibility that a sincere friendship was all he might ever be offered. Only time would tell. And time, sadly, was against him at present.

Abbie must leave. He had to let her go, and yet by doing so he was in no doubt that, sooner or later, he might lose her to someone else. But better that, he reminded himself, than risk placing her in danger by inviting her to remain at the Court. All he could do to minimise the time they must spend apart was concentrate all his efforts on trying to uncover the identity of the person or persons who seemed hell-bent on making his life as unpleasant and hazardous as possible.

With this determination now very much in the forefront of his mind, Bart wasted no time in riding to the village. He quickly discovered that Major Wetherby had left earlier to pay a visit on Lord Warren, and had no hesitation in turning his mount in the direction of the Hall in pursuit of his quarry.

Fortune then favoured him, and he discovered Major Wetherby, still happily ensconced in the well-stocked library, enjoying a glass of port in the company of his host who, after furnishing him with a drink, tactfully withdrew once he realised that Bart's reason for calling was to seek an interview with his guest.

'Your arrival is most opportune,' Major Wetherby confessed. 'It has saved me the trouble of calling upon you. My men will not be remaining in the locale for very much longer. I received orders to leave early next week.'

Bart wasn't unduly surprised. 'In that case, Major, I'm pleased to have the opportunity to speak to you now, and shall come straight to the point. I want you to cast your mind back four years, to the time when you first arrived in the Peninsula and were assigned to the Provost Marshal.'

Just a hint of a smile pulled at the Major's full lips. 'If

my memory serves me correctly, Cavanagh, you didn't hold the Provost in the highest esteem, and were not reticent in airing your views. I seem to remember you were one of those who spoke out vociferously against the method adopted for dealing with men who stole from our allies.'

'True,' Bart concurred, meeting the Major's faintly sardonic gaze with one of his own. 'I could never bring myself to countenance hanging a man for the mere purloining of a chicken. And never shall. However, during my years in the army, there was one man about whose neck I could happily have placed the noose myself.'

Having successfully gained the Major's full attention, Bart rose to his feet and went to stand before the window, his mind's eye having little difficulty in conjuring up many unpleasant images from the past. 'I understand from Miss Graham that, having uncovered no serious pockets of dissatisfaction in the area, you are firmly convinced that the instances of damage to property were motivated by revenge, directed against one person in particular—namely myself.'

'I said as much when we dined together here a couple of weeks ago,' the Major reminded him, 'and I've discovered nothing since to make me alter my opinion. However, I can tell you this much, Cavanagh, I haven't encountered anyone who has betrayed the least animosity towards you personally. Quite the contrary, in fact.'

Bart drew his eyes away from the magnificent park to cast the Major a wry grin. 'The reasons for your having come to the area must be common knowledge. Only a halfwit would betray any ill feeling he might be harbouring towards me in your presence.'

'True,' the Major agreed. 'But I do recall from our several past encounters in the Peninsula that you were never afraid to speak your mind. Therefore, unless you have changed to any significant degree, and I don't imagine you have, it's not inconceivable that you have ruffled a few feathers since leaving the army. All the same, I do recall that not only your fellow officers held you in high esteem, but also the men under your command.'

'The majority, yes. But certainly not all,' Bart enlightened him, once again turning to stare out of the window. 'After I had attained my Majority, I was assigned a company of men that included a loathsome piece of humanity by name of Septimus Searle, whom some mindless fool had seen fit to make up to sergeant.' His lip curled. 'Hardly surprising, really. By devious methods he had somehow managed to gain approval.'

'But not yours,' the Major prompted when silence lengthened between them.

'No,' Bart admitted. 'It didn't take me long to get his measure. I had him flogged, after he was caught stealing, and his stripes taken away and given to an Irishman who was far more worthy to sport them on his jacket. Soon afterwards we were involved in the capture of Ciudad Rodrigo. And we all know what took place in the aftermath of that confrontation, and then again a few weeks later at Badajoz.'

The Major shrugged. 'Not altogether shocking when you consider the majority of those who made up the army. Wellington's opinion of them was common knowledge.'

'Yes, rogues, thieves and liars. But not all were murderers and rapists. Septimus Searle, however, most definitely was. I know for a fact that he was one of those actively involved in the very worst of what took place at Badajoz. Afterwards he, like many others, deserted. And that is when you came upon the scene.'

Once again Bart experienced flashing images from the past as he continued to stare sightlessly across the park. 'The day you left camp to round up those deserters, I set out for Lisbon on some long-overdue leave. I was informed on my return to Spain that your mission had been a resounding success, that you had located the deserters' hideout, an abandoned village tucked away up in the hills. Wellington, having sustained considerable losses in recent engagements, was, I remember, prepared to allow those who gave themselves up voluntarily to rejoin the ranks, without fear of reprisals. Those who put up any resistance, if not killed in the attempt, were to be brought back to camp and hanged. I assumed, perhaps erroneously, that because he wasn't among the rank and file, Septimus Searle had received his just deserts.'

Major Wetherby gave vent to a bark of derisive laughter. 'Surely, Cavanagh, you don't expect me to remember whether this man Searle was among those brought back to camp and subsequently executed as an example?'

'Naturally not,' Bart assured him. 'But I would like you to cast your mind back and tell me everything you can remember about that particular assignment.'

For a moment it seemed as though Major Wetherby would not oblige, then his rather harsh features were surprisingly softened by a lopsided grin. 'Well, you're lucky, because I do happen to recall that particular mission very well, as it was my first.

'We located the hideout without too much trouble,' he continued, after substantially reducing the contents of his glass. 'The village was little more than a few derelict buildings, ransacked by the French some months before. Most were only too willing to give themselves up. The twenty or so who put up resistance were either shot or brought back to camp.'

Bart frowned heavily. 'Searle would never have given himself up, of that I'm sure.'

'What makes you so certain? As I told you, the French had scoured the hills only months before. There was little food to be had.'

'Maybe not. But Searle wouldn't have wanted to come face to face with me again, or the men in my company, who had more reason for despising him than I had.'

'In that case he might well have been one of those who put up a fight, or maybe…'

'Maybe what?' Bart prompted, when the Major fell silent.

'As I mentioned, many of the deserters were in a pretty poor state. It took us five days to get back to camp. On the second night, four men stole some provisions and took off. Three were recaptured and subsequently hanged. The fourth killed one of my men by slitting his throat, and then made off with his horse.'

Bart stared speculatively across at the Major. 'Aside from his loathsome character, there are two things I particularly remember about Searle—he was very handy with a knife, dangerously so, and he spoke with a pronounced Yorkshire accent. I discovered only the other day that a tavern on the Evesham Road is now owned by a man heralding from that particular county. And, unless I'm much mistaken, the new owner took possession at the beginning of the year, just prior to when all this trouble began. Although it may be mere coincidence, I think I'll pay a visit. If the innkeeper is Searle, I'll recognise him.'

'In that case, Cavanagh, you'll oblige me by delaying your visit for a while. I have one or two matters I must discuss with Lord Warren before I leave. I'll then return to the village, collect some of my men and ride directly over to you. If it is Searle, I'll be only too happy to take him into custody, doubly so if he should turn out to be the one who escaped from me four years ago, and murdered that young lieutenant in the process. He happened to be a particular friend of mine.'

'In that case, Major, I'll await your arrival at the Court.'

Abbie took a step back from the portrait to consider the finished result yet again. She had completed the work at the beginning of the week, but couldn't resist coming in every day to study the result of all her efforts. She was pleased, and hoped Bart would be too. It was a good likeness, and a fine piece of work, even though she did say so herself.

Yes, she had definitely succeeded in capturing that certain look, that softer expression he sometimes wore when he wasn't precisely smiling, and yet it was clear something had pleased him. It was high time the subject of the painting was informed that his likeness was finished and viewed it for himself. Why she hadn't informed him of its completion before she couldn't imagine. No, that wasn't strictly true, her conscience corrected. She had thought... hoped that by keeping it a secret she might succeed in delaying her departure for a while longer, but Bart seemed determined she should go. And perhaps it was for the best. The last thing in the world she wanted was to outstay her welcome; to make him think she was taking advantage of his kind hospitality.

The mere thought of going left her feeling hollow. She could deny the truth no longer—she loved this house, but nowhere near as much as she had grown to love its master.

Yes, the unthinkable had happened—she had fallen hopelessly in love with the very being whom she had vowed never to wed. What irony! she mused, steadfastly refusing to give way to the tears that might lessen the misery for a while, but could never hope to bring lasting relief to the torment she would carry with her through the years. If she had not been so proud, so naïve, so very prudish, she would indeed have been mistress of this fine house by now; married to a man who was neither saint nor depraved sinner, a man who, though annoyingly dictatorial and forthright on occasion, was essentially kind-hearted and considerate; she would have been married to a man who was so very right for her.

Through the haze of unshed tears, she stared once again at the likeness that, without being aware of it, she had lovingly created. One day soon, she hoped, it would find a permanent position, maybe in the library, above the fireplace. She would never see it hanging there. But then, she reminded herself, she would never need to. That face, that certain expression it had worn so often when they had been alone together here in this very room, would have a permanent place etched in her own memory.

Alerted by footsteps along the landing, she quickly covered the painting with its protective sheet. She had no desire to be caught, misty eyed and gazing adoringly at Bart's portrait, by one of the servants; or worse still by the master himself. No, it wouldn't do for Bart to discover how she now felt about him. Being the man he was, he just might feel obliged, out of misguided gallantry, to ask for her hand a second time. If she could be sure her feelings were reciprocated, she wouldn't need to think twice about accepting him. But the fact of the matter was she wasn't sure. And she could not, would not accept him on any other terms.

By dint of long practice Abbie was able quite easily to maintain the outward appearance of contentment when she left the room and went downstairs to join her godmother in the parlour, where they discussed plans for their return journey to Bath. When she suddenly announced her intention of going out for a ride, she didn't believe she aroused any suspicion, for Lady Penrose well knew her fondness for that particular form of exercise. Josh too wasn't in the least taken aback when she appeared in the yard, demanding her usual mount, and was soon leading her favourite grey mare and a gelding from the stable.

'There's no need for you to accompany me,' she told him. 'I've no intention of going far, at least no farther than the boundary of Mr Cavanagh's property, so if you've work to do here, Josh, then do not feel obliged to neglect it for my benefit.'

Just for an instant she thought she detected a slightly guarded expression, before he led the mare to the mounting block. 'I would be neglecting my duties if I *didn't* go with you, Miss Abbie. And I don't want to get into Mr Cavanagh's black books now I'm working for him.'

It was a timely reminder, and she didn't hesitate to assure him how pleased she was that he had secured himself a permanent position. 'I do so hope you'll be happy here, Josh.'

'Happen I will, miss. It's a nice place. Makes you feel comfortable, like.'

She knew precisely what he meant, only too well, but steadfastly refused to become maudlin. Hurriedly changing the subject, she suggested they make for the home wood, which had become, quite early in her stay, one of her favourite places to visit when out riding.

The August day was oppressively warm, and Abbie was grateful for the shelter from the sun's harsh rays the instant they entered the wooded area of land where Bart went shooting rabbits, when he could find the time. She had heard him remark on several occasions that it was one of his favourite spots. And that, she mused, as she led the way along one of the wider tracks, was perhaps why she too had become so fond of the place.

She could imagine him, gun over his arm, walking along a track, that alert gaze of his searching for any sud-

den movement in the undergrowth. She wished he had
suggested an afternoon's shooting during her stay, but he
hadn't, and it was unlikely now that she would be granted
the opportunity to exhibit her own prowess with a firearm, a skill her somewhat eccentric grandsire had seen fit
to impart when the bond between them had been so much
closer than it was now.

The regrettable thought had just passed through her
mind when Abbie caught sight of a rough wagon half-
hidden among the trees. Josh noticed it too, and suggested
it might be estate workers replenishing the log store in
readiness for the cold autumn and winter nights. Abbie
might have agreed, and not given the matter another
thought, had it not been for the conspicuous absence of
men at work and no sound of an axe or saw being applied
to a felled tree.

Curiosity having quickly got the better of her, she rode
over to take a closer look. The distinct absence of wood
chippings in and around the cart suggested that it hadn't
been used to transport logs, at least not recently, and the
sad condition of the poor beast between the shafts did little to stem her growing unease. The cart was empty except for a pile of sacking concealing something at one end,
which she did not hesitate to raise in order to reveal what
was hidden beneath.

Josh, like Abbie, wasn't slow to recognise the evilly
formed metal objects. 'Lord save us, miss!' he burst out.
'The master's never gone and ordered them 'eathen things
set on his land?'

Concerned though she was, Abbie couldn't suppress a
wry smile. If that selfsame question had been put to her
several months before she would have needed to ponder
long and hard before giving an answer. Now, she didn't
even need to think about it at all.

'No, Josh, Mr Cavanagh would not,' she assured him, one hundred per cent certain in her own mind that she was right. 'Your master might be concerned about what has been happening in recent months, but he would never risk maiming an innocent man or animal by laying such barbaric devices. Which makes one wonder,' she added, 'why these mantraps are here on his land? Who brought them here and why, if not to set them?'

Grim-faced, Josh had dismounted before Abbie had finished speaking. 'Happen I should take a look around, miss, and see if I can't discover someone about who shouldn't be.'

Abbie didn't attempt to dissuade him as she was of a similar mind. 'But be careful, Josh,' she adjured. 'We don't know how many of these dreadful things have been set already.'

Waiting until her groom's broad form had disappeared from view, Abbie slipped to the ground and once again turned her attention to the poor beast between the shafts. If she had needed absolute proof that Bart had not ordered the setting of mantraps, she was looking at it now. Half-starved and bearing marks of further needless cruelty across its flanks, the gelding took the morsel in her outstretched hand, the treat she had intended giving to the mare after her ride. She proceeded to stroke the gelding's dusty neck as it munched away on the offering. It betrayed no sign of enjoyment at the show of affection. But then, Abbie reasoned, perhaps he had experienced so few acts of kindness during his miserable life that he wasn't perfectly certain what was happening.

She shook her head, appalled at such wanton cruelty. For all that Bart, and her grandfather, come to that, could be overbearing and downright obstinate on occasions, neither would treat a creature with such neglect. Which made her wonder who was responsible for the animal's poor condition. She was destined not to remain in ignorance for much longer.

The sound of a twig cracking behind her had her swinging round on her heels to discover not her groom, as expected, but the dullard whose position Josh had filled and the man for whom he now worked.

The look of unholy satisfaction she couldn't fail to see in the older man's pitiless dark eyes sent her heart-rate soaring, and prompted her to ask the question that even to her own ears sounded singularly foolish.

'What do you imagine you are doing here?'

'Happen you know the answer to that already,' Dodd's companion answered, peering in the cart at the contents that she had left uncovered.

He turned his attention back to her, his gaze insolently assessing as he looked her over from head to foot. 'Who would have thought when we set out this morning that such a fine piece of merchandise would fall into our hands, eh, Doddy, lad? Told you I felt lucky today, when you said as how we should wait for the soldiers to move on before doing owt else to Cavanagh.'

Fearing she would never reach her mare in order to effect an escape, Abbie swiftly suppressed the impulse to try. Instead, she focused her attention on Dodd, determined to brazen it out until Josh returned.

'Have you given any thought at all to what will happen when Mr Cavanagh discovers you've been on his land? You didn't leave his employ upon the best of terms,' she reminded him.

Dodd, betraying his unconcern at the prospect of possible repercussions, merely shrugged, and left it to his companion to give voice to their complete indifference at being discovered.

'Happen the Major'll have far too much to worry about to trouble 'imself over a few traps, pretty lady.'

She resented the over-familiar tone almost as much as the insolent way he continued to regard her, as though she were some tasty morsel on his plate. Most worrying of all, though, was that, although a relative stranger in these parts, he seemed to know a deal about the master of Cavanagh Court. His knowledge of the rank Bart had held in the army led one to suppose that he and Bart were not total strangers. Was this person responsible for the recent malicious acts? His uninvited presence on Bart's land suggested strongly that he could well be.

'Evidently you are acquainted with Mr Cavanagh?'

'Oh, aye, lassie,' he acknowledged, seemingly quite happy to satisfy her curiosity. 'The Major and me, we goes back a long way.' There was a faint rasping sound as he rubbed dirt-ingrained fingers back and forth across the stubble on his chin. 'Not that we've seen much of each other in recent years. But I never forgets me friends. Nor me enemies, come to that.'

Just for a second Abbie allowed her eyes to slide past the stranger's left shoulder to scan the woodland beyond. Where was Josh? Why hadn't he returned? She began to experience the most uneasy feeling, but maintained her self-control as she said, 'And I strongly suspect that Mr Cavanagh falls into the latter category.'

'Well, let's just say there be no love lost between us, lass.' Lips drew back to reveal an incomplete set of badly decayed teeth. 'I'm thinking, though, the Major's feelings for you be a mite warmer than they were for any of those Spanish beauties he had out in the Peninsula. But then he did always 'ave an eye for a pretty woman. Happen he'll pay reet 'andsome to 'ave you back safe and sound.'

His intent could not have been plainer, and Abbie instinctively took a step away, only to find her back pressed against the side of the cart. Escape seemed impossible without help of some sort. 'You forget that I didn't come here alone.' She knew she was grasping at straws, hoping that one of Bart's workmen, perhaps even his gamekeeper, would just happen along and offer aid.

Sadly Dodd's unexpected bark of laughter didn't precisely boost her flagging confidence. 'That dolt Arkwright won't be of no use to yer,' he told her bluntly. 'I 'it 'im 'ard. It'll be a long time afore he comes round…if ever he does.'

It would have afforded Abbie the utmost satisfaction to have been able to slap the self-satisfied smirk off Dodd's unpleasant face. Unfortunately the opportunity to make the attempt was denied her by his companion who, having edged closer, had her upper arms clasped in a firm grip, before she could make even a token attempt at escape.

Her valiant struggles were in vain. She was no match for the two of them. They swiftly had her wrists and ankles bound, and Dodd's neckerchief covering her mouth, effectively stifling her belated screams for help. She then found herself airborne, before being tossed unceremoniously into the cart, and covered with several layers of filthy sacking.

Abbie was now firmly convinced that it had been none other than Dodd himself who had been responsible for many of the malicious acts perpetrated against Bart. She was equally convinced that he had been carrying out the orders of his companion. Just why the stranger bore such a grudge against Bart remained a mystery. What had been made frighteningly clear, however, was that his thirst for revenge had yet to be satiated.

During the mercifully short journey, Abbie was too preoccupied trying to stop herself from coming into contact with the sharp metal edges of the traps to concern herself overmuch with her ultimate fate. Understandably, fears returned with a vengeance when the cart came to a halt in the yard behind the neglected tavern and she was carried into the ramshackle building that functioned as a stable.

The lascivious gleam in the men's eyes, after they had tossed her down on to the pile of filthy hay, which resulted in her skirts rising above the knee, only served to increase her apprehensions. Yet her fears proved groundless, at least for the present, for, apart from ogling his fill of her slender, shapely legs, Dodd's companion merely grasped her from behind and dragged her back towards one of the upright wooden roof supports.

'First things first, Doddy, lad,' he said, after securing Abbie to the beam with a length of rope, wrapping it several times about her waist. 'We'll have our fun, never you fear, but not afore we've got Cavanagh 'ere to see us enjoying his wench.'

The gleam of hatred in his dark eyes was unmistakable. 'I've waited a long time to get even. I want to hear 'im beg. He wouldn't for himself…' he looked briefly at Abbie before rising to his feet '…but he would for her. And afore I kill him he'll suffer. Oh, I'll make him pay with much more than just the golden guineas he'll give us to see the lass again. We'll get 'er to write a letter, so he's in no doubt that we 'ave 'er. But first we'll drink to our good fortune and to the man who'll make sure we can live comfortably for a while to come afore he meets his maker.'

The taunting sound of malicious laughter seemed to echo off the stone walls long after the sounds of rusty bolts being thrown across the wooden doors and heavy retreating footsteps had died away.

Tears born of frustration and anger blurred her vision, but Abbie managed to hold them in check, as she attempted to free herself from her bonds. The fact that she had only herself to blame for her present predicament didn't precisely improve her flagging spirits. Fully aware of recent happenings, she had blithely gone to investigate when she had stumbled upon something suspicious. Most disturbing of all was the knowledge that, if she couldn't manage to effect her own escape, she would be placing Bart in the gravest danger.

This very real possibility forced her to ignore the painful chafing of her wrists as she strained against the ropes, until finally she was forced to admit defeat, and acknowledge that she would never get free without help. The trouble was that no one, with the possible exception of Josh, would have an inkling of where she might be. And poor Josh, if Dodd was to be believed, might never be able to reveal what he knew. And then there was Bart. When he received that letter, he would be walking straight into a trap, unless...

For a few moments Abbie toyed with the idea of flatly refusing to do her captors' bidding, but then thought better of it. She didn't doubt that they would resort to force. Besides which, there was just a chance that she might be able to pen some cryptic warning in the missive. Dodd, she felt sure, was illiterate. Unfortunately there was no guarantee that his vengeful companion was. He could in all probability read sufficiently well to be able to decipher what had been written. There was just the chance, though, that he might overlook the occasional misspelled word wherein she might be able to offer a clue as to her whereabouts. Given that there was precious little else she could do, it was worth a try.

Abbie was quick to hear the sound of footsteps again. Evidently her captors were eager for her to pen the ransom note, and she was now very willing to oblige them. But it might be a mistake to appear so, she swiftly decided, as one rusty bolt was drawn back far more slowly than it had been thrown a short time before. The last thing in the world she wanted was to ruin what was likely to be her one and only chance of warning Bart of the danger awaiting him should he attempt a rescue.

Chapter Fourteen

Exerting immense will power, Bart successfully resisted the temptation to pay a visit to that certain poorly maintained wayside inn on the Evesham road on his way home. It wasn't that he felt in the least daunted at the possibility of coming face to face with the black-hearted wretch whom he had been unfortunate enough to have under his command for a few short months when fighting in Spain. He did, however, appreciate his own limitations, and very much feared that the desire to mete out the justice the Army had lamentably failed to do during the Peninsular Campaign might prove too strong.

Consequently he made directly for Cavanagh Court. Turning his mount off the main road, he took advantage of the highly convenient short cut through his wood, as he had every intention of arriving in good time to partake of the last luncheon he would enjoy in Abbie's company. The good Lord only knew how long it would be before he was in a position to commence his courtship in earnest. If, however, his instincts proved correct, and his nemesis did turn out to be none other than Septimus Searle, perhaps it wouldn't be too long before he was journeying to Bath again.

It was a highly pleasing prospect upon which he could happily have dwelt had it not been for a sudden movement off to his left capturing his attention. He turned his head, surprised to discover not the deer he had been expecting to see foraging in the undergrowth, but the mount Abbie had always favoured riding. Not too far away from the dapple mare, and equally happily engaged munching the sweet grass, was the gelding used by the stable lads when undertaking the duties of escort and groom.

Abbie had remarked that she enjoyed riding through this wooded area of land, and the fact that she had chosen to take full advantage of the shelter provided by the trees on this very warm day came as no real surprise. What he found a touch disquieting, though, was that both Abbie, and her protector, undoubtedly Josh, had left their mounts unattended, and free to wander. It was so unlike the stable lad to be so neglectful; Abbie, too, come to that.

Bart's unease increased when no response was forthcoming to his several calls, and after securely tethering the horses, including his own, he decided to take a look around. For several minutes all he could hear were snatches of bird song and the occasional sound of some frightened scurrying creature, then he detected that certain sound all too frequently heard in the aftermath of a battle, that guttural moan from a man in pain.

Bart wasted no time in locating Josh's whereabouts and managed to force some of the contents from his flask, which he habitually carried with him when out riding, between the young groom's bluish-tinged lips. The crust of blood now forming in the blond hair was proof that Josh had sustained a severe blow. Blessedly the brandy quickly revived him, and a glimmer of recognition was not slow in coming to his eyes.

He made to rise, but Bart, easily restraining him, coaxed

him to sample more of the brandy before finally allowing him to sit unsupported. 'Just take your time, lad,' he urged gently, when Josh made to rise again, 'and tell me what happened to you?'

Bart experienced the uneasy feeling that Josh's injury might be severe indeed when he caught the hushed response to his question. 'Mantraps?' he echoed, totally at a loss to understand to what the groom was alluding.

'Aye, sir. Miss Abbie and I saw 'em in that there cart. She were certain sure you wouldn't 'ave ordered the laying of such 'eathen objects. Thought someone were up to mischief, so I took a look around. That's all I can rightly recall.'

As there was no sign of a cart now, Bart could only assume that Abbie had left the wood in that conveyance, and he very much feared that she hadn't done so willingly. She would never have callously abandoned Josh, unless she had been forced to do so.

Bart betrayed none of his rapidly mounting fears as he asked, 'And you've no idea who attacked you?'

Josh shook his head, wincing as he did so. 'Came at me from behind, sir, so I didn't get a look at 'im, 'cepting…' He took a moment to frown down at the ground between his boots. 'I could swear I 'eard 'im laugh before I blacked out, and it put me in mind of that stupid barking laugh o' Dodd's.'

Bart didn't wait to hear more. He rose at once to his feet, his mind working rapidly. Abbie's abduction, and he was in no doubt that she had been taken against her will, changed everything. He had to get to her without delay, for he was sickeningly aware of what would be her fate if she remained in Septimus Searle's hands for any length of time. There was no question now of waiting for Major Wetherby.

Offering his support, Bart assisted Josh to rise. Clearly the groom was in no fit state to go careering about the countryside on horseback. But what other choice was there? Time simply wasn't on his side, and he wasn't prepared to waste a precious second in returning to the Court to get help.

The walk back to the horses wasn't achieved speedily, for not only was Josh understandably unsteady on his feet, but both men were scanning the path immediately ahead for any sign of a lurking trap, which would effectively thwart any possible rescue attempt. Thankfully both successfully reached their goal unscathed, and Bart wasted no further time in asking the question at the forefront of his mind.

''Course I can ride over to Lord Warren's, sir. Have no fear. Once I'm in the saddle I'll stay there.'

Bart wasn't so sure, although by the time they had reached the fork in the road, where they were destined to part company, he was experiencing a degree more confidence in the injured groom's ability to reach Warren Hall, and apprise those present of what had occurred. He was certainly in no doubt at all that Wetherby would come to his assistance at once. No matter what he thought of him personally, he knew Wetherby to be a conscientious officer who never shirked his duties. Nevertheless he had no intention of delaying for the time it took for the Major to marshal his troops and come to his assistance, and set off along the Evesham road the instant Josh had turned his mount in the direction of the Hall.

By the time he had reached the wayside inn Bart had formulated a plan. He would begin his search for Abbie in the outbuildings. He couldn't imagine Searle being so foolish as to imprison her in the inn itself, where her whereabouts might just be stumbled upon by one of the patrons, even though it was highly unlikely that the ill-kept inn was ever well patronised.

Tethering his mount some distance away, Bart circled round to the back of the buildings, careful to take advantage of stone walls, hedges and trees in the hope of concealing his approach. As luck would have it he found the yard deserted except for an undernourished, work-weary horse harnessed to a cart, of which he didn't hesitate to make full use by crouching down below the high wooden side of the vehicle while he carefully threw back the bolts on the barn's rotting wooden door.

Bart masterfully suppressed a shout of pure joy at the variety of emotions he saw clearly mirrored in those gorgeous blue eyes after he had taken a step inside the barn. Truth to tell, he was experiencing a degree of astonishment himself, for he had never supposed for a moment that he would discover her whereabouts without encountering some opposition. Most rewarding of all was finding her, apart from dishevelled, appearing none the worst for her ordeal, a fact that she wasn't slow to confirm the instant he had knelt down beside her and had removed the hated gag.

'How on earth did you manage to find me?' Abbie asked, experiencing not the least degree of maidenly modesty as he blithely raised her skirts, and she felt the touch of those shapely hands brush against her ankles as he proceeded to release her from her bonds. 'Did someone witness my abduction? Was it Josh?'

'No, I found the poor lad just coming round, after the blow he'd received to the head.'

'Then how?' she persisted, determined to have her curiosity satisfied.

'Well, I suppose in a way it was you.' Bart couldn't forbear a smile at the mingled exasperation and disbelief clearly writ across her face. 'No, I'm not spinning you a yarn, my little love,' he assured her. 'It was you who urged me to think long and hard about the past and consider anyone who might well bear me a grudge.'

'And the owner of this inn does?'

'If it's the devil I think it is…then yes.'

'Well, he's certainly a most unpleasant fellow,' Abbie assured him, experiencing a tingling in her toes now that the bond had been removed. 'It was his intention to extort money from you for my safe return.' She had no difficulty either in interpreting the look on his face before he turned his attention to the rope securing her to the wooden support. 'No, I didn't suppose for a moment that he had any intention of releasing me once he had managed to lure you here.'

Abbie cast an anxious glance towards the door before returning her attention to the rugged features which, against all the odds, she had grown to love. 'They might return at any moment, Bart. You didn't come here alone, I trust?'

The note of concern in her voice was crystal clear. 'Don't worry. Josh has gone to the Hall, so help is on the way. Besides…' Delving into his pocket, Bart drew out a pistol, which he placed on the ground between them. 'I never ride out unarmed, a habit one swiftly acquires when in the army.'

And Abbie for one was glad of it. Yet she couldn't help but feel that it hadn't been wholly sensible to come alone… But then it wouldn't have crossed his mind for a moment to consider his own safety.

Lowering her head, she bit down hard on her lip to stop its trembling. Now was not the time to give way to foolish emotions, she told herself sternly. Unfortunately the silent reprimand did little to help, and she found herself plagued by a veritable barrage of self-recriminations. How she could ever have thought so ill of Bartholomew Cavanagh she would never know. He hadn't a cowardly bone in his body. Avarice and conceit were foreign to his nature. Nor was he in the least petty-minded. She wasn't now so blinkered by her regard that she could no longer see his faults. Yet she loved him as much for his imperfections as she did for his many wonderful qualities. He was quite simply a man, and a very fine one withal.

She felt the telltale pricking at the corners of her eyes, and closed them tightly, determined not to give way to those all too frequent recurring feelings of regret and self-pity.

She could hear Bart's occasional sharp intake of breath as he struggled with the occasional stubborn knot. Then she detected another sound close at hand, and opened her eyes. Unfortunately her stifled warning scream came just a fraction too late. Dodd wielding a heavy stick caught Bart a stunning blow across his temple as he half-turned, making to rise, sending him crashing to the dirt floor, clearly revealing the pistol he had only minutes before placed on the ground.

This time Abbie's reactions were far quicker. By moving her left leg slightly, she successfully concealed the weapon beneath the folds of her skirts before Dodd had noticed it was there. Still half-stunned by the blow, Bart was endeavouring to rise to his knees and was fortunately holding his attacker's full attention, a circumstance of which Abbie didn't hesitate to take full advantage. Blessedly Bart had succeeded in loosening the knots sufficiently for her to be able to move her wrists. Striving to ignore the pain, she strained against the bonds until her own attention was captured by the arrival of Dodd's accomplice, brandishing a pistol of his own.

His expression was ugly, and grew more menacing still

when his gaze fell upon Bart's half-kneeling form. 'Why, if it ain't my old, gallant Major,' he sneered. 'How I've been looking forward to meeting up with 'ee again!'

For answer Bart seated himself beside Abbie and, easily interpreting the silent message in her eyes, placed his hand beside the skirt of her habit, before fixing his attention on the unkempt figure by the door.

Abbie, watching closely, was amazed at what she saw. She knew Bart didn't try unduly to conceal his feelings. He was far too candid by nature to dissemble. She had seen him betray annoyance and anger on numerous occasions since their reunion in Bath, but never before had she glimpsed such an expression of utter loathing on his face.

She couldn't help but feel that it wasn't entirely wise to betray antipathy at such a time. With any luck Josh might already have reached the Hall, and help would hopefully not be long in arriving. Surely it was better to attempt to stall for time by distracting the villains than risk an immediate attack by showing hostility? All she required was a minute or two more in order to prise her hands free. Then she might possibly be of help by putting up at least a token resistance.

'You have the advantage of me, Bart,' she said, having swiftly decided on pinning her hopes on delaying tactics. 'Aren't you going to introduce me to this gentleman?'

'Gentleman?' Bart snarled. 'Gentlemen do not commit cold-blooded murder, Abbie.' If anything, his expression grew increasingly contemptuous. 'Oh, Septimus Searle had a splendid war, until I took command of the company. One of his more despicable exploits was to force the wives of the men to sleep with him in order to spare their husbands a flogging for some false charge, which in my book is tantamount to rape. It didn't take me very long to get his measure and put an end to his sickening pleasures.'

'Aye, you served me a reet bad turn there, Major. And I've never forgotten it neither. My life weren't worth living when you took away my stripes. It were a case of deserting or being killed sooner or later by the men in the ranks. I asks you, what choice did I 'ave?'

If he expected a show of sympathy, he was doomed to disappointment. Bart's expression remained a contemptuous mask, and Abbie experienced nothing but a surge of revulsion towards the being who clearly experienced no remorse for his misdeeds, though she had no intention of betraying the fact. Searle seemed locked in the past, content to reminisce, and Abbie was more than happy for him to continue doing so. The longer he was allowed to lament over what he evidently considered to be his ex-commanding officer's grave injustices, the more likely it was that help would arrive in time

''Course, when I escaped from the Preventives,' Searle continued uninterrupted, 'I swore I'd 'ave my revenge on you once the war were over, if the Frenchies didn't get you first. It took me some time to get back to dear old England and cost me most everything I'd—er—put aside while I were a soldier. Managed to do all right for myself since I've been back, mind,' he revealed with a noticeable degree of smug satisfaction. 'And as soon as I'd money enough I sets about finding you.'

'No need to ask how you acquired the means to do so,' Bart muttered loud enough for Searle to hear. Fortunately he seemed to find the disparaging remark amusing.

'Aye, you're a downy one and no mistake, Major. Pity, really, you decided to make me your enemy. Reckon you and me would 'ave got on reet well iffen we'd become friends.'

'There was never any likelihood of that,' Bart didn't hesitate to assure him. 'I select my friends with care.'

'Expect you do, Major.' Searle's gaze slid to Abbie. 'You always had your pick of the womenfolk, at any rate, not like us poor common soldiers. We 'ad to make do wiv any old trollopy camp follower. Always 'ad a mind to sample a bit of what you'd tasted.' The sinister leer returned to his eyes, betraying his intent. 'What do you say, Doddy, lad? Fancy a tumble with that there piece of flash goods? You'd best be quick, mind. There's no saying when they'll start searching for the Major, 'ere, and 'is ladylove. We'll need to get rid o' their bodies reet quick.'

Abbie didn't know what sickened her more—Searle's callous declaration of intent, or the sight of Dodd's grubby fingers fumbling with the buttons on his breeches. She had no intention of allowing herself to be violated without putting up at least a token struggle. And blessedly she could do so now! Quite unobserved, she had succeeded in freeing one of her wrists during the verbal exchanges between Bart and his sworn enemy. It was an easy matter to slip her right hand free from the ropes.

But before she had even attempted to rise, Bart's voice, icy cold and controlled, successfully checked Dodd's evil purpose. 'So much as lay a finger on her, and I'll kill you.'

'I've got 'im covered, lad,' Searle assured him. 'Have yer fun, but be quick about it.'

Had he glimpsed the pistol, he might not have given such poor advice, for Bart's skill with firearms had been common knowledge throughout the army. One moment Dodd had been dropping to his knees, eager once again to satisfy his lust; the next his lifeless body lay sprawled on the floor.

Hardly had the deafening report died away than Bart was rising and hurling the pistol across the barn. Unfortunately Searle recovered in an instant from the painful blow he had received to his arm, and had his own weapon steadily levelled before Bart could bridge the distance between them.

For a few brief seconds it was as much as Abbie could do to watch in horrified silence as Searle's finger curled round the trigger, and his unpleasant mouth twisted into a malicious, self-satisfied smirk. Bart had succeeded in placing himself directly in line of fire, his intention clear. He would take the bullet so that she just might survive.

But how could she let him? She didn't want to live… couldn't live without him…

Bart hardly knew what had happened. One moment he had been poised, about to make what would undoubtedly have been a final, and possibly fatal, attempt to disarm Searle; the next, Abbie had cannoned into him, sending him stumbling sideways, while a second deafening report was ringing in his ears.

Instinctively he reached out and caught Abbie before she slumped to the floor, his eyes quickly focusing on the unmistakable dark trickle of liquid steadily seeping through the charred portion of her gown.

As she lay there, motionless, like a lifeless rag doll in his arms, Bart would have given everything he owned to be able to reject the evidence of his own eyes, to have been able to believe that she had merely fainted, that those delicate lids would flicker open at any moment and he would find himself the recipient of that lovely teasing gaze. Sadly he wasn't the kind of man who couldn't accept cruel reality. Nor was he the type to succumb to the emptiness born of grief when his strength was needed to finalise an unpleasant task.

Tenderly placing Abbie on the ground, Bart could feel white-hot rage going some way to fill the chasm of despair that was growing ever wider within him, as he caught sight of his adversary attempting to slink unobtrusively away.

Galvanised by an overwhelming desire for revenge, he was on his feet in an instant and easily caught up with Searle halfway across the yard.

A life of dissipation having taken its toll, Searle was no match for Bart, who overpowered him in a trice, effortlessly bringing him to the ground. For several moments mercy didn't enter into Bart's thinking. Wrapping one strong arm about Searle's neck, he was determined to mete out the punishment the army had failed to do years before. Then, unbidden, some inner voice reminded him that he had once been a courageous soldier, taking life only on the field of battle, not some cold-blooded killer, bent on revenge. He found the muscles in his arm automatically relaxing, as his ears detected the sound of approaching horses. Yet it wasn't until urgent fingers began to tug at his jacket and a more urgent voice succeeded in penetrating the layers of numbness that still clung to him that he at last released his hold and rose to his feet.

'You'll find your mistress in the barn,' he managed finally to reveal in response to Josh's repeated enquiry.

'Are there any more of them?' Major Wetherby asked, after ordering his men to take Searle in charge.

Bart gestured towards the barn. 'Yes, in there. He's dead.'

The Major's intention to discover for himself was checked by Josh who, dashing out of the barn, almost cannoned into him. 'Sir… Mr Cavanagh, sir, oughtn't you to be getting Miss Abbie to the doctor?'

Bart's initial reaction suggested that he hadn't heard a single word. He just stood there, with the hunched posture of a desolate, broken man, staring dumbly at the ground. Then very slowly he raised his head, and it seemed to the two men avidly watching him that a bright lamp had suddenly been ignited behind his eyes.

Before either could move or utter anything further, he had brushed past them. Not daring to hope or believe, he dropped to his knees beside Abbie and stretched out decidedly unsteady fingers towards the slender neck. It took several moments, but eventually he was certain he had detected that pulsating throb—faint, certainly, but blessedly there.

Early that evening, as he sat in his library, Bart appeared at first glance much the same as usual—dispassionate, a man in full control of his emotions. Perhaps only those who knew him well would have suspected that all was not as it should be; maybe only a few highly observant souls would have detected the evidence of tension along the line of the jaw, and the anguish, partly concealed, behind the half-hooded lids.

From the instant he had realised that life still throbbed in Abbie's veins, he had taken complete control, issuing instructions to Major Wetherby and his men as though he himself had been in command. That he had taken every precaution, done everything humanly possible to ensure Abbie's continued existence, now brought scant comfort.

Not daring to risk jolting her on horseback, he had travelled back with her in that tumble-down old cart, holding a pad over the wound in the hope of stemming the flow of blood. The journey had seemed interminable, and there had been times when he had thought the undernourished horse would fail to reach the Court. Thankfully, under Josh's skilful handling and gentle coaxing, it had.

The doctor, summoned by one of Major Wetherby's men, had been awaiting their arrival, and the servants, forewarned, had everything prepared. That Lady Penrose, ably assisted by her highly efficient maid, had taken immediate charge of the sick room had brought little solace either; and he hadn't needed the dour, though highly skilled, local practitioner to confirm his worst fears.

'Well, Cavanagh,' he had announced, on entering the library an hour before, 'I have managed to extract the lead shot and clean the wound, and can confirm that it touched no vital spot. However, the young woman has lost a considerable amount of blood, and is very weak. If no infection sets in, there's a chance she'll survive.' Here he had paused, the inference only too painfully clear. 'I shall be able to tell you more in the morning.'

His venture into the sick room, shortly after the doctor's departure, had done nothing to improve Bart's state of mind. The sight of her lying there, motionless, the blue tinge about her lips the only vestige of colour in her beloved face, had added substantially to the heavy burden of guilt.

Why hadn't he checked for signs of life at the outset? Yet again that damning question passed through his tortured mind. Had he been so obsessed by a desire for revenge that he had been incapable of rational thought? Why had he not taken a moment to consider her dishevelled state? With what she had been forced to endure, her clothing had become crumpled. But when he had caught her in his arms the bodice of her habit had stretched across her breast, giving the impression that the wound had been fatal, when in fact the ball had entered her body several inches higher. Precious minutes had been wasted dealing with Searle—time he ought to have spent with Abbie, attempting to stem the flow of blood.

The sound of an arrival interrupted his distressing reflections. He had given strict instructions, after Major Wetherby had called to assure him that Searle was now safely behind bars, awaiting trial, that no more visitors were to be admitted to the house. Consequently he was surprised when the normally efficient Barryman entered to inform him that a gentleman insisted upon seeing him.

'Be assured, sir,' he went on apologetically, 'that in the normal course of events, I would not have hesitated in denying admittance, but—'

He got no further. The door behind him was thrown wide, and a tall, distinguished-looking gentleman with a decidedly military bearing came striding into the room, demanding without preamble, 'What the devil do you mean, sir, by sending me that damned impertinent letter?'

Chapter Fifteen

Abbie, supported by a mound of pillows, sat up in bed, dutifully awaiting the return of one or other of her self-appointed gaolers in order to gain permission to rise. It wasn't that she was incapable of dressing herself, far from it in fact. Unlike those early days of her convalescence, when she had been as helpless as a babe, unable to so much as feed herself, she was now sufficiently restored in health to do most everything for herself. Yet, sensible of how much she owed both her godmother and Felcham for nursing her so tirelessly during the past month, she had no intention of undoing all their good work by attempting to do too much too soon, even though she felt it was time to regain at least some of that treasured independence.

In truth she could recall little of those early days when, under the influence of laudanum, she had slept for much of the time. She had discovered from Lady Penrose how Bart and Josh had brought her back to the house in a cart. From Dr Phelps she had eventually learned just how critical her condition had been and how her life had hung in the balance for several days. Her most vivid recollection had been waking to discover her grandfather, pale and drawn, a mere shadow of his former self, seated beside the bed.

Needless to say, in face of the touching concern he had displayed throughout her recovery, she had found it no difficult matter to forgive his past behaviour towards her. He wasn't a man given to displays of emotion, at least not the more tender ones. All the same, she was in no doubt now of just how much she really meant to him. How she wished she could be as sure of quite another gentleman's feelings towards her!

From her godmother's own lips she had learned how Bart had spent many hours watching over her during those first days. She vaguely recalled seeing a tall, shadowy figure seated beside the bed; vaguely remembered, too, the comforting clasp of a warm hand about hers. That, of course, might well have been her grandfather, for Bart hadn't made a habit of visiting her regularly since her strength had begun to return. When he had put in a brief appearance, it had always been when someone else had been present.

A sharp knock on the door forced her to abandon her melancholy reflections, and she looked up to find her grandfather striding purposefully into the room, his attire clearly revealing how he intended occupying his time that morning.

'So, you are going out riding, Grandpapa,' she said, after receiving the loving salute he had never failed to place upon her cheek each morning during these past weeks. 'How I wish I could accompany you!'

'It will not be too long before you're able to do so. Believe me, my darling child, you cannot possibly look forward to the occasion more than I.' For once he chose not to avail himself of the chair beside the bed. Instead he took up a stance at the window, before adding, 'Which prompts me to raise a matter we must discuss—namely, your future.'

Abbie clearly detected the note of reserve in his voice

that she had grown increasingly accustomed to hearing in recent years. Only this time she knew that it wasn't because she had fallen from favour. She strongly suspected the reason for the slight constraint stemmed from discomposure and bitter regrets.

Colonel Graham wasn't slow to corroborate this presumption. 'I've been a crass fool these past years, child,' he burst out. 'And I can only ask…beg you to forgive me for the unhappiness I've caused you.'

Abbie would have given much to hear him say that before she had left Foxhunter Grange, but not now. He had been so right in his belief that she and Bart were well suited. It ought to be she begging forgiveness.

She was therefore able to respond with total sincerity, 'There's nothing to forgive, Grandpapa.'

'Oh, but there is, child,' he countered softly. 'I came here full of self-righteous indignation, and preconceived notions that were foolishly unjust. I was more than happy to point the finger of blame at you for persuading Bart to write what I considered a damned insulting letter. Needless to say, he wasn't slow to set me right on several points.'

'I imagine not. Bart isn't one to hide his teeth.' Abbie couldn't prevent a wry smile, even though she thought the confrontation should have been avoided. 'You and Bart are very similar in many ways, Grandpapa. Both of you have strong, determined natures, and are never afraid to speak your mind.'

'Very true,' he concurred, smiling briefly himself now. 'But at least we're not too proud to own when we have been at fault. And I have been most unjust in my dealings with you, Abbie, my dear,' he continued, as he came to stand beside the bed, so that not only could she hear the deep regret in his voice, but also see the sadness in his eyes. 'Bart forced me to acknowledge that on the night I arrived here.

He freely admitted that your refusing to marry him six years ago was the right decision, that it would have been a grave mistake if you had formed a union.'

This wasn't precisely what Abbie wished to hear, even though deep down she had suspected it was true. 'Although Bart would never hurt my feelings by admitting as much, I do not believe my refusal caused him much heartache. In fact, I believe his offer of marriage came more from a desire to please you, Grandpapa, than himself.'

'You are possibly right, child,' he said, unaware of just how much it had hurt her to be so candid. 'I do recall that he appeared rather surprised when I broached the subject quite out of the blue that evening. With hindsight I now realise it would have been wiser to have waited a year or two. But, as I remember, Bart was due to leave us the following day, and I had no real idea how long it would be before he visited us again. As things turned out he never did, as he decided to join the army.'

Although Abbie had paid her grandfather the common courtesy of listening to everything he had to say, one salient point had remained in her mind—namely, the timing of the proposal. Unless she much mistook the matter, her grandfather hadn't touched on the subject of marriage until after Bart had returned from his assignation with Lady Fitzpatrick in the summerhouse.

She favoured her grandfather with a searching stare. 'When precisely did you first raise the subject of marriage with Bart?'

'Oh, good heavens, child! I cannot recall precisely. It was over six years ago.' The flicker of irritation swiftly faded from his eyes and was replaced by one of contrition, as though he regretted his mild show of impatience. 'Well, let us see if I can remember... I do believe he'd been out for much of the day. So it must have been early evening, just prior to going in to dinner.' He paused to watch an odd expression flicker over her face. 'Is it important?'

It might have been at one time, Abbie mused, smiling to herself, but certainly not now. It didn't matter a whit. 'No, Grandpapa, it isn't important.'

'In that case, may I now turn your thoughts to the more urgent matter of your future?' All at once he seemed ill at ease, and reluctant to meet her gaze. 'Will you grant me the dearest wish of my heart and return to Foxhunter Grange? Of course I'm happy to remain here until you feel able to undertake the journey. And—and I do not want you to think it will be—be as before,' he continued, with less than his customary aplomb. 'It shall not. You will, I'm sure, wish to visit your godmother now that the two of you have become reacquainted. And then, too, I should like for us to visit the capital. Perhaps this autumn, if you are agreeable?'

Once she would have given much to be offered the opportunity of meeting a gentleman of her own class with whom she might form an attachment. Much, however, had changed in the space of a few short weeks. The only man with whom she would ever willingly share her life resided right here, in this very house. So why waste her time and her grandfather's money in the hope of one day meeting Bart's equal? She never would, and in truth she felt not the least desire to try.

Feeling the need of their support, she fell back against the mound of pillows. 'I see no reason why we shouldn't leave at the end of the week.'

Evidently she had sounded far more enthusiastic at the prospect of leaving the Court than she truthfully was, for she instantly won a smile of approval.

'Capital! When I've returned from my ride, I shall begin to make arrangements. Even though Bart has shown excellent hospitality, I dare say the boy won't be at all sorry to have the house to himself again.'

Abbie was spared the necessity of responding by the arrival of Lady Penrose, which in turn prompted her grandfather's immediate departure. Although the two were unfailingly polite to each other, at least within her hearing, Abbie had gained the distinct impression that Colonel Graham had yet to win favour in her godmother's eyes.

'Felch will be along presently to help you dress, child,' Lady Penrose revealed the instant they were alone. Receiving no response, she cast a swift glance down at the bed and wasn't slow to note her goddaughter's wan expression. 'I sincerely trust your grandfather hasn't tired you. I sometimes think he forgets how gravely ill you've been.'

'No, he hasn't tired me in the least.' As though adding credence to the assertion, Abbie swung her feet to the floor, and reached for her robe. 'In fact, I think I shall take the opportunity of enjoying some late summer sunshine by sitting in the garden this morning. It's high time I entered the real world again. You see, I intend to accompany Grandpapa when he leaves the Court at the end of the week.'

Nothing in her demeanour betrayed the fact that Lady Penrose was not best pleased to learn this. The instant she left the bedchamber, however, it was a different story. Her expression changed and no one could have been in any doubt that something had occurred to vex her deeply.

It wasn't that she objected to Abbie leaving the confines of her room. In fact, she was very much in favour of it, and perhaps later would suggest that she eat with the rest of them in the dining-room from now on. On the other hand, this notion of leaving the Court at such a time could well prove a grave mistake, adversely affecting her goddaughter's future happiness.

So what on earth had prompted the girl to agree? True enough, Colonel Graham's attitude towards her had definitely changed. He was now all touching concern. But surely Abbie had overcome her former dislike of Bart? Yes, of course she had, Lady Penrose decided a moment later. The girl knew she belonged here at the Court with him. So what was persuading her to leave? And now that she came to consider the matter, why on earth had the master of the house shown no inclination to declare himself?

Suddenly realising she was standing stock-still in the middle of the passageway, Lady Penrose was about to continue towards the stairs, when she felt a draught coming from the chamber adjoining her goddaughter's room. Evidently one of the maids must have been cleaning and inadvertently left the door ajar. About to rectify this oversight, she reached for the handle, checked, hand in mid-air, and then very slowly pushed open the door, curious to see a certain object that she had not viewed since her arrival at the Court.

Usually all it would take was a good gallop across his land to clear Bart's mind and lift his spirits. Today, however, had proved the exception. And small wonder, after the news his godfather had imparted! Even so, he flatly refused to give way to depression. Nor was he prepared to neglect his duties as host during the time his guests remained under his roof.

Consequently, on arriving back at the house, he led the way into the library in order to furnish the Colonel with a glass of burgundy, only to stop dead in his tracks at the unexpected sight of Lady Penrose seated by the hearth, drumming her fingers impatiently on the arm of her chair.

Although she had never once attempted to invade his private sanctum throughout her stay in his house, her mien suggested that her reason for doing so now stemmed from pique rather than an impending crisis. 'Ma'am, is something amiss?'

'You might say so, yes,' she didn't hesitate to confirm. 'The problem also concerns you, sir,' she added bluntly, thereby arresting Colonel Graham's tactful withdrawal.

Successfully suppressing a smile at the clipped tone, Bart went over to the decanters. Although immensely good natured for the most part, Lady Penrose wasn't above bearing a grudge. Her behaviour towards Colonel Graham since his arrival had been, to say the least, slightly cool, a clear indication that she, unlike himself, had not been willing to forgive and forget the Colonel's past behaviour towards his granddaughter.

'Can I tempt you to join us in partaking of some refreshment, ma'am? A glass of ratafia, perhaps?' he asked in the hope of thawing her a little.

'You can. But I should prefer port,' was her prompt response, which instantly drew a frown across the Colonel's brow, evidence enough that he did not wholeheartedly approve her choice.

Bart, having for some inexplicable reason become far more tolerant in recent weeks where the fair sex was concerned, merely smiled as he handed her the chosen tipple. Then, without further ado, he enquired what had prompted her to seek him out.

'My charge,' she answered without preamble. 'Oh, you needn't worry,' she added, noting with a degree of satisfaction the look of concern that instantly sprang into dark eyes. 'She hasn't suffered a relapse. In point of fact, she's ventured out of doors for the first time today. She's at present sitting in the garden enjoying the fresh air.'

This did little to ease Bart's mind. 'Is that wise, ma'am?

The doctor insisted that she does not exert herself unduly for some time yet.'

Lady Penrose dismissed this with a wave of her hand. 'The girl is all but fully recovered. Which is perhaps just as well,' she added, favouring the Colonel with a blatant look of disapproval herself now, 'since she will be forced to undergo the rigours of a long journey in a few days.' She transferred her gaze back to their host. 'If you permit her to leave, that is.'

Like an echoing taunt, Lady Penrose's last words seemed to hang in the air. Colonel Graham, whose colour had increased alarmingly, appeared to be battling to contain his wrath. Bart too was not altogether pleased, as his suddenly compressed lips revealed, before he swung round to stare resolutely out of the window.

'You forget yourself, ma'am,' he said, in a milder tone than he might otherwise have used had he not held the lady in such high regard. 'I have no say in the matter.'

'A feeble excuse!' Lady Penrose scoffed, clearly undaunted by the coolness of his reply. 'I would never have supposed a man of your stamp, Cavanagh, would calmly stand by and allow the woman he loved to walk out of his life.'

This brought his head round, as she knew it would, hope and uncertainty clearly mirrored in his eyes.

'Surely you don't imagine that your feelings are not reciprocated? Good God, man! Have your wits gone begging? The girl came perilously close to losing her life in order to save yours.'

'That is something I'm never likely to forget,' Bart responded softly. 'But it isn't as simple as you seem to suppose.' Tossing the wine down his throat, he set the glass aside. 'There are reasons, ma'am...obstacles that must be overcome before I—'

'Bah!' Lady Penrose interrupted crudely, before following his example by consuming her wine in one go. 'Tell me, Bart,' she added, rising to her feet so that she could face him squarely, 'have you ever viewed the portrait you commissioned Abbie to paint?'

The abrupt change of topic surprised him, and he didn't attempt to hide the fact before he shook his head.

'I thought not,' she said, appearing smugly satisfied. 'Well, if it is proof positive you require before taking action, then I suggest you follow me. You too, Colonel,' she added, favouring him with a look that dared him to refuse. 'Hopefully it might persuade you not to commit yet more folly.'

Like a galleon at full sail, Lady Penrose majestically glided out of the room and up the stairs, leading the men on their journey of discovery. She had taken the trouble earlier of removing the protective sheet and turning the easel so the painting could be viewed the instant one entered the chamber. Thus, Bart found himself for the second time that morning halting momentarily on the threshold of a room.

Colonel Graham too, betrayed a marked degree of surprise. 'Fine piece of brushwork,' he opined, after taking a few moments to study the portrait more closely. 'Takes after her grandmother,' he added with simple pride. 'She was a very gifted artist too.'

'For once we are in complete accord, Colonel,' Lady Penrose announced, while staring resolutely in Bart's direction. 'It is a fine piece of work. She has captured that certain look so very well, don't you agree? That certain tenderness of the gaze, that marked softening to the set of the mouth. But then she shouldn't have found it too difficult a task. After all, it is a look she has observed often. A look, I have noticed, reserved for her alone.'

Lady Penrose smiled when the Adam's apple in Bart's

throat protruded further than usual as he swallowed hard. 'If I have one slight criticism, then it is that dear Abbie has had a tendency to flatter the subject by making him appear rather better looking than, in fact, he is. But then, one must make allowances, mustn't one…? She does, after all, view him through the eyes of love.'

For several disappointing moments Lady Penrose thought she had failed to remove those shackles of uncertainty. Then, quite without warning, she was imprisoned in a pair of strong arms and lifted quite off her feet to receive a smacking kiss on one plump cheek.

'You will forgive me if I leave you now,' Bart announced, already halfway to the door. 'There's a matter requiring my urgent attention.'

'Don't give us another thought, dear boy,' Lady Penrose urged him. 'I'm sure the Colonel and I can manage to rub along together reasonably well until your return.'

In truth, Bart wasn't unduly concerned whether they would succeed in doing so or not, for already that tiny voice advocating caution was making itself heard, regenerating those old doubts. Against all the odds, Abbie loved him—yes. There wasn't the least doubt in his mind about that any longer. But it did not automatically follow that she would be any more willing to marry him now than she had been six years ago.

Part of her endearing charm, and what set her quite apart from most other females of his acquaintance was her sense of proportion, her level-headedness. She wasn't a young woman prone to flights of fancy or given to foolish starts. She would consider long and hard before making a decision that would effectively alter the course of her life. Ergo, it was not inconceivable that she might retain grave misgivings, that she would reject his suit a second time.

The alternative, though, was to watch her walk out of his life, and perhaps not for a short time either.

Coming upon her sitting in the garden in that peaceful way of hers succeeded in bridling his qualms, if failing to eradicate them completely. Abbie, catching sight of him a moment later, would never have supposed for a moment that the mere sight of her had instantly restored some of his spirits, for as he drew nearer she detected the crease between his dark brows, clearly revealing concern over something.

'I sincerely trust you haven't been sent out to scold me for remaining in the garden too long? The truth of the matter is I've been making the acquaintance of your latest acquisition.'

Refusing to be daunted by his lack of response, Abbie smiled as he lowered himself on the bench beside her. 'You don't fool me any longer, Bartholomew Cavanagh. I know well enough that beneath that stern exterior lurks a great soft-hearted fellow. Most gentlemen would have had no compunction in consigning that poor beast to the knacker's yard. Though I must confess he bears little resemblance to the undernourished creature I encountered a month ago. He's prancing round the paddock at this very moment like a playful colt.'

Although Bart didn't attempt to feign ignorance, he wasn't prepared to accept credit for the gelding's vastly improved state either. The truth of the matter was he hadn't given the animal he had purloined on that eventful day a single thought, after he had carried Abbie back inside the house. It was almost a week later, when he was certain she was out of danger, that he had once again taken up the day-to-day running of his property and had paid a visit to the stables.

Thankfully Josh had not been so negligent, and had

taken it upon himself to care for the late Septimus Searle's maltreated horse, and under his tender care the animal's general health had improved dramatically. Bart couldn't deny, however, that he simply hadn't the heart to dispose of the gelding after its heroic labours in returning them to the Court.

He smiled crookedly. 'Well, I dare say he'll earn his keep when he's eventually put to work.'

'Which means that you're content to let him remain idle for the most part.' Recalling an oversight on her part, Abbie was suddenly serious. 'I've never yet thanked you, Bart, for putting your life at risk by seeking my whereabouts that day. You possibly saved my life.'

His smile was crooked. 'Yes, I might possibly have done so,' he conceded. 'But you definitely saved mine, you foolish girl.'

It might have been intended as a criticism, but to Abbie's ears the stricture sounded more like an endearment, so softly had he spoken. 'Well, you'll not need to put up with my stupidity for much longer,' she said, desperately striving to keep her tone light, and ignore the painful ache that had suddenly attacked her throat. 'Has Grandpapa mentioned that we intend to leave on Friday?'

A long silence, then, 'Don't go!'

It wasn't so much the command itself that persuaded Abbie to remain seated beside him, when she had been about to rise, as the raw feeling she couldn't fail to hear in his voice. 'Why…? Is there something else you wish to say to me?'

'Don't go, Abbie,' he repeated, lowering his head to stare fixedly at a spot between his boots. 'Don't leave me here alone to dwindle into a lonely, irascible old man. I should, you know, without you. I need you to coax me out of my ill humours, reprimand me if I become overbearing, tease me if I grow too arrogant.'

No clearer declaration of love could have been given, and all Abbie could do as the silence between them lengthened was to watch through the mist of unshed tears when he rose abruptly to his feet, the response she so longed to utter suppressed by the painful obstruction that had lodged itself in her throat.

'Don't think me so insensitive that I cannot appreciate your misgivings,' he continued, staring straight ahead of him across his land. 'I can understand how disgusted… insulted you must have felt years ago when I—'

He got no further. Abbie was beside him, the fingers of her left hand pressed gently against his lips. 'Don't you dare apologise to me for being a man, Bartholomew Cavanagh,' she managed to force past that lingering constriction. 'I don't want a paragon… I only want you.'

Abbie watched dawning wonder replace disbelief in dark eyes before Bart lowered his head and kissed her, at first with infinite tenderness before suppressed passion demanded release.

'I shall never give you cause to regret it, my darling,' he vowed, keeping her a very willing prisoner in his arms.

She didn't pretend to misunderstand and smiled lovingly up at him. 'If I thought for a moment that it was your intention to stray, Bart, I shouldn't consider marrying you,' she admitted with total sincerity, but couldn't resist adding, 'However, I think it only fair to warn you that should you ever succumb to temptation, you'll rue the day you ever met—'

It was Bart's turn to silence her this time, and he did so very comprehensively, blissfully unaware that his peerless display of masculine passion was being witnessed by the two people who had once again taken refuge in his library.

'By gad! What is going on out there, do you suppose?'

Lady Penrose favoured her companion with a look of comical dismay. 'I should imagine, Colonel, that they have just become betrothed. And without any assistance from you this time.'

'By gad!' he said again. 'Well, this is a turn up for the books. Not that I didn't always consider they would suit admirably.'

'Yes, Colonel, and you may have the satisfaction of knowing that you have been proved right,' Lady Penrose responded, exerting admirable self-control. 'The mistake you made was imagining that you could decide the matter for them. All things considered, though, I believe you can be forgiven.'

Wisely she chose not to elaborate, especially as he appeared to be having a little difficulty in comprehending the very favourable turn of events. Instead she suggested that he might like to order a bottle of champagne brought up from the cellar in readiness for the perfectly matched couple's return to the house.

'Of course, I suppose I must not neglect my duties by leaving my goddaughter unchaperoned for too long,' she added, taking refuge in one of the comfortable chairs. 'In the meantime, I think you and I might enjoy a celebratory tipple while we await the arrival of the champagne, don't you, Colonel?'

'By Jove, I think we should too, ma'am!' he agreed heartily. 'Port, was it not?'

An expression akin to approval spread across her ladyship's plump features. 'Colonel Graham, I actually think I'm beginning to find you most agreeable!'

* * * * *

Introducing...

MILLS & BOON
Swoon ♡ Club

The new way to enjoy your favourite
Mills & Boon books, conveniently delivered
to you every month.

Enjoy 50% off
the first month!

Call Customer Service on **1300 659 500** and
quote the code **SWOONCLUB***

or visit **millsandboon.com.au/swoonclub**

**No lock-in
Contracts**

**Free
Postage**

**Exclusive
Offers**

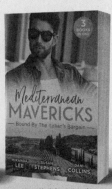

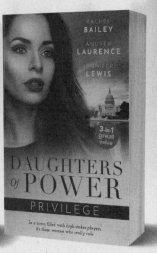

LET'S TALK ABOUT BOOKS!

JOIN THE CONVERSATION

MILLSANDBOON
AUSTRALIA

@MILLSANDBOONAUS

ESCAPE THE EVERY DAY AT
MILLSANDBOON.COM.AU